The Book of Death

A novel (probably)

Anonymous

Copyright © The Bourbon Kid 2012

The right of the author (under the accredited pseudonym The Bourbon Kid) to be identified as the author of this work has been asserted by him/her in accordance with the Copyright, Designs and Patents Act 1988.

This novel is entirely a work of fiction. The names, characters and incidents portrayed in it are the work of the author's imagination. Any resemblance to actual persons, living or dead, events or localities is entirely coincidental.

All rights reserved. No part of this publication may be reproduced, stored in a retrieval system, or transmitted by any means, without the prior permission in writing of the publisher, nor be otherwise circulated in any form of binding or cover other than that in which it is published and without a similar condition including this condition being imposed on the subsequent purchaser.

Cover designed by Sophie Montemagni

ISBN 978-1500384425

The Book With No Name
The cover and pages of *The Book With No Name* were created using wood from the cross on which Christ was crucified. Any vampire that touches part of the cross is destroyed. The book is a vital weapon in the war against the undead.

The Eye of the Moon
The Eye of the Moon is a precious blue gemstone with incredible power. Anyone wearing the stone becomes immortal. It can also be used to control the orbit of the moon, change weather patterns, heal wounds and transform vampires back into humans.

The Devil's Graveyard
The Devil's Graveyard is an area of desert where people go to cut deals with the Devil. Buried in the Graveyard are the undead corpses of many of those who sold their souls in exchange for fortune and fame.

The Book of Death
The Book of Death was created to log the names of the dead. The Egyptian ruler Rameses Gaius cursed the book so that he could write the names of his enemies in it. They all died on the dates specified in the book.

The Bourbon Kid would like to thank the following people by writing their names in The Book of Death.

Sophie Montemagni, Jack Safarian, Caroline Vallat, Toby Buchan, Jennifer D, Fabienne Reichenbach and Don Murphy. Also thanks to the wonderful people at Sonatine Editions, Bastei Luebbe and Ediciones B and many other foreign publishers for their excellent publications of my work.

List of works by Anonymous –

The Book With No Name (2007)
The Eye of the Moon (2008)
The Devil's Graveyard (2010)
The Book of Death (2012)
Sanchez: A Christmas Carol (2014)
The Red Mohawk (2015)
The Plot to Kill the Pope (2016)

The author can be found on Facebook and Twitter as Bourbon Kid.

Dear Reader,

You have opened *The Book of Death*.
Appearances can be deceptive. Read carefully.

Anonymous

Prologue

A teenage girl ran through the dark, murky back alleys of Santa Mondega, her lungs working harder than ever before. Her pursuer had not given up the chase. She could hear him behind her, his footsteps mostly softened by the snow underfoot. She hadn't dared to look back ever since he had first leapt out of the shadows at her. She had seen the whites of his eyes clearly, standing out within the large black patches of paint covering much of his face. Dressed all in black, at first he had looked like a giant shadow with eyes. Then she saw his teeth. They were huge vampire fangs. She ran for her life.

Screaming for help wasn't an option, because the vampires in the streets outnumbered the humans. Something big was going down in the city right now, and calling out would only attract more of the undead. She needed somewhere safe to hide. As she charged out of the end of an alleyway and into one of the city's main streets she saw a place that might offer sanctuary.

The Santa Mondega City Library.

She raced across the road and up the steps to the front entrance. The doors were wide open, inviting her in. She wasted no time and charged through them into the library foyer. The foyer had a marble floor and a very high ceiling. The sight should have been familiar to her because for months her parents had been encouraging her to visit the library to study for her exams. Straight ahead of her was a set of large wooden double doors secured with a large bronze padlock and chain. That left her with one option. She raced over to a staircase on the left.

As she struggled up to the upper floor, the soles of her sneakers left a trail of snow behind her. If the vampire followed her in he would easily track her down. She knew she risked cornering herself by hiding in the library, but she couldn't outrun the vampire forever. If he was anything like the vampires in Twilight he'd be able to leap through the air, covering huge distances with ease, catching up with her whenever it suited him. Maybe this particular vampire was revelling in the thrill of the chase, excited by the sound of panic in her erratic breathing.

At the top of the stairs she risked a look behind her. There was no sign of her pursuer. Maybe he had given up the chase or found an easier victim to prey on. Even so, she wasn't willing to hang around. She staggered into the large hall of books, hoping to find a maze of aisles to hide in. There was no one manning the reception desk, and no sign of anyone browsing through the ceiling-high shelves of books. Directly ahead of her was an open area filled with tables and chairs, but that too was deserted.

She hurried over to the Reference section and ducked behind the shelves. The aisle was dark and even though that probably wouldn't deter a vampire, it seemed like her best option. At least, it did until she saw something at the other end of the aisle that made her blood run cold.

On the floor, lying in a pool of blood was the body of a teenage boy. His head had been smashed to a bloodied pulp. Of far greater concern, though, was the man leaning over him, a man she had heard rumours about. Concealed from head to toe in a long black robe with a hood pulled up over his head was the Bourbon Kid. As he looked up at her she noticed that his hands were covered in the boy's blood.

After gawping at his hands for a second Caroline looked back up. Her eyes met his. She stood rooted to the spot, her body and brain shut down at the sight of the notorious killer. She watched in horror as he rose to his feet and reached inside his dark robe. His bloodied hand pulled out a large handgun. He took aim, pointing it at her head. A red laser sighter on the top of the gun shone brightly, aimed right between her eyes. She wondered if she had just taken her last breath, but before he squeezed the trigger, the Bourbon Kid said two words in a distinctive gravelly voice straight from the depths of hell.

'Get down.'

For a moment Caroline remained frozen. Then she did as instructed and ducked down, burying her head between the knees on her blue jeans. She put her hands over her ears and closed her eyes.

BANG!

The sound of the gunfire was almost deafening, even with her ears shielded. As it continued to echo around the vast hall of books, she slowly uncovered her ears. Behind her she heard the sound of a body crumpling to the floor. She remained in her crouched position for a few seconds before tentatively opening her eyes and looking up at the Bourbon Kid. He had replaced his gun within his dark coat and was once again looking down upon the blood-soaked body of the dead boy on the hardwood floor.

Caroline stood up slowly. Lying flat on his back on the floor behind her, minus a large portion of his head, was the vampire who had been chasing her through the streets. Smoke was pouring out of the gaping hole in his head and blood was seeping out across the floor in an ever-expanding puddle. She backed away from it and turned back to the Bourbon Kid.

'Thanks,' she mumbled. 'He'd been chasing me for a long time. I don't know who he is.'

The Kid did not respond. Caroline took a step towards him and spoke a little louder. 'Do you know what's going on here?' she asked. 'Did the vampires get that boy?'

The Kid seemed to have forgotten she was there. At the sound of her voice he glanced over at her. 'That guy chasing you was a Panda,' he said.

'A what? Panda?'

'Yeah.'

She paused, unsure what he meant. It made no sense.

'The black paint on his face, around his eyes, it means he's a member of the Panda clan of vampires. Or at least, he was til I blew his fuckin' head off.'

Caroline heard what he said, but she found herself distracted by the body of the dead boy on the floor. 'Oh my God, that's Josh. He goes to my school. Did the Pandas do that to him?' she asked.

The Kid shook his head. 'No. This ain't vampire style.'

'So who did it then?'

The Kid ignored her and reached inside his robe again. He pulled out the gun he had used to kill the vampire. He looked like he was ready to use it. He strode towards her, his eyes staring right past her as if she wasn't there. She stepped aside, her back pressing hard up against a shelf of books behind her in an effort to keep as much distance between herself and the Kid as possible. He walked past her, his robe brushing gently against her leg. At the end of the aisle he stopped and peered both ways, his gun pointed and ready for action.

Caroline tentatively called out to him. 'Is it safe to go back outside?'

'For me it is.'

'Can I come with you? I'm scared to go on my own.'

He glared at her. 'You'll be safer here.'

Caroline pointed at the dead boy on the floor. 'But what about whoever killed Josh?' she asked. 'What if they're still here in the library?'

The Kid was already walking toward the exit as he replied. 'The man who killed him has gone already.'

'Do you know who it was?' she called after him. 'And are you going to kill him?'

'He's on my list.'

One

The gutters overflowed with rainwater, sewage and blood. In the disquieting hush that had overtaken the city, these were the final remnants of the massacre that had laid siege to Santa Mondega for the last twenty-four hours. Ravaged by thunder, lightning, and death, Halloween had never been more chaotic. And that was saying something in Santa Mondega.

Had it been any other town, police and press would be roaming the streets, looking for clues and witnesses. But if any cops were still alive, they wouldn't resurface until daylight. The city was normally crawling with vampires, a high percentage of which were cops. But on this night the cops and the vampires (and in particular, the vampire cops) had been the victims of the massacre. The residents of Santa Mondega would wake to a city with virtually no law enforcement.

At four a.m. two figures roamed the ghost-like streets. The young couple stayed mostly in the shadows. The girl, aged in her early twenties, wore jeans and a grey sweatshirt. The bloodstains on the front looked black in the darkness. The blood was mostly her own, dribbled there from a wound in her neck which she hid well beneath her long dark hair. Her partner, a male of similar age, was the cause of the wound. He'd transformed her into a creature of the night like himself just after midnight.

Since then they had traipsed across town and had just spent several minutes in the shadows outside the police station, the scene of some of the night's more unpleasant carnage, checking for signs of any life inside.

The male, Dante Vittori, eventually stepped out of the shadows and into the light that shone down from the streetlights. The lights showed up the heavy bloodstains on his light blue police officer's shirt that hung untucked over a pair of dark blue pants. He gestured to his partner to join him. The police station looked totally desolate and unoccupied. Dante walked unashamedly towards it, secure in the knowledge that anything that might be lurking nearby would not dare harm him. His girlfriend Kacy slipped from the shadows and chased after him.

'I'm not convinced this is the best place to be right now,' she called out to him as he made his way up the concrete steps that led to the glass double doors at the front of the station.

'Trust me,' he said, pushing the glass door on the right open. 'There's something here you're gonna like.' He peered around the door to check if anyone was around.

Kacy wasn't convinced. 'Unless it's a cure to turn us back to normal I doubt I'm gonna like it.'

'Come on. There's no one here,' said Dante waving her in through the door as he held it open for her.

Kacy stepped inside and waited for him to lead the way. The reception area inside the station was a mess. And eerily quiet. Dante headed towards an elevator on the far side of the reception, past several unmanned desks. Blood covered the desks, walls and much of the floor around the reception area. The corpse of a police officer lay on the floor by the right hand wall. The top half of his head was missing.

'I wonder what happened to him?' Kacy asked, stepping clear of the body.

'The monk Peto knocked him out.'

'The monk who had his head cut off earlier?'

'Yeah, Peto. He was a good guy.'

'I hope the cops find the person who cut his head off.'

'I bet they don't even find the head.'

Kacy frowned as she stared at the corpse on the floor. 'How did knocking this guy out leave him in this state?'

'After Peto knocked him out, the Bourbon Kid shot him in the back of the head to make sure he didn't wake up.'

'Nice,' said Kacy, taking one last look at the body before following Dante over to the elevator. 'Where exactly is the Kid now? Can we find him? Would he help us?'

Dante shook his head. 'Nah. The Monk used the Eye of the Moon to help the Kid get his soul back or something. It turned him all queer and then he just drove off and left us.'

'Asshole.'

'Yeah. I wouldn't call him that to his face though.'

Dante pressed a button in the wall by the elevator to call it up to their floor. As the gears of the elevator began to churn, Kacy became aware of a foul stench in the air.

'What on earth is that smell?' she asked.

'Shit.'

'What?'

'That smell is shit.'

The elevator made a pinging noise and the doors opened, revealing an elevator carriage with walls covered in blood and shit.

'Oh my God,' Kacy put her hand over her mouth and reeled back, not just at the shock of the sight but also at the stink.

'See,' said Dante pointing at some of the browner patches. '*Shit*. Kid rammed a shotgun up a cop's ass and blew his guts out. Shit went everywhere. Real nasty.'

'Can we take the stairs?' Kacy asked.

Dante stepped into the elevator and pressed a button on the keypad on the right hand side.

'Come on in,' he said. 'It's just shit. And blood.' He glanced at a spot on the floor out of Kacy's eye line, before adding, 'and a testicle by the looks of it. Real hairy one.'

'I'm taking the stairs,' said Kacy. 'What floor are you going to?'

'Basement.'

'See you there.'

The elevator doors closed and Kacy hurried over to a door on the right that led to a flight of stairs. She rushed down them and arrived in the basement a good few seconds before the elevator.

The basement was a disused locker room. It had seen better days and was in need of some serious modernisation and a good clean up. There were several long wooden benches nailed to the walls with unlocked grey metal sports lockers above them. The floor was covered in blood (similar to the floor in the reception area above) and black burn marks. And much like the elevator, the place stank of shit and death. The walls too, were stained with a ridiculous amount of blood. Dried blood though, not the kind that would satisfy the lusting that Kacy was beginning to feel. The sight of it made her incredibly hungry.

The elevator made another pinging sound, the doors parted and Dante stepped out. He looked around at his surroundings.

'Why are we here?' Kacy asked.

'There's something here you might like. Or certainly need anyway.'

'Like what? A dirty jockstrap?' asked Kacy looking around once more at the foul locker room.

Dante kissed her on the cheek then walked past her to a row of lockers on the wall. He peered along the floor beneath the wooden bench that ran beneath the lockers. About two thirds of the way down the wall, maybe twenty lockers along, he leaned down and scoured the floor beneath the bench. He reached beneath it and pulled out a package that had previously been concealed from view. He turned around and grinned at Kacy. Two of his top teeth slowly extended into tiny fangs.

'What's that?' Kacy asked pointing at the package in his hands.

'Catch.'

He threw the package towards her. As it flew through the air Kacy realised it was a bag of liquid. Dark liquid. She caught it competently. Once it was in her hands she soon realised she was holding a fairly hefty bag of blood. The mere sight of it set her pulse racing. She felt her own vampire fangs grow a little in length. An urge came over her, an almost uncontrollable urge. Suddenly without giving it a second thought she lifted the bag up to her mouth and used her razor sharp teeth to rip it open. She began to pour the blood recklessly into her mouth. Much of it missed its target and dribbled down her face. But every single ounce that slid down her throat brought on a sensation like nothing she had ever known. A feeling of pure adrenaline raced through her bloodstream and she became lost in her inner self. She closed her eyes and let the feeling of power and lust flow through her body. For a brief time she felt at one with the universe, yet oblivious to everything around her, until she felt Dante's hand grab hers.

'Hey, save some for me,' she heard him say.

She opened her eyes and took a deep breath. Dante took the bag of blood from her. Like her, once the blood was in his hands his self-control seemed to vanish. He poured some into his own gaping mouth. Kacy saw that he too was experiencing the same orgasmic feeling that she had just enjoyed.

After finishing off the remains of the bag, Dante stood still, breathing slowly and blinking. He had a look of extreme pleasure on his face, the likes of which Kacy had never seen before. She then became aware of the fact that she had a huge beaming smile across her own face. Maybe being a vampire wasn't so bad after all.

'That was awesome, wasn't it?' she said.

'Incredible,' said Dante. 'I mean, when I bit you and turned you into a vampire earlier, I drank some of your blood, but it was *nothing* like this. No offence, babe.'

'None taken.'

'That shit was better than heroin,' Dante said.

'When did you ever try heroin?'

'I didn't. I'm just saying.'

Kacy wiped her finger across her cheek and licked up a small dribble of blood. 'Where did this blood come from?' she asked. 'We should get some more of it.'

Dante shrugged. 'We just found it down here earlier. One of the vampires the Bourbon Kid killed had it in his pocket. We just chucked it under the lockers. Never thought I'd be drinking it a few hours later.'

Kacy looked at the bag and noticed that there was a white sticker on it that had remained intact in spite of her ripping the bag open with her teeth.

'What's that sticker say?' she asked, pointing at it.

Dante unravelled the bag and took a look at the sticker. It was a label with some black typed lettering on it.

'It says it's the blood of someone called Archibald Somers,' Dante said with another shrug of his shoulders.

'Archibald Somers,' said Kacy. 'I recognise that name. Who was he?'

'No idea, but I could drink the guy's blood all day. I've never felt anything like this. How about you?'

Kacy agreed. 'I feel incredible. Where can we get some more?'

Dante appeared to be deep in thought for a moment, which was unusual for him. Deep thoughts and Dante weren't two things normally associated with each other. Eventually he spoke up. 'I think I know a place,' he said.

'Really? Where?'

'It's the nightclub, The Swamp. Vanity, the leader of the Shades clan, owns it. He could help us out. He might even have some blood there that we can drink.'

'Can we trust him?'

'I think so. I mean, I'm already part of his clan. The rest of the Shades got killed, so he'll probably be pleased to see me, especially now I have you. He might be grateful I've brought him a new recruit.'

'But will he know that you teamed up with the Bourbon Kid and the monk last night?'

'Only one way to find out. Let's go see him.'

Kacy looked at her watch. 'It's well past four o'clock,' she said. 'Do we need to worry about the sun coming up?'

'No. The sun always comes up, doesn't it?'

'That's not what I meant you idiot. I mean, if we're outside when the sun comes up are we going to melt or something like that?'

'I have no idea.'

'Then let's get a move on!'

They hurried back up the stairs to the reception area. It was still eerily quiet up there and thankfully still dark outside. As they sidestepped their way through the blood and mess on the floor on their way out, a face appeared at the glass double doors at the entrance. It was the terrified face of a young boy, no more than eight years old. He banged hard on the glass doors and appeared to scream something like *"Help me!"*

Before either Dante or Kacy could react, a second figure appeared behind the boy, swooping out of the darkness. It grabbed him around the waist and dragged him back away from the doors. A second later the boy and his much larger assailant had vanished.

'Fuck me,' said Dante. 'Did that really just happen?'

Kacy tried to process the image in her head. It had happened so fast. 'Did you see who that was that grabbed the boy?' she asked.

Dante nodded. 'Yeah, that's some fucked up shit. I guess we're not the only vampires out at this time of night.'

'Have you seen that guy before?'

'Yeah, but only with you, and he wasn't a vampire then.'

Two

Beth woke from her gentle slumber. Her bed was warm and cosy. Warmer than usual because she had shared it with JD, finally reunited after eighteen years apart. She couldn't remember ever waking up feeling so happy. She had allowed him to fall asleep before her simply because she had been so happy to just stare at him, knowing that it was real that he had come back to her. She rubbed her eyes and rolled over to look at him again. The duvet on the other side of the bed had been pulled back.

JD was gone.

Her heart missed a beat. Had it all been a dream? Had he really reappeared at the end of the pier where she was waiting? Where she'd waited every Halloween night all those years?

She thought hard. Her head felt fuzzy and she was still coming to terms with waking up so early. The curtains were drawn and it was still dark outside. She reached over and felt the bed where the duvet had been pulled back. It was still warm. She decided she couldn't have dreamt it. It wasn't possible. The whole thing had been so real, right down to the moment when she had fallen asleep in his arms.

She spied a small piece of brown cloth resting on the pillow on the other side of the bed. She grabbed it and held it up in front of her face to get a good look at it. Sewn into the centre of it was a dark red heart. In the centre of the heart in blue letters were the initials JD. It was a relief to know she wasn't going crazy. This was the proof she needed to confirm that the previous night hadn't been a dream. But what was the significance of the cloth? Did it mean he'd left? Was it a goodbye note of some kind?

In one swift move she jumped up from the bed, wrapping herself in the duvet as she did so. Her bedroom suddenly seemed cold and empty where it had felt warm and full of life only moments earlier. She scurried around the bed and opened the bedroom door. Peering out into the poky living room in her one bedroom apartment she saw no sign of anyone. Just as she was beginning to panic, dreading the thought that she might be all alone again, the door to the apartment opened. In walked JD. He was wearing the same jeans, black T-shirt and black leather jacket as he had when he'd turned up near the pier the night before. He saw the worried look on her face and calmed her instantly with a gentle smile.

'Sorry, did I wake you?' he asked.

Beth breathed a sigh of relief. 'I thought you'd gone.'

'Just went outside for some fresh air. I couldn't sleep.'

He took off his jacket and threw it on to the back of her green two-seater sofa, then plonked himself down on one side of it, facing the TV. He picked up the remote and flicked the TV on. A late night action movie came on.

Beth shuffled over to the sofa, holding the duvet close to keep herself warm. She sat down next to him and kissed him on the cheek. 'I thought for a horrible minute that I'd dreamt last night.'

'Maybe you did. Maybe you're still dreaming.'

'Well then I hope I don't wake up. Ever.'

He kissed her back. 'It's no dream, I promise you,' he said. 'I'm back. And I'm back for good.'

'I can't begin to tell you how great it is to hear you say that. I had this horrible feeling for a minute there that you might have just come back for the one night. Like maybe you had a girl in every town.'

'I do have a girl in every town. I travel around on an eighteen-year circuit. You're my girl in Santa Mondega.'

Beth gave him a playful shove. 'In your dreams!'

'I promise you, if I'm going anywhere, you're coming with me.'

'For now, how about just coming back to bed with me? It's cold in there without you.'

'Sure. I was just gonna watch the news for a bit.' He changed the channel over to the local news station. A reporter in the news studio was reading out the latest news with a grave expression. Even his voice sounded grave. Beth looked at the TV screen and frowned. 'Wait a sec,' she said. 'What's that about?'

A scrolling yellow bar at the bottom of the screen read –

HUNDREDS DEAD AS BOURBON KID KILLS AGAIN

'Oh my God,' she gasped. 'I hope no one I know has been killed.'

As if to confirm her worst fears the reporter reading out the news announced that one of the Bourbon Kid's victims had been her boss at the museum, Bertram Cromwell.

Beth was horrified. Cromwell was one of the only people in the city who she could genuinely call a friend. She put her hand over her mouth. 'I don't believe it,' she said, 'Cromwell was the nicest man in town. He's the only reason I have a job. And now the Bourbon Kid has murdered him. His wife will be devastated. This is awful.'

JD rubbed her back to comfort her. 'Maybe this is a sign that you should quit the museum,' he said. 'In fact, how about quitting this shithole town altogether?'

Beth barely heard what he said. Her thoughts were only of Bertram Cromwell and his family. 'I hope they catch the Kid and give him the electric chair.'

JD squeezed her in close. 'I think the Kid was killing off all the local vampires. I doubt he had anything to do with Cromwell's murder.'

'Vampires?' said Beth, snapping out of her maudlin thoughts. 'Like that thing that attacked us that time on the pier?'

'Yeah.'

'Was that really a vampire though? I mean, I've never come across a vampire since then. I was beginning to wonder if I'd imagined it.'

'The city was rife with them. Bet they're all dead now.'

'Yes but the Bourbon Kid is still at large. He's a bigger menace than the vampires, I think.'

The scrolling yellow bar on the news program suggested otherwise.

BREAKING NEWS – BOURBON KID APPREHENDED AND KILLED BY SPECIAL FORCES

JD pulled her in towards him and kissed her again, this time firmer than before. 'See, you're safe. The Bourbon Kid is dead, gone forever. And so are all the vampires. There's nothing to be afraid of.'

Beth forced a smile. Her thoughts suddenly returned to the piece of cloth with the heart sewn into it. She had it in her hand. 'You left this on your pillow,' she said, holding it up.

'That's for you,' said JD.

'What is it exactly?'

He paused. 'What do you think it is?'

'A piece of cloth with your initials on.'

'Then that's what it is.'

'There's more to it than that,' she said, slapping him across the arm. 'This was a sign to let me know you were coming back, right?'

He smiled. 'Yeah. Keep hold of that. I'll always come back for it. And you won't have to wait eighteen years again, I promise.'

'So I can keep it?'

'It's all yours.'

Beth looked down at the heart sewn into the cloth. She now had something of his that carried some meaning. Just holding it in her hand made her feel safe. As long as she had it, JD's heart belonged to her.

Three

Vanity's club The Swamp was far more impressive than its title made it sound. Kacy was expecting a real dive bar in a back alley somewhere. In fact it was a five-storey building on the South side of the city, situated on a street corner. As they approached the front entrance, something landed gently on the ground in front of them.

'Is that snow?' Kacy asked.

'Can't be,' said Dante, dismissively. 'It's never snowed in Santa Mondega.'

'What the hell is it then?'

'I don't know, but let's hurry up and get inside.' He pushed at the black door at the front of the place. The door opened easily. 'There's all kinds of creepy fuckers around this place usually, so stay close to me,' he added.

'Great.'

He led the way up several flights of stairs. There wasn't a soul in sight. Not one single creepy looking person. Not even a Depeche Mode fan. It was as empty as the streets outside.

'This place is dead,' Kacy whispered.

'Weird,' said Dante. 'Last time I came here there were vampires hanging around on the stairs doing all kinds of shit. I wonder where they've all gone?'

A voice from above answered him. 'They've gone to the Casa de Ville.'

They both stopped and looked upwards. A vampire with shoulder length dark hair, wearing wraparound shades and sporting a neatly trimmed goatee beard was staring down at them from the landing a few floors up. Dante recognised him straight away.

'Hey Vanity, how you doing?' he said, waving.

Kacy recognised the outfit Vanity was wearing. He had on the same black leather jacket that Dante had been given when he had infiltrated the Shades clan of vampires a few days previously. Underneath it he wore a plain black T-shirt, his outfit topped off with a pair of black jeans and matching ankle boots.

'Come on up!' Vanity called down to them. 'I'll get you some clean clothes. And you can tell me what the fuck you've been doing all night.'

Kacy grabbed hold of Dante's hand and followed him up to the landing where Vanity had been. By the time they reached it he had moved into a large hall. It was a pool hall with numerous tables scattered around and a long bar against one wall.

'Through here,' said Dante. 'I've been in here before. Had a fight with some clowns the other day.'

'Why does that not surprise me?'

Inside the pool hall Vanity stood beside one of the pool tables in the centre of the room. He had tossed a couple of black leather jackets on the table. The words "The Shades" were sewn into the back in gold lettering. *Tacky as hell,* Kacy thought, but she kept her opinion to herself out of politeness.

Vanity took off his sunglasses. His eyes were unlike anything Kacy had ever seen. They flickered between three different colours. Like a rotating disco ball they flickered from gold to black and then silver to black before repeating the routine. The image was practically hypnotic. He stared at her for a moment before turning to Dante.

'So who's the girl?' he asked.

'She's a babe I just picked up,' Dante replied. Kacy let go of his hand and allowed him to walk up to Vanity and slap hands with him. 'She's kinda cool. You'll like her.'

Vanity pursed his lips and looked Kacy up and down. 'What's your name, honey?' he asked.

'Kacy.'

'Kacy. Nice name,' he said looking her up and down again. 'Fit too. She'll go down well in the initiation orgy. All the guys will love fucking her.'

Kacy felt her blood run even colder than when she had become a vampire hours earlier. 'What?' she spluttered.

Vanity grinned. 'I'm kidding.'

Kacy breathed a huge sigh of relief. She saw Dante wipe a bead of sweat from his brow. He had obviously fallen for Vanity's dubious wisecrack too.

'Here,' said Vanity tossing a leather jacket to Kacy. 'Put this on. The three of us gotta haul ass. All vampires have been summoned to the Casa de Ville by Rameses Gaius.'

'What for?' Dante asked.

'You heard about all the shit that's gone down tonight, right?' said Vanity.

'Heard the Bourbon Kid killed a lot of people,' Kacy chimed in, saving Dante from having to reveal where he was when it had all kicked off.

'Yeah,' said Vanity nodding. 'Turns out Déjà Vu was the Bourbon Kid. Did you know that, Dante?'

Dante was putting on one of the leather jackets from the pool table. He pretended not to have heard Vanity's question for a few moments, dusting off the jacket as he considered his answer. At this point it was hard to know whether or not Vanity knew that he knew this information already and was testing him. Kacy jumped in and provided the answer for him. 'We heard the word on the street,' she said. 'Everyone's talking about it.'

'No shit,' said Vanity. 'Did you hear that they caught him though?'

Dante answered immediately this time. 'Seriously? They caught the Bourbon Kid?'

'Yeah. Some military guys that Gaius hired caught up with him and cut his fucking head off.'

'Shit,' Dante couldn't hide how shocked he was at the news.

Kacy wasn't nearly as concerned as Dante. She was far more interested in how her new leather jacket was going to look on her. She slipped her arms into the sleeves and discovered to her delight that it fitted perfectly. Vanity then tossed her a pair of sunglasses.

'The fact they caught him and killed him has probably saved our necks,' Vanity said. 'I doubt the powers that be are too impressed with us right now.'

'Maybe we should stay here for a while then?' Kacy suggested, looking at the sunglasses in her hand and wondering how she would be able to see with them on.

'We're in enough trouble already,' said Vanity. 'But the fact that the Bourbon Kid killed hundreds of vampires earlier tonight means that Gaius is low on numbers at the moment. He's assembling an undead army to take over the city. The lack of other experienced vampires should be enough to keep us alive for now.'

'Is it safe to go out at the moment?' Kacy asked. 'I mean, won't the sun come up soon?'

Vanity shook his head. 'Gaius says not. He's found some way to keep dark clouds over the city. So for a while we're all daywalkers.'

'Really?'

'Yeah. Archie Somers tried in vain for years to turn the skies dark permanently. Gaius did it in no time.'

Kacy perked up. 'Who was Archie Somers?' she asked.

'The old boss. Chief bloodsucker, one of the original daywalkers.'

Dante blurted out what was on Kacy's mind. 'We just drank some of his blood.'

'What?'

'We were scoping out the police station earlier for any potential victims and we found a bag of blood with the name Archie Somers on it.'

'*Archie Somers?* Where is it now?'

'We drank it all.'

Vanity eyed them suspiciously. 'Are you bullshitting me?'

'No,' said Dante. 'It was fucking good stuff.'

Vanity sighed. 'You know, if I was you, I'd keep quiet about stuff like that,' he said. 'Don't let Jessica or Gaius hear you say shit like that. Gaius will fire fucking laser bolts from his fingertips at you. And Jessica, well, she'll just rip your fucking insides out!'

'Who's Jessica?' Kacy asked, cautiously.

'You'll see her when we get to the Casa de Ville. Now we gotta make a few stops before we get there. See if we can find any more of our clan alive. Safety in numbers an' all that.'

'Great,' said Kacy, unable to mask her lack of enthusiasm.

Vanity slipped his sunglasses back on and nodded towards the exit. Kacy saw Dante slip on a pair of sunglasses too so she followed suit and was surprised to find that she could see just as clearly as before even though it was dark.

Vanity walked past her and jumped over the banister at the top of the stairs. He disappeared out of sight. Kacy rushed over and peered over the banister. Vanity was dropping gently to the ground floor. She looked back at Dante.

'Can *we* do *that?*' she asked.

Dante grimaced. 'I guess so. Shall I go first?'

'You'd fucking better!'

As he was about to hurl himself over the balcony Kacy grabbed his arm. 'Baby, are we about to go and join a vampire army?' she asked.

'I think so.'

'Are you sure we want to do this?'

'Well, we are vampires at the moment. I say we go with the flow.'

'I'm not sure I'm ready to go around killing people just yet.'

Dante pulled her in towards him and planted a kiss on the long dark hair on the top of her head. 'We're vampires now, babe,' he reminded her. 'Until we find the Eye of the Moon and transform ourselves back into humans I say we go with the flow.'

'I suppose,' said Kacy. 'But Vanity said the vampire army is going to take over the city. Do we really want to be a part of that?'

'I dunno, babe, but with the Bourbon Kid out of the picture, there's nothing to stop the undead from taking over the city. At least we'll be on the winning team.'

'Yeah, but I still can't get the image of that little boy being dragged away at the police station out of my head.'

'Thanks, I'd just about managed to forget about that.'

'Well I can't. It's still bugging me.'

'Try to think about something else.'

'Like what?'

'Baseball.'

Kacy sighed. 'It's not just the image of it that's bothering me. It's what it represents.'

'Huh?'

Dante wasn't getting her point so she spelled it out for him. 'I could never hurt a child. What if the craving for blood makes us kill kids?'

'You'd never hurt a kid, Kace, and neither would I.'

'I know, but what if that changes? I don't want to hurt anybody's kids. I think I want to go back to being human again.'

Dante kissed her on the forehead. 'All right, babe. I'll tell you what, next time we see a vampire try to kill a kid, I'll kick that vampire's head in.'

'And I'll help you do it.'

'Okay, but you know our first priority has to be finding a way to get the Eye of the Moon back.'

'Have you got a plan?'

'No. When have I ever had a plan? Plans are for suckers.'

It was at times like this when Dante talked passionately yet with no sense of what danger lay in wait for him that Kacy remembered why she fell in love with him in the first place. He might well be a foolhardy moron, but he was as brave as any man she'd ever met.

'I love you, you know,' she said.

Dante grabbed her ass and squeezed it hard. 'I love you too,' he said. 'This vampire shit will just be temporary. Trust me.'

Four

Sanchez hated snow. Until now he'd only ever seen it on television but that was enough to make him hate it. And waking up on November 1st after the previous awful day's events, the last thing he wanted to see was snow-covered streets. It had fallen thick and fast overnight, settling two inches deep on the roads. The local kids were overjoyed and were busy building snowmen in the streets. And someone (Sanchez suspected his paperboy) had thrown a snowball at him when he was walking to his car. Little fucker. The only good thing about the cold weather was that it had given him the opportunity to wear his replica *Top Gun* jacket. He'd bought it on the Internet, but it had always been too hot in Santa Mondega to merit wearing it out in public. Up to now it had only ever been worn in his bedroom when he was pretending to be Tom Cruise in front of the mirror.

His drive to the Ole Au Lait for breakfast took a little longer than usual. Partly because the snow made the roads a little more dangerous, but mostly because Sanchez veered off the road a few times in order to knock down some of the snowmen that the local kids had built on the sidewalks.

He arrived at the café at just after nine o'clock in the morning. Experience had taught him to get there early before all the local seniors showed up. The elderly seemed to like nothing more than to sit themselves at the tables next to him and break wind while he tried to eat.

He walked through the door, carrying a black satchel over his shoulder. If he wanted a breakfast this morning, he knew he was going to have to settle a debt he had with Rick the owner of the Ole Au Lait. On the previous day, Rick had called him with some useful information and in return Sanchez had agreed to give him a bottle of liquor. He had the bottle in his satchel, although he secretly hoped Rick wouldn't be there to accept it. Also in his bag was a book that he had stolen from the library, a book called The Book of Death. It had provided none of the clues he had been hoping for in his quest to find out more about Jessica or The Book With No Name. In fact, the only mention of Jessica in the book had been written in there by Sanchez. Rick had informed him of her full name and also that of an acquaintance of hers named Rameses Gaius. Sanchez had noted their names down on a blank page of the book and carried out an Internet search to see if he could find more about them. He had found nothing.

As he approached the counter he became aware of an unpleasant smell of piss. Slumped over in a table by the window was a drunken Santa Claus impersonator. He looked half asleep, but he still managed to mutter something to Sanchez that sounded like "spare me some change". Sanchez ignored it and instead forced a fake smile for Rick who was standing behind the counter, counting the notes in the till. Rick looked full of beans. He wasn't wearing his usual chef outfit. Instead he was dressed to go out in a pair of jeans and, rather annoyingly, a leather Top Gun jacket exactly like Sanchez's. Bastard. He looked up when Sanchez arrived and forced a fake smile back.

'Mornin' Sanchez. Nice jacket,' he said.

'Yeah, you too,' said Sanchez, inwardly seething.

Rick peered over at the satchel. 'I hope you've got that bottle of Jack Daniel's for me,' he said his fake smile expanding into a broad grin.

'I sure have,' Sanchez replied. 'It's in here.'

'Hand it over then.'

Sanchez reached into his satchel. The bottle of Jack Daniel's had slipped to the bottom, beneath The Book of Death. He pulled the big black hardback book out first and placed it on the counter.

'What's this?' Rick asked.

'Just some book I gotta take back to the library later.'

Rick turned the book around to get a look at the title. 'The Book of Death? What's it about?' he asked.

Sanchez pulled the bottle of Jack Daniel's out and placed it on top of the book. 'Not really sure what it's about,' he said. 'Just a list of names, in some sort of diary format.'

'Oh,' Rick sounded disappointed. 'Well, I'm going to the library this morning. I can drop it back for you if you like?'

'That'd be great,' said Sanchez. 'Don't check it in though, just slip it back on the shelf in the Reference section.'

Rick raised an eyebrow. 'Why's that then? Didn't you check the book out?'

'Yeah, but I kind of wrote some names on one of the blank pages.'

'Why?'

'I didn't have any other paper to hand at the time.'

'Well that's hardly a crime is it?' said Rick coolly.

'Actually it is. Defacing a public library book is considered a fairly serious offence.'

'To whom?'

'Have you seen the woman that works in the library?'

Rick grinned as he grasped what Sanchez was getting at. 'Yeah. She's pretty much a bitch, isn't she?'

Sanchez despised Ulrika Price and agreed wholeheartedly with Rick's assessment of her. 'That's the nicest thing I've ever heard anyone say about her,' he said.

Rick picked up the bottle of Jack Daniel's and unscrewed the lid. He took a sniff. 'Smells like good stuff,' he commented.

'What did you expect?'

'I thought it might be some of your homebrew.'

Sanchez did his best to look offended. 'I have no idea what you mean.'

'Sure,' said Rick. 'That Santa in the corner smells just like your homebrew.' He had a point.

'Anyways,' said Sanchez. 'It's breakfast time and I'm hungry.'

Rick took the hint and shouted out to the back room. 'Yo, Flake, customer!'

Rick's head waitress Flake, appeared, complete with a notebook and pen. Her long brown hair was neatly scraped back into a ponytail. And as usual she was wearing the uniform that Rick insisted all his female members of staff wore. Sanchez approved of it too. It consisted of a short black dress and stockings, a look that suited Flake's petite figure nicely.

'Good morning, Sanchez,' she said beaming a bright white smile at him. 'Twelve item breakfast and a large coffee?'

'Yes please, Flake.'

She pointed to a table on the opposite side of the café to the piss smelling Santa. She clearly knew Sanchez well. He liked to eat his breakfast as far away from other customers as possible, particularly smelly ones. 'I've just cleaned that table up for you and left a newspaper over there,' she said with a wink.

'Thanks.'

Rick picked up The Book of Death, tucked it under his arm and walked around the counter. 'Right, Flake, I'm off to town. You can go when Sanchez is done with his breakfast.'

'You closing up early?' Sanchez asked.

'Wouldn't have even opened at all if it wasn't for the fact I knew you'd be dropping by with my bottle of JD,' said Rick, flipping the closed sign up on the front door. He pulled the door open and as he walked through it he looked back at Sanchez and winked. 'Don't let Flake get you into any trouble.' With that he closed the door behind him and headed out into the snow.

'I'll bring your coffee over in a second,' said Flake. 'Make yourself comfortable.'

As he walked over to the unusually clean table in the corner by the window, Sanchez eyed Flake suspiciously. Was she building up to asking him for something? Beneath that fresh faced glow on her pink cheeks and those big inviting brown eyes she could be plotting something. Or hoping for a tip.

'What's got you so cheerful today?' he asked her.

'I'm just pleased to see you, Sanchez,' she replied. 'After all the killing yesterday it's nice to see that you weren't one of the victims.'

'Well, I did have a run in with the Bourbon Kid and some werewolves.'

'Yes, I heard about that. You survived another shootout. You're so lucky.'

'Not that lucky. He killed all my customers again. The bastard.'

'Was it because you poured piss in his drink again?'

Sanchez sat down and picked up the newspaper to glance over the front page headlines. 'I didn't get a chance to this time. I would have, but I'd just served it all to the werewolves.'

The front page, as expected, ran with the story of the latest massacre. The death toll looked like it might even run into the thousands this time. Sanchez tutted to himself as he thought about all the potential customers he must have lost.

When he looked back up he noticed that Flake looked different. She was still stood behind the counter, wearing the same outfit, but she had now removed the white apron from the front of her dress and had also let her hair down. It now hung freely around her shoulders. She had beautiful long brown hair to match her eyes. Sanchez couldn't help thinking that Flake letting her hair down while working in an establishment that served food seemed somewhat unhygienic. Nevertheless, he knew she cooked a good sausage so he kept his thoughts to himself.

He continued to read the newspaper shaking his head occasionally as he came across details of the demise of more potential customers. Eventually Flake wandered over with his mug of coffee. As she set it down on the table, she spoke again.

'You're the only person I know who's brave enough to serve the Bourbon Kid a glass of piss,' she said. After saying it she seemed to suck in a deep intake of breath. It made her chest jut out over the top of Sanchez's newspaper as he lowered it to take a look at his coffee. He couldn't help but notice that she had a particularly fine pair of boobs.

For a few seconds he stared, gawping at them, before remembering she had just spoken to him.

'Brave?' he said aloud, failing to hide his confusion at being called such a thing. She was definitely on drugs.

He quickly recovered from the unexpected compliment and attempted to act like he was downplaying it. 'Yeah well, some people are afraid of the Bourbon Kid,' he shook his head, '…but I'm not. I think he knows not to mess with me. I show no fear when he's around. Think he respects that.'

'Wow. You should join the police, Sanchez. They could use someone like you.'

He shrugged. 'Well, the town would be a safer place. That's for sure.'

'So join up!' Flake sounded genuinely excited at the idea.

'I would,' said Sanchez, pretending to read the newspaper while he took another sneaky glance at Flake's chest. 'Believe me, if they were recruiting, I'd be first in line. This town needs someone to clean up the streets.'

'Brilliant!' her voice went up a few octaves. She slammed a white paper flyer down on to the table by his coffee. 'Look, you can sign up today!'

Sanchez stopped pretending to read the paper and glanced down at the flyer. His eyes settled on the black bold lettering at the centre of it.

POLICE RECRUITING TODAY

'I'll have my eggs sunny side up today please,' he said, hoping to change the subject.

'Oh, okay,' said Flake. 'But what do you think of the flyer?'

'And I'd like my sausages burned, please.'

'Okay, no problem. So what do you think of the…'

'And an extra piece of bacon.'

'Okay, anything else?'

'That should do it.'

Flake was very persistent, much to Sanchez's irritation. 'See they're allowing just about anyone to join the police now,' she said pointing at the flyer. 'Just as a temporary measure, until they can get some real cops in from out of town. So, you gonna sign up?'

'Actually, did I mention I wanted white toast?'

'You always have white toast.'

'Just making sure you hadn't forgotten.'

Flake giggled. 'You're so funny,' she said, gazing at him with big hopeful brown eyes. 'So are you going to sign up or what?'

Sanchez sighed. 'I'd love to,' he said. 'But I'm not tall enough. I don't meet the height restrictions.'

'There are no height restrictions,' Flake said, her voice sounding more excited with every syllable.

'I'm too old then.'

'No age restrictions either. Great, isn't it?'

'I have a criminal record.'

'Doesn't matter! Look, read the whole flyer. They're taking anyone. This is your big chance!'

There was no doubt about it. She had to be on drugs. No one should be that enthusiastic in the morning. Particularly not when they were serving breakfast. Still, Sanchez decided to play along for now. He was willing to tell Flake whatever she wanted to hear, as long as it meant he got to eat his breakfast in peace.

'Well, that's great news isn't it?' he said disingenuously. 'I'll be down there as soon as I've finished my breakfast. Just try and stop me.'

'Brilliant,' said Flake, clapping her hands together with glee. 'We can go together. I'm signing up too. I'm so glad I'll have someone to go with. This will just be the most fun, won't it?'

'What?'

'I'll drive us there as soon as you've finished your breakfast.'

'Huh?'

'I'm so excited! My horoscope said this would happen!'

'Wait, hold on a—'

'In fact, I'm going to buy your breakfast for you this morning.' With that, Flake dashed off back to the kitchen to make his breakfast. She sure did seem excited. Sanchez figured he'd let her pay for his breakfast, as it was obviously important to her. But then, once he'd finished eating it, he'd come up with a way of getting out of signing up for the police force.

Five

Dan Harker was having a hell of a day already. In the early hours of the morning he had been summoned to the Mayor's office and deputized as the new Captain of the Santa Mondega Police Department. His first day wasn't going to be a gentle bedding-in, either. Most of the city cops had been murdered the previous day so he wasn't going to have much help dealing with any crimes. The Mayor had done all he could to help by placing advertisements all over town requesting members of the public to sign up, but that just meant Harker would have to spend half the day recruiting.

Investigating the most recent Bourbon Kid massacre and totaling up the number of victims was going to be one hell of a job. The only good news was that according to a number of eyewitnesses the Bourbon Kid had been gunned down and beheaded in a hotel corridor just after midnight, so by rights the killing should have come to an end.

Before heading to the station to introduce himself as the new Captain, Harker first had to stop off at the local museum. The mayor had informed him that the security department at the museum had some CCTV footage of the Kid murdering their manager, Professor Bertram Cromwell.

When Harker arrived at the museum, Elijah Simmonds, the deputy manager, greeted him in the reception area. Harker had only met Simmonds on one previous occasion. It had been at a charity event held by Bertram Cromwell over a year earlier. Simmonds had struck him as being a bit of a dick. He'd worn a cheap ill-fitting suit and he had a horrendous ponytail that really didn't suit his narrow face.

Simmonds welcomed him with a warm handshake and a cursory smile, so it wasn't as if the guy was totally devoid of qualities. Unfortunately though, he still had the ponytail and the poor taste in suits. His face wasn't quite as narrow as before. In fact he appeared to be in the process of growing a second chin.

As the two of them walked along a narrow corridor on the way to the security office, Simmonds surprised the new Police Captain with an observation Harker wouldn't have made himself.

'You and I have a lot in common,' he said.
'How so?'
'Well, we obviously both like to dress well,' Simmonds smiled and hesitated a moment waiting for Harker to make an agreeing sound of some kind. He didn't. Harker's black three-piece suit was impeccable

and fitted snugly, unlike Simmonds's ill-fitting grey number. 'And then of course there's the obvious,' Simmonds continued.

'What's that then?'

They arrived at a door in the left wall of the corridor and Simmonds turned the handle of it, pushing it open before continuing. 'Both of us have just landed ourselves a promotion, courtesy of the Bourbon Kid's killing spree yesterday.'

Harker threw a look of disapproval at Simmonds. The comment was in rather poor taste under the circumstances. Simmonds recognised the look.

'Obviously it's not how I would have wanted to get my new job. I would much rather Bertram Cromwell was still alive, of course, as I'm sure you wouldn't have wished death on the previous Police Captain.'

Simmonds stepped inside the security office and held the door open for Harker to follow him through.

'The last Captain was a Grade A prick and I'm glad he's dead,' said Harker, stepping into the room.

'Oh.'

'Can you just show me the CCTV tapes please? Then I'll be on my way. I've got a hell of a busy day ahead.'

'Of course.'

Inside the security office, sitting in a rather knackered looking blue chair was a guard in a grey uniform. He was watching a bank of television monitors on the wall in front of him. He was a big, broad shouldered fellow with blond wavy hair and striking blue eyes. Simmonds strolled over to him and placed a hand on his shoulder.

'James, did you manage to make a copy of the murder footage for the police?'

The security guard sat upright. 'Sure did, sir.' He picked up a CD in a plastic case that was on the desk in front of him. 'It's all on there.'

Simmonds took the CD and held it out for Harker.

'Thanks,' said Harker, snatching the CD away from him. He peered over the security guard's shoulder at the bank of monitors he was watching. They showed live footage of the goings on all around the museum.

'Say, James,' Harker said. 'Could you get the footage of the murder up on screen for me now? Be useful if I could take a quick look at it before I leave, just in case I spot anything I'd like to ask you guys about. I wouldn't wanna be two miles away watching it and wishing I could ask you what I'm looking at.'

'Sure thing sir,' said James. He pressed a few keys on a keyboard on the desk in front of him and then pointed up at a monitor on the right. 'Should be coming up on this screen here.'

Harker leaned over James's shoulder to get a closer look at the footage on the black and white monitor. The image wasn't especially clear. He was able to make out the figure of Bertram Cromwell sitting in a comfy chair in the museum's staff room. The professor was watching the news on a television. After about ten seconds, Harker saw a tall figure in a hooded robe enter the room. Cromwell stood up from his chair and a brief exchange of dialogue followed, none of which was available due to the lack of audio provided by the CCTV camera. The dark hooded figure of the Bourbon Kid then pulled a machete out from within his robe. Harker winced as he watched the Kid hack Cromwell to pieces. It was as violent a death as the new Police Captain had ever witnessed, and he had seen a fair bit of violence in his time. It seemed like an extremely unjust way for such a decent man to die. At the end of the slaying, the Kid walked calmly out of the room. James the security guard pressed a button on his keyboard and the image froze on screen showing Cromwell's dead body lying in a pool of his own blood on the floor.

'It gets worse every time I see it,' said Simmonds, visibly shuddering.

'Yeah, I'm sure,' said Harker. Something had caught his eye at the bottom of the screen. He stared closely at it for a moment, recalling something the Mayor had said when they had spoken earlier. 'Is that clock right?' he asked, pointing at the time display in the bottom corner of the screen.

James the security guard nodded. 'Yep. Two thirty-seven. That's about right I think. I saw the Professor about twenty minutes before that. I recommended that he go home but he was totally glued to the news, watching all the updates about the murders and stuff.'

'Interesting,' said Harker, scratching his chin. 'The Bourbon Kid was reported dead not long after midnight. We got a whole bunch of eyewitnesses to back that up too.'

Simmonds looked surprised. 'Really?'

'Yeah. He was gunned down and beheaded by a bunch of military guys in an apartment block. I was under the assumption that Cromwell was one of his last victims before they caught him. This kind of complicates things.'

'So the Bourbon Kid is still alive?'

Harker nodded. 'So it would seem. I'll take this CD and be on my way. If the Bourbon Kid is still at large I'd better make sure the press are aware. The public have a right to know that the streets are still unsafe.'

'You might want to tell those military guys that they beheaded the wrong person too.'

Harker smiled. 'I'm hoping they'll see it on the news before they leave town, if they're even still around.'

Six

Snow was falling from the skies over Santa Mondega for the first time that Dante could remember. He marvelled at it as Vanity drove him and Kacy to the Casa de Ville.

"Cool car, ain't it, babe?" Dante heard Vanity say to Kacy. "Ford Ranger. Brand new, too."

"Pity it's blue," Kacy said in a bored tone as she looked out of the window.

From his seat in the back Dante smirked. Kacy wasn't the sort to be impressed by a car that wasn't stolen. As it happened, he was pleased they were in the Ranger. The roads were more dangerous than usual. Dark clouds were forming over the city too. Big ones.

What looked like a huge medieval castle rose up in the distance.

"What the hell is that?" Kacy asked.

"That's the Casa de Ville," Vanity replied.

"It's a bit fucking big, isn't it?' said Dante.

"It's gonna need to be,' said Vanity. 'There's gonna be a helluva lot of vampires in there in a minute.'

Dante shook his head. The sight of Case de Ville getting larger and larger as they drew closer rendered him speechless for once.

Vanity parked the Ranger in a large car park around the back of the main building. Dante and Kacy followed him back around to the front of the building where a vampire wearing some curious black eye makeup let them in through the front door and directed them to the main hall.

The main hall was magnificent in size. Its ceiling stood fifty metres high and had a balcony running around the walls halfway down. At the far end of the hall stood a large set of very wide marble stairs that led up to the landing and the balcony. It really did feel like a castle. The only major difference Dante had spotted were the obvious CCTV cameras recording every move. The fucking things were everywhere you looked. The hall was already buzzing with noise. Literally hundreds of vampires were standing around chatting amongst themselves.

'Wow, something big is definitely going down,' said Vanity. 'Let's hang at the back. After that whole thing with Déjà Vu being the Bourbon Kid I think a low profile is the way to go.'

'I'm down with that,' said Dante.

The crowd of vampires in the hall resembled the audience at a rock concert. There were all kinds of strangely dressed freaks from every vampire clan in the city, all congregated in this one huge room staring up at the marble staircase at the end of the hall. Dante recognised some of the clans, such as the Clowns, of which there were quite a few. There weren't too many of the Filthy Pigs and Rastafarians from the Dreads clan around this time; of course, there weren't many of the Shades around either. Apart from Dante, Kacy and Vanity, only Cleavage and Moose had survived the recent massacre. The two female members of the Shades were present in the hall, but they had naively ventured to the front of the crowd to get a good look at what was going on.

The majority of the audience now seemed to be made up of what Vanity informed them was the Panda clan, a group of vampires like the one who had let them into the building. They all had black face paint across their eyes giving them a look much like a bunch of human pandas, albeit carnivorous fanged bloodsucking pandas. One of the other dominant clans was the Black Plague, a group that usually stayed on the outskirts of the city. They all wore ninja style black outfits complete with black masks that revealed just their eyes and a small amount of dark skin around them. No doubt lethal predators at night, Dante thought.

After a twenty-minute wait, the huge imposing figure of Rameses Gaius appeared at the top of the staircase. The chatter in the hall beneath him hushed to a silence. Dante recognised Gaius immediately. He shuddered at the memory of Gaius kidnapping him and Kacy a week earlier. He had travelled under the name Mr E at the time and had claimed to be a member of the Secret Service. He had given Dante the mission that involved infiltrating the Shades clan to discover the whereabouts of Peto the monk.

Dante peered over his sunglasses at Kacy. She peered back over hers. It was obvious that she too recognised Gaius as Mr E.

Dante nudged Vanity in the arm. 'Is that really Rameses Gaius?' he asked.

Vanity nodded. 'Yeah. Don't mess with him. He'll snap you in half.'

Gaius wore a shiny silver suit (as he had when Dante had met him before) and a pair of dark sunglasses. His head was bald and his olive skin as smooth as a billiard ball. Both Dante and Kacy lowered their heads in the hope that he wouldn't spot them at the back of the crowd.

'Hey,' Vanity nudged Dante back. 'That's his daughter Jessica behind him. Total babe. Queen of the vampires.'

Dante glanced back up and saw that standing behind Gaius on the steps was none other than Jessica the Vampire Queen. The very same woman he had fired a shitload of bullets into at the Tapioca during the eclipse the previous year. The Bourbon Kid had been gunning her down at the time, so Dante had joined in and then they had left her for dead. It wouldn't do to be spotted by her either.

Up ahead, Gaius raised his arms to grab everyone's attention. 'Thank you all for coming,' he said. 'I have big news for you today. After all that happened yesterday, when we lost a number of our brothers and sisters to that scumbag the Bourbon Kid, we now have reason to be cheerful. And very excited.'

A wave of muttered conversations swept around the hall briefly before Gaius continued.

'At just after midnight last night we captured and beheaded the Bourbon Kid. He is no more!'

A huge cheer went up from the crowd and Gaius gestured quickly for them to quieten down again.

'With him now out of the way, it is time for us to make our move. Soon we will be able to reveal ourselves to the world. I have set in motion a plan which will enable each and every one of you to hunt by day. No more sneaking around in back alleys and clubs at night. We will soon take over the city of Santa Mondega. *This is our time!*' The crowd cheered even more boisterously than before. After hushing them, Gaius continued. 'The local police force is now crippled, and with the Kid out of the picture I want everyone here to be ready to carry out my instructions to take over the city. You may have noticed that it is snowing outside and that there is a large formation of dark clouds settling over the city. This, my friends, will become permanent very soon.'

A woman's voice shouted out from the crowd below. 'How so?'

Gaius removed his sunglasses and a huge gasp went up from the crowd, including Dante and Kacy. In his right eye socket was a glowing blue stone: The Eye of the Moon.

'Yes. That's right,' said Gaius. 'I have the Eye of the Moon once again. It is secured back in its rightful place.' He tapped the eye gently and smiled at his watching audience. 'With the powers of the Eye I have brought together all of those clouds. At the current time I estimate that ninety percent of the sunlight over Santa Mondega is being blocked out. By the end of the day tomorrow I expect that to be one hundred percent. And it will stay that way. We don't need an eclipse to block out the sun, my friends. I can do that for you using the power of my Eye. Once the clouds have intensified sufficiently to block out the sun entirely, we shall come out from the shadows and take over the city. The snow will incapacitate our enemies and once we have complete control of Santa Mondega, we will look to expand our empire and increase our numbers. The humans will be harvested and grown for *your* consumption. Now I know most of you don't need reminding of this, but do not feed upon the children of this city. We will need them in the future. They will live simply to create more of their kind for our future survival.' There were more mutterings from the crowd below, mostly voicing their approval. Gaius waved them down and continued. 'Now, I ask one thing of you. Go out into the streets and hills of Santa Mondega and round up all of your vampire brothers and sisters. I want the werewolves informed too. They will make useful allies in the early days as we seek to conquer. Get the word out to everyone. Tell them to congregate here tomorrow night. This will be the staging point of our war on humanity. Tomorrow night will be the beginning of a new dawn where the undead will rule the world!'

He shook his fist in the air as he finished his speech. A huge roar went up from the watching crowd. Vampires high-fived each other and slapped one another on the back. There were fanged smiles all round in fact. Except for Dante and Kacy.

Kacy tugged at Dante's arm, dragging him back away from the crowd and out of earshot. 'He's got the Eye of the Moon in his head,' she said, her voice largely drowned out by the cheering mob around her.

'I know,' said Dante. 'I thought things were *really* bad before but this is worse than I thought.'

'How much worse?'

'It's *very* bad.'

Kacy frowned. '*Very* bad is worse than *really* bad?'

'Yeah.'

'Are you sure?'

'*Really* sure.'

'Well, let me know when you're *very* sure.'

Dante peered over his sunglasses at her and raised his eyebrows. 'I'll tell you what I *am* sure of. If we try to get the Eye out of his head, we'll most likely get killed. But if we don't get it out of his head, the whole world is gonna end.'

Kacy looked around at the cheering mob of vampires surrounding them. 'This is *very* bad,' she muttered.

Seven

Upon arriving at the police station for his first morning as the new captain, Dan Harker was disappointed to find that the place was a horrible mess. The aftermath of the previous day's massacre was still in evidence. Although there were no dead bodies around, the reception area was still covered in blood. An elevator at the back of reception was covered in blood and faeces.

He eyed the elevator warily and took the stairs on his way to the Forensics department on the third floor. Most of the forensics guys had survived the previous night's massacre and one of them, William Clay, had even turned up for work. Harker found Clay at the first desk inside the office.

Clay was a tall, gangly, socially awkward scientist type with round glasses and a shaved head that neatly disguised a thinning patch on the top of his head. He was sitting behind his desk in the same long white coat he wore every day. As Harker came through the door, he looked up and then immediately closed down a window on his computer monitor.

Harker greeted him cordially. 'Hi, Bill,' he said. 'Is this a bad time?'

Clay smiled. 'Nah, fine. You caught me by surprise. What can I do for you, Lieutenant Dan?'

'It's Captain Harker from today, thank you.'

'I know, just kidding. Congratulations by the way. You pleased?'

'Ecstatic.'

'I'll bet. Get a good raise?'

'I did okay.'

'Good, 'cause you know the last two Captains were killed by the Bourbon Kid. Let's hope he's not looking for a hat trick.'

'Don't you watch the news? Bourbon Kid's dead.'

Clay peered over the top of his glasses. 'He's not though, is he? I can tell just by the look on your face.'

Harker pushed the door shut behind him and walked over to Clay's desk. 'It looks like he somehow faked his death. An hour or so after he was beheaded he showed up at the museum and killed Bertram Cromwell.'

'How do you fake having your head cut off?'

'You get someone who looks like you to take your place.'

'I'm not sure I've got a friend that would give up their head to save me.'

'Me either. But the Bourbon Kid had one. I have no idea who it was. Just another John Doe to add to the list of victims, I suppose.'

'Which includes most of our colleagues,' Clay sighed.

'Not all of whom will be missed.'

'That's harsh.'

Harker rubbed his chin. There was no easy way to make his next revelation without Clay thinking he was insane, so he decided to simply blurt it out. 'Did you know the last Police Captain was a vampire?'

'What?'

'I said –'

'I heard what you said.' Clay frowned. 'You just implied that Captain De La Cruz was a vampire.'

'I didn't imply it. I came right out and said it.'

Clay looked shocked, and unsure of whether or not he was being teased. 'You mean vampire, as in, sucks blood and turns into a bat?'

Harker looked around the room and spotted a plastic chair nearby. He grabbed it and sat down opposite Clay. 'I don't imagine the bat thing is real, but he was definitely a blood sucker.'

'Seriously, you think he was drinking people's blood?'

'I know he was.'

'I hear the rumours of vampires in the town all the time, but I assumed it was *at worst* just a group of people drinking blood and pretending to be vampires or something like that.'

'It's very real.'

Clay didn't look convinced. 'So I could have killed De La Cruz with a crucifix or some garlic then?' he said with a hint of sarcasm.

'He would probably have preferred that to the way he was killed last night.'

'Yeah, I heard. A shotgun up the asshole. Shitty way to go.'

'Yeah, his lunch is all over the elevator. I'm gonna have to get some poor sucker to clean that up later.'

'Don't look at me.'

'Don't piss me off then. Anyway, I didn't come here just to talk to you about dirty elevators and vampire's assholes.'

'So what can I do for you?'

'I spent half an hour on my laptop this morning going through De La Cruz's private files. There's one particular case he was working on that stood out. I can't work out how it's never been on the news. His files say he spoke with you about it on a couple of occasions. I want to know what you've got on it.'

Clay leaned back in his chair. 'It's the child killer case isn't it?'

'Yeah. How d'ya guess?'

'Because it's been pissing me off how De La Cruz never did anything with it. And like you, I can't work out how it never made it onto the news.'

Harker liked the fact that his colleague seemed to care as much as him. 'I've got a theory on that. I think De La Cruz was protecting the killer.'

'I can believe that, but why?'

'I suspect it was another vampire.'

Clay screwed his forehead into a contorted frown. 'That would actually make sense. The evidence would back it up too.'

'Good. So what have you got? Any DNA or anything?'

'Not exactly,' said Clay turning back to his computer. He started tapping away at the keyboard as he spoke. 'However, there've been seventeen murders that I know of.'

'Actually it's more like eighty six.'

Clay raised an eyebrow. 'Like I said, seventeen that *I* know of. But in terms of DNA we've got nothing, no saliva, blood traces or anything like that. What we do have to link all seventeen of the murders i—'

Harker interrupted. 'A green tongue and bite marks on the neck?'

'How did you know?'

'Like I said, I've been going through De La Cruz's files. The bite marks yells vampire at me, but I don't get the green tongue part.'

'It's a kind of poison. All these kids were drugged by an unidentifiable green solution. It causes almost instant paralysis.' He paused and peered over his glasses once more, no longer tapping on his keyboard. 'But there's something else. Something that De La Cruz dismissed out of hand as coincidence, but quite clearly it's a huge clue in the case.'

Harker perked up in his seat. 'What?'

'For twelve of the seventeen victims we found something else. Grey hairs. Usually only one, sometimes two or three, but on several occasions the victims had the grey hairs underneath their fingernails.'

'Like they fought back before the paralysis set in?'

'Exactly.'

'Well can you get a DNA match for the hair?'

Clay grinned. 'Good question. De La Cruz was taking away all the hairs away to analyse them himself, but he never returned any of them. Kept claiming I'd never given them to him and all kinds of other excuses. But, lucky for you, I kept the most recent one. Never told him about it. I knew he would make it vanish if he got his hands on it, so I kept it here and did some analysis.'

'And?'

'It's not human hair.'

Harker raised his eyebrows to emphasise his surprise at the remark. 'What?'

'It ain't human hair. It's goat hair.'

'Goat hair?'

'Goat hair.'

'And?'

'And nothing. It's goat hair. You're the detective, not me.'

'So, it's like a trophy or something? A calling card to identify the killer?'

Clay shrugged. 'Like I said, you're the detective. Personally I would have said the green poison and the bite marks were a perfectly adequate calling card. No need to leave the goat hairs intentionally too.'

'True.' Harker scratched his chin. 'So why goat hair? I guess I can go looking for someone who owns goats. This could be a fairly useful clue.'

Clay smiled. 'Yeah, all you gotta do is find a vampire who happens to be a goat herder in his spare time.'

'You got any better suggestions?'

'*Jesus*, Harker, you're slow.'

'What do you mean?'

'It's not a goat herder or a shepherd you need to be looking for.'

Clay turned the monitor on his computer around for Harker to get a good look. He stared at the screen for a few seconds, puzzled by the picture of a person he recognised. Then the truth hit home. He shook his head. 'Of course,' he said. 'Goat hairs. Sonofabitch.'

Eight

Ulrika Price had encountered numerous problems during her time as Head Librarian at the Santa Mondega Library, but right now she had possibly the most serious crisis of her career. She had lost The Book of Death. Rameses Gaius, her master, had entrusted her as the keeper of the book with two simple instructions, log names in it when instructed to and never under any circumstances lose it. The previous day she had logged three names in it at his request, but then she had carelessly left the book unattended and it had vanished.

She had suffered a sleepless night tossing and turning as she tried to cast her mind back to the previous day's events. She had wracked her brain trying to work out what could have happened to it. Eventually in the early hours she had come to the conclusion that her teenage assistant, Josh, a dimwit of the highest order, must have stuck it on one of the shelves somewhere by mistake.

Fortunately the following morning the library was quiet, which afforded her the time to hunt for the book. For two hours she had searched in vain. It was nowhere to be found. After one last look around her desk area she gave up and decided to phone Josh to see if she could get any sense out of him. These were desperate times indeed. She was relying on Josh, a total idiot, to remember something from the day before. Normally he couldn't remember anything from five minutes before.

She sat at her desk and dialled his home number on the office phone, tapping impatiently on the desk with one of her long bony fingers. Eventually after about eight rings, Josh's mother answered the phone.

'Yeah,' she said.
'It's Ulrika Price at the library.'
'Fucking hell. Hang on a minute. I'll go get him.'

Josh's mother knew better than to waste time making idle small talk with Ulrika. The two of them had exchanged harsh words in the past after Ulrika had once described Josh as a mindless baboon in one of her written appraisals of his performance at the library. Through the phone's earpiece Ulrika heard some shouting and cussing and the sound of someone dropping the phone.

Eventually Josh's irritating voice came through loud and clear. 'Hello, Miss Price.'

'Hello Josh, you moron. I need to know what you did with The Book of Death yesterday.'

'The what?'

'There was a book on my desk yesterday, it's called The Book of Death, and it's gone missing. You must have put it somewhere, or given it out to a customer.'

'Oh.'

He sounded as gormless as ever, much to Ulrika's annoyance. 'Well,' she snapped. 'What have you done with it?'

'I don't remember.'

'Try to remember, please.'

A brief silence followed before Josh replied. 'Was that the Sesame Street annual?'

'No. Why would a Sesame Street annual be called The Book of Death?'

'That's what I was wondering when I put it back on the shelf.'

Ulrika perked up. 'So you *have* seen it?'

'Yeah.'

'What did it look like?'

'It was a big black book, just said The Book of Death on the cover. You're the one who said it was a Sesame Street annual.'

'Why would I say that?'

'I don't know, but you told me to put it back on the shelves before I went home last night. I remember because it's the last thing I did.'

Ulrika breathed a sigh of relief. 'Okay, so you thought it was a Sesame Street annual. Therefore is it safe to assume you stuck it on a shelf in the children's section?'

'No. I think I stuck it in Reference.'

'Why would you stick it there?'

'Because I stick all the books in the Reference section.'

'Prick.'

'I did put it under A though, for Anonymous.'

Ulrika rolled her eyes. Talking to Josh was exasperating. 'Well that's something. Thank you. By the way, don't bother ever coming back to work here, Josh, you're not welcome.'

'Fine by me. Is that all?'

'Yes, goodbye and thanks for your incompetence.'

'Oh, Miss Price, before you go, there's one last thing.'

'What's that?'

'You smell.'

Josh hung up. Ulrika slammed the receiver down in frustration. However, in spite of Josh's rudeness and general ineptitude, at least she now knew where to find the missing book. She hurried over to the

Reference books and began scouring the section marked A for Anonymous.

There were some pretty decent books written by anonymous authors, but the only one Ulrika was interested in was The Book of Death. Unfortunately after scouring the shelves for ten minutes, she came up empty handed. Either Josh had given her incorrect information or someone had borrowed the book from the library after he'd stuck it on the shelf.

The only person who had come into the library after Josh had left the night before was Sanchez Garcia, the bartender from the Tapioca. Ulrika thought back to his appearance. She had caught him loitering suspiciously in the Reference section, and then he had borrowed a book called The Gay Man's Guide to Anal Sex, an odd choice of book for him, she thought. Although Sanchez struck her as being completely inept with women, he didn't strike her as a homosexual either. On the contrary, she'd caught him staring at her cleavage on several occasions, and his dress sense was shit.

She rushed back to her desk to check the computer logs to see if anyone else had been in around the time Josh left. If no one had, then Sanchez might just be the prime suspect in the disappearance of the important book.

As she sat down at her desk the telephone rang. She answered it with an impressive level of politeness considering how irritated she was.

'Hello, City Library.'

'Ulrika?'

She recognised the voice. It was Rameses Gaius. A shiver ran down her spine.

'Hello Rameses,' she said, her voice betraying her anxiety.

'Did you write those names in The Book of Death yesterday as I asked?'

'Of course.'

'Read them back to me please. I need to clarify what names you wrote.'

'Um, oh,' Ulrika tried to cast her mind back to the names she had written in the book the previous day.

'Get on with it,' Gaius snapped. 'Have you not seen the news? They're saying the Bourbon Kid is still alive. This is important. What names did you write down?'

Ulrika cringed. She couldn't remember the names, certainly not under this kind of pressure. 'One of them was John Doe,' she said.

'That's correct.'

'I can't remember the other two,' she said.

'Well look them up in the book for goodness sake!'

Ulrika swallowed hard. 'I can't find it at the moment,' she said softly.

'What?'

'I think it's been borrowed by someone.'

'Borrowed by someone? Since when the fuck did you start allowing people to borrow The Book of Death?'

'I don't. My assistant messed up. But I think I know who has it. I'm just going to track him down. I'll have it back within the hour.'

She could tell by the sound of his breathing that Rameses Gaius was furious. 'If you don't get that book back by lunchtime, I'll send my daughter Jessica to come help you look for it. And I gotta tell you, Jessica really doesn't like you.'

'Yes sir.'

Gaius hung up the phone. Ulrika sat still for a few moments, taking deep breaths to calm her nerves. The book was missing and she had less than two hours to find it.

'Morning Ulrika,' said a man's voice. She looked up and saw Rick from the Ole Au Lait walk past her desk on his way out. She hadn't even seen him come in because she had been so engrossed in her conversation with Rameses Gaius. She didn't like Rick any more than she liked anyone else in town, so she ignored him until he was halfway down the stairs and heading out of the library before she responded with a veiled *"Fuck off"* under her breath.

Her top priority was to get The Book of Death back urgently. And her prime suspect was Sanchez Garcia.

Nine

Beth had received an early phone call from the museum's new manager, Elijah Simmonds. Although he was only in temporary charge, he now had the authority to fire her. He had insisted she drop by the museum even though Bertram Cromwell had given her the day off. Chances were high he was calling her in to relieve her of her position as a cleaner.

She and JD arrived at the museum to find a medical crew outside lifting a stretcher up onto the back of an ambulance. The face of the person on the stretcher was concealed beneath a green blanket. Beth could tell it was Bertram Cromwell. She didn't need to see the gory details. The sight of the blanket pulled over the face of the body was enough to set her mind racing with all kinds of unpleasant images.

JD put his arm around her shoulder and squeezed her in tight as they walked up the steps to the front entrance of the museum. In doing so he shielded her from the sight of the body. Having his arm around her shoulder made her feel safe, and warm too. She had a blue cardigan on over her white T-shirt but with the sudden arrival of snow in Santa Mondega the cardigan wasn't offering as much warmth as usual. She could feel the cold around her legs too because her black jeans had a few tears in them and not for fashion reasons either. They were just bloody old and knackered and she couldn't afford a new pair. With her hair down and the wind blowing it all over the place she actually had a rather cool grungy look going on. She was quite pleased about that because it seemed to be a look that JD liked. He was still wearing his clothes from the night before, blue jeans, black T-shirt and black leather jacket. Beth was hopeful that they looked like a well-matched couple. And secretly she was keen for some of her colleagues to see the two of them together.

Just inside the museum reception area, one of the security guards rushed over. Beth knew him only as James. He was a broad muscular fellow and like every other security guard that had ever worked there his grey uniform looked a size too small. Maybe in his case it was by choice because it looked like he wanted to show off his large pectorals. He was a big guy in his early twenties with a blond wavy haircut and stupidly large shoulders. A nightstick hung from a belt at his side, but in truth he didn't look like the kind who would need it. His fists were big enough to deal with most things.

'Beth, have you heard the news?' he asked with a look of genuine concern on his face.

'About Cromwell? Yes. Terrible, isn't it?'

'Yeah. Shocked the hell out of me.' James seemed to suddenly notice that she wasn't on her own. He stared at JD for a second, then looked back at her, his face showing signs of confusion. 'What you doing in today anyway? Aren't you supposed to be off?'

'Simmonds called me and asked me to come and see him about something.'

James grimaced. 'Oh. He's in his office. You can go straight in. He's on his own.'

'Where's his office?' Beth asked. She couldn't recall Simmonds ever having an office.

'Cromwell's old office. Down there.' James pointed down a corridor that Beth knew well. Her thoughts turned back to Cromwell, one of the nicest men she'd ever met, in a city full of horrible people. He had been the only person to make her feel welcome at the museum. The thought of him being brutally slain by a psycho with a machete was almost too much to bear. It made her more grateful than ever to have rediscovered JD.

'Poor Bertram,' she sniffed, feeling an outbreak of tears coming on. 'He was such a nice man.'

'Yeah. Simmonds will be a good replacement though. He's already got big plans for this place. He's gonna have a real shake up.'

Beth's heart sank. Her time at the museum was surely at an end. Simmonds, the high-flying, pony tailed, scrotum scratching slimebag, didn't like her. Cromwell had been her only ally at the museum.

JD rubbed the small of her back. 'Hey don't worry, I'll come with you,' he offered.

'You can't,' James interrupted. 'It's staff only down there. You'll have to wait here.'

JD kissed her on the forehead. 'You gonna be okay on your own if I wait here with this guy?'

'Yeah.' Beth looked up at him, unable to mask the worried look on her face. She was about to head into a confrontation with Simmonds and she was going to have to do it on her own. 'I'm probably going to get fired,' she whispered.

'You'll be all right,' said JD. 'Just be confident.' He stroked her hair and kissed her on the lips, bringing a gentle smile back to her face momentarily. He still knew exactly how to make things better for her just with a simple gesture. After a deep breath and a squeeze of his hand, Beth headed off down to Cromwell's old office to see her new boss Elijah Simmonds.

JD stood in the reception hall with James the security guard and watched her walk away. Her body language spoke volumes. The walk to the new boss's office clearly filled her with dread.

Once she was out of sight, James wandered over to him and slapped him gently on the shoulder. 'I doubt she'll be very long, buddy. Simmonds gets to the point very quickly.'

'Is she gonna lose her job?'

'Probably.'

'Why? What's this Simmonds guy got against her?'

James laughed quietly, almost to himself. 'You don't know her all that well, do you?' he said. 'I can tell, you've clearly only just met her.'

'Kind of, yeah. Why? What do you mean?'

James patted him on the shoulder again. 'No offence, buddy, but you'll find out soon enough, so I might as well tell you anyway, she's known around town as Mental Beth. She's not quite right in the head.'

'What?'

'Seriously, man. Ask if you can meet her friends.'

'Why? What's wrong with her friends?'

'Nothing, man. It's just that she ain't got any! No one around here likes her. If I can give you some advice, I'd say get out of here quick. Give her a wide berth. She's bad news.' He lowered his voice slightly before adding, 'She killed her own mother.'

JD nodded. 'I see what you're saying.'

'Yeah, you can do a lot better,' said James, patting him on the shoulder one more time. 'Right, I've got other places to be, see you later, man.'

As James walked away, JD followed after him. 'Hold on a sec,' he said catching up with the security guard.

'Whassup?' James asked.

JD pointed at James's chest. 'You've got something on your shirt.'

Ten

Sanchez wasn't entirely sure how it had happened, but somehow he'd ended up in a Volkswagen Beetle with Flake. And he was on his way to the police station to enrol as a member of law enforcement. Not a proper officer by any stretch, but if he couldn't work out an acceptable way to weasel out of it pretty soon, he was going to find himself in a uniform as one of those useless part time cops with no authority.

Flake babbled on at a hundred miles an hour about how excited she was to be joining the force. She spoke so bloody quickly that Sanchez couldn't get a word in. He'd had to accept a ride from her after discovering to his dismay that some local kids had vandalised his car outside the Ole Au Lait. All four of his tyres had been slashed. *"No doubt unprovoked,"* he thought.

Flake had promised she would drop him off at the tyre repair place. But it now seemed that her plan was to go there after they'd been to the police station. As a contingency plan to avoid joining the police, Sanchez was fully prepared to pull out the old "bad back" excuse.

Flake drove like she spoke too. This girl didn't stop for anything. Red lights, stop signs, pedestrians, snowmen, she just zipped through, over or around them. Her constant chatter would have done Sanchez's head in under any normal circumstance. At the moment he was unable to concentrate on anything other than clenching his butt cheeks and pressing both hands against the dashboard. As if to make travel that much more terrifying, the passenger side of Flake's old white Beetle wasn't fitted with a seat belt. So Sanchez actually felt somewhat relieved when they arrived at the police station. Flake steered the car down the wrong side of the road for a hundred yards or so, before pulling a completely unnecessary handbrake turn which spun the car around and pulled it perfectly into a parking spot directly out front of the station.

Throughout the manoeuvre Sanchez had gripped the dashboard so tight that his fingers had gone white. He was also stuck with a wide-eyed look of terror imprinted on his face. It was a look that would take a few seconds of deep breaths to shift.

Flake switched off the engine. 'Come on, Sanchez,' she said. She gave him a gentle shove on the arm as if she thought he was faking the look of terror.

'I think we just travelled back in time,' Sanchez muttered.

'You're so funny,' said Flake, slapping his arm once more. 'Come on. Stop joking around and let's get in there before it's too late.'

Sanchez definitely wanted to be out of the car. He knew that much. But he didn't particularly want to be walking up the steps to the police station. As the blood began to flow back into his fingers he peeled his hands back off the dashboard and reached over to open the door. Flake was already up and out of the car by the time he had hauled his ass up out of the seat. Closing the door behind him he took a deep breath and with his left hand reached slowly around to his back. He started to rub it slowly and pretended to wince in pain.

Flake looked genuinely concerned. 'Are you okay?' she asked.

'Old war injury,' said Sanchez grimacing. 'Not sure I'll make it up them steps.'

Flake's face dropped. 'Oh.'

Before she could add anything else, a police officer came rushing down the steps from the front of the station. He was a rugged fellow in his mid-forties with a full head of neatly combed brown hair. And he was dressed smartly for a cop too. He had on a pair of black trousers and a white shirt with a black waistcoat over it. Sanchez was surprised to see an officer in such good shape, considering the obligatory diet of donuts that all the local boys in blue stuck to so rigidly.

The officer yelled at Flake as he approached her. 'You got a license for that vehicle miss?'

Sanchez recognised the officer. It was Dan Harker, a fairly decent, hard-working detective who had never really made it as far up the ranks as he should have. If memory served correctly he was one of the less corruptible cops, not as easily open to bribes as most of the others. He'd dropped by the Tapioca numerous times to question Sanchez about various unsolved crimes.

At the sound of his voice Flake turned around. 'Hello, Mr Harker,' she said. She knew him too. The Ole Au Lait wasn't exactly crime free either.

'Flake, you drive like a freakin' lunatic. I could book you for dangerous driving and illegal parking right now!' Harker said, shaking his head.

Sanchez nodded in agreement with Harker, although he brought the nodding to an abrupt end when he thought Flake had caught sight of it out of the corner of her eye.

'I'm sorry Dan,' said Flake smiling. 'We've come to sign up for the police force and I was hoping to impress you with my driving skills, you know? I'm good in a high speed pursuit.'

Dan Harker's look of disapproval vanished. 'Oh,' he said. 'Good. I mean, excellent. You're the first two to come and sign up. Come on in. I'll get your forms filled in.'

'I've got a bad back,' said Sanchez, once more rubbing his back and wincing.

Harker ignored him and spoke to Flake, 'There's a thousand dollar incentive for the first two people to sign up.'

Sanchez perked up and looked around him. There were a few other people milling around in the street. No sense in waiting for one of them to race up the steps and get into the station before him. Straightening up, he rushed out of the icy road and onto the snow-covered sidewalk, then bounded on to the steps and up towards the glass doors at the front of the station.

'Gosh, he's keen,' said Harker.

Flake rushed up the steps after Sanchez. 'We're both very keen to do our duty,' she said.

Sanchez reeled back in shock when he saw the state of the reception area in the station. The place was a bloody mess. Literally. In fact it was one big crime scene. The walls and floor were covered in blood. And it smelled like the Tapioca after a curry night. Harker followed them in.

'It's a real mess in here,' he said walking briskly past Sanchez and Flake. 'One of your first jobs will be cleaning this place up. We've had forensics in to collate all the evidence, now we just need someone to wipe the blood off the walls.'

'Sanchez will be good at that,' Flake said.

'That's true,' Sanchez agreed. He'd cleaned blood and piss off the walls of the Tapioca numerous times. And for a thousand dollars, he'd clean up just about anything.

Harker smiled and reached into a drawer on the main reception desk. He pulled out a thick blue hardback book and slapped it down on the desk. 'I just need you both to sign this register,' he said opening the book up. 'You sign this each day and it grants you the authority to arrest, harass and intimidate local civilians at your leisure. You get paid a thousand dollars up front for being the first two recruits. After that it's a standard five hundred dollars a day.'

Sanchez picked up a pen from the desk and grabbed the book before Flake could get to it. He filled in a few details and signed his name then looked up at Harker.

'You paying cash?' he asked.

'For the first day, yes. After that it's bank transfer.'

'Good enough.'

Flake began filling in her details in the register. Harker took a few steps back and stared at his new recruits, looking them both up and down. 'Right,' he said frowning. 'I'm going to nip upstairs and get you two some uniforms. Should be easy for you Flake, you're a fairly common size. It might take me a while to find a pair of pants for you though, Sanchez.'

'I'm a medium,' Sanchez said defensively.

'And I'm an astronaut,' said Harker. 'I'll find you some pants, don't worry. Now, while I'm upstairs getting your uniforms you can get started. Flake, you man the reception desk. Deal with any phone calls or anyone who comes in off the street to report a crime. If you're not sure what to do, just bullshit them.'

Flake looked genuinely enthusiastic. 'I can do that,' she said smiling.

Harker turned back to Sanchez. 'You can start by cleaning the elevator. There's a mop and bucket over there in the corner. There's soapy water in it already. All you gotta do is…'

'I know how to mop, thank you,' said Sanchez.

'Fine. Then I'll expect that elevator to be spotless by the time I get back.'

Harker turned on his heels and headed for the door that led to the stairs. Sanchez pulled a face at him behind his back and mumbled a quiet impersonation of him under his breath.

'Isn't this exciting?' said Flake.

'Exhilarating,' said Sanchez sarcastically. He walked over to the mop and bucket and picked it up. Then he wheeled it over to the elevator and pressed a grey button in the wall to call it. The doors opened immediately and Sanchez was overwhelmed by the stench of shit. The elevator was covered in blood, brains and shit from floor to ceiling. It looked worse than the toilets in the Tapioca after a Saturday night. Shaking his head in disgust, he pulled the mop out from the bucket and shoved the head of it into the floor. This would be no five-minute job. The stink alone would take weeks to eliminate.

Two minutes into his mopping task, Sanchez heard someone approaching the reception desk behind him. Then he heard a lady's voice speak. It was a voice he recognised.

'I'd like to report the theft of a book from the library,' it said.

Ulrika Price. The bitch.

Sanchez stepped into a now clean part of the elevator and turned around. His eyes immediately met Ulrika's. The librarian had obviously come straight from work because she was wearing a woolly brown cardigan over a flowery dress, standard attire for annoying librarian types. She loomed ominously over the reception desk, with Flake seated in front of her, with her back to Sanchez. Ulrika's piercing green eyes opened wide when she saw Sanchez.

'It's him!' she hissed. 'He stole it!'

Sanchez shook his head. 'No. Not me,' he mumbled.

Ulrika strode around the reception desk. Flake stood up. 'You can't go back there,' she said.

Without taking her eyes off Sanchez, Ulrika shoved Flake in the face, knocking her back into her chair. Then to Sanchez's utter horror, she opened her mouth to reveal a set of rapidly expanding vampire fangs.

Just as he'd suspected in the past, this evil bitch was a vampire. And right now, she had her eyes set on Sanchez as her first meal.

There was only one thing to do. Press a button in the elevator and get the hell out of there. Sanchez looked down at the keypad. All of the buttons were covered in shit apart from one. The button for the basement. He pressed it six times in less than a second. Through the closing doors he saw Ulrika's feet leave the floor as she flew towards him, fangs wide open.

Eleven

Beth arrived at Cromwell's office and was saddened to find that the nameplate on the door had already been changed. Instead of CROMWELL it now read SIMMONDS in bold silver lettering over the black plaque.

She knocked twice on the door and soon heard Simmonds's voice call through from the other side.

'Come in.'

She reached for the large brass doorknob and twisted it first one way and then the other. It didn't open so she tried pulling hard as she twisted it this way and that. She could never remember if the door opened inwards or out. Eventually she was relieved to find that it opened when she pushed it and turned the knob to the right simultaneously. Breathing a sigh of relief she entered the office and closed the door shut behind her.

Simmonds was sitting in the large black leather chair behind the shiny oak desk. And he looked smug. Even by his own smug standards as the undisputed King of Smug Town. He had his blond hair scraped back into its traditional greasy Steven Seagal style ponytail.

'Hello, Elijah,' Beth said smiling tentatively.

'It's Mr Simmonds to you, Lansbury,' he replied coldly.

She approached one of the two seats on the near side of the desk opposite Simmonds.

'Don't bother sitting down,' he said waving a dismissive hand at her. 'This isn't going to take long.'

'Umm, okay.'

'Terrible news about Bertram obviously, but life goes on. I hope you're not too upset.'

'Are you kidding? Mr Cromwell was a lovely man.'

'Yes, the emphasis there being *was*. Unfortunately now he's dead, but the museum is not. And I, as the new manager am going to have to make all the changes that Cromwell was too weak to make.'

Beth nodded, knowing what was coming. 'Okay.'

'We have to cut costs and I'm afraid that means that some staff will lose their jobs.'

'Oh dear, how many?'

Simmonds grimaced. 'I was hoping you wouldn't ask that. Basically we only need to lose one head, and, well, it's you. You'll be paid up to the end of the week, but I'd prefer it if you left now.'

Beth's heart sank. She'd known this would happen the second she'd heard about Cromwell's death. 'I think my contract says I get paid up to the end of the month if I lose my job.'

Simmonds shook his head. 'You've got some nerve, haven't you?' he said with a look of disgust on his face. 'Bertram Cromwell is dead, murdered at the hands of the Bourbon Kid, in cold blood, with a machete, and all you can think about is yourself and how to take advantage of your contract.'

Beth was taken aback. 'No, it's not like that.'

'Well that's how it looks, Lansbury. God, you disgust me sometimes. It's not enough that you killed your stepmother, you now want to trample all over the memory of a great man like Bertram Cromwell, after all he did for you.'

'That's not fair.'

'Take it up with the union.'

'I didn't know we had a union.'

'We don't. Now get out. I can't bear to look at you. Honestly, did it never occur to you to cover up that scar on your face when you came to work? It upsets everyone else here having to look at it.'

Beth could feel tears welling up in her eyes. The scar ran deep for many reasons. She tried to downplay it though, so as not to give Simmonds the satisfaction of knowing he had gotten to her. 'It's just a scar,' she said.

'Yes, but that scar represents the struggle of your stepmother trying to defend herself when you stabbed her to death doesn't it? Awful, just awful. I don't know how you have the nerve to walk around with it on display like that.'

Beth had no further response. A tear trickled down her right cheek, slipping into her scar and sliding along it towards the corner of her mouth. Simmonds gestured towards the door and then looked down at some papers on his desk to signify that their meeting was over.

'Go on, run along,' he said. 'We're done here.'

Beth felt her bottom lip tremble. Being fired was a humiliating experience at the best of times, but to be ridiculed in this manner was too much to take.

'What about my uniform and stuff. What should I...'

Simmonds looked up. 'Are you still here?' he sneered.

'Yes, I just...'

'Oh God, you're not going to cause a scene, are you? Seriously, if there's one thing I can't stand, it's people coming into my office and causing a scene. If you want a drama, go join an acting club or something, don't do it in my office.'

Beth turned away. She'd had all she could take. She grabbed the doorknob. There was an awkward three or four seconds as she fumbled with turning and pulling it before it opened. Luckily it came open just before she began sobbing out loud. Being humiliated by a bully like Simmonds had really gotten to her. Bullying didn't get any easier to take as an adult. Her only comfort was that now unlike in the past, at least she had JD to offer an arm of consolation or a kind word to make it all better. She trudged back up the stairs to reception, wiping away the tears as she went, in the hope of not looking like too much of a mess when she got back to him.

What she discovered when she arrived back in reception made her forget about her tears quite quickly. JD was still there, smiling at her as she hurried back to him. But lying on the floor at his feet in a state of unconsciousness was James the security guard.

Forgetting about her tears for a moment, she hurried over and peered down at James. He was laid out, completely motionless on the floor. She looked back up at JD.

'What happened?' she asked, her voice revealing her obvious concern for the security guard.

'I think he fainted,' said JD shrugging. 'How was your meeting?'

'His face is covered in blood,' Beth said, staring at the terrible state of James's face. She leaned down to take a closer look at the stricken security guard. 'How did that happen?'

'He had a nosebleed. I think the sight of his own blood is what made him faint.'

Beth frowned. 'But his nose looks broken and his eyes are swollen.'

'Yeah. Weird. So what did your boss say?'

'I got fired.'

JD reached out and stroked her hair away from her face. He could see she'd been crying. 'It's just a job. Not worth crying about. Look on the bright side, now we've got no reason to stay in this shithole town.'

'It's not being fired that bothers me so much as the way he did it.'

'Why? What did he do?'

Beth sniffed. The tears were coming back. 'He said my scar bothers everyone here and I should be more considerate and cover it up.'

'Fucking cunt.'

JD stormed past her in the direction of Simmonds's office.

Simmonds was glad to see the back of Beth Lansbury. Now that the museum was under his control there was absolutely no need to be employing women with facial disfigurements. It made him shudder to think that Cromwell had been so foolish as to employ her in the first place, what with the fact she was a convicted murderer too. What a ghastly image for the museum. A scar-faced murderer working there. Well not any more. Firing her had been fun too. He was still congratulating himself on making her cry when the door to his office flew open and one angry looking dude stormed in.

'Who are you?' Simmonds asked.

'Are you Simmonds?'

'Yes. And I'll ask again, who are you?'

'I'm JD, the guy that's come to ram your face up your own ass.'

Simmonds sighed and rolled his eyes. 'Have you come to cause a scene?' he said nonchalantly. 'Because if you have, I'll get security to have you removed.'

JD approached Simmonds desk and leaned over it to get into his personal space. 'Security's lying on his back upstairs with a broken nose.'

'So you have come to cause a scene then? Well you should know this. I know karate,' Simmonds said coolly. He demonstrated a few slow motion karate chops with his hands. 'These hands are deadly weapons.'

JD reached over the desk and grabbed him by the throat, hauling him up out of his seat, so that the two of them were eyeball to eyeball. 'Try using those hands now,' he growled.

Simmonds swallowed hard and responded in as brave a voice as he could muster. 'Get out of my office before I call the police.'

'You think it's funny to take the piss out of someone for having a scar on her face? How about I slice your face up and then take the piss outta you?'

Simmonds smirked and nodded at the doorway behind JD. 'Don't make me embarrass you in front of your girlfriend.'

JD looked back over his shoulder. Beth was standing in the doorway behind him. Simmonds could see that she'd been crying. She looked as bereft of self-confidence as she always did. The girl really was a pathetic excuse for a human being. Simmonds couldn't work out quite how she'd ever managed to murder someone. She looked too timid.

'JD, leave him,' she pleaded. 'It doesn't matter. He's not worth the trouble.'

JD looked back at Simmonds. He looked like he wanted to say something, but instead he slowly and reluctantly released his grip on the manager's throat. Simmonds slouched back into his leather chair with a satisfied smirk across his face.

'I carry a lot of sway around this city these days you know,' he bragged.

'I don't give a—'

Beth jumped in to cut him short. 'JD, please let's just go. I don't want any trouble with the police.'

'See,' said Simmonds. 'With her criminal record, she can't take any chances, and neither should you. Listen to Tony Montana. She knows what she's talking about.'

JD furrowed his brow. 'What did you just call her?'

'Tony Montana. That's what everyone calls her around here. You know, Scarface.'

Before JD could lunge over the desk at Simmonds, Beth grabbed him by the arm.

'Please let's go,' she said. 'I'm glad I'm not working here any more. You wouldn't want me to have a job working for this guy, would you?'

'No, but I'd feel better if I knocked him out.'

'But I won't. I don't want to lose you again just because you've beaten up this loser and been arrested. Come on, let's go.'

JD eyeballed Elijah Simmonds for a few more seconds before Beth dragged him away. He managed one last comment. It was almost lost under his breath but it was just loud enough for Simmonds to pick up on it.

'This isn't finished.'

Simmonds's face broke out into a huge grin. 'Yeah, good one,' he called after them as they left his office without closing the door behind them. 'See ya, JD. What's that stand for anyway? Juvenile Dick?'

JD didn't answer. Simmonds got up and closed the door behind them then sat back at his desk and congratulated himself on wielding a little more of his newly acquired power. He turned back to his computer to check on the local news to see if there was any announcement about his appointment as the Museum's new manager. The news mentioned the demise of Bertram Cromwell but had no mention of Simmonds replacing him. As he scoured through the article he came across some breaking news. It said:

CCTV footage of the Bourbon Kid found. Click here to see what he looks like.

Simmonds clicked on the link expecting to see the footage he had provided to Captain Dan Harker. Instead what he saw was some different footage of the Bourbon Kid walking into the local police station with two other guys dressed as cops. He recognised one of the cops as Dante Vittori, a former employee at the museum. But that wasn't what really caught his eye. He recognised the face of the Bourbon Kid too. It was JD, the man who had just left his office with Beth Lansbury.

Twelve

Even though the elevator doors had closed before Ulrika Price got anywhere near him, Sanchez knew it was only going to be a brief reprieve. Having pressed the button to take him down to the basement he was now faced with two options. He could either get out when the doors opened and make a run for it, or stay in the elevator and press one of the shit covered buttons to head back up to one of the higher floors. Problem was, if Ulrika had called the elevator back to the ground floor, the doors would open when he got there and she'd be upon him. And all he had to defend himself from any attack was a dirty mop. Time was not on his side, so when the elevator doors opened he decided to head straight out. He was greeted by the sight of a disused locker room. The place (much like the elevator) was covered in blood, mostly on the floor, but there were also specks sprayed across the walls and doors of the lockers.

As the elevator doors closed behind him he began retreating down through the rows of lockers, watching the elevator to see if it went back up. He was backing himself into a corner with only a damp mop covered in blood, shit and a touch of soapy water as protection.

After a few seconds he heard the gears churn and the elevator started moving upwards. He continued edging back from it, keeping one eye on the door in the wall next to the elevator in case Ulrika charged through it. He couldn't see a single decent hiding place either. His options seemed limited to the lockers or the benches in front of them. And Sanchez was in no kind of shape to be fitting himself into a locker, or under a bench for that matter.

Glancing behind him he saw that he was heading towards a communal shower area. This had potential. Maybe if he turned on all the showers he could create some steam to hide in? If Ulrika showed up and followed him in, he could catch her with his mop and make a break for it. It was lame. Not a plan that even Sanchez was proud of, but what else did he have? And why was Ulrika taking so long to get down to the basement? Maybe she was killing Flake?

Damn, Sanchez had forgotten all about Flake in his haste to escape from Ulrika. If Flake perished at the hands of Ulrika, he'd have to find another ride home if he made it out of the station in one piece. Flake made a pretty damn good breakfast too. Sanchez hated the thought that he might have to get his early morning fry up from somewhere other than the Ole Au Lait.

As he pondered every trivial matter that came to mind, he backed into one of the shower switches. What followed was a grinding sound from behind. He spun around and saw the wall behind him sliding to one side. A secret compartment had opened up for him. What a stroke of luck! A clear sign if one was needed that Sanchez's infrequent visits to church had paid off.

The room behind the door was actually quite a substantial size. And it had a long wooden table in it. No bloody chairs though. Sanchez was about to congratulate himself on finding the secret room when he realised he couldn't see a switch anywhere to close the wall back up again. No use being in a secret room if everyone can see in. He looked around frantically for some kind of switch inside the room. There didn't seem to be anything remotely resembling a switch. Maybe moving the table would trigger something off?

He leaned his back against the table to see if he could shift it. It moved back easily enough. But as it did the elevator at the other end of the locker room made a pinging noise and its doors parted slowly. Ulrika Price stormed out. She clocked Sanchez right away.

'Where's my book, you thieving bastard?' she screamed.

Sanchez pushed back hard against the table and succeeded in forcing it back against the wall. It achieved nothing. The secret doorway remained open. He watched in terror as Ulrika launched herself towards him at great speed. Her feet left the ground and she flew through the air, her arms outstretched. Sanchez had seen some unpleasant stuff in his time, but the sight of a crazy librarian bitch flying at him, was right up there with the worst of them. He grabbed a firm hold of his mop and lifted his ass up on to the table behind him. Then climbing to his feet, he stood firm on the table and held the mop out to fend off the onrushing vampire.

Ulrika landed back on her feet at the entrance to the secret room and sneered at him. 'That mop won't save you!' she hissed.

'It's got shit on the end of it!' Sanchez warned. 'And I'll shove it in your face! I'm warning you. Stay back!'

It didn't deter Ulrika who once again leapt from the floor and flew up towards Sanchez's head. Bracing himself for the impact of her attack, he thrust the mop at her from his position up high on the table. Being pretty useful with a mop, he successfully caught her full in the face with the shittiest part of the mop head. It knocked her off balance, forcing her back. She landed upright on her feet and Sanchez retracted the mop, ready to go back in with another lunge if needed.

Ulrika's face was covered in blood, shit, soap and oddly enough a small piece of sweetcorn. She wiped most of it away with one swipe of her long bony right hand.

Sanchez warned her again. 'This mop has a lifetime supply of filth. Come one step closer and it goes on your shoes, bitch.'

Ulrika lowered her head and bent her knees to make herself a smaller target so she could avoid the prods of his mop as she looked for the best way to attack him. It didn't take her long to work it out. She lunged down at the table beneath him and grabbed a hold of one of the legs on the near side. She yanked it hard. As she pulled at it, Sanchez swung the mop head at her once more, catching her on the side of the head. But Ulrika was strong. The strength of her pull on the table moved it swiftly and violently towards her causing Sanchez to lose his footing. He tumbled forward off the table. In order to avoid smashing his face on the floor he had to manoeuvre the mop head so that his face landed on it to cushion the blow. He heard a horrible squishing noise as the remains of what was left on the mop splashed over his face. There was no time to lie around whining about it though. Keeping a tight grip on its handle he clambered to his feet and saw Ulrika on his right, lunging towards him. He prodded the mop at her feet, just as he'd threatened to. If he was going down he was taking that bitch's shoes with him. The mop connected with her comfy red lesbian shoes and unbalanced her just enough to buy him the time to turn and run. He knew that Ulrika would most likely catch up with him before he reached the elevator, but he had to make a break for it.

He ran down through the rows of lockers as fast as he could. Unfortunately that wasn't particularly fast, and the mop made things particularly awkward. He only made it past three lockers out of a row of thirty, before he was confronted by Ulrika again. She had somersaulted over his head and landed in front of him, blocking his only escape route out of the locker room. Her face looked murderous, and a little shitty. Her hair was unkempt and her eyes full of spite. This was one riled-up bitch. Sanchez had no option but to swing his mop again. This time Ulrika was too quick for him. She grabbed a hold of the mop handle and yanked it out of his hands. Then she tossed it to the floor and revealed her vampire fangs once more. She spat out a hiss and then launched herself at him again. Sanchez cowered down and raised an arm to fend her off, but it was to no avail. Ulrika pounced on his back and pushed him down to the floor, pinning him there with her knee pressed into the small of his back. It knocked the wind out of him and left him powerless to fight back.

He felt her breath on the side of his face as she leaned down to speak in his ear. 'I've never liked you, Sanchez. Now tell me what you've done with my Book of Death!'

'I don't know what you're talking about,' he protested.

'You won't be able to lie to me when I rip out your jugular,' she hissed.

'Rick from the Ole Au Lait has it.'

'Bullshit.'

'Honest.'

Ulrika grabbed a clump of his hair and pulled his head up off the floor, almost breaking his neck. 'I don't believe you,' she said sniffing his neck for a good spot to bite. 'I can smell a lie you know.'

'Are you sure it's not the shit from the mop?'

'You think you're so funny, don't you?' she hissed. 'Let's see how funny you taste, shall we?'

Sanchez closed his eyes and winced in readiness for whatever pain was about to follow. Ulrika let out another sickening animalistic hiss right by his ear.

A gentle thud followed.

And then a longer hiss. *A really loud hiss.* Sanchez suddenly felt like his back was on fire. The burning feeling lasted little more than two or three seconds as the cowardly bartender lay eyes closed on the floor waiting for the moment of truth.

There was another gentle thud as something landed on his back. Then he heard Flake's voice speak out from behind him. 'Are you okay honey?'

'Huh?'

Sanchez opened his eyes and peered back. Flake was stood over him. She lifted a thick brown hardback book off his back and dusted it off.

'What the hell?' Sanchez asked aloud, baffled at the lack of any sign of Ulrika Price. 'Where's the psycho bookworm gone?'

Flake tucked the brown book under her left arm and held out her right hand to offer him a lift up from the floor. Sanchez took a hold of her hand and hauled himself up. Flake was smiling, looking very happy about something.

'What's going on?' Sanchez asked again.

'I hit that bitch over the head with this book,' said Flake holding out the brown hardback book.

'So where'd she go?'

'She burst into flames and then turned into ash. Look.' She gestured at a patch of thick black ash, most of which was settling on the floor, and some of which was no doubt on Sanchez's back.

'What the fuck?' Sanchez was still confused.

'This book kills vampires, I guess,' Flake said with a shrug.

'But how did you know?'

'I didn't. My horoscope today said that I should use a book for something other than reading.'

'You do everything your horoscope tells you?'

'Oh yeah, I live my life by Big Busty Sally's horoscope.'

'God bless Sally. Did she tell you to come down to the locker room too?'

Flake laughed. 'No I just followed Ulrika down here to try and help you. When I got here she was on top of you. Then I saw this book sticking out of one of the lockers over there and I thought about what my horoscope had said. So I hit her over the head with it. As soon as it made contact with her she just spontaneously combusted.'

Sanchez dusted himself off. 'Wow. You did that because of a horoscope?' he asked, failing to mask the surprise in his voice.

'Well partly,' said Flake. 'But you and me are a team. We've got to watch each other's backs. You led her down here so that we'd have her cornered, right?'

Sanchez coughed. 'Well yes. Obviously. I had to get her away from you, so that you'd be safe. I knew she'd follow me down here.'

'You're so clever Sanchez. I'd give you a kiss, but it looks like you have poo on your face.'

'Never mind about that,' he said wiping his face. 'Next time just don't take so long to get down here.'

'Sorry,' said Flake. 'I shudder to think what might have happened if I hadn't found this book. We might both be dead by now.'

She had a point. The discovery of the book was a stroke of incredibly good fortune. 'What's the deal with that book anyway?' Sanchez asked aloud.

'Maybe vampires are allergic to books?' Flake suggested.

'She was a librarian.'

'Oh.'

'Yeah. That woman's had her filthy hands on every book in the city. So I figure that one you just dropped on her must be a bit special. A book that kills vampires, eh? It could be worth a fortune. We could auction it on eBay!'

Flake clearly disagreed. The look on her face said as much. 'If it's really a deadly weapon that kills vampires I think I'd rather keep quiet about it. Ulrika was looking for a book and she was willing to kill you for it. Let me do some research on the Internet to see if I can find anything out about *this* book. The last thing we need is more librarians coming down here!'

She had a point. 'This is a worry,' said Sanchez. 'It's dark outside. Vampires could be all over the city. Maybe something big is about to go down?'

Flake grimaced. 'If that's the case, then this book might be the most important thing in the world. Let's keep it to ourselves for now.'

Thirteen

In spite of what appearances might suggest, Silvinho was a great lover of culture and the arts. A giant of a man dressed in military gear and sporting a six-inch high pink mohawk haircut, he certainly didn't look like your typical art lover. But having just recently completed the latest Shadow Company mission, one that involved gunning down and beheading the Bourbon Kid, he wanted to take in the sights at the Santa Mondega Museum of Art and History before he and his team left town. Life as a mercenary suited him just fine. He'd spent years in war zones killing men behind enemy lines, often going months at a time without seeing a piece of art. Fortunately his new role as a mercenary travelling the world with his Shadow Company comrades allowed him the chance to sample the best art that the world had to offer, in between beheading the odd person here and there.

He was in one of the museum's many art halls admiring a magnificent colourful Eugene Delacroix painting of a young lady when his cell phone rang. The display on the phone indicated that the call was from his boss, Bull, so he answered it without hesitation.

'Hey, what's up boss?'

'You seen the news?'

'No.'

'Well it turns out that the guy we beheaded last night wasn't the Bourbon Kid. We got the wrong guy.'

'Who did we kill?'

'Just some freak who looked a bit like him.'

Silvinho grimaced. 'Oh dear. It's a pity we didn't notice that before we shot him and cut his head off.'

'Yeah well, I'm over it already. Where are you now? I need you back here at the Casa de Ville.'

Silvinho took a look around at the paintings on the wall to remind himself he was in a place of great beauty. 'I'm just at the museum. Got some lovely paintings here.'

'Is that the Art and History museum?'

'Yeah. Why is there another one around here?'

'No. But according to the news the Bourbon Kid showed up there just after two o'clock this morning and killed the museum's manager.'

'Oh. Want me to ask around here? See if anyone knows anything about it?'

'Yeah. Ask to see if they have any security camera footage of the killing. And find out if he had a motive to kill the manager there. It might be a clue that leads us to him, or his next victim.'

'Sure thing boss. Anything else?'

'Just give me a call if you find anything out. If you don't then just head back to base.'

'Will do. Later.'

Silvinho hung up the phone and took one last look at the Delacroix painting before reluctantly heading back to the reception area.

In the reception hall he saw a security guard with a badly swollen nose and a pair of black eyes. The guard looked like he'd had a pretty bad day so far and was ready to go home. He was the perfect guy to interrogate.

'Excuse me,' said Silvinho, approaching him. He glanced at the guard's security badge. 'James,' he announced. 'My name is Silvinho. I'm from the U.S Special Forces. I understand the Bourbon Kid dropped by here last night. Is that correct?'

The guard's response was less than enthusiastic. 'You got any ID?' he asked.

'Sure.' Silvinho reached inside his coat and grabbed his wallet. He opened it and pulled out a plastic ID card. He handed it over to James who took it and eyed it suspiciously.

'How do I know this is real?' he asked.

'I could render you unconscious in about three seconds flat, if you like? Would that validate me?'

James looked as though he wanted to dare him to back up the threat with actions, but after gently rubbing his broken nose he handed the card back to Silvinho.

'I'll take you to Elijah Simmonds's office. He can answer any questions you have. He's already told the police everything though, and given them a copy of the CCTV footage.'

'You *have* CCTV footage?'

'Yep. If the boss okays it, I'll make you a copy.'

Silvinho smiled and slapped his right hand down on James's shoulder, squeezing it hard. 'I'll tell you what,' he said. 'How about you direct me to your boss's office and while I'm there you can get me a copy of the footage, you know, to save time.'

He squeezed James's shoulder just a tiny bit harder, which was all it took for the security guard to agree to the proposition.

'Just head right down that corridor,' said James pointing the way. At the end of it you'll see Simmonds's office. You can't miss it. It's got his name on the door.'

'Thanks. I'll see you there shortly.'

Silvinho released his grip on the other man's shoulder and made his way down to Elijah Simmonds's office. Sure enough it was exactly where James had indicated it would be. He knocked twice on the door and then turned the doorknob to open it without waiting for Simmonds to answer. The door opened inwards and he was greeted by the sight of Elijah Simmonds sitting behind a desk with a laptop computer in front of him. He looked startled at the sight of a giant soldier with a pink mohawk striding in.

'Can I help you?' he asked.

'You Simmonds?'

'Yes.'

'I'm Silvinho. I work for Special Forces. Come about the Bourbon Kid. Mind if I ask you a few questions?'

Simmonds spun his laptop around. 'The Bourbon Kid,' he said pointing at a face on the computer screen. 'You mean this guy?'

Silvinho stared at the screen. 'Is that him?' he asked.

'Yep,' said Simmonds.

'The picture's not very good is it?'

'No. But it's good enough that I recognize him as a man who was in this office just a few minutes ago.'

'What?'

'I just fired his girlfriend and he came down here to berate me for it. He tried to cause a scene and ended up embarrassing himself.'

'The Bourbon Kid has a girlfriend?'

'Yes. And in exchange for the reward they're offering on the television for information that leads to the arrest of the Bourbon Kid, I'll gladly give you her home address.'

Silvinho pulled bone-handled knife from inside his jacket. The blade was almost a foot long and had serrated edges. He ran his index finger along the smooth part of the blade and eyeballed Simmonds.

The museum's manager looked deeply concerned. 'There's no need for any violence,' he said nervously. 'I just want the reward that's advertised.'

'Forget the reward,' Silvinho snapped. 'Just give me the address, or I'll cut your fucking balls off.'

Fourteen

Beth stared out of the car window at the sleet and snow shooting down from the sky outside. Since the thunderstorm from the night before had ended, the snowfall had been relentless and had settled two inches thick on the ground. The clouds that had formed overhead were the darkest she had ever seen and they seemed to cover the whole sky. Occasional intermittent shafts of sunlight slipped through between clouds here and there, but generally Santa Mondega had become a city bathed in darkness overnight.

Being driven slowly through the icy streets in JD's super cool black V8 Interceptor made her feel like a teenager again. This is what the pair of them should have been doing in their high school years. Going for drives in his car, taking walks along the pier and just generally hanging out and having fun.

Nothing in her life ever worked out as she planned though, and now that she found herself without a job, she worried that she wouldn't be able to pay the rent on her apartment. She could probably survive for a few weeks, but then what? Ask JD to help out with the rent? Or ask him to move in? Or move in with him? Where did he live anyway? He wasn't very clear on where he'd been and what he'd been doing for the last eighteen years. Travelling mostly, he'd claimed, and left it pretty much at that.

The car radio had been playing Christmas songs for the whole journey, inter-spliced with news updates, one of which announced that the Bourbon Kid was still alive. It seemed that to alleviate all the bad news, the local radio station had jumped into an early festive mood brought on by the sight of the snow, even though it was only one day after Halloween.

JD hadn't spoken since the song *Have Yourself a Merry Little Christmas* by Judy Garland began playing. As the song was coming to an end, the deejay's voice spoke over it. Beth recognised him as Mad Harry Hunter, a local radio star with an annoying knack of dragging out every word. He interrupted the end of the song with an announcement that the police were hiring new recruits and paying them a handsome daily rate until new cops could be drafted in from out of town.

Beth considered the possibilities of becoming a cop. 'Maybe I should try out for the police force?' she suggested, hoping to gauge JD's thoughts on the matter before committing to it.

'Fuck the police. Bunch of corrupt fuckers,' he muttered, not taking his eyes off the icy road ahead.

The uneven road they were on was covered in icy puddles and littered with potholes, many of which were hidden under patches of snow and ice, making the road even more dangerous than usual. It didn't help that cars were parked on either side of the road, leaving little room for manoeuvring around the hazards. The only blessing was that there was hardly any other traffic about.

'They're pretty desperate by the sounds of it though,' Beth carried on. 'And I'm out of work now. It could be worth doing for a few days, at least.'

'Yeah.'

He seemed disinterested but she carried on regardless. 'A lot of officers were killed by the Bourbon Kid last night. The streets aren't really safe without a visible display of law enforcement.'

'Those cops got what they deserved.'

There was something about the way JD spoke that revealed a real lack of compassion for the dead officers and their families. He seemed to be missing the point that even though some of the dead might have been bad people, they still might have young kids or partners who would be suffering. Her thoughts turned to Bertram Cromwell again momentarily.

'And Cromwell? Did he get what he deserved?' she asked.

'Who knows?'

'The answer is no,' she snapped. JD seemed so distant suddenly, as if he weren't really listening. 'I hope the Bourbon Kid gets caught and they stick him in the electric chair!'

'Shut up a minute,' said JD, twisting a knob on the radio to turn up the volume.

Beth caught the end of Harry Hunter announcing that there was a development in the Bourbon Kid case.

"The local news has obtained some video footage of the Bourbon Kid taken from the police station last night. We urge everyone to check out the footage on the local news or on our Radio SM website. Anyone who spots the man in the picture is advised to steer clear and call the Bourbon Kid hotline. The number is…'

JD switched off the radio before Harry Hunter could read out the number.

'Wow,' said Beth. 'I'm going to check that out when I get home. I wonder what he looks like?'

'Probably looks like everyone else in this town,' said JD. 'Black and white camera footage is a waste of time.'

'Even so. I'd still like to see the face of the man who murdered Cromwell last night.'

JD seemed agitated. He rubbed his chin and took a moment to respond. 'You know what,' he said. 'Now that you're out of a job why don't we just get the hell out of this place? Leave today. Right now.'

Beth was taken aback by the suddenness of the suggestion. 'What? Leave Santa Mondega altogether?'

'Yeah. I only came back here for you. Now that you have no ties to this place, there's nothing to stop you and me from moving away, starting a new life somewhere else. Somewhere with no fucking vampires for starters.'

'Really?'

'Yeah. Unless you can think of a good reason to stay?'

Beth loved the idea. Leaving Santa Mondega and travelling the world seeing different places with JD had been a distant dream less than twenty four hours ago, but now that dream could become very real. 'Well, when were you thinking of leaving?' she asked.

'No time like now.'

'That would be great, but my landlord needs four weeks notice before I move out.'

'Fuck your landlord. You can't pay him if you're in New Mexico.'

'We're going to New Mexico?'

'We could do. We can go wherever you want, babe. Anywhere's better than here.'

'That's true enough.'

JD pulled the car over. They had arrived at the apartment block Beth lived in. He stopped the car by the kerb right outside the entrance and turned the engine off. He looked at her, his face revealing he was deadly serious. 'Yeah. Go pack up your clothes and essentials and I'll pick you up in an hour.'

'What are you going to do?'

'I'm gonna go get my shit together then I'll be back.'

He leaned over and kissed her on the lips, a slow lingering kiss that made up her mind for her. 'Come on, before I change my mind,' he said.

'You sure? Really?'

'Yeah.'

'I'll need more than an hour to pack though.'

JD sighed. 'What have you got that you're gonna need on the road? You can leave most of your stuff behind. Just bring the basics and the sentimental stuff you can't live without.'

Beth smiled and kissed him back. 'I suppose, most of my furniture either belongs to the landlord or isn't worth much anyway.'

'Great,' said JD. 'It's agreed then. Start packing straight away. No time to make coffee or watch TV right? Just pack and let's be gone within an hour.'

'Okay. One hour.'

'If you're not ready when I get here, I'm leaving without you.'

Beth reached into a pocket on the front of her jeans and pulled out the small cloth he had given her earlier that morning. 'I've still got this, remember?' she said, smiling.

JD's eyes settled on the cloth. His face revealed a look of sadness. It passed all too briefly, replaced by a smile, but Beth had seen it and sensed something was wrong. 'What is it?' she asked.

'Nothing.'

'Is there something I should know about this cloth patch? You looked kind of sad then for a second.'

He smiled. 'It's okay. It's kinda silly really. My brother Casper made it for me. He wasn't too great at making anything and he was real pleased with himself when he made that.'

Beth unfolded the cloth again and looked at the stitching on the letters JD. It was a little amateurish, but knowing that it was of personal value added to its charm. 'How is your brother these days?' she asked. 'I never got to meet him, did I?'

'He was murdered.'

'Oh my God! I'm so sorry. What happened?'

'I'd rather not talk about it. But that cloth, that's the only thing I have to prove he ever existed. Everything else is gone. No photos, nothing.'

Beth felt a lump in her throat and was overwhelmed with guilt at having brought the subject up. 'I'm so sorry,' she said, glancing awkwardly at the cloth in her hands.

'It's okay,' said JD. He leaned over and stroked her cheek. 'Now you know why I'll always come back to you if you've got that piece of cloth. Make sure you take good care of it.'

'I will, I promise.'

'Good.' He glanced in the rear view mirror momentarily, as if he'd seen something moving behind them. 'Now hurry up. You've got one hour, remember.'

Beth opened the door to get out of the car. 'I'll be ready,' she said slipping the cloth patch back in her pocket.

She stepped out into the sleet and snow and slammed the car door shut behind her. Then she ran up the front steps that led to her apartment block. Through the darkened skies she took a long look up at the building she had lived in for the last eight months. It was a drab, depressing six storey grey building. Not a place she would miss when she left town. As the sleet lashed down against her face and hands she fumbled around in her pocket for her keys. She pulled them out and held them up, waving them towards JD's car to let him know she had found them and was heading inside. He obviously saw the gesture because he started up the engine on his car. A second later she watched his V8 Interceptor pull away from the kerb and cruise off down the road. She slipped the key in the lock on the front door of the apartment block and turned it. Beneath the noise of the sleet crashing against the windows, she barely heard the click as the door unlocked. She pushed it open and stepped inside into the cold entrance hall.

It wasn't the most inviting entrance hall around. It had hardwood flooring and there was an old fashioned stairway on the right with a dirty yellow carpet on it. The stairs were extremely steep so she was never keen to use them because her apartment was all the way up on the fourth floor. So even though the unreliable old elevator at the end of the hall was a potential death trap, she headed over to it and pressed the button.

After a thirty-second wait that ate into the first minute of her one-hour packing time, the elevator arrived and the doors parted. Inside was one of her fourth floor neighbours, an elderly black man known as Jerry Rockwell. He was a smelly old drunken former cop in his seventies who somehow managed to drink a bottle of whisky every day and never feel any the worse for it. He just looked a day away from death all the time. He had an unhealthy complexion to match the grey trousers and musty green cardigan he was wearing. Beth actually quite liked Mr Rockwell in spite of his faults because he was always polite and helpful, and as long as he'd been drinking he was always in a good mood too.

'Hi Mr Rockwell. How are you?' she asked, running a hand through her hair to wipe out the sleet and snow. His scruffy appearance had made her only too aware of her own suddenly.

'Fine thank you, Brenda. Is it still raining out?'

'My name's Beth.'

'Whatever. Is it still raining?'

'I'm afraid it's worse than that. It's snow and hail stones.'

Rockwell stepped out of the elevator and staggered past Beth out in to the hall corridor. He reeked of booze. She watched him steady himself by pressing his hand against the wall as he made his way to the front door.

'You go easy, Mr Rockwell,' she called after him. 'It's very slippery out there. Might be best to stay home for a while.'

'I gotta stock up on whisky,' he called back. 'Been waiting for it to stop raining all mornin'. Can't wait no more.'

'It's not raining, it's snowing.'

'Whatever.'

Beth spotted the elevator doors closing and quickly stuck her arm through the gap to prevent them from meeting. The doors reopened and she stepped inside. She pressed the button for the fourth floor and turned back to watch Rockwell walking slowly towards the front door. As he reached the door he looked like he was falling over headfirst but he somehow managed to grab a hold of the doorknob to hold himself up. He twisted it and opened the door. It swung open with surprising force. Someone had pushed it hard from the outside. The door caught Mr Rockwell full in the face, knocking him to the ground. Beth was about to rush out to offer him some help when she saw the person who had pushed open the door from the outside appear in the doorway.

He was a giant of a man, soaked through from the downpour outside. His most distinguishing feature was a long pink streak of hair down the middle of his otherwise shaved head. After walking through the door he looked down at Jerry Rockwell who was lying on the floor in a daze.

'You okay, old man?' the hulking figure asked.

Beth heard Rockwell respond with something that sounded like, "I landed on my balls." The man with the pink hair leaned down to offer Rockwell some assistance before recoiling and holding his nose.

'Jeez, you fuckin' stink,' he said, stepping back from the old man on the floor.

As the elevator doors began to close the man looked over at Beth. Their eyes met for a second. She realised that she recognised him as one of four military guys she'd seen in the Tapioca on the previous night. A second later his eyes seemed to reveal that he recognised her too. He started walking towards the elevator. Before he reached it, the doors closed and it began moving upwards.

Beth had no idea why this man was in her apartment block, but she didn't like him and was glad he hadn't made it into the elevator with her.

Fifteen

Vanity had parted company with Dante and Kacy shortly after the morning meeting at the Casa de Ville. They had other business to attend to moving themselves into the Swamp. They had told him that their clothes were still in a hotel room somewhere, so Vanity left them to it and went out with Cleavage and Moose to try and find some new members of his clan. Unfortunately he'd barely gotten started when he received a phone call summoning him to the office of the great Rameses Gaius. He'd been told it was urgent so there had not been time to change into a suit or anything smart to impress the new boss, so he turned up in his jeans and his black leather Shades jacket. This wasn't likely to make a great impression.

    He arrived at Gaius's office knowing that his days could well be numbered. He was head of the clan that had been infiltrated by the Bourbon Kid. That wasn't something that was going to make him popular with the vampire hierarchy. Gaius had some serious anger issues and Vanity might be about to feel the force of his wrath. He hoped he would be given time to explain himself before Gaius passed sentence on him. History had shown that the former ruler of Egypt was a merciless killer, one who didn't usually offer his victims the time to make their excuses before he killed them. It was rumoured he could absorb and control energy sources, granting him the power to expel such things as electricity from his hands. Vanity was hoping not to be on the receiving end of a demonstration of any such power.

    Standing guard outside Gaius's office was one of the vampires from the Panda clan, a fairly decent looking female with an athletic build. Vanity approached and did his best to look confident.

    'Hi. I've been summoned to see Rameses Gaius,' he said.

    The Panda girl's expression gave away nothing. 'He's expecting you. Go on in.'

    'Thanks.' He took a deep breath. He wondered if he looked as nervous as he felt. Before reaching for the door handle he slipped his hand inside his jacket and pulled out a small hand mirror. He pretended to check his reflection in it.

    The Panda girl shook her head. 'You're a freak,' she said, finally revealing a playful grin.

    Vanity ignored her and continued staring into the mirror, stroking his goatee and flicking his wavy dark hair behind his ears. As a vampire he had no reflection, but the mirror gag always went down well with the females.

'Maybe you and I could have dinner some time?' he suggested, winking at the Panda girl.

She shook her head. 'I couldn't go out with a man that carries a hand mirror around with him. You're just too vain.'

'Don't diss the mirror,' said Vanity, trying not to sound offended. 'This thing's an antique, handmade in Egypt by a powerful witch doctor. It's indestructible. Even your ugly reflection couldn't break it.'

Panda girl sighed. 'If they cut your head off while you're in there, I'll ask for it as a souvenir. Go on in, you freak.'

He slipped his mirror back into his pocket and reached for the door handle, adding one last comment as he turned it. 'I can see why you've got a pair of black eyes.'

Inside the office, Gaius was sitting at his desk wearing the same sharp silver suit he had worn during his rousing speech in the main hall earlier in the day. He was still wearing his dark sunglasses too. His olive coloured skin gave no indication that he was a fully paid up member of the undead. No creature of the night would normally have a tan that healthy. Except maybe for Vanity who had never been one to worry about applying a thin layer of fake tan.

'Good day to you, Mr Gaius,' he said courteously, stepping inside the office. The Panda Girl pulled the door shut behind him, making him jump inwardly.

'Please take a seat,' said Gaius gesturing to a seat opposite him at the desk. Vanity sat down and took off his sunglasses.

Gaius leaned back in his black leather chair. 'You really fucked up,' he said.

'I know,' said Vanity raising his hands in defence. 'But if you'll…'

'Normally you'd be dead already. You know that, don't you?'

'I was expecting to wake up with a horse's head on my pillow.'

'As opposed to a moose head?'

'Hey, that's just a rumour!'

Gaius took off his sunglasses and tossed them down onto the desk. Vanity tried once more not to get caught staring at the bright blue eye, which looked kind of weird. He hoped that Gaius would put his glasses back on.

'You're alive because I kinda like you. You're the only guy in town with weirder eyes than me,' Gaius went on. 'And as I understand it, you're pretty good in a fight.'

'Thank you.'

'But the Bourbon Kid was hiding in your clan.'

Vanity nodded. 'Yes sir. I can only offer my apologies for that. He blended in well. He actually *was* a vampire, and seeing as we didn't know what the Kid was supposed to look like, we had no way of knowing it was him.'

Gaius reached down below the desk and hauled something up from the floor. He then placed it down on the desk in front of Vanity. It was a severed head. One that Vanity recognised, just.

'Whose head is this?' Gaius asked.

Vanity grimaced at the sight of the shrivelled head. 'That's Obedience.'

'Obedience?' Gaius didn't sound convinced.

'Yeah. He looks pretty messed up, but the CUNT tattoo on his forehead is the big give-away. Not too many people have those.'

Gaius frowned. 'So why was he dressed as the Bourbon Kid?'

Vanity shrugged. 'I didn't know he was.'

'I was told that the Bourbon Kid was in your clan, using the name Déjà Vu.'

'That's what people are saying, but I haven't seen Déjà Vu since everything kicked off yesterday. I thought it was him you'd beheaded.'

'We *all* did. But as you've just confirmed for me, we beheaded the wrong guy. So do you know where I can find Déjà Vu?'

Vanity shook his head. 'I'd say he's gone. Sonofabitch killed the rest of my clan too. Apart from Cleavage, Moose and a couple of new recruits called Dante and Kacy.'

'What?'

'I've only got a handful of members of the Shades clan left, and two of them are new recruits.'

'Did you say Dante and Kacy?'

Vanity sensed a real irritation in Gaius's voice. 'Yeah. You know them?'

'Those two idiots are supposed to be dead. His name was supposed to be in The Book of Death!'

'You've lost me. What are you talking about?'

'Dante Vittori was hired by me to try and flush out the monk who was hiding in one of the clans. He's not even a vampire. I had him injected with a serum so he could blend in with the clans. Jesus, Vanity, you've had everyone hiding in your fucking clan. How shit are you when it comes to spotting impostors? His girlfriend wasn't even injected with the serum, surely you can see she's not a vampire?'

Vanity tugged at his chin beard again. 'That's weird,' he said. 'They're definitely vampires. They even told me that they drank the blood of Archie Somers last night.'

It was Gaius's turn to look confused. 'What?'

'I know I thought it was weird too. Said they found a bag of blood with Archie Somers's name on it. They found it at the police station. No idea what it was doing there.'

Gaius stood up from his desk. His face was thunderous. 'You know what Archie Somers did to me, don't you?' he bellowed.

'Erm, he married your daughter against your will?' Vanity suggested in as careful a manner as possible, knowing that there was an element of truth in it.

'Archie Somers, when he was better known as Armand Xavier, betrayed me. He's responsible for me being drugged and then mummified for hundreds of years in that godforsaken tomb at the museum.'

'Oh. Guess he's not on your Christmas list then?'

'Fucking right he's not! When he was killed, the curse on me was broken and that's when I was able to break free from the tomb at the museum.'

'Well it's good to see the story has a happy ending.'

Gaius ignored the remark and stared around the room for a few moments, deep in thought. 'This is interesting,' he said finally. 'At least they didn't drink his blood from the Holy Grail. I know that because I've got it in my trophy cabinet.'

'The Holy Grail? Seriously?'

'Yes, not that it's any of your concern. The important thing here is that I never thought I'd get the chance for revenge on Armand Xavier. But now you're telling me that his blood is flowing through the veins of Dante Vittori and that whiny girlfriend of his. This is an opportunity for some payback. Revenge on Xavier, as well as those two annoying kids. Where are they now?'

'I told them they could move into the Swamp with me. Right now they've just headed back to a hotel they were staying at. The girl wanted to pick up some clean clothes. Once they've packed up all their stuff they're heading back to the Swamp. Want me to get them to come here?'

Gaius waved a dismissive hand. 'No that won't be necessary,' he said. 'I have much bigger plans for them. Gain their trust for now. This is your chance to redeem yourself, Mr Vanity. In fact, you just might be able to earn yourself more than a reprieve. You could seriously work your way up the vampire hierarchy if you help me out here.'

Vanity had long since given up hope of weaselling his way up through the ranks in Gaius's organisation. The opportunity for more power and the benefits that it might bring appealed to him immensely.

'Okay, he said, trying his best to hold back a huge grin. 'What have you got in mind?'

'Just play along with them to start with. Use that legendary hypnotic charm of yours. Feed them whatever bullshit you have to, and see if you can get them to the Santa Mondega Museum of Art and History. I'll get my old tomb prepared for them. Then Armand Xavier and those two idiots keeping his blood alive can get a taste of what it's like to be encased in a tomb for hundreds of years.'

'You're going to have them mummified?'

'Poignant, don't you think?'

Vanity finally allowed himself to unleash a beaming grin across his face. 'I like it,' he said. 'It's seriously evil.'

'Yes it is,' said Gaius, in a more serious tone. 'But know this, if you fuck this up, if you cross me, or if I even suspect you're not on the level, I'll rip your insides out and hang them from the walls of that shitty nightclub of yours. You're in the last chance saloon, you bearded fuck, and the Devil is ready to call time on you. Is that clear?'

'Crystal clear, sir. I won't let you down on this. In fact, I'm looking forward to it.'

'Good. Now get the fuck out of my office, you cunt.'

Sixteen

Beth stepped out of the elevator and on to the fourth floor of her apartment block. Her one bed apartment was at the end of the corridor. She headed towards it at a slightly quicker pace than usual, her heart pounding with excitement. Her new life with JD outside of Santa Mondega was less than an hour away. Her head was filled with thoughts of what things she needed to pack and what she could afford to leave behind. Starting a new life with JD in a far away place was the dream she thought would never come true. She still remembered how wonderful the feeling had been eighteen years earlier when they had kissed for the first time. That had been followed by eighteen years of hell including ten in prison for the murder of her stepmother. The law courts hadn't taken into consideration the fact that the murder was in self-defence. Her stepmother had attacked her with a knife, causing the horrible facial scar she had as a permanent reminder, but in the tussle her stepmother had fallen on the knife and cut her own throat.

 The sight of the military guy with the pink mohawk entering the building downstairs had set alarm bells ringing in Beth's head. There was no reason to suspect he was after *her*, but she was acutely aware of the fact that she had no idea what enemies JD might have made over the eighteen years they had been apart. In the few hours they had been together she had been so happy to have him back she hadn't dared to probe him about exactly why he had been away for so long. And what he had been doing. Add to that the fact she was pretty sure he'd had something to do with James the security guard at the museum being knocked unconscious, and she was rightly paranoid.

 She reached her apartment and fumbled to get the key into the lock, such was her haste to be out of the hallway quickly. After a few painfully long seconds she managed to turn the key and the door opened. As she stepped into her apartment, she heard a voice call out from down the corridor.

 'Excuse me, miss. I'm looking for someone. Can you help?'

 It was the huge guy with the pink mohawk. He was walking briskly towards her with a gentle smile on his face.

 'Umm, sure. Who are you after?' she asked.

 The man didn't respond straight away, but carried on walking towards her. Eventually when he was just a few feet away he replied. 'Beth Lansbury. That's you, isn't it?'

 Beth wanted to dive inside her apartment and bolt the door shut, but she was caught in two minds. Technically she had nothing to fear from this man. He was acting in a friendly manner, and they were in an open corridor. She only had to scream for help if he did try anything nasty.

'Uh, yeah. I'm Beth Lansbury.'

The man stopped in front of her. 'Also known as Mental Beth?' he asked with a smile.

'Huh?'

'That's what the fat bartender at the Tapioca called you the other night.'

'Oh.'

'Says you killed someone. That true?'

'Umm, who are you?'

The line of questioning was making her nervous. Who was this guy? And what did he want with her? Was he a threat? Or simply someone who had heard much of the local gossip about her?

'Oh God, I'm sorry. My name's Silvinho,' he said holding out a hand. 'I didn't mean to alarm you. That probably wasn't the best way to introduce myself, was it?'

Beth tentatively slipped her hand into his and allowed him to shake her hand. 'What can I do for you?' she asked.

'I'm looking for JD. Is he here?'

He hadn't let go of her hand yet. Although he had stopped shaking it. 'JD?' she asked, in a manner that she hoped wouldn't give away whether she knew him or not.

'Yeah. I heard you know JD. Me and him are old friends. Is he around?'

'He doesn't live here.'

'Know where I can find him?'

Beth was unsure how to answer the question. Was JD in some kind of trouble with this guy? Would it be foolish to admit that he was coming to pick her up in an hour's time? A few awkward seconds passed while she pondered her answer. Before she stammered out her latest "umm" a voice from down the hall answered for her.

'I'm right here.' It was JD. He had come up the stairs the same way Silvinho had and was now walking down the corridor towards them.

Silvinho let go of Beth's hand and spun around to face him. 'You're JD?' he asked.

'Yeah. Who are you? And what the fuck is that on your head?'

Silvinho arched his shoulders back as JD approached. The man's attempt at a pleasant aura had gone. He had taken on an aggressive stance. 'What's JD stand for?' he asked.

'Mind your own business.'

'Does your girlfriend here know your face is all over the news?'

JD walked up to Silvinho and stopped two yards in front of him. Then he spoke in a gravelly tone that Beth had not heard from him before. 'Who sent you?' he growled.

'Bull.'

'Bullshit.'

'No, Bull Thompson actually.'

Something about the name Bull Thompson set both men off. Silvinho stepped forward and lunged at JD's face. Beth watched on in shock as JD ducked out of the way and responded by swinging a punch straight into Silvinho's midriff. The big man took the blow in his stride, throwing a punch of his own that crashed down hard on top of JD's head. The blow threw JD off balance and he staggered back, almost losing his footing.

Beth screamed. 'STOP IT!'

Neither man seemed to hear her. They both flew at each other. Silvinho was the taller and more muscular of the two. His biceps were huge. As JD hit him with another blow to the ribs, the big hulk grabbed him in a headlock and swung him around, off his feet. He threw JD against the wall. In response JD simply used the wall as a springboard and launched himself back into Silvinho, knocking him into the opposite wall. Silvinho once again grabbed high and wrapped his huge right arm around JD's neck. He twisted him around and it began to look as if he would close off JD's windpipe with ease. Beth thought about what to do. She had a baseball bat under the bed in her apartment just in case she ever heard burglars. She had no intention of using it, but if she could just grab it and brandish it in a threatening manner maybe she could make Silvinho leave.

She dashed inside her apartment and raced through the living room and down the hall to her bedroom. The door was closed but she burst through it and dived down onto the floor by her bed. She felt around under the bed until she touched upon the wooden bat. She grabbed it by the narrow end and pulled it out, hauling herself up from the floor immediately. She raced out to the living room again, unsure quite what she would do with the bat once she reached the corridor outside. When she got there she stopped dead in her tracks. The fight was already as good as over.

Silvinho was sat on the floor with his back leaned up against the wall opposite her, his face a bloodied mess. JD stood over him, holding a large bone handled knife with razor sharp edges pointed at his face.

'Who the fuck sent you?' he growled at his fallen enemy. Beth felt the hairs on the back of her neck stand on end when she heard his voice. It dripped with venom.

'I'm not telling you anything,' Silvinho, spluttered, blood dribbling from his mouth.

The scene reminded Beth of the time she had been prostrate on the floor with her stepmother standing over her brandishing a knife, with the intent to kill. It sent shivers down her spine. Then JD did something she would never forget. He leaned forward and thrust the knife straight into Silvinho's throat. Right through his Adam's apple.

Beth immediately threw up. Her stomach launched itself up towards her lungs as the vomit spewed from her mouth. She dropped to her knees and sprayed sick all over the floor in front of her. The image of the blade entering Silvinho's throat raced through her mind over and over. How could JD do such a thing? Was this really the same man she had spent the last eighteen years longing for? A cold-blooded killer?

Hauling herself back up, she looked over at him. He was still staring down at the dead body of the man he had just slain, the blade in his hand, both his hands covered in blood.

'What have you done?' she spluttered, tasting the sick in her mouth as she spoke. 'You've killed him!'

JD turned around slowly. There was blood on his face as well as his hands. He was taking deep breaths too, his chest heaving. He looked over at her. 'We've gotta get out of here now,' he said in his new gravelly voice. 'I'll explain on the way.'

Beth shook her head in disbelief and stared open mouthed at the dead man in the corridor. 'You stabbed him,' she mumbled. 'You stabbed him in the throat.' Her voice rose. 'Why would you do that? He was incapable of defending himself.'

'You stabbed your stepmother didn't you?'

Beth swallowed hard, once more tasting vomit. 'What?'

'Well you *did*, didn't you?'

'In self defence!' She suddenly felt very angry at JD. This was not the man she thought she knew. How could he do what he had just done? And not seem to care?

'I did that for you,' he said.

'I didn't ask you to.'

'He'd have killed us both.'

'You don't know that.'

'I couldn't take the chance. He had to die.'

Beth stared again at the corpse of Silvinho. 'You did that without even blinking,' she said.

JD nodded. 'Yeah. Used to be, I coulda killed him with one punch. I made real hard work of that. I'm not a killer any more. This was just self-defence.'

'Any *more?* You've killed before?'

'Yeah. It's a long story.'

'Who have you killed before?'

JD leaned down and wiped the blood off the blade onto Silvinho's shirt. 'Vampires mostly,' he said. 'Some werewolves too. A few zombies. And a few people who pissed me off. It's all in the past now though. I don't kill any more.'

Beth was astonished at his blasé attitude to the killing. And his confession of other murders seemed to be lacking in any remorse. 'Why were you killing though? Were you a hitman or something?'

'No, nothing like that.'

Beth pointed at Silvinho. 'So why did he say your face was on the news?' As soon as she asked the question, the answer hit her. 'Oh my God, you're...'

'Not any more.'

'You're...' she couldn't bring herself to say it out loud.

JD shrugged. 'Look, don't overreact,' he said. 'But, yeah, I was...'

Beth shook her head. 'No.'

'Yeah.'

'No. You can't be.'

'It's no big deal. I'm not like that any more.'

'You're the Bourbon Kid. You killed Bertram Cromwell!'

'No, I didn't.' JD approached her, still brandishing the now clean knife.

Beth raised her baseball bat in self-defence. 'Where were you this morning? When I woke up and you'd gone out? You said you went out for some fresh air? Where did you go?'

'I just went for a walk.'

'Oh my God, you went out to kill Cromwell didn't you? That's why you want us to leave town isn't it? Your face is all over the news. You wanted me to leave with you before I found out who you really were.'

His voice suddenly returned to its usual calmer manner. 'Beth, put the bat down. Come on, we've gotta go. If this guy tracked you down, there'll be more of them. They'll find you and kill you.'

She backed away, holding the bat up to keep him at a distance. 'You're not the man I thought you were.' She looked back down at the dead body of Silvinho one last time. 'I don't think I want to be around you any more. What happens when we have an argument? Are you going to stab me in the throat too?'

'Come on, don't be stupid. I would never do anything to hurt you. I'm done with killing. This guy was a one off.'

She took a deep breath. 'But *you* attacked him first. He hadn't done anything to me. He was just asking me where you were?'

JD seemed to lose his patience. 'Oh come on,' he snapped. 'Don't be so naïve. Look at him. You can tell he's bad news the minute you lay eyes on him.'

Beth shook her head. 'Look at yourself,' she said. His face was covered in spatterings of blood, his hands and shirt too. And he was holding a knife in an aggressive stance. He looked every bit like the mass murderer she had heard about on the news.

Outside, the sound of heavy sleet and snow was suddenly punctuated by the blaring of a police car siren.

JD held out his hand to Beth. 'Come on. We gotta get outta here. Cops are coming.'

She recoiled in horror. 'I'm not fleeing from a murder scene again. And certainly not with you. How could you do that?'

He stepped towards her, his hand still outstretched. She backed inside her apartment door. 'Get away from me. I'm not going anywhere with you.'

'Fucking cops are coming. We gotta go! Come on!'

Beth shook her head one last time. 'You've ruined everything.' She reached into the front pocket on her jeans and pulled out the cloth patch he had given her earlier. She threw it onto the floor at his feet. 'You may as well have that back,' she said. 'I wouldn't want you thinking you had a reason to come back for me. Goodbye, Jack.'

As he looked down at the cloth patch at his feet she stepped back inside her apartment and closed the door in his face.

A second later he banged on the door and yelled through it. 'Beth, take some time to think this through! Half the cops in this city are vampires and those that aren't are scumbags. You know that. And you know *me*.'

'No I don't!'

She heard him sigh in frustration, before speaking through the door once more in a calmer voice than before. 'Listen, I'm gonna go pack up some stuff and be back in an hour. Just like we planned. Take the hour to think things through. My face is all over the news. I have to leave town, with or without you.'

Beth felt tears running down her cheeks. All those years waiting for him to return had been for nothing. Eighteen years had been wasted living in the misguided belief that a guy she had met one night at a Halloween ball was her soul mate. She had been infatuated with a man she knew nothing about. A man that had turned out to be the Bourbon Kid, a renowned serial killer and ruthless murderer of innocent people.

'Just go, Jack,' she said, sobbing. 'And don't bother coming back in an hour. I won't change my mind. I don't want to see you ever again.'

Seventeen

An hour had passed since Flake and Sanchez had toasted Ulrika Price in the locker room below the station. Flake had taken the mysterious Book with No Name back up to reception to hide it in her desk drawer. They had agreed not to tell Dan Harker or anyone else about what had happened. After all, technically they had just murdered Ulrika Price. There were no witnesses and fortunately there was no corpse either. Even so, neither Sanchez nor Flake was willing to have it known around town that they had killed a vampire and particularly one that was quite possibly of fairly high significance in the undead community.

Sanchez had stayed down in the locker room and done his best to mop up all the evidence. If his mopping skills were as good as he believed then none of the other officers would ever find out what had happened. He was well aware that vampires had infiltrated the police force in the past so discretion about the murder of Ulrika was vital. Not that there were many officers still alive by the sound of it. Those that weren't out on the streets demonstrating that there was still a police presence in the city were up on the higher floors probably filling out paperwork. Mind you, Sanchez had a suspicion that there were free donuts somewhere upstairs and the rest of the force were joyfully tucking into them.

Just as he had finished mopping all the blood and shit out of the elevator, Captain Harker reappeared. He came down to the locker room via the stairs and threw a black bin liner full of clothes at Sanchez. It hit him in the chest and landed on the floor just outside the elevator.

'That's your uniform, Sanchez,' said Harker. 'You're an awkward size, so until we get a custom made one for you, that'll have to do.'

'Thanks,' said Sanchez, dreading what he might find in the bag.

Harker stepped into the elevator. 'You've done a great job here,' he said inspecting the walls for any evidence of the previous night's bloodshed. When he was satisfied that everything was spotless he pushed Sanchez back out into the locker room. 'Stick your uniform on and then meet me up at reception,' he said pressing a button on the elevator keypad. The elevator doors closed behind him and Sanchez was left alone in the locker room with a black bin liner containing his new law enforcement outfit.

He opened the bin liner expecting something completely inferior to what all the other officers had. He was right. It would be inferior to most people, but not to Sanchez. He couldn't wait to get it on and see how it looked.

It was a beige coloured highway patrol officer's outfit, complete with a matching Stetson hat and a nightstick. The pants were a bit tight and in danger of ripping up the ass if he bent over too quickly, but they still looked cool. The shirt was equally tight and showed off his man boobs a little more than he would have liked, but with the Highway Patrol badge on the right breast pocket it looked awesome. The hat fitted snugly on his head, which was pleasing, but the best part of the outfit was undoubtedly the pair of mirrored sunglasses. Even though he was indoors and it was overcast and snowing outside, Sanchez was keeping those beauties on at all times.

After strutting up and down the locker room for a few minutes quoting lines from Dirty Harry he called the elevator down and stepped inside. As the elevator headed back up to the ground floor he checked out his reflection in its mirrored back wall. He looked the business all right.

When the elevator doors parted he saw that he wasn't the only one with a new uniform. Flake had her back to him and was bending over the reception desk, reaching for something. She was now dressed in a standard blue cop uniform. Tight fitting it was too, but in a good way. It certainly fitted better than the outfit Sanchez was wearing. In fact with her ass up in the air it suddenly became clear to him that she was in fact in extremely good shape. Great legs, great ass. In fact, tidy all over.

He strutted out of the elevator towards her tapping his nightstick against his leg as he walked. It alerted Flake to his presence and she turned around, kicking shut the bottom drawer on her desk with the heel of the black boot on her right foot.

'Look at you!' she said smiling. 'You look like Poncharello from that TV show. What's it called?'

'CHiPs!'

'That's it. You're a dead ringer for Erik Estrada!'

Sanchez shrugged. 'I know. And you look like Heather Locklear when she was in T.J. Hooker.'

Flake's face lit up. 'You think?'

'Yeah. That waitress outfit you wear normally wasn't doing you justice. You look hot!'

The compliment obviously went down well because Flake's face lit up. 'You know,' she said dryly, 'because you're wearing those shades, I can't tell if you're kidding or not.'

'That's why I'm keepin' 'em on.'

It suddenly dawned on him that they were flirting. How had this happened? Flake was quite fit (particularly now she had on the uniform), so why was she flirting with him? Fit women never did that unless they wanted free drinks in the Tapioca. Odd. He'd definitely have to keep a close eye on her, he decided. Particularly her ass.

As if she suspected he'd be wondering about the whereabouts of The Book With No Name, Flake kicked the bottom drawer of her desk. 'The book's in there,' she said. 'I'm going to ask around later to see if there's any vampire folklore about magic books or anything. I'll also try an Internet search to see if I can find out who wrote it.'

'Good luck with that,' said Sanchez. 'I think you'll have more chance of finding out who wrote the Bible.'

'Worth a try though,' said Flake.

Sanchez barely heard her. Something else had grabbed his attention. Something far more important. Someone had just walked into the station through the glass doors at the front. It was a lady he recognised. The woman of his dreams.

Jessica.

She was wearing a black catsuit and she looked as hot as ever. Her dark hair positively shone and her milky white skin looked as soft as silk. Sanchez had feared he might never see her again ever since she had gone missing from his spare room above the Tapioca. He'd had her safely tucked away up there for months while he had nursed her back to health. But then she'd just recently come out of a coma, only to then vanish while he was out shopping. It really was a relief to see her alive again. And he was particularly pleased that she'd turned up while he was wearing a super cool highway patrolman's outfit. If he could get himself a motorbike too, he'd be irresistible to any woman.

'Jessica,' he said strolling nonchalantly towards her. 'Where have you been? I was worried. Thought you might have been shot by the Bourbon Kid again.'

She obviously hadn't recognised him straight away, but he could sense that she recognised his voice. And she smiled too. A good sign. She walked up to him with her usual sexy swagger.

'Well, hello there Paunch-a-rello,' she said patting his stomach. 'How's tricks?'

'Great,' said Sanchez. 'How's your memory today? Have you got amnesia again? Because you should know, we've become quite close.'

She smiled. 'My memory is just fine. How could I forget you, Sanchez? After all you've done for me?'

This was a great sign. Chances were high she was single again. Her previous lover Jefe had been killed the same day she had slipped into her latest coma, so finally, the timing might be just right for a romance with Sanchez.

'Have you come here just to see me?' he asked.

'Actually I've come to report a theft.'

From behind Sanchez, Flake called out, 'I can help with that. Please take a seat, miss.'

Jessica sauntered past Sanchez and took a seat on the customer side of Flake's reception desk. 'Who are you then, sweetcheeks?' she asked.

'Officer Munroe,' said Flake in an official sounding voice. 'And you are?'

Sanchez answered on Jessica's behalf. 'Jessica Xavier,' he said.

Jessica turned her head and eyed him suspiciously. 'How do you know my surname?' she asked.

It was a good question. Sanchez had hired the services of Rick from the Ole Au Lait to find out the information from some seedy contacts he had in the press. Best not to admit to that, though.

'You talk in your sleep,' he replied, relieved that he was wearing his sunglasses, which would hide the deceit in his eyes.

Flake had been typing the name into her computer. After hearing the revelation that Jessica talked in her sleep she looked up. 'You two have slept together?' she asked.

Jessica grinned at Flake. 'Oh yes, lots of times. Sanchez is a real animal in bed. Didn't you know?'

'No, I didn't.'

Sanchez frowned. He'd never slept with Jessica. Maybe she thought they had? She certainly seemed to be bigging him up to Flake. Maybe this meant she was into him? If she genuinely thought they had already slept together then he really did stand a chance.

'We go way back,' he said insouciantly.

'Okay,' said Flake, not sounding convinced. 'So Miss Xavier, what is it that you'd like to report stolen?'

'A book.'

Sanchez's ears perked up at hearing about yet another stolen book. He quickly butted in. 'What's it called?' he asked.

Jessica kept her gaze fixed on Flake who was still tapping away on her keyboard. 'It's called The Book of Death,' she said.

Well, this had Sanchez confused. Jessica was looking for the same book as Ulrika Price. The same book that Sanchez himself had stolen, but then given to Rick to return to the library. Why would Jessica be reporting it stolen?

Flake remained calm and didn't give away the fact that she, like Sanchez, was only too aware of the fact that Ulrika had reported the book missing earlier. And they had turned Ulrika to dust and ash, the remains of which were now in the bin.

'Do you know where it was stolen from please?' Flake asked.

'The local library.'

Flake tapped away some more on her keyboard before asking. 'You work there?'

'No.'

'Was it your book?'

'Yes.'

'Why was it at the library then?'

'Because that's where I liked to keep it.'

Flake looked confused. 'Have you questioned the librarians about it?' she asked.

'The chief librarian is a bitch.'

Sanchez nodded. 'Right. Good riddance to her.'

Jessica spun around on her chair. 'What do you mean, good riddance? Have you seen her?'

'Umm, well, y' know…'

Flake jumped in to bail him out. 'What he means is, they used to date.'

Jessica turned back to Flake. Sanchez frowned. What the fuck was Flake talking about? Jessica didn't seem convinced either.

'You what?' she asked, glaring at Flake.

Flake shrugged. 'Oh yeah. You know Sanchez. He's a real ladies' man. He met Ulrika and just swept her away. But she turned a bit psycho, so he recently dumped her. Didn't you, Sanchez?'

Sanchez nodded. 'Like I said, she was a bitch. Good riddance to her.'

Jessica eyed them both suspiciously for a moment. 'Fine,' she said. 'But if you see her, I'd like to know about it. She might have the book I'm looking for.'

'Certainly,' said Flake. 'Can you tell us what this book looks like?'

'It's a big black hardback book.'

'That's it? Just black?'

'As far as I know. I've never actually seen it.'

Flake looked puzzled. 'What do you mean you've never actually seen it? I thought it was your book. Surely you must know what it looks like?'

'It's actually my father's book. A family heirloom that will rightfully be mine one day.'

Flake stopped tapping on her keyboard and pursed her lips, deep in thought for a moment before responding. 'Look, Miss Xavier, I don't mean to sound obtuse, but surely, if this is just a book with a black cover and you've never even seen it, wouldn't it be easier just to go to the shop and order a new copy?'

'It's one of a kind. There was only one copy ever printed.'

'Are you sure?' Flake asked.

'Yes I'm sure.' Jessica's voice indicated a touch of impatience.

Sanchez tried to appease the situation. 'Maybe it's available on the Kindle?' he suggested.

'IT'S NOT AVAILABLE ON THE FUCKING KINDLE!' Jessica snapped.

'It wouldn't hurt to check though?' Sanchez suggested.

Jessica took a deep breath. 'It's a hand written book. It's centuries old. And it's worth a lot of money. To me, anyway. I'm advising you two about it, because I'm offering a fifty thousand dollar reward for its return.'

Sanchez's eyes lit up. 'Fifty thousand?'

'Yes. Fifty thousand.'

'Where d'ya get that kind of money?'

'My father is a wealthy man,' Jessica said, her irritation visibly increasing at all the questions. 'If you get the book, bring it to me. I'll be staying at my father's new home on the edge of the city.'

Flake tapped the keyboard once again. 'Do you have the address please?' she asked.

'Yes. It's the Casa De Ville.'

Sanchez was taken aback. The Casa De Ville was the former home of El Santino, the recently deceased crime lord of Santa Mondega. And it was a nasty place too. Scary looking from the outside. It was practically a castle. Anyone who could afford to live there must have a serious amount of cash. Really serious.

Before he could comment, he heard a door open behind him. Captain Harker walked in through the door at the rear of the reception. He was holding a small piece of paper in his right hand. He headed straight for Sanchez.

'You, Sanchez, I got a job for you.'

'What?'

'There's been a murder on 54th Street. The ambulance crew are already there. The residents are saying that the boyfriend of the woman in apartment 406 stabbed some guy in the throat. I need you to question the woman in 406. Find out who her boyfriend is and why he stabbed the guy, and see if you can find out where he went. The woman's name is Beth Lansbury. You think you can do that? And get me something useful?'

Sanchez shrugged. 'Yeah, s'pose so. Mental Beth, huh? Who knew she had a boyfriend?'

'Not me,' said Harker handing Sanchez the small slip of paper and a set of car keys from his pocket. 'That's the keys to your squad car, number seven. It's parked out back. And the address is on that piece of paper. If there's any street cops anywhere in the vicinity of the murder I'll get them to stop by and take over from you.'

Sanchez took the piece of paper and looked at the details. 'Do we know who the victim was?' he asked.

Harker shook his head. 'No one local. Some dude with a pink mohawk haircut apparently. Probably drug related.'

From behind Harker, Jessica perked up. 'Did you say it was a guy with a pink mohawk?' she asked.

'Yeah. Freaky, huh?'

'What was his name?' Jessica asked.

Harker frowned as he tried to remember. 'Ambulance people said his name was Silver or something.'

'Silvinho?'

'Yeah, that was it. You know him?'

'I did.' Jessica stood up from her seat. 'He was a real hardass. Ain't many folks around here that could get close enough to him to stab him in the throat.'

'Well, somebody did,' said Harker.

Jessica brushed past him and grabbed the slip of paper from Sanchez's hand. 'Right,' she said. 'I'm coming with you, Sanchez. I'd like to meet this Beth Lansbury myself.'

Sanchez couldn't believe his luck. This was a sure sign that Jessica was keen to hang out with him. It had to be something to do with the uniform. *Chicks dig the uniform*, he thought to himself. It was only his first day as a stand in police officer and already he was taking Jessica on a ride along. This was going to be the start of something big.

Eighteen

Sanchez had never driven a police squad car before. He'd ridden in the back a few times, but being the guy in charge of the siren and the flashing blue lights was awesome. Having Jessica in the car with him only added to the experience.

'Hey Jessica, watch this,' he said, slowing the car down to a crawl on one particularly icy street. He steered it over towards the sidewalk where an elderly lady with a walking stick was struggling to stay on her feet as she hobbled through the snow. As the car pulled in just a few yards behind her, Sanchez flicked a switch on the dashboard and turned on the siren. It blared out at a deafening level, causing the old lady to jump in shock. She slipped on the ice and fell backwards, landing flat on her back, screaming out in pain. Sanchez turned off the siren and sped off again. He nudged Jessica who was sat shaking her head in disapproval in the passenger seat.

'Pretty funny, huh?' he said.

'Hilarious. How about just getting us to the crime scene now though, huh?'

'Yeah, good idea. Shout if you see any more old people though. Or young children for that matter. Or cats.'

Jessica let out a deep sigh. 'You know, Sanchez, it's times like this when I wonder how it is that you're single. You're a real catch.'

'Yeah, well,' he said straightening his sunglasses. 'While I've been nursing you out of a coma for the last few months I haven't had time for anyone else.'

'That's too bad.'

'I'll tell you what else is too bad. Did you know that your old boyfriend Jefe got shot in the face during the eclipse last year?'

'Oh, did he?'

'Yeah, he must be gutted.'

'He can't be gutted if he's dead.'

'I would be.'

'Whatever.'

Jessica didn't seem too bothered about Jefe's death. *That's what being in a coma for months will do to you*, thought Sanchez. This was most definitely an opportunity to put forward his own case. 'So, I guess with Jefe dead, it means you're single too? Maybe we should go out on a date?'

Jessica stared out of her passenger side window. 'Can we talk about something else?' she said.

'If you like.'

Sanchez hit the brakes as they approached a red light. The car skidded a few times before eventually stopping just before the lights. He looked over at Jessica. She was still staring out of the window at the snow. 'I wonder what this crime scene will look like when we get there,' he mused.

'Bloody, probably,' said Jessica. 'If it really is the Silvinho that I know then it'll be messy. He's no fool. Not many people in this town could have killed him.'

The traffic lights turned green and Sanchez pulled away, driving with a little more care this time. 'So how do you know this Silvinho guy anyway?' he asked. 'And who would want to kill him?'

'The Bourbon Kid.'

'You think?'

'Yeah,' Jessica pointed at the road up ahead. 'We're nearly there. I can see an ambulance parked outside that building. That must be it.'

Sanchez looked to where Jessica was pointing. Sure enough, a hundred yards down the road was an ambulance with its blue lights flashing. There was a crowd of people on the street outside the building, even though it was snowing outside.

'Where the hell am I gonna park?' Sanchez muttered aloud, looking for a space.

'Over there,' said Jessica pointing at a space on the opposite side of the road to the ambulance.

'Good spot,' said Sanchez. 'Right outside the Dirty Donut shop too.'

He pulled the car over and in spite of the front wheel riding up onto the sidewalk briefly, he slipped it into the space just fine.

Jessica was quick to open the passenger side door. 'Why don't you grab us some donuts?' she suggested as she climbed out. 'I'll head up to this Beth Lansbury's apartment and make sure the coast is clear. You might spot the killer escaping while you're buying the donuts.'

'Great idea,' said Sanchez, pleased that she had made the suggestion. 'Any particular donut you'd like?'

'Surprise me.'

Sanchez climbed out of the car, grateful to be wearing his new Stetson hat, which did a great job of sheltering him from the snow, which was at last showing signs of easing up. By the time he'd stepped onto the sidewalk, Jessica had vanished. She obviously didn't feel like hanging around outside in the cold weather.

The ambulance outside Remington Tower had quite a crowd around it, yet the medics themselves were nowhere to be seen. There was another police squad car parked further down the road too, which was a relief. It would mean Sanchez wasn't the first officer on the scene and therefore the potential for fucking up a crime scene was limited. Anyhow, more importantly, he had to work out how many donuts he could afford.

The guy in the donut shop looked like he enjoyed a cake or two himself. And a lot of beer and pizza too. He was a short, rotund fellow with a curly brown mullet haircut. His stained white DIRTY DONUTS T-shirt fitted so tightly to his curves it looked as if it had been tattooed on. Clearly this guy was eating the profits.

'Got any special offers on?' Sanchez asked as he approached the counter.

'I recommend the Fat Boy Pick and Mix,' the man suggested.

'What's that then?'

'A box of ten donuts of your choice. Only five bucks.'

'That sounds like donut heaven. I'll take one.'

Sanchez spent five minutes or so deciding which donuts to have. The variety on offer was extremely impressive. So much so that he bought two boxes, one to take up to the crime scene and another to stick on the back seat of the squad car for later.

By the time he'd stored the spare box on the back seat and crossed the road to head towards the crowd of onlookers stood outside Remington Tower, it had stopped snowing. Jessica hadn't come back down, and no dead body had been carried out by any medics either.

'Step aside please. Officer coming through,' he said pulling his nightstick out with his free hand and prodding people with it as he made his way through the crowd and up to the front of the building. The door at the entrance was slightly ajar. To avoid crushing any of his donuts he backed into it and forced it open with his ass cheeks.

Once inside, he kicked the door shut behind him to stop anyone else from getting in. The corridor wasn't much warmer than the cold wind outside. *"What a shitty apartment block this is!"* he thought. He slid his nightstick back into its holster on his belt and opened the box of donuts. He pulled out a pink iced ring and took a large bite. It was as tasty as it looked. Next decision, stairs or elevator? He remembered the stink in the elevator at the station and decided the stairs would be a better option. Plus the stairs would take longer and he'd be able to eat at least two more donuts by the time he made it to the fourth floor. Maybe three more.

When he eventually made it to the fourth floor he was met by an eerie silence. If this was the floor on which the murder had taken place, then why was it so quiet? It ought to be buzzing with onlookers, ambulance crew and cops. He stepped off the staircase and into a long hallway. At the end of the hall he could see the crime scene. The dead body of a guy with pink hair was slumped against the wall. Even from where Sanchez was he could see that the guy was a mess. There was an awful lot of blood on the floor and over the wall behind him. Sanchez shoved the rest of his third donut into his mouth, then pulled his nightstick back from its sheath, ready for action.

He edged slowly down the hallway towards the apartment at the end. The walls of the corridor reminded him of the walls in the Tapioca after a typical visit from the Bourbon Kid. They were covered in blood and stank of death. Aside from his own footsteps, the eerie quiet remained. Where the hell was Jessica? Or Mental Beth? He could see the door to Beth's apartment was slightly ajar, but no sounds were coming from within. He edged ever closer, wondering exactly what he would find inside

With his back against the wall he sidled up to the doorway and peered through the gap. He couldn't see anything of interest, but he was really wishing he had a gun instead of a stick. He poked a leg out and kicked at the door. It creaked as it opened slightly. Nothing seemed to have been disturbed so he kicked the door again, a little harder this time, keeping his distance, just in case. It opened fully this time. He counted to three in his head then peered around the door into the apartment, with his nightstick drawn and ready for action.

His eyes darted around at the sight in the apartment before him. Nothing was moving so he lowered his nightstick and stepped inside.

His jaw dropped open as he saw the carnage in front of him.

This was a bloodbath.

Nineteen

The Santa Mondega International Hotel looked as impressive as ever, which was quite a feat considering Peto the Hubal monk had been beheaded in the lobby the night before. And of course, Dante had shot Robert Swann in the head at the foot of the steps out front. Add to that the small matter of Kacy shooting Agent Roxanne Valdez in the face in one of the upstairs corridors and it had to be said that the place was in remarkable shape. Any new visitors would be none the wiser about what had gone on there in the last twenty-four hours.

The lobby was a tad quieter than usual, but so were most places in Santa Mondega, simply because the population had dropped considerably overnight.

Dante strolled up to the reception desk with Kacy following on behind. He recognised Benito the receptionist. Benito was wearing the shitty pink porter outfit that Dante himself had once had to wear during his time as an employee there.

'Mornin', Benny,' Dante said brightly. 'Lost my room key, can you give me another please?'

Benito looked reasonably pleased to see him. The two of them had gotten on well enough in the past. 'It'll cost twenty dollars for a replacement,' he said apologetically.

'That's okay. Just bill it to the room.'

'Sure thing.'

Benito tapped a few keys on a keyboard on his desk and then grabbed a keycard from a drawer by his right leg. He tossed it over the counter to Dante.

'Try not to lose that one,' he said. 'The fine goes up to thirty dollars next time.'

'Thanks.'

When Dante turned around Kacy was already heading for the stairs. 'Don't you wanna take the elevator?' he called after her.

'No. Do you?'

He pondered the idea for a second. Elevators were bad news in Santa Mondega. 'Nope,' he said. 'I'm right behind ya.'

As he followed her up the stairs, admiring her ass for most of the way, Dante wondered what they might find in their hotel room. Would it be as they left it? Would the cops be there investigating the deaths of Robert Swann and Roxanne Valdez? Were there even enough cops left alive to investigate anyway? His name was on all the bills and there was only supposed to be him and Kacy staying in the suite, so as things stood, there was no reason why anyone would be checking the place for evidence. When they arrived at their suite he was pleased to see that nothing much had changed other than the beds had been made by one of the hotel chambermaids.

'Pack only the stuff you really need,' he told Kacy, recognising that she would not want to discard too many of the clothes from her wardrobe.

Naturally she pretty much ignored him and set about filling a large suitcase with clothes. She had the case laid out on the bed and was rifling through a chest of drawers. And she seemed to be packing everything. Dante on the other hand was happy to fill a smaller suitcase with just a couple of pairs of boxers, two pairs of jeans and a few T-shirts.

'Remember you won't need anything woolly,' he pointed out as Kacy picked a brown fleece out of the drawers. 'We won't be feeling the cold much these days.'

Kacy hesitated a moment, but then folded the fleece and slipped it into her suitcase. 'If we become human again, we'll need all the warm clothes we can get our hands on,' she said. 'What with all the snow and everything.'

Damn! She had a point. Dante turned back to a chest of drawers with some of his warmer clothes in and started rummaging through them. 'You know, Kace,' he said. 'Sometimes I think you're even smarter than I am.'

'*Sometimes?*'

'Yeah. This is one of those times.'

'Are you kidding? You couldn't tie your fucking shoelaces without me.'

'I don't wear laces.'

'And I know why.'

'Fine. If you're so clever, then how come it's *me* that has to come up with a plan for how we're gonna get the Eye of the Moon out of that guy's head?'

'Because you got us into this fucking mess!'

'So?'

Kacy exhaled noisily. 'Maybe Vanity will have some ideas?'

'We can't ask him.'

'You can't, but I could.'

'How?'

'I can turn on the charm with him a bit.'

'Turn on the charm? How so exactly?' Dante asked, more than a hint of suspicion creeping into his voice.

'Not like that. I just mean, he must know stuff about Gaius. Maybe if I act a bit ditzy I can quiz him a bit? I might find out something useful.'

'Useful? Like what?'

'Like maybe Gaius has a dog he takes for walks on his own.'

'A dog?'

'Hey, I'm just spitballing here. If we have any chance of stealing that Eye, it'll be when Gaius is on his own, or even better, when he's asleep.'

Dante sneered. 'That is lame.'

'Fuck off,' said Kacy, playfully throwing a pair of rolled up socks at him. 'I'm just trying to think of some scenarios.'

'I know, babe. I'm just kidding.'

He zipped up his own suitcase, comfortable that he had packed enough stuff. Out of the corner of his eye he spotted something in one of the open drawers that contained the clothes of the now deceased Robert Swann. It was a bottle of clear liquid and a syringe. He recognised them immediately. It was the bottle containing the serum that had lowered his body temperature sufficiently enough to walk undetected among the vampires before he had actually become one. The syringe had been used to administer the injections of the serum.

'I'd better pack this,' he said waving the liquid and syringe at Kacy.

'Why?'

'Because, well, it's pretty rare stuff. And who knows when we might need it again?'

Kacy pulled a face. 'I can't imagine any reason we'd need to use it.'

'Well neither can I right now, but things do have reasons, you know.'

'*Do* they?' said Kacy sarcastically.

'Yes they do.'

'So give me a reason why you might need the serum. Go on, give me a good one.'

Dante scratched his chin and looked deep in thought, not a look that he used often. Eventually he spoke, albeit somewhat tentatively. 'What if we get the Eye and get cured? If we were human again we might need the serum to escape from the vampires in this city?'

Kacy gasped. 'Oh my God. You just said something sensible.'

He frowned. 'I did, didn't I?'

'Yeah. That's gotta be our cue to get outta here. Who knows what other miracles might be about to happen!'

Dante tucked the syringe in a pocket inside his jacket, then slipped the small bottle into a pocket on the front of his jeans. 'Come on, let's get outta here. You got everything?' he asked, zipping up his suitcase.

Kacy took one last look around the bedroom before zipping up her own suitcase. It was relatively tidy and there didn't seem to be any evidence of any wrongdoing on display. The only possible problem was that some of Robert Swann's clothes were left behind, but that didn't seem significant enough to worry about.

They headed back down the stairs to reception. By the time they reached the bottom Kacy was complaining about the weight of her suitcase.

'Can you carry mine for me?' she whined as they strode into the reception area.

'Are you kidding? We've got about a fucking two-mile walk to the Swamp.'

'Oh God. I can't walk all that way.'

'Okay, so why don't I go pick a car from the parking lot? Save some time and energy.'

'I'm all for that,' Kacy agreed. 'Don't know about you but I'm feeling kinda weak. Could really use another drink, if you know what I mean?'

Dante did know what she meant. The thirst for human blood was hitting him again too. Was this what it was going to be like as a vampire? Constantly craving the thrill of drinking blood? 'I'm thirsty as hell,' he said, leading the way out to the rear car park.

Once they were outside in the car park, Dante surveyed the vehicles available. The car park was pretty full. Cars were lined up in rows of twenty stretching back about ten rows.

'See anything in particular you like?' he asked.

'Are you kidding? They're all covered in snow. They all look the same.'

'Fair enough. I'll choose then.'

He picked out his car of choice very quickly. 'Wait here and keep an eye out for any cops' he said to Kacy. 'I'll be back in a sec with a car.' Dropping his own suitcase at her feet he vanished in between the rows of cars.

Kacy knew that Dante was a good at breaking into cars. He might well be pretty stupid and lacking in such simple skills as discretion, but he could break into and hot-wire a car in less than thirty seconds. Her confidence in him was proven correct when after less than a minute she heard the sound of a car engine starting up. Moments later she saw a car moving through the rows, heading towards her. She slapped her forehead in frustration when she saw Dante's smiling face behind the wheel on the driver's side.

He'd picked a police squad car.

The car crawled through the snow and pulled up alongside her. Dante wound down the driver's side window.

'Chuck the luggage in the back and hop in,' he said, accidentally sounding the siren momentarily as he wound the window back up.

Knowing that there was no time to argue or point out the stupidity of stealing a police car, Kacy jumped in and soon they were heading out of the hotel car park and out into the icy streets of the city.

'You couldn't have found anything less discreet?' she asked.

'Always wanted a cop car.'

The police radio crackled into life as they headed down the main street towards the Swamp. A voice came through loud and clear.

'This is Detective Sanchez Garcia. Request for backup. I'm on the fourth floor at Remington Tower on 54th Street. I've got some unidentified dead bodies here. And there's blood everywhere. I think the killings have only just occurred and the killer could still be in the vicinity. I'm on my own. Please send backup otherwise I'm getting the fuck outta here.' There was a pause before he added, 'I've got donuts.'

Dante and Kacy exchanged a quick look.

Kacy said what was on both their minds. 'He just said there was blood everywhere. Fresh blood. Are you thinking what I'm thinking?'

'Dante nodded. 'Yeah. Fresh blood and we wouldn't have to kill anyone.'

'Remington Tower is only a couple of blocks from here,' said Kacy.

Dante pushed his foot down hard on the accelerator. 'I'll get us there in two minutes,' he said.

Twenty

The pool of blood on the hardwood floor was edging slowly towards Sanchez's feet. He glanced back at the dead guy with the pink hair in the hall. The poor bastard's throat was hanging out and blood was still seeping out down the front of his shirt. But it looked like he'd gotten off easy in comparison to the dead woman just inside the door of apartment 406. Sanchez reckoned she was probably in her early thirties, but her face was such a mess it was hard to be sure. Her eyes had been gouged out and her face was caked in blood. She had a bit of a big chin too, he thought inconsequently. There was blood running all down it, due in no small part to the fact that her tongue had been ripped out. A quick scan around the room revealed that she wasn't the only victim. There were two other corpses inside the room, both of them in a similar state. But no sign of a killer. Or, for that matter, Jessica.

The bloodied blouse on the dead woman had been ripped open and she had vicious deep gashes across her chest. In fact Sanchez was pretty sure one of her nipples was on the floor near his feet. Closer inspection of her blouse showed that it had the local hospital logo on it and the word "MEDIC" sewn in green lettering on the right breast pocket. Using his new detective skills, Sanchez came to the conclusion that the dead bodies were that of the ambulance crew.

The two other bodies in the apartment were in pretty bad shape too. One of them, wearing a standard white medic's uniform, was on all fours with his head stuck through the television screen. Another, a black guy from the ambulance crew, was lying on his back in a crucifix pose staring up at the ceiling. Well, he would have been staring if he had any eyes. Someone had gouged them out and all that was left were two gaping holes. His white uniform was also stained as badly as that of the woman Sanchez was in the process of stepping over.

Unsurprisingly the place absolutely stank. At least one of these corpses had shit their pants, Sanchez decided. The stench made him want to spray some Forest Fresh air freshener around the room. It was also noticeable that the apartment was as cold as the streets outside.

The reason for the cold became evident when a huge gust of wind from outside blew the curtains open.

'What kind of a moron keeps their windows open in this weather?' he pondered, gripping the end of his nightstick tightly.

Then, behind the sofa, he spotted two more dead bodies. Both were men dressed in standard blue police uniforms.

What the fuck?

There was no sign of a bullet wound on anyone. The murders reminded him of the slayings of his brother Thomas and his wife Audrey. He had found them murdered in a similar state a year earlier. The two cops were covered in blood, their eyes were missing and their tongues not particularly visible. What the hell had gone on here? He leaned over the nearest dead police officer to get a better look. It was a forty-something overweight donut-loving fellow with grey hair. In a holster by his ribcage he had a small pistol. Sanchez replaced his nightstick on his belt and reached down to the pistol. He slipped his fingers around the handle, hoping to avoid getting any blood on his hands, then slid it out of the holster and took a look at it. It was largely blood free, or at least, the handle was, so he gripped it tightly in his right hand. If there was a killer nearby he needed to be ready to point it and look like he might fire it. He had a pretty dismal record with handguns, but it was better to have one for show and not need to use it, than to not have one at all.

Looking for other items that might be of use he noticed that the cop also had a CB radio on his belt. Sanchez had wanted a CB radio ever since he was a kid. He hadn't been issued with one by the department, so seeing as the dead cop wouldn't be needing his any more it seemed logical to relieve him of it. He picked it up and secured it on his belt next to his nightstick. Then he resumed his assessment of the crime scene.

'Jessica?' he called out rather tentatively. 'Jessica? You in here? Hello? Anyone?'

He received no answer, apart from another billowing from the cream coloured curtains. On his right there was a kitchen area and in the corner was an open door that led to a narrow corridor. At the end of the corridor was a closed door. Gun in hand, Sanchez decided to investigate. There could be more dead bodies behind that door, or worse still, the killer could be hiding in there. But, on the off chance that Jessica was in there, it was worth taking a look. And where was Beth Lansbury? Maybe *she* had killed everyone? After all, she was mental. And this was her apartment.

As he stepped into the corridor, he noticed another door in the wall on the left. A bathroom perhaps? He reached for the doorknob and turned it slowly with his free hand, keeping his gun at the ready just in case. The door creaked as it opened inwards. Directly in front of him, he saw a white toilet. Using his newfound detective skills he deduced that it was indeed a bathroom. And there were no signs of any violence in it, not even so much as a skid mark down the back of the toilet.

Peering right around the door he was pleased to see that there was no one hiding inside.

He backed out of the bathroom and tiptoed towards the door at the end of the corridor. By now he could feel his heart pounding in his chest. His breathing was louder than he would have liked too. Dreading what he might find, he took a deep breath and turned the doorknob. He threw the door open and jumped back, pointing his gun into the room, just in case. No noise came out. All he could see was a blue coloured wall opposite and the end of a bed on the left. He edged forward and peered around the doorway. There was nothing of any interest inside, just a perfectly made bed, a dresser and a walk in wardrobe. The room seemed completely untouched by the carnage that had gone on in the living room area. Breathing a sigh of relief he tucked the gun into the back of his pants and stepped back out, closing the bedroom door behind him.

It looked as though the killer had fled, possibly at the sight of Sanchez arriving to investigate, so he was in the apartment on his own. This would be a good time to call for back up, he supposed. He pulled the CB radio from his belt and radioed in to the police frequency.

'This is Detective Sanchez Garcia. Request for backup. I'm on the fourth floor at Remington Tower on 54th Street. I've got some unidentified dead bodies here. And there's blood everywhere. Reckon the killings have only just occurred and the killer could still be in the vicinity. I'm on my own. Please send backup otherwise I'm getting the fuck outta here.' Sensing that no one would come without a decent incentive, he added. 'I've got donuts.'

But first things first, now that the adrenaline rush brought on by checking the apartment for signs of the Bourbon Kid was subsiding, he felt a desperate need for a piss.

He walked back into the bathroom and lifted the seat on the toilet. He tucked his gun into the back of his pants and unzipped his fly. There was nothing quite like unleashing his special homebrew on the world to relieve a tense situation. As he listened to the sound of piss hitting water in the toilet below, he pondered what might have become of Jessica. Maybe she had escaped through the open window in the living room? That was a possibility. She was a resourceful young lady. In fact maybe she was out there hanging off the window ledge waiting for him to come to her rescue? It was definitely worth checking.

He finished his piss and zipped up his fly. As he reached forward to flush the toilet, the handgun that he had tucked neatly into the back of his pants slid out. No, it was pulled out.

Uh-oh.

He heard a loud click. Someone had released the safety clip on the gun.

Fuck.

As the toilet made a loud flushing noise, Sanchez turned around slowly. Stood behind him, pointing the gun at his face was a man he recognised. The man wore casual clothes, just a pair of jeans and a white T-shirt under a black leather jacket. Not his usual attire, but even so, Sanchez recognised him straight away. It was the Bourbon Kid.

He raised his arms in surrender. The Kid never looked anything other than murderous, so Sanchez hoped his lucky streak of surviving unscathed every time the pair of them met would continue. The Kid's face showed some genuine anger. Maybe he lived here? If so, Sanchez hoped that he wouldn't notice a small patch of piss on the floor where he'd missed the toilet at one point. All it would take was one squeeze of the trigger on the gun, (which was inconveniently pointed at his face) and Sanchez's time would be at an end.

The Kid spoke first. 'Where's Beth? What the fuck has happened here?' He looked Sanchez up and down, then added. 'And why the fuck are you wearing a gay cop outfit?'

Sanchez was somewhat baffled by the questions. Clearly the Kid must know more about what had happened in this apartment than him? After all, he must have done the killing, right?

'Why are you asking me?' he asked. 'I mean, I'm guessing you killed all of those people out there? And Jessica too? What have you done with her?'

The Kid looked confused. 'What?'

'Jessica. Where is she? She came up here before me, but when I got here she was gone and there were all those dead people on the floor. What have you done with her? And why do you keep trying to kill her?'

The Kid lowered his gun. 'Jessica was here?' he said.

'Well, yeah. Didn't you see her?'

'I killed her during the eclipse last year. She's dead.'

'No,' Sanchez protested. 'I nursed her back to health after you shot her. She's okay now. Or, at least, she was. Can't find her now though. She must be here somewhere.'

The Kid raised his gun again, pointing it at the end of Sanchez's nose. 'Where the fuck is Beth?'

'Mental Beth?'

'What?'

'Beth Lansbury.'

'Yeah, Beth Lansbury. Where is she?'

Sanchez shrugged. 'I dunno. She wasn't here when I got here.'

The Kid lowered the gun again and walked back out of the bathroom. He headed for the bedroom at the end of the hall.

'There's nothing in there,' Sanchez called out. 'I just checked.'

He heard the Kid open the bedroom door to take a look for himself. Sanchez lowered his arms and walked to the door. He peered around it to see what the Kid was doing. A second later the Kid reappeared from inside the bedroom and came storming back down the corridor towards him. Sanchez retreated back into the bathroom. The Kid rushed past the door and back into the living room area. Fortunately it looked as if killing Sanchez wasn't high on his list of priorities. And it also seemed as though the Kid had no idea about what had happened to Jessica. Sanchez could only guess that she had seen the Kid and escaped through the open window.

Watching his step, he crept back into the living room, making sure he made no sudden movements. The Bourbon Kid was at the window, peering out into the snow-covered streets below. He turned around and looked at Sanchez.

'Did you open this window?' he asked.

'No,' Sanchez replied, raising his hands in surrender again. 'It was already open when I got up here. Anything out there?'

'Just some footprints in the snow.'

'I guess Jessica got away from you again.'

The Kid shook his head. 'And she's got Beth with her.'

'They both escaped, huh?'

The Kid pointed at the bodies strewn across the floor. 'Who d'ya think killed all these fuckers?' he asked.

Sanchez wondered if it was a trick question. 'I'm guessing you did?' he ventured.

'How fuckin' dumb are you? Jessica will have killed them all.'

'That's ridiculous.'

'No it ain't.'

'Okay.'

The Kid peered out of the window again at the streets below and reached into a pocket on his jeans. He pulled out a cell phone and dialled a number. This was just the opportunity Sanchez needed. There was still a second dead cop on the floor, one who might have a gun somewhere about his person. With the Kid distracted and staring out of the window, Sanchez crept over to the body and reached down to see if he could pick the guy's gun out of his holster without drawing attention to himself. An almighty loud clap of thunder from outside startled him. It was followed by a flash of lightning and the sound of hailstones landing on the metal stairs outside the window. The Kid remained unfazed by it as he stared out of the window with his phone pressed against his ear.

Sanchez reached down to the pistol in the cop's holster. It came out smoothly. This was his chance. He could feel his heart beating fast and his hands trembling. Was he really about to do this? To shoot the Bourbon Kid in the back? And save Jessica from his wrath once and for all? He took a deep breath and raised the gun, pointing it at the back of the Kid's neck. Before he had a chance to squeeze the trigger he heard a beeping noise behind him. Someone's cell phone had gone off.

The Kid spun around to see where the beeping sound had come from. He ignored Sanchez and walked briskly past him. On the floor by the sofa was a cell phone. The Kid picked it up. He still didn't seem to have realised Sanchez had a gun. The tubby bartender-cum-replacement cop once again pointed it at the back of his neck and readied himself to fire. The Kid was reading a text message on the phone. Whatever it said, it riled him up. He threw the phone across the room and it smashed against a wall. Without looking at Sanchez he spoke.

'Put the gun down, you fat bastard.'

Sanchez lowered the gun, but didn't drop it. 'Whose phone is that?' he asked the Kid.

'Beth's. She's gone. She's fucking gone.' He turned to face Sanchez, his face revealing a look of desperation. 'Next time you decide to nurse someone back to health, try checking to see if they're a vampire first, you dumb fuck.'

'Huh?'

'Give me the gun.'

Sanchez held out the gun and the Kid snatched it from him and checked to see if it was loaded. Something Sanchez hadn't done. After checking the barrel and noting that it was indeed loaded he looked back up at Sanchez. 'Where does Jessica live?' he asked.

Sanchez shrugged. 'Don't know.'

The Kid pointed the pistol at his head.

'She lives in Cinnamon Street.'

'Last chance.'

'Casa de Ville. She said she was staying at the Casa de Ville.'

The Kid lowered the gun and shoved Sanchez hard in the chest, knocking him back against the wall. He headed for the window and began to climb through it.

'Where are you going?' Sanchez called after him.

'Where d'ya think?'

The Kid vanished through the window and out into the snowy streets below. Sanchez breathed a sigh of relief as he looked around at the dead bodies in the apartment. There was no way Jessica could have killed these people. Nor could she possibly be a vampire as the Kid had intimated. It had already been reported that a man had killed Silvinho, so the only logical explanation was that he had killed the others too. And now he was going to kill Jessica.

Sanchez would have to warn her. And get The Book of Death back to her.

Twenty-One

When the flashing blue lights on the ambulance outside Remington Tower came into view up ahead, Dante steered the stolen police car off the main road and down a back alley. He parked up next to some industrial sized wheelie bins and turned off the engine.

'Why are we parking here?' Kacy asked.

'Discretion.'

Kacy gasped loudly and grabbed his hand. 'Oh my God. You're like Skynet!'

'What?'

'You've become self aware.'

'What are you talking about?'

'You've learned to be discreet. You couldn't possibly believe how proud of you I am right now.'

'You're taking the piss aren't you?'

'A little bit.'

He pulled his hand away from hers and climbed out of the car. By the time Kacy had jumped out of the car too, he was at the end of the alley staring around the corner into the street. Kacy caught up with him and peered over his shoulder.

There was a crowd of people loitering around by the ambulance outside Remington Tower, although there was no sign of any actual ambulance crew.

'What d'ya think?' Kacy asked. 'Is it worth a look?'

Dante didn't answer. He was staring across the street at something. Kacy looked at where he was staring but could see nothing unusual.

'What is it?' she asked.

Dante stepped out of the shadows provided by the alleyway and pointed at a car across the street. 'That's the Bourbon Kid's car,' he said. 'He's here somewhere.'

'That would explain the ambulance then,' said Kacy. 'He's probably killed someone.'

'I hope so. If he's back to his old self and killing innocent people again then he might be a really useful ally to have. Let's go check out his car. I'll see if I can break in to it.'

Kacy was unsure of the benefits of breaking into the car, but she knew Dante just loved doing it. He headed over to the black car and grabbed the door handle on the driver's side. Kacy followed on behind, checking to see if anyone had noticed them, knowing full well that

Dante would have the door open in a matter of seconds. Sure enough he did. He climbed in and reached over to the passenger door, unlocking it. Kacy opened it and climbed in to find he was already in the process of hot-wiring the car.

'Why are you starting the car?' she asked.

'If we can hide his car from him he can't jump in and drive off without us.'

'Would he do that?'

'Let's just say his track record ain't good.'

'What if he comes back and catches you?'

'He'll be okay about it. I think.'

Kacy pulled the car door shut. The snow outside was still falling hard. Had she not been a vampire she suspected she would be feeling the cold. 'Hurry up will you?' she urged. 'I don't wanna get caught.'

A second later the car's engine burst into life. 'Listen to that,' said Dante. 'This is a fuckin' beautiful car.'

A figure appeared at Dante's window. The driver side door swung open.

Kacy screamed. 'LOOK OUT!'

Dante turned to see who had opened the door. Before he could speak, a large hand grabbed him by the hair and dragged him out of the car. Kacy opened her door again and jumped back out into the street. She raced around the car and found Dante on his backside on the sidewalk, at the feet of the man who had dragged him out of the car.

Dante looked up at her. 'Kace, this is the Bourbon Kid.'

The Kid ignored Kacy and instead grabbed Dante's hand. 'What the fuck are you doin' tryin' to steal my ride?' he asked, hauling him up from the sidewalk.

'We been kinda looking for you, man,' said Dante dusting himself off.

'Why? What do you want?' The Kid took a step back and took a long hard look at both Dante and Kacy. 'And when in the fuck did you become a vampire?' he asked.

'Last night,' Dante replied. 'Right after you ditched me and drove off.'

'What happened?'

'I got bit by a fuckin' vampire. You were supposed to come with me to rescue Kacy from the fuckin' Secret Service guys, remember?'

The Kid shrugged. 'Sorry, man. I had other places to be.'

'Yeah, well we're both stuck as fucking vampires now. Unless we can get the Eye of the Moon back from this Rameses Gaius guy.'

'Rameses Gaius?'

'Yeah, some kinda mummy. He's running the show around here now. He's planning to take over the city, then the world. He's amassing a huge undead army.'

'How do you know all this?'

'We were summoned to the Casa de Ville this morning. That's where he's staging all this from.'

'The Casa de Ville?'

'Yeah.'

'Fuck. And there's a whole army of vampires there?'

'Yeah. And they're getting the werewolves in on it too.'

The Kid looked rattled. 'Didn't I kill all the fucking vampires yesterday?'

'Evidently not. You got most of the Shades, Pigs and Dreads, but there's fucking loads of these Pandas and Black Plague dudes around.'

'I fucking hate Pandas.'

Kacy butted in, hopeful of an answer to Dante's earlier question. 'So can you help us get the Eye of the Moon back from Gaius?'

The Kid frowned. 'How the fuck did a Mummy get his hands on the Eye of the Moon?'

'They got it from Peto,' said Dante.

'The monk?'

'Yeah.'

'And where's he now?'

'They cut his head off.'

'Good,' said the Kid. 'That monk was a cunt anyway.'

Kacy asked again. 'Can you help us or not?'

'I got problems of my own. My girlfriend is either dead or about to be dead. If she is alive, she's at the Casa de Ville,' he started moving towards his car then added, 'and from what you've just told me, the place is gonna be a fucking fortress.'

Dante stepped aside to allow the Kid to get to his vehicle. 'It's a bitch when someone's holding your girlfriend hostage, ain't it?' he remarked.

'Guess it is.' The Kid climbed into the driver's side of his car and reached out to the pull the door shut. Dante grabbed a hold of it.

'Hold on a minute,' he said. 'You want a hand rescuing your girlfriend?'

'No.'

Kacy stepped forward and leaned into the car. 'If we help you, can you help us get the Eye of the Moon back from this mummy?'

The Kid looked up at them both and was obviously pondering their offer. After a few seconds he spoke up. 'You ain't getting that Eye back. Ain't no way that Gaius character is gonna let you anywhere near it.'

'Then we'll have to kill him, won't we?' said Dante.

'Good luck with that,' said the Kid, tugging at the car door to pull it shut. Dante kept a firm grip on it much to his obvious annoyance. 'Let go the fucking door, man!'

'Pull it shut,' Dante challenged him.

The Kid pulled hard at the door. It didn't budge. Dante was stronger than him and continued to hold it open with ease.

'See,' said Dante. 'You need us as much as we need you. You ain't the hardass you once were. Remember using the Eye of the Moon to make yourself into a regular guy last night?'

'Let go of the door.'

'I'm stronger than you now. And I'm guessing so is Kacy. You want to get your girlfriend back, you're gonna need our help. And in order to kill Rameses Gaius, we're gonna need yours.'

The Kid looked somewhat irritated at the suggestion that he was no longer the hardass he once was. Once he came to terms with the fact Dante wasn't going to let him shut the door he stopped pulling at it. 'Get in,' he said.

Kacy didn't need a second invitation. She raced back around to the passenger side of the car. 'Shotgun on the front seat,' she called out.

The Kid nodded at Dante. 'Your chick's pretty sharp, huh?'

Kacy stood patiently waiting by the passenger door, snow settling on her hair as she held the door open for Dante to climb into the back seat. He climbed in and she slipped into the front seat closing the door behind her.

The Kid pulled the car away from the sidewalk and out into the icy street, then sped off down the middle of the road. The heavy sleet, snow and some traces of hailstones crashed against the windscreen, making visibility of the road ahead virtually impossible. Kacy made a snap decision to put on her seatbelt.

After they had driven for a couple of minutes, she made a polite observation. 'Isn't the Casa de Ville back the other way?

'Yeah. We gotta stop off at a bar first.'

'Why?'

'I need a drink.'

Twenty-Two

Police work was proving to be quite tiresome. Sanchez had spent a further hour in Beth Lansbury's apartment explaining to another officer exactly what he believed had happened there. A camera crew from the local news station had also turned up to report on the murders. He gave them a quick interview explaining how the Bourbon Kid had murdered everyone but fled when he had burst in and scared him off. Everyone seemed quite impressed and Sanchez was looking forward to seeing himself hailed as a hero on the evening news. It was about time he received some recognition for his public services.

It was early evening when he arrived back at the police station to find Flake still alone in the reception area. She was sitting behind the reception desk reading a book. She didn't notice him arrive and it wasn't until he was only a few yards from the reception desk that she looked up.

'Hey Sanchez, how did it go?' she asked.

He took his Stetson hat off and wiped some sweat from his brow. Even though it wasn't very bright in the station he kept his sunglasses on because, well, they made him look cool. He fanned himself with the hat a few times and rolled his tongue around in his mouth to build up some tension before relaying the tales of his adventures to Flake. Eventually when he was convinced she was desperate to hear what he had to say he began to tell her about his action packed afternoon. 'Well, I lost Jessica, bumped into the Bourbon Kid and saw a whole load of dead bodies. You know, the usual shit.'

Flake looked impressed. 'Are you being serious? Who's dead? And what happened with the Bourbon Kid?'

Sanchez perched his ample butt cheeks on the edge of her desk. 'The ambulance crew and a couple more cops were dead as well as the guy with the pink hair.'

'Oh God. *Really?*'

'Yeah. I had to put in a call for some more ambulance people. Then I had to give an interview to the press, y'know, 'cause they think I'm a hero an' all that.'

'Wow. Are you gonna be on the news tonight?'

Sanchez shrugged. 'Maybe.'

'Cool. I hope you've remembered all the details. And don't forget you'll have to file a report for the Captain.'

'You think?'

'That's protocol isn't it?'

'Well, a guy from forensics turned up eventually and I left him to clear up the mess. He'll probably do the report. I'll do one if Captain Harker asks me to, but it's an open and shut case. The Bourbon Kid killed everyone there and fucked off out the window when I arrived. I scared him off I think.'

'Wow,' Flake gasped. 'You're having quite a day!'

'Much the same as any other,' said Sanchez nonchalantly.

Flake slipped a thin black leather bookmark onto the page she was reading and closed the book in order to give him her full attention. 'So what happened to Jessica? How did you lose her?'

'She'd gone on ahead of me. She must have seen the Kid and made a break for it in case he tried to kill her again.'

'Do you think she's okay?'

'I'm guessing she's headed back home to the Casa de Ville.'

'You're not going to go over there tonight are you? What with the Bourbon Kid being on the loose again. And the vampires!'

Sanchez shook his head. 'No, not tonight. I'll get The Book of Death for her first. It'll cheer her up if I turn up there tomorrow with the book she's been looking for.'

Flake looked unconvinced. 'Do you think you'll be able to find it?'

'I had it this morning.'

Flake laughed. 'You're so funny.'

'No, seriously. I borrowed it from the library,' he paused and looked around to check if anyone was nearby, before adding, 'without actually checking it out.'

Flake gasped. 'Oh my God. You're the one who stole it!'

'Shhh,' said Sanchez looking around again. 'I gave it to Rick to take back to the library this morning, just before you made my breakfast.'

'Why give it to Rick?'

'So I didn't have to face the wrath of that librarian bitch Ulrika. Why d'ya think?'

'Oh, of course.'

Flake took in a deep breath through gritted teeth, in the manner of a mechanic who was about to give a quote for some new brakes. 'I'd be wary about being seen with that Book of Death if I was you,' she warned.

'What do you mean?'

She pointed at the thick hardback book that she had been so engrossed in reading when he entered. 'I've been reading this book,' she said. 'And it's got a bit in it about a book called The Book of Death.'

'Really? What does it say?'

She opened the book and began flicking back through the pages. 'It says it's an ancient Egyptian book that was used to record the names of the dead,' she said, struggling to find the page she was looking for. 'It also says that there was an ancient ruler of Egypt who dabbled in the dark arts. Apparently he found a way to write the names of the dead in it before they actually died.'

Sanchez slid off the desk and stood beside Flake, peering over her shoulder at the book. 'How could he do that?' he asked.

Flake continued to flick through the pages until she eventually found the passage she was looking for. 'Look here,' she said pointing at a short paragraph at the beginning of one of the chapters. 'It says here that he used to write the names of his enemies in The Book of Death. According to this, his enemies would then be cursed to die on the date specified on the page in the book.'

Sanchez scratched his chin and thought about what Flake was saying. 'The Book of Death that I gave to Rick was full of names, and there were dates on the top of each page, but they were all in roman numerals or something. I couldn't work them out.'

Flake shook her head. 'Don't you think a book like that should be destroyed?'

'I dunno,' said Sanchez. He nodded at the book on the desk. 'What's this one you're reading anyway?'

'It's that one I used to kill the librarian.'

'What's it called again?'

'It's doesn't have a name.'

Sanchez stepped back from the desk. 'Oh my God! You're reading The Book With No Name?'

'Yeah.'

'Fuck! You never told me earlier that it was The Book With No Name.'

'Why? What difference does it make?'

'That book was mentioned in the news a while back. Everyone who ever read it died. The cops never figured out why. I was looking for a copy of it at the library yesterday when I picked up The Book of Death instead.'

'I've read about a hundred pages of it now,' said Flake. 'Does that mean I'm going to die?'

'It might. I don't know.'

'Weird, isn't it?'

'What?'

'There's two books that seem to be causing people to die.'

Sanchez thought about it for a few seconds. 'I suppose,' he agreed eventually.

'Which one's worse, do you think?' Flake asked.

'I figure they're both pretty bad.'

Flake grimaced. She looked genuinely concerned for her wellbeing. 'I think I'd rather have read the first hundred or so pages of The Book With No Name, than have my name written down in The Book of Death,' she decided eventually.

Sanchez took off his sunglasses and slipped them into his breast pocket to take a better look at The Book With No Name. 'Have you told Captain Harker about this?' he asked.

'No. He's real busy with some kind of child killer case. He's been on the news all day talking about it.'

'Child killer, eh?'

'Yeah, someone's been poisoning kids and draining their blood.'

'Bloody vampire, I'll bet.'

Flake nodded in agreement. 'Yeah. Harker reckons there could be hundreds of victims, mostly orphans.'

'Well, we're lucky we're adults, aren't we?' said Sanchez finding something positive to take from the distressing news.

'Terrible though, isn't it?'

'Absolutely. What happens when he runs out of kids to kill? He might move on to adults. Then we'll be in trouble.'

Flake frowned. 'I hope he does try his luck with us. We've got this book that kills vampires, remember.'

'Oh yeah, good thinking,' said Sanchez. Flake really was pretty smart sometimes, for a waitress. He glanced at his watch. 'The library will be closed now. I'll go tomorrow morning and take back another book I borrowed yesterday. I'll look for The Book of Death while I'm there.'

'I'll come with you,' Flake offered.

'It's okay. That's not necessary.'

'You could pop by the Ole Au Lait first and we could have breakfast together,' Flake suggested.

Sanchez slipped his hat back on as he contemplated her offer. She clearly had plans to share in the reward on offer for returning The Book of Death to Jessica. He slipped his sunglasses back on to hide the deceit in his eyes.

'Yeah, okay. See you there at about nine o'clock tomorrow morning.'

'Great!' she beamed. She continued babbling on about something or other as Sanchez made his way out of the station. He had no intention of stopping off at the Ole Au Lait for breakfast. Getting to the library first thing in the morning was his top priority.

Twenty-Three

Kacy hadn't set foot in the Tapioca for a long time. The place hadn't changed much. It was still a shithole. The walls were a disgusting yellow colour, it stank of cigarette smoke and although it wasn't very busy, everyone in there looked like a criminal. The only major difference was that there wasn't a fat guy behind the bar this time.

She followed Dante and the Bourbon Kid up to the bar. Before they had even taken a seat, the Kid called out to the barmaid.

'Get me a bourbon. And fill the glass.'

Kacy grabbed a stool and sat down at the bar. The barmaid set a whisky glass down on the bar and began filling it to the top with bourbon from a dirty brown bottle of Jim Beam.

Dante nudged Kacy. 'Watch what happens once he's downed it. Those four guys at the table in the corner are most likely gonna get wasted.'

Kacy glanced over at the table in question and saw four greasy lowlifes supping at bottles of beer. She made eye contact with one of them and immediately looked back to the bar. The Kid had thrown a five-dollar bill at the barmaid.

'Keep the change,' he muttered.

As the barmaid began ringing the sale up in the till at the back of the bar, he picked up the glass of bourbon and took a long hard look at it, inspecting the contents. The glass wasn't particularly clean and the bourbon didn't look particularly special, but he was definitely going to drink it. He put the glass to his lips and poured the contents down his throat. Then he slammed it back down on the bar.

From all that she had heard about him, Kacy expected to see him turn into a giant psycho, or pull out an arsenal of weapons. What actually happened was distinctly underwhelming. He simply stared down into the empty glass, deep in thought.

Eventually he looked over at them. 'I feel nothing,' he said. 'Something's gone. Right now I should be looking at those four guys in the corner and deciding on how I'm gonna kill 'em.'

'What do you mean?' Dante asked.

'I can't think of a good reason to kill them.'

'Since when did you need a reason?'

'Since now.'

Kacy gestured over to a table by the entrance. 'Why don't we take a seat and talk about this,' she suggested.

The three of them made their way over to the table and each sat down on one of the creaky wooden chairs around it.

'What's different?' Kacy asked sympathetically.

'I don't feel the same,' the Kid said, looking confused. 'I used to get a major adrenaline rush after a drink. You know that feeling where you just wanna kill everyone you see?'

'Not really,' said Kacy.

'Well, something used to take over after I'd had a drink. It was brought on by the memories of the moment when I killed my mother.'

'You killed your mom?' Kacy couldn't mask the shock in her voice.

'She turned into a vampire. Begged me to kill her. I had to have a drink first. Drank a bottle of bourbon, ploughed about six bullets through her heart. After that the only thing that ever made me feel alive was drinkin' bourbon and killin' folks. Especially vampires.'

'And you're not getting that feeling any more?'

'No. Not since…' he trailed off.

Dante finished the sentence for him. 'Not since he used the Eye of the Moon to get his soul back last night. Now he's a regular guy. Got a conscience like everyone else.'

The Kid reached inside his jacket and pulled out a pack of cigarettes. He used his teeth to pull one out of the pack and sucked hard on the end of it. It lit up brightly and he replaced the pack in his jacket. 'There's some shit I can still do,' he said. 'Don't go thinking I'm all washed up. I still know everything I knew before, I've just lost a bit of my inner rage.'

Dante looked at him. He looked like a regular guy. Something was missing and it wasn't just the dark hooded coat. There was something missing from his eyes. Those eyes used to reveal a look of contempt for everything and everyone, but now they looked just like anyone else's.

Without realising he was doing it, Dante shook his head scornfully as he looked at the man opposite him. 'So how are you gonna help us kill Rameses Gaius and get the Eye of the Moon back?' he asked.

'You can't kill Gaius.'

'Why not?'

'You said he's got the Eye of the Moon in his head. It's a part of him, like a pulse or a living organism that gives him his strength, so he's totally immortal. And a mummy. Those fuckers don't die. There's only one way to deal with him.'

'And what's that?' Kacy asked.

'You send him back where he came from.'

Kacy looked at Dante. He appeared to have no idea what the Kid was talking about either. 'Where does he come from?' she asked.

The Kid took a drag on his cigarette and blew the smoke back out through his nostrils. 'A tomb. You gotta wrap that fucker up in bandages and bury him alive in a tomb.'

'You're kidding, right?' said Kacy.

'Nope. That's why you're gonna need my help.'

'So what are you gonna do?' Dante asked before Kacy had the chance.

'I'm gonna head out of town for a while. Can you two get into the Casa de Ville and meet me there tomorrow?'

'Yeah,' said Dante. 'We were there this morning. Big place. Fucking lot of vampires there. Heavily guarded too. I'm not sure how you'll get in there. No offence, but unless you can get back to your bad old self, you won't even make it past the front gate. There's an undead only policy there at the moment.'

'Wait a minute!' Kacy butted in. 'He'll get in if he's a vampire.'

Dante raised an eyebrow. 'You wanna turn him into one then?'

'Won't need to,' she replied.

'Huh?'

She tapped Dante on the leg. 'Give him that serum you brought back from the hotel.'

Dante's eyes lit up as it dawned on him what she was getting at. 'Good idea.'

'What serum?' asked the Kid.

Dante pulled a syringe and a small bottle from his pocket and slid it over the table to the Kid.

The Kid looked at it and frowned. 'What the fuck is that?'

'That's what'll get you past the front gates.'

'Care to elaborate? 'Cause I don't wanna have to read your mind.'

'This is the serum I was using to lower my blood temperature when I was undercover with the vampires. It's what helped me walk among them unnoticed. Inject yourself with that before you get to the Casa de Ville and they'll think you're one of them.'

The Kid picked up the bottle of liquid and looked closely at it. 'This stuff didn't work that well for you. I spotted you right away when you were undercover.'

'Maybe so,' said Dante. 'But the rest of the clan fell for it. It's worth a shot.'

'Fine,' said the Kid. 'You got a cell phone?'

'I have,' said Kacy.

The Kid slipped the syringe and bottle into a pocket inside his jacket and pulled out a cell phone. He handed it to Kacy. 'Stick your number in here so I can contact you if I need to.'

Kacy took the phone and began inputting her number.

Dante prodded the Kid in the arm. 'What do you want us to do while we're waiting for you?'

'See if you can find out what happened to my woman. If she's still alive I wanna know about it. If she's dead, I wanna know about it too. Send me a text, okay?'

'Sure thing,' said Kacy.

'What about Gaius?' Dante asked. 'He's mounting a whole fucking army at the Casa de Ville. How can we deal with that? There could be a million of them by the time you get there?'

'Let me worry about that.'

'Normally I would. But you aren't exactly demonstrating *army destroying* skills right now, if you don't mind me saying.'

'I *do* mind you saying, since you ask.'

'Sorry, but I'm only callin' it as I see it.'

'You'll see it differently tomorrow.' The Kid got up from the table. 'Right now I've got a conscience. I'll be back to my old self once I get rid of it. I'll see ya later.'

As he walked towards the exit, Kacy called after him. 'So where exactly are you going?' she asked.

He stopped short of the door and turned around. He pulled a pair of sunglasses from inside his jacket and slipped them on. Then he answered her question with two words that meant nothing to her.

'Devil's Graveyard.'

Twenty-Four

Gaius burst into his office and found Jessica sitting in his black leather chair behind his desk with her feet up. Her black knee-high boots were resting on his favourite notepad. She was wearing an all black outfit as usual, with a plunging neckline on the top, revealing a fair amount of cleavage, much to her father's disapproval.

'You'd better have found The Book of Death!' he grumbled.

'Nope,' said Jessica nonchalantly. 'Got something better.'

'I seriously doubt that.'

She gestured to a cream sofa set against the wall behind him. He looked over at it and saw a woman slumped across it. She was lying face down and was wearing a pair of tatty ripped black jeans and a blue cardigan. This was not the usual kind of riff-raff Gaius expected to see in his office.

'Who the fuck is that on my sofa?' he asked.

'That's Beth Lansbury.'

'Who's Beth Lansbury?'

'She is.'

'Very funny. Seriously, who is Beth Lansbury and why is she in my office, taking a nap on my sofa?'

Jessica took her feet down off the desk and stood up. She pointed at Beth and smiled. 'That there little lady is the Bourbon Kid's girlfriend.'

Gaius raised an eyebrow and half a smile. 'Is that so?'

'Yep.'

'Did you kill her?'

'Nope. No sense in that. Look what happened to those three idiot cops who killed his brother.'

'Okay. So why is she here in my office?'

'Leverage. If he cares about her as much as I think he does, then he'll try and rescue her. When he shows up, we give him a choice, his life or hers.'

Gaius was unimpressed. 'I fail to see how this is better than bringing me The Book of Death.'

'You're getting cranky.'

'No I'm not.'

'You are. And you're getting paranoid again too. You've been keeping that Eye in your head for too long. It's making you all paranoid, just like the last time you had it.'

Gaius squinted suspiciously at her. 'Who's been saying I'm paranoid?' he snapped.

'Just me.'

'Are you sure?'

Jessica sighed. 'See, you're being all paranoid now. That Eye is having a bad effect on you. You need to take it out for an hour or two here and there, otherwise it makes you all vengeful and you make bad decisions based on all your pathetic personal grudges. That's what got you in trouble all those years ago and it's why you ended up being mummified for centuries. Take it out and think for yourself, for fuck's sake!'

'I am fucking thinking for myself, thank you very much. Now are we going to kill this woman on my sofa or not?'

Jessica strolled across the room to the sofa and gave Beth a prod in the back. She didn't stir. Jessica turned back to Gaius and smiled. 'Calm down, father, and just listen to me for a minute. Before I put her to sleep I managed to extract some information from her. She didn't even know her boyfriend was the Bourbon Kid until today when he killed Silvinho. She knew him by another name. His real name.'

'Which is what?'

'Jack Daniels. Corny, huh?'

Gaius nodded. 'Very. We finally know his name but we've lost the fucking book. Does anything ever go according to plan around here?'

'No, but that's why it's always good to have a backup plan.' Jessica leaned down and stroked Beth's hair. 'You put too much faith in that book, father. With her as bait we can kill him without having to worry about whether or not his name is in your precious book.'

Gaius walked over to his desk and sighed rather loudly as he sat down in his black leather chair. 'Jessica my dear, the reason I want The Book of Death isn't simply to kill the Bourbon Kid. He's a mere irritation. I could kill him easily with my bare hands. I need that book for far more important matters.'

'Such as?'

'Insurance. Once my undead army is established and my plan to conquer the rest of the world is underway, the leaders of the free world will attempt to take us out with nuclear weapons and all kinds of other shit. But once I've demonstrated to them that all I have to do is write their names in my book to kill them, those world leaders will soon come around to my way of thinking. I'll have them all in my back pocket. We'll be able to waltz on in to any country we wish, uncontested. Our army won't need to fight anyone, we'll just travel freely around the world, conquering.'

Jessica looked surprised. 'Wow, I had no idea you had such big plans. I'm mildly impressed.'

'As you should be. Right now though, there's no sign of the book, or Ulrika Price. Which reminds me, I'm going to have to make a stop by the library to kill her at some point.'

Jessica shook her head. 'See, there you go getting all personal and vengeful again.'

'Oh, shut up about that. You don't like Ulrika Price anyway. I thought you'd be glad to see the back of her.'

'For all we know that bitch might have gotten big ideas and decided to write our names in the book. I'm amazed you trusted her with it, what with you being all paranoid and stuff. Or maybe she sold it and skipped town.'

Gaius could feel himself grinding his teeth in frustration. 'As I keep saying, it's imperative that we get The Book of Death back. These are testing times. With all the murders that have just occurred in this city it's only a matter of time before the rest of the world discovers that Santa Mondega is rife with the undead. The minute the word gets out about us, the governments of the world will start sending armies here. We'll be blown to bits before we've even gotten going. So, yes, great though it is that you've kidnapped this woman, it's nowhere near as important as finding The Book of Death before word gets out about what we're up to here.'

'Oh dear,' Jessica had a troubled look on her face. 'In that case you're not going to like this.'

'Like what?'

'We're kind of all over the news already.'

Gaius could feel himself becoming extremely agitated. He ran his right hand back and forth over his smooth bald head. If he'd had any hair he would have been pulling it out about now. 'What do you mean?' he snarled.

'There's been a piece running on the local news channel for the last hour. It's picking up steam and causing a fair amount of public outrage.'

Gaius took a deep breath through his mouth and exhaled slowly through his nostrils. 'What is it? Go on tell me!'

'There's a child killer on the loose.'

'Why should I care about that?'

'Because it says that the victims were all poisoned and have bites on their necks. There are mutterings that it's the work of vampires. We haven't exactly been discreet in recent times, but now that someone's killing kids, it's becoming very high profile.'

Gaius slammed his fist down on the desk. 'For fuck's sake!' he yelled. 'This will fuck up everything. If that story goes national, we'll have armies from every fucking nation in the world sending troops down here! Who the fuck is doing it?'

'Well, that's the other thing, the news flash says that some of the kids who were killed had goat's hair under their fingernails.'

'Goat's hair?'

'Yeah.'

Gaius sighed. 'I should have fucking known.'

Jessica reached a hand into her cleavage and pulled out a cell phone that had been concealed within it. She pressed a few buttons, then approached her father's desk and handed it to him. 'Just press dial,' she said.

Gaius snatched the phone from her hand and pressed the dial button. The phone rang twice before it was answered.

'Hello,' said a voice on the other end of the line.

'Well, hello there. This is Rameses Gaius. Is there something you want to tell me?'

There was an uneasy silence on the other end of the phone for a few seconds. Eventually the other person answered. 'No. I don't think so.'

Gaius couldn't contain his rage any longer. 'YOU'RE ALL OVER THE FUCKING NEWS, YOU IDIOT!'

'Oh.'

'Yes, *oh*. You promised me no more kids. Not while I'm planning world domination. You've disobeyed me for the last time!'

'I'm sorry. I thought I was being discreet.'

'You're about as discreet as a fart in a library.'

'Huh?'

'For fuck's sake,' said Gaius, exasperation evident in his voice. 'I'm having the day from hell already. The Book of Death has gone missing, the Bourbon Kid is on the loose somewhere, and then on top of that, you're all over the news for killing kids!'

'The Book of Death has gone missing?'

'Yes. Not that it's really any of your concern.'

The voice on the other end of the line took on a less apologetic tone. 'I know who has The Book of Death,' it said. 'I can get it back for you.'

'Seriously?'

'Yeah. But if I get it for you, can I carry on killing kids?'

'Sure. Who has the book?'

'Just a local idiot. He's only a stone's throw away from me at this very moment. Getting it back will be a piece of cake.'

Twenty-Five

Rick's day had been a tiring one. With Flake signing up to join the police force, he'd had to close the Ole Au Lait for most of the day, and in trying to find a replacement for her he'd barely had five minutes to himself. According to some stupid local bylaw there was nothing he could do about Flake joining the police force in an emergency either.

When he'd finished all of his extra chores, he locked the front door of the Ole Au Lait behind him and stepped out into the snowy streets once more.

The dark clouds that had been looming over the city for the last twenty-four hours showed no signs of clearing. He hadn't minded the heavy rain and occasional thunder from the night before. But the non-stop downfall of snow over the course of the day was a real pain in the ass. There sure was some strange shit going on in town. Lots of kids were complaining about a hit and run driver mowing down the snowmen they had built around the streets. There had also been numerous elderly people taken to hospital after slipping and falling over on the icy sidewalks.

As night fell the streets were deserted, which was hardly surprising. It was late, it was dark and above all it was fucking dangerous to be out. In spite of the rumour that a shitload of vampires had been slaughtered on Halloween, Rick still worried that there might be a few lurking around. Thinking about it made him pull the collar on his raincoat up to cover his neck.

His apartment was only a block away from the Ole au Lait, and normally he wouldn't fear a vampire attack. Any of his customers leaving late in the evening could well expect to become food for the immortals, but being the café's owner, Rick was generally left alone. If any vampire killed him then his café would close down. In the same way that none of the undead ever touched Sanchez, Rick knew he was safe because they needed the blood of his customers. No Ole Au Lait, no late night coffee drinkers. No Tapioca, slightly less drunken assholes.

As he turned the corner at the end of the block he almost slipped on a manhole cover that was hidden beneath some black ice. Fortunately no one was around to see him stumble slightly except the drunken tramp dressed as Santa Claus who was lying in a shop doorway on the other side of the road. The tramp looked fast asleep. His white beard had turned a horrible grey colour and the front of his red outfit was stained with rainfall, sleet, specks of snow and no doubt some booze that he would have spilled from a bottle he had resting on his lap in a brown paper bag.

'Poor old bastard,' Rick muttered to himself. It had to be desperate times indeed for that particular tramp. It was only November, so the guy had another month to wait before people started to take pity on him and throw some cash his way in the build up to Christmas.

By the time Rick reached his house he was soaked through from the steadily falling snow and chilled to the bone thanks to the icy winds. He hurried down the five concrete steps that led down to his front door below the sidewalk and pulled a set of keys from his pocket. He fumbled for the correct one, his frozen fingers struggling to get a suitable grip on the key he required. When he eventually settled on the right one, he slipped it into the door's lock and turned it. The door clicked and he pushed it open. The hallway inside looked warm. He stepped inside and onto the brown welcome doormat. The house was much warmer than outside and he placed his hand down onto the radiator on the wall. It was suitably warm, but would no doubt need turning up before the night was through. His shoes were soaked and carrying all kinds of debris on the soles. He rubbed them on the mat and turned to push the door closed behind him. That was when Rick realised he had a visitor. And not a pleasant looking one. He was greeted by the sight of a giant man in red lunging through his front door, his mouth wide open revealing an enormous set of vampire fangs.

'Shiiiiiiiiiiiit!'

A huge dark dirty hand slammed over Rick's mouth, silencing any attempt at a cry for help. Rick was now staring right into the crazy black eyes of a vampire dressed as Santa Claus. What had looked like a perfectly helpless drunken tramp only a minute earlier when slumped in a doorway down the road, was now a full blown, bloodsucking maniac. And this motherfucker looked thirsty. The Santa was strong and pushed Rick back into his hallway, keeping its hand pinned over his mouth. Rick's eyes opened wide as he got a close up look at some thick streaks of blood in his intruder's bushy grey beard.

The Santa pulled him in close and then hooked a leg around the back of Rick's knees and pushed him again causing him to fall back on to the hardwood floor. Rick heard the front door slam shut as the Santa kicked it back with one of his heavy black boots.

'I own the Ole Au Lait,' Rick spluttered, hoping it would buy him a reprieve.

'I know you do,' growled the Santa. 'That ain't what's gonna save you.'

Rick looked up at his tormentor, finally getting a really good look. The Santa was a fearsome looking guy indeed. Behind his dirty grey beard was a blotchy red and purple face. And unless he was wearing fake padding, he was decidedly overweight too. But he had big arms and a head the size of a pumpkin. His red Santa hat was definitely an extra large and the top part of it hung down next to the side of his face.

'Please,' said Rick in his most pleading and desperate voice. 'I'm a good guy, I swear.'

Santa leaned over him. 'I've met lots of children lately who've been good all year,' he said. 'It didn't save them and it won't save you.'

Rick grabbed at the Santa's beard. This was no way to hurt him though. As he pulled at it, it came away from his attacker's face. The beard was a fake, made from animal hair and held on by an elastic band wrapped around his ears. It smelled unpleasantly of goat.

'Please,' Rick begged in desperation. 'I'll give you anything. Just let me go.'

'You can start by telling me where The Book of Death is.'

'The Book of Death?'

'That's right. You had it this morning. I saw you with it in the Ole Au Lait. Where is it now?'

Rick swallowed hard. 'I took it back to the library,' he spluttered as the grey beard brushed against his face.

The Santa leaned down even further, getting his face in close to take a good look at Rick to see if he was telling the truth. The smell of stale booze was overwhelming as the monster breathed over him before finally responding. 'I went to the library already. They said it was missing.'

'I didn't check it in with the librarian. I just stuck it on the shelf in the Reference section.'

'Why? Why not hand it in to the librarian?'

'I was returning it for my friend Sanchez. He said he'd borrowed it without permission so I had to stick it back on the shelf myself.'

The Santa slapped Rick around the face. 'I don't believe you!' he hissed.

'I can take you back there in the morning and show you where I put it.'

The Santa sat down on Rick's chest, pinning him to the floor. 'You just said it was in the Reference section. I can find it myself.'

'Okay, fine. We're good then, right? You can leave me alone now?' said Rick, hoping that the situation was resolved.

The Santa reached inside his red jacket and pulled out a brown paper bag. From within it he pulled out a small silver hip flask. He reached down with his spare hand and grabbed Rick's nose, pinning his nostrils shut and pushing his head down onto the floor. He put the bottle to Rick's lips. 'Open wide,' he said. 'You'll like this!'

Rick could feel his lungs gasping for oxygen. Having his nostrils held shut brought on a feeling of helplessness and panic. All he could do was open his mouth and hope to suck in some air. Instead, as he opened his mouth he watched on in terror as the heavy set vampire in the Santa outfit held the bottle over his mouth and poured a small amount of a warm green liquid down his throat. The liquid had a lemony taste to it, not totally unpleasant. Certainly better than some of the piss Rick had been served by Sanchez over the years.

The Santa eventually stopped pouring the green liquid into his mouth and eased his grip on his nose, allowing him to suck in some air. It caused him to cough and choke a little and he felt the taste of the liquid in his throat and nostrils.

To his surprise the Santa stood back up. It relieved the pressure on Rick's chest for a moment. He took in a deep breath, only to then feel his chest begin to tighten again. A warm sensation came over him. It was a relatively pleasant feeling after the cold wet weather outside and the suffocation incident of a few seconds earlier. However, the warm sensation lasted only momentarily. It was followed by a numbness that swept from his shoulders to his toes in a matter of seconds. He tried to speak, only to find that his mouth and tongue didn't move to say the words he wanted, which would have been *"What's happening?"*

The Santa took off his red hat, revealing a head of thick dark dirty greasy hair. Then he grinned his huge vampire-fanged smile at the stricken coffee shop owner.

'What you're experiencing right now is a form of paralysis brought on by what you just drank,' he said. 'I want you to lie there and enjoy yourself while I go to work on you. I usually save this stuff for kids, but I'm making you a special case. You'll feel all the pain as I drain your blood from your veins. You just won't be able to react to any of it. It should only take a few hours.' He unleashed an evil smile, then added, 'Merry Christmas.'

Twenty-Six

Kacy awoke from a very deep sleep. She was naked beneath the covers of a bed in a room she didn't recognise. She felt hung over too. As the recollection of the previous night's events came back to her she realised why. After leaving the Tapioca and the Bourbon Kid, she and Dante had headed out in search of some fresh blood. They had found it a lot harder to come by than either of them had expected. Neither of them wanted to murder an innocent person and drink their blood, so after some half-hearted attempts at attacking strangers they had headed back to the Swamp empty handed. As it turned out they needn't have worried because Vanity kept fresh bottles of blood behind the bar in the pool hall.

They had arrived at the pool hall to find an after hours drinking club in full swing. Vanity had invited along the other surviving members of the Shades clan and a few other hard drinking vampires. He was a generous host so there were free bottles of a drink named "Bloodweiser" available all night. It was a blood based drink designed to look like Budweiser beer. It hadn't been anywhere near as satisfying as the blood of Archie Somers, but it had done enough to cure the craving that both Dante and Kacy had.

Kacy had found Vanity to be a pretty reasonable guy and quite a charmer. The guy knew how to throw a party and make the guests feel welcome and he didn't come across as terrifying in the way she had imagined a vampire to be. But then, she too was a vampire these days and she didn't consider herself to be a blood crazed lunatic either.

Alongside her in bed, Dante was still sleeping. She got up and showered in the en-suite bathroom without waking him. He'd always been a late riser, particularly after a night of drinking, so she was able to make as much noise as she liked without worrying about him waking.

The bedroom Vanity had given them to share was on the top floor of the Swamp. It had no windows in it, presumably so that any vampire waking up in there in the morning didn't get an unexpected taste of sunlight for breakfast.

After drying her hair and dressing in a comfy pair of blue jeans and a red sweatshirt, she decided to go see if the snowfall outside had gotten any worse.

She opened the door into the living room and peered around it to see if Vanity was around. He was sitting on a sofa with his back to her watching something on the large television screen on the far wall. Fortunately it wasn't porn and his pants weren't around his ankles. He was wearing a crimson coloured dressing gown and a pair of matching slippers, hardly what one might expect from a fearsome vampire. The television was playing a home video of a wedding reception. Kacy loved a good wedding, so she stepped out into the living room and gently closed the door behind her. Vanity obviously heard her because he twisted his neck around sharply.

'Oh hi,' he said looking surprised to see her. 'You sleep well?'

'Yeah, great, thanks.'

'What about Dante?'

'He's still asleep. Probably will be for another hour or two yet.'

'Had a good time though. You both seemed to enjoy yourselves last night.'

'Yeah, it was a blast. Where did everyone else go?'

Vanity smirked. 'Well we listened to you two fucking for a while, then the others all went home for the night.'

Kacy felt herself beginning to blush. The lusting brought on by the blood drinking the previous night had made her and Dante somewhat horny. They'd lost their inhibitions and had one almighty loud and energetic fuck in Vanity's spare bedroom. As she cast her mind back to some of the things she'd screamed out in the throes of passion, she decided a change of subject was required.

On the television screen on the far wall, she spotted a face she recognised. 'Is that you?' she asked.

'Yeah,' Vanity reached for the remote to turn the television off.

'Is this your wedding day?'

'Uh huh.'

'Oh wow! Do you mind if I watch it with you for a minute?'

Vanity looked surprised and put the remote back down on the coffee table. 'Sure, if you want. It's not exciting or anything.'

Kacy looked closely at the bride. She was a beautiful brunette aged about twenty-five. The groom, Vanity, looked similar to how he did now, only he was dressed smarter in a black suit with a white shirt and black bow tie.

'Your wife is really pretty,' Kacy said, perching herself on the edge of the sofa.

'Yeah, she is.'

'Are you still together?'

He shook his head. 'Nah. She didn't want to become a vampire.' His voice hinted at a deep rooted sadness.

'Why? What happened?'

Vanity paused the video just as he and his bride were sharing a kiss for the camera. 'I wasn't a vampire back then,' he said. 'Some fucker bit me on our honeymoon. Emma, my wife, didn't want to become a vampire too, so I had to get the hell outta there or I'd have bitten her. I promised her that one day when I found a cure and became human again, I'd go back for her.'

'How long ago was it?'

'Four years.'

Kacy tried to imagine what four years apart from Dante would be like. Not very nice, she decided. She stared hard at the happy couple on screen for a few seconds before asking Vanity another personal question. 'And what about Emma? What's she doing now?'

Vanity stared at the screen in a daze as he spoke. 'She's never remarried or anything, but she's twenty-nine now, the same age as me. In a few months time she'll be thirty. Me, I'll always look twenty-nine. Our dream of growing old together died the day I was bitten.'

'I'm so sorry.'

'Yeah, me too. Dante's real lucky to have you, but you've made one hell of a sacrifice by becoming one of us.'

'I know. It was a spur of the moment decision. But I can't live without Dante. We've been together forever.'

'I can tell,' said Vanity smiling. 'When he said he'd just picked you up the other night, I knew he was lying right away. You're very comfortable with each other.'

Kacy realised she'd been a little too open and honest with Vanity. She couldn't help herself though. She felt a bond with him. He was the only vampire friend she'd made so far and he understood what she and Dante were going through. Even though he had no doubt killed many people in order to survive as a vampire, Vanity seemed full of remorse, not necessarily for the killings, but for the fact he had no chance to go back to his old life.

Kacy probed a little deeper. 'If you could go back to being human, would you do it? And go back to your wife?' she asked intrusively.

'In a heartbeat. I hate being a vampire. I'd give absolutely anything to be human again.'

Kacy took a deep breath then blurted out what was on her mind. 'Did you know the Eye of the Moon can make you human again?'

Vanity smiled. 'Yeah, but Rameses Gaius would never allow any of us to use it for that. Trust me, if I could work out how to get the Eye of the Moon out of his head, I'd do it. Problem is, he'd kill me before I got anywhere near it.'

'Wouldn't it be great if we could get hold of the Eye though?'

'Yeah, but seriously, forget it.'

'Why?'

'It'd be suicide.'

'But if we *could* get it, you could become human again and go back to your wife.'

Vanity frowned and then looked back over at the television. He stared for a second at the frozen frame picture of him and his wife. Then he picked up the remote and switched the TV off.

'Would you and Dante be willing to risk it?' he asked.

Kacy shrugged. 'If it was possible, I'd want to try. Wouldn't you?'

Vanity sat staring at the blank screen on the television for a while, deep in thought. Eventually he took a deep breath and turned to Kacy. 'You know what?' he said. 'I think I know a way we can get hold of the Eye. It's dangerous though.'

Kacy was all ears. 'Really? How?'

'I heard that Gaius is going to the museum tonight. He's planning on having the Eye cleaned by a special diamond polishing machine they've got there. If we could somehow be there when he removes the Eye from his head, we could snatch it away. The three of us, you, me and Dante could pull this off, I think. It'll be the only chance we'll ever get because he's not gonna take that Eye out very often.'

Kacy felt very excited. 'Oh my God. Do you really think we could do it?'

Vanity nodded slowly, almost as if he was convincing himself. 'Actually, you know what? I really think we could. Without the Eye he's nothing. Not a threat to us at all. The three of us would be more than a match for him.'

Kacy jumped up from the sofa. 'Oh my God,' she squealed. 'I'll go and wake Dante and tell him.'

'Cool.'

She raced back into the bedroom to tell Dante the big news. As soon as she was out of sight, Vanity pulled his cell phone from his pocket. He dialled the number for Rameses Gaius. Gaius answered within one ring. His voice sounded as irritated as ever.

'What do you want?' he snapped.

'It's done,' said Vanity. 'I'll have them both at the museum tonight. You wouldn't believe how easy it was.'

Twenty-Seven

Sanchez arrived at the library just after nine o'clock and raced up the steps at the front of the building. He reached the large wooden double doors at the entrance just as they were being opened. Josh, the young lad who worked as assistant to the now deceased Ulrika Price, pulled open the door on the right and was in the process of unbolting the second door as Sanchez barged in. Josh winced as the cold air blew in through the open door. His librarian uniform consisted only of a pair black trousers and a thin white shirt so the fresh air would have raced right through to the bone on the fresh faced teenager. He looked quite surprised to see anyone arriving so early too, particularly someone like Sanchez who was not exactly a regular bookworm.

'Morning, Sanchez,' he said, his brown hair blowing up out of his face courtesy of a gust of wind from outside.

'Good day to you, young man,' said Sanchez with an air of officialdom in his voice. 'It's Detective Garcia to you though. I'm here on official police business.'

Josh looked surprised, but he looked Sanchez up and down, no doubt admiring his uniform. Then he shrugged. 'Sure thing, Detective. Is this about Ulrika Price?'

'No. Why would it be?'

'Well, she's gone missing. I'm not supposed to even be working here any more because she fired me yesterday morning.'

'What a bitch.'

'Yeah. Apparently just a few minutes after firing me she vanished off the face of the planet. I thought if she'd been reported as a missing person I might be on your list of people to question?'

Sanchez pondered what he'd said for a moment before answering. 'It's okay. That's not why I'm here. Although if she *has* been murdered I would imagine you'll be the prime suspect in any investigation, so don't go leaving town any time soon.'

'Yes sir. So what can I do for you now?'

Sanchez headed to a staircase on the left-hand wall that led to the first floor and the Reference section. 'I'm fine thanks. Shouldn't need any help,' he said. 'Just got to relieve you of a book to help with an investigation.'

'What book is it?'

'Never you mind.'

He walked briskly up the stairs and left Josh behind to stick the OPEN sign up in the front window by the entrance.

The upstairs section of the library looked as daunting as ever. There were countless aisles full of books and plenty of tables and chairs in which students could sit and read for free. On Sanchez's last visit he had smuggled The Book of Death out by tucking it into the back of his pants so Ulrika Price wouldn't see it. There would be no need to do that this time. He was now an officer of the law, and Ulrika Price wasn't on duty.

The Reference section was full of shelves that carried on all the way up to the ceiling, filled with hardback books about all kinds of boring subjects. It was a blessing that the books were sorted alphabetically by author name, well, more or less. He headed straight to the first row of shelves and began scouring the spines of the books written by authors whose surnames began with A. It seemed that the Reference section was the graveyard for all the unclassifiable books that were dumped by Josh when he didn't know where to put them. Aside from not being in particularly good alphabetical order there were also all kinds of non-referential books in sight. Sanchez flicked through the titles until he came to one by Anonymous. It was called Primary Colors. Scouring along the shelf to the right he saw several more books, some with the name Anonymous along the spine and others with no name at all. It baffled him how anyone could be so stupid as to go to the trouble of writing a book and then forget to put his or her name on it.

There were varying titles, some of which were further reference books in the "Gay Man's Guide To..." series. During his last visit to the library Sanchez had mistakenly picked up a copy of The Gay Man's Guide to Anal Sex and ended up borrowing it to prevent Ulrika Price from noticing he was stealing The Book of Death at the same time. The guide wasn't due back for another week so he had left it back at the Tapioca. In fact he wasn't sure how he was ever going to get around to returning that book, simply because of the embarrassment of being seen with it in public.

After scouring over a hundred books, he finally spotted the familiar black binding on The Book of Death. The title was written in a white font, which had faded quite badly. He felt his heart race in his chest. This was it, the ticket to fifty thousand dollars in reward money and a place in Jessica's heart. If this didn't impress her, nothing would.

He pulled the book out from where it had been wedged in by Rick the day before. Resting it on the edge of one of the shelves he flicked it open at about halfway. It was definitely the right book. It was full of names, just as he remembered. He flicked through the pages until eventually he came to the one where he had written Jessica's name along with two others. Checking both ways along the aisle to see if anyone was watching, he grabbed a firm hold of the page and tore it out of the book as quietly as he could. He crumpled the paper up and stuck it into one of the front pockets on his pants. Everything seemed to have worked out perfectly. He breathed a sigh of relief and tucked the book under his arm, then he strolled confidently back out of the aisle and out into the open area near the reception desk. Josh was now sitting behind the reception desk. He nodded at Sanchez when he saw him.

'Find what you were looking for, Detective?' he asked.

'Yes I did, thanks.'

'Can I ask what it is, please?'

Sanchez thought about it. He had nothing to hide this time. He wanted the world to know he had been the one to locate the book. If by some chance anyone else tried to take the credit for discovering it, he would have Josh as a witness. In fact, he decided, it would be worth checking the book out in his own name, just to make things official.

'It's The Book of Death, by Anonymous,' he said. 'Please log it against my account.'

'Certainly, sir,' said Josh reaching down to type on a keyboard in front of a monitor on the desk. Sanchez waited by the desk to make sure he did it properly.

After a few seconds of typing, Josh looked up. 'It says here you already have one book out,' he said frowning. 'The Gay Man's Guide to Anal Sex?'

'Police business,' Sanchez retorted.

Josh raised an eyebrow. 'Researching the great buggery case from nineteen eighty-four?'

'Are we done?' Sanchez asked in a firm voice.

'Yep. When should I expect both books back?'

'When I've finished my research. Good day.'

With The Book of Death tucked firmly under his arm, Sanchez marched out of the doors and headed down the stairs. The whole process had actually been much easier than he had expected (aside from the unfortunate revelation about the buggery book). As he hurried down the steps he contemplated what he would say to Jessica when he showed up at the Casa de Ville with the book. He was so deep in thought that he barely noticed the large gentleman dressed as Santa Claus coming up the stairs. The two of them bumped into each other. The collision caused Sanchez to drop The Book of Death. It bounced onto the edge of one of the steps behind the Santa and then continued to bounce down the stairs to the bottom. Sanchez looked up at the Santa who stared back at him with a look of surprise on his bright red face. Both men spoke at the same time and uttered the exact same words:

'Watch where you're going, ya fat bastard!'

The Santa actually looked pretty fearsome, and Sanchez noticed specks of blood in his dirty grey beard. He also smelled of stale booze, a smell Sanchez knew only too well. It's how most of his customers at the Tapioca smelled when they arrived for the day. Considering the level of booze, Sanchez was surprised that the Santa was even up so early in the morning. Whatever the reason, it was obvious that the guy wasn't much of a morning person because he looked about ready to rip Sanchez's head off. His face contorted with rage at the fat bastard comment from the law enforcement officer. An apology of sorts was required.

'Er, sorry,' said Sanchez. 'Didn't realise you were a man of God an' all that.' He reached inside his jacket and pulled out his silver hip flask. He held it out to the angry Santa. 'Here, have some Christmas spirit on me,' he said with a fake smile.

The Santa looked down at the hip flask and eyed Sanchez suspiciously. 'What's in it?' he asked.

'It's similar to eggnog, so it'll probably taste very familiar to the likes of you. And you can keep the flask. Merry Christmas.'

The Santa took the flask. The angry look on his face softened. 'Merry Christmas to you too, officer,' he said. Then he carried on his way up the stairs.

Sanchez breathed a sigh of relief and hurried on down to the bottom of the stairs where The Book of Death had landed face down on the ground in a patch of dirt and snow just inside the front doors. The dirt had most likely been brought in on the boots of the fat angry Santa (who by Sanchez's reckoning would be even angrier once he took a sip from the hip flask). He picked the book up and brushed the snow and dirt off the cover then headed back out into the street.

Up in the library, Josh was busy trying to fathom whether or not Sanchez was really a cop or just a homosexual who liked dressing up as a member of the Village People, when he was confronted by the sight of an angry looking Santa Claus.

'Can I help you, sir?' he asked.

The Santa leaned over the desk. He had an unpleasant smell emanating from his breath. 'I'm looking for the Reference section. Where is it?' he asked.

'Over there,' said Josh pointing over the Santa's right shoulder. 'Are you a member here, sir?'

'No.'

'In that case I'll have to get you to fill out a new members form once you've chosen a book.'

The Santa curled his top lip up, revealing a fairly sharp set of teeth. He unscrewed the lid on a silver hip flask he was holding and eyeballed Josh. 'I'm looking for The Book of Death,' he said in a husky voice unbefitting of a man so universally loved by children the world over. 'I'm told it's in the Reference section. You seen it?'

Josh knew where it was all right. Sanchez had just taken it away for official police business. So why did this guy want it? Was he a criminal? And what was the big deal with The Book of Death anyway? As Josh pondered his answer, the Santa took a swig from his hip flask. A second later his eyes bulged open wide and he spat the contents out over Josh's face and shirt.

Josh reeled back and wiped the spittle from his face. 'What the fuck?' he groaned, sniffing the liquid on his hands. It smelled like piss. Normally that would have made him react very angrily but looking at the size of the Santa he decided to show some restraint and just answer his enquiry instead. 'Sanchez Garcia has the book you're looking for. He just left. You probably passed him on the stairs. Short fat guy in a gay cop outfit.'

The Santa was still retching from the drink that he had just spat out. 'What?' he snarled.

'Sanchez. He has the book.'

The Santa threw the hip flask at Josh. It hit him hard on the forehead and some more of the contents spilled out over him. A smell of piss filled the air. Sanchez's legendary finest homebrew had struck again.

'I'll fucking kill him!' the Santa growled.

By the time Josh had finished wiping the piss out of his eyes the Santa was halfway down the stairs in pursuit of Sanchez.

Twenty-Eight

JD had lost track of how long he'd been on the road. His mind had been filled with numerous different scenarios of how the journey might end. And what had become of Beth. He had no way of knowing if she was alive or dead. All he did know was that he, JD, was not the man to carry out any kind of rescue mission, or if necessary a revenge mission. That was a job for the Bourbon Kid, the man he used to be. Others might look at him and see the mass serial killer, but deep down inside he knew that he was nothing of the sort. He was now a man with a conscience and more importantly a soul. That soul was all he would have to bargain with in the Devil's Graveyard.

The drive had flown by, much like the scenery, until finally he found himself on a familiar stretch of road. He'd been down this particular highway before, almost a decade earlier. The highway still looked the same and the desert plains surrounding it were still barren and desolate. The sky overhead was clear blue, a stark contrast to darkened cloudy skies above Santa Mondega. As he sped down the middle of the highway all he could hear was the roar of the engine on his dust covered black V8 Interceptor.

When he passed a burned out old police car on the side of the road he knew he was close. It reminded him of a high-speed chase he'd been involved in with the cops on his last visit to the Devil's Graveyard. He'd rammed several of their cars off the road and fired off plenty of rounds at them, usually hitting his mark whether it be a tyre or a cop's face.

A few miles further down the road he zipped past the decrepit and abandoned gas station with the imaginative title Joe's Gas and Diner. As it disappeared from sight in his rear view mirror he slowed the car down. There was a crossroads up ahead.

The Devil's Crossroads.

He eased off on the accelerator and pulled over at the side of the road just before the junction and turned the engine off. There was no one in sight. Not a soul. But this was definitely the place to be. He had to cut a deal here. The kind that Robert Johnson had cut with the Devil back in 1931.

He opened the car door and stepped out onto the dusty highway. The silence outside in the Devil's Graveyard was eerie. Not the usual quiet one found anywhere else. There was a silent breeze blowing, he could feel it on his face. But the only thing in the desert making any kind of sound was him. His footsteps crunching on the gravel stones beneath his black ankle boots offered the only evidence that he wasn't in a dream.

The crossroads looked just as he'd remembered it. The signpost that was supposed to show where all the turnings led was missing, just as it had been all those years before.

So where the hell was the man with the directions?

He stood at the central point of the junction and looked around. If he remembered correctly, the now non-existent Hotel Pasadena had been a few miles down the road after a right turn. So where did the other turnings lead? He looked to his left. There was nothing to see but more desert wasteland and some high orange coloured mountains in the distance. It was the same in all four directions. It was while staring out into this abyss that he heard the voice he'd been waiting for.

'I wondered when you'd be back,' it said.

It was Jacko. The blues man.

His old acquaintance was walking towards him along the middle of the road, from the East, carrying a black guitar case.

The young black singer was still wearing the black suit, fedora hat and aviator sunglasses that he'd been given by the Bourbon Kid for his performance as a Blues Brother in the Back from the Dead singing contest all those years before. He hadn't aged a day since they had last met, still looking every bit like the fresh-faced young musician looking for his big break.

'You owe me a pair of shades,' JD reminded him.

'Nice to see you too.'

'You know why I'm here?'

'Sure.'

He was relieved to know that he wouldn't have to explain himself to Jacko (who, he recalled, could be quite a tiresome and cryptic individual). The fact that Jacko was well aware of the reasons for his reappearance in the Devil's Graveyard didn't surprise him. He'd always suspected that their paths would cross again. It was a small matter that both men had been only too aware of when they had last met.

'What happens now?' JD asked him.

'I can arrange a meeting.'

'So do it.'

Jacko shook his head slowly and smiled. 'Do you seriously want to end up like me?' he asked. 'Wandering out here in the Graveyard for the rest of eternity?'

JD shrugged. 'The only downside I can see to it is that you'd be here.'

'You don't change, do you?'

'As a matter of fact I do. If I hadn't changed I wouldn't be here.'

'You were always gonna come back, you just didn't know it back then.'

'Just make the introduction.'

Jacko set his guitar case down in the road. 'Who do you want to see?'

'Who d'ya think?'

'It's not for me to say.'

'I think I'm looking for a man in red.'

A voice spoke out behind him. 'I'm right here. All you had to do was call me out.'

JD reached into his jacket and pulled out a gun. He spun around and pointed it in the direction the voice had come from. Stood leaning against his black V8 Interceptor was a large black man in a red suit with a red bowler hat and a big grin across his face. His teeth created a glare as the sun reflected off them. His eyes were yellow like the sand in the desert.

'How's this work then?' JD asked, keeping the gun trained on the man.

The man in red held out his hand and waited for JD to take it and shake it. What other options did he have at this point?

None.

He slipped his gun back inside his leather jacket. He'd come all this way to see this man to make a deal. He was going to have to shake his hand at the very least. Looking the man in red deep in the eyes he reached out and took his hand. The two men shook hands. It was a firm handshake but one that JD was eager to end, so as soon as the other man softened his grip he pulled back.

The man in red leaned back on the car and hoisted himself up onto the hood in a comfortable sitting position with the sun glaring over his right shoulder. 'I've wanted to meet you for a long time,' he said. 'Last time you were here you didn't stay long enough for us to get acquainted.'

'I don't have much time to chat this time either. Can you help me? Or what?'

'Of course I can. But whatever I do for you will come at a price.'

'If it's my soul you're after then it's all yours. I got no need for it.'

The man in red's grin broadened. He was a master at negotiations, particularly when the odds were stacked in his favour. It was clear that the deal he offered would be shitty. He raised a quizzical eyebrow and spoke. 'JD, it may surprise you to know this, but I don't want your soul. You have something of far greater value to me than that.'

This wasn't part of the script. JD had expected him to accept the offer of his soul, but even so, he hadn't come all this way to walk away without accepting the terms on offer, no matter how unreasonable they might be.

'Just name it,' he said.

The man in red shook his head. 'Tell me what you want from me first. Then I'll tell you the price.'

'All I want is to get back to being the man I was.'

'The man you were last week?'

'Yeah. I wanna go back to being a murdering sonofabitch. You gonna make it happen? Or you gonna sit there like a smug cunt talking cryptic bullshit?'

The man in red laughed a fake yet hearty laugh. 'Hahaha! I want you to be that evil sonofabitch too. You were far more interesting back then. These days, if you don't mind my saying, you're a bit dull. Something of a nonentity, by all accounts.'

'Having a soul and a conscience will do that to a man. That shit, it ain't for me.'

'Glad to hear it.'

'So can you make it happen?'

The man in red sat back with both his hands on the hood of the car. He crossed one leg over the other. Then he took off his red hat and placed it on his lap. Underneath the hat he had a thick head of curly black hair.

'Of course I can make it happen,' he said. 'You see, you and I share a common interest.'

'Which is?'

'Hell dodgers.'

'What?'

'Hell dodgers.'

'I heard what you said. What's your point?'

'It's the vampires. I can't stomach those hell-dodging weasels. The werewolves too and most of all, that fucking mummy! You know, that Rameses Gaius, he was stuck in Purgatory for centuries until you lifted that curse on him. I really thought he was gonna be mine one day. And I gotta tell ya, I'm still aching to have him at my table.'

'Good for you.'

'But Jessica, she's the one.' The man in red became very animated as he spoke of Jessica. He was clearly passionate about her in some way. 'She's eluded me for as long as I can remember. And boy oh boy, there have been times when you so nearly delivered her to me. Honestly, how she's evaded me for so long really is nothing short of a miracle.'

JD was surprised by the man's revelation, but pleased to hear it none the less. 'So you'll help me kill her?' he asked.

'I'll give you back what you had, and I'll even up the odds for you,' the man replied. 'But I can't help you kill her. That's all down to fate.'

'Fate won't kill her. I will.'

The man in red shook his head. 'If you were gonna kill her, you'd have done it already.'

'What's that supposed to mean?'

'Just think about that when you come face to face with her.'

'Enough with the cryptic bullshit. What do you want from me in return?'

From behind him JD heard Jacko speak up. 'It'll be something you won't like,' he warned.

The man in red slipped his bowler hat back on and slid off the hood of the car. He walked towards JD. 'On the contrary,' he said, 'it'll be something you'll love.'

'So what is it?'

The man in red placed a warm hand on JD's shoulder. 'All in good time,' he said. 'But, first of all, before I give you what you want, I'd like a little something from you. A deposit if you will. Non refundable, of course.'

'Okay.'

'Your wheels.'

JD looked at him suspiciously. 'My car? If I give you my car, how the hell am I gonna get back to Santa Mondega?'

'Oh my boy, I'll get you there quicker than any car!'

'Fine.' JD reached into his pocket and pulled out his car keys. He tossed them to the man in red. 'I just gotta grab a few things out of the trunk though.'

The man in red took the keys and carried on grinning. 'You don't need anything from the car. Everything you need, you'll find down that road,' he said pointing up at a signpost by the crossroads. The missing signpost with its four white wooden panels pointing in different directions was back where it belonged at the roadside. It now had a destination painted in black lettering on the panel pointing West. It read one word, PURGATORY.

JD turned back to the man in red. 'What the fuck is in Purgatory?' he asked.

'A test of sorts,' said the man in red with his usual smug grin. 'While I go and draft up a contract for you to sign, you go pass the test.'

JD looked back down the deserted highway. 'Where's the test?' he asked.

He heard no reply. Instead he heard the sound of a car door opening. He turned around and was dismayed to see that the man in red was already in the driver's seat of the black V8 Interceptor. The engine roared into life seconds later. The man in red winked at him and revved the engine a few times before inducing a loud screeching wheelspin, which blew up sand and dust in all directions. JD watched on as the car sped off down the road towards the area where the Hotel Pasadena once stood.

He turned back to see Jacko behind him. The blues man had taken his guitar out of its case. He now had the sleek black blues guitar hanging around his shoulders, ready to play. He strummed one note on it and began to sing.

'Down to the crossroads...'

JD reached inside his jacket and pulled out his gun again. He pointed it at Jacko's face. 'Shut. The. Fuck. Up,' he snarled.

Jacko stopped playing and pointed up at the sign marked PURGATORY. 'Keep walking 'til you find yourself ready to start over.'

Twenty-Nine

With The Book of Death tucked securely underneath his left armpit Sanchez trudged through the snow on his way back to his squad car, which he had parked just around the corner. He'd parked in a disabled bay even though there were spaces nearer the library. There were far too many locals with disabled permits that they didn't deserve, so now that he was a police officer and could park where he liked, he'd gone straight for the disabled zone. In hindsight it was a decision he was beginning to regret because the air was biting cold. He couldn't recall Santa Mondega ever being so cold before. It was still fucking dark everywhere too. The only consolation was that with the streetlights on and the snow settled on the ground, the place did look quite festive for once. Not that Sanchez was a fan of Christmas. It just gave more people an excuse to beg for money or badger him in the street to donate to the homeless who apparently suffer worse than usual in the holiday season. Sanchez couldn't see quite how, because they seemed to get free stuff all year round and at Christmas they just got more. It still rankled with him that the tramps could get free soup at the local homeless shelter, yet he was only allowed to smell it from afar.

This morning's soup was chicken flavour, judging by the inviting aroma coming from the polystyrene cup that a tramp sitting at the corner of the street was sipping from. He was an old guy in a tattered green raincoat and a pair of torn grey pants. He had no shoes either, just thick grey socks with holes where his toes poked through them. Sanchez pretended not to see him in the hopes that he could make it past without being harassed for any money. As he walked past him though, the tramp looked up.

'Spare some change officer?' he asked. 'For a cup of coffee.'

'Sorry, haven't got any.'

The tramp reached out with one hand and grabbed hold of a handful of cloth on Sanchez's pants. He tugged at them, causing Sanchez to almost lose his footing. He had a pretty tight grip for an old guy too. Sanchez tried to shake him off in the same manner that he would have shaken off a randy dog trying to hump his leg, but this old fucker wasn't going to let go without a struggle.

'Listen stinky,' Sanchez snapped. 'If you don't let go of my leg, I'll arrest you and have you charged with vagrancy!'

The tramp ignored the threat. 'I just need enough for a cup of coffee. I'm freezing to death out here. You wouldn't want an old man to freeze to death, would you?'

Sanchez sighed. He reached into one of the front pockets on his pants to see if he had any change. He had plenty, but also in that particular pocket he had a Zippo lighter and the page he had ripped from The Book of Death. That page needed to be destroyed at some point, so Sanchez had an idea.

'I've got something that will warm you up,' he said.

The tramp's grey sullen eyes suddenly lit up and he let go of Sanchez's pants, looking up at him like an excited puppy waiting for a treat. Sanchez grabbed his Zippo and pulled it out from his pocket. He held it up in front of the tramp's unwashed but excited looking face and flipped it open. A sizeable flame lit up in the gloomy air. The tramp still looked eager, hoping maybe that he was about to receive the lighter, which was worth a few bucks. Alas, Sanchez pulled out the page he had ripped from The Book of Death. He uncrumpled it as best he could, while still trying to keep the book tucked tightly under his arm. The tramp frowned, no doubt wondering what he was doing. Once the page was as flat as he could get it, Sanchez held it up and dipped the bottom of it into the flame on his lighter. The page lit up immediately and the flame began racing upwards.

'Here,' said Sanchez, holding the burning paper out to the tramp. 'This will keep you warm.'

The tramp pulled his outstretched hand away and balked at the offer.

'It's all I have,' said Sanchez placing the burning page down on the ground at the tramp's feet. The tramp scowled but then held his grubby hands out over the flickering flame in the hopes of getting some warmth from it.

'Tight ass,' he muttered.

'Thank you,' said Sanchez, pleased to hear the words tight ass instead of fat ass for once. He closed the lighter, slipped it back in his pocket and carried on his way, turning the corner and heading towards his car, safe in the knowledge that his good deed for the year was done.

As he was strutting down the street, he was suddenly hit on the side of the face by something cold. It exploded into his hair and all over the side of his face, splashing water into his eyes. And it made his ear feel numb from the cold.

Stopping to wipe his face dry, he realised that someone had thrown a snowball at him and caught him real good with it too. He looked over in the direction it had come from and saw on the other side of the road an old lady in a long dark blue coat with a walking stick. She looked familiar. In fact, as she flipped him the middle finger and shouted *"Asshole!"* at him, he recognised her as the old bag that had fallen in the street when he'd switched on the police siren in his squad car to impress Jessica. The stupid old witch obviously couldn't take a joke. But right now Sanchez had neither the time nor the patience to deal with her, although he did plan on giving her the siren treatment again, if an opportunity presented itself.

The impact of the blow from the snowball could have caused him to lose his footing, such was the precarious state of the ice and snow underfoot, so with that in mind he exercised more caution in the remainder of his walk to the car, taking high steps and pressing his boots down hard onto the ground. When he reached his squad car he set The Book of Death down on the roof next to the siren and fumbled in his pocket for his keys. As he pulled the keys out they snagged on his Zippo lighter and it flew out and fell into a thick pile of snow just below the kerb.

'Fuckin' hell,' he mumbled to himself.

He crouched down to retrieve the lighter from the sludge, doing his best not to kneel in the snow. It was cold enough already without getting his uniform wet. The lighter had landed just under the car, almost out of reach. As he pawed at it, he caught sight of a dark shadow looming over him in the snow. Even in the already gloomy light provided by the dim streetlights, this shadow was dark, and large. He leaned back and looked over his shoulder. There, stood behind him and now looking quite a fearsome sight was the Santa Claus he had bumped into in the library.

'You want something?' Sanchez asked, climbing to his feet.

The Santa opened his mouth wide. On his upper set of teeth he had a large set of fangs. The guy was a fucking vampire. A big bastard one at that.

The big ugly Santa hissed at him, his foul breath wafting out from the pit of his stomach. Sanchez reeled back instinctively at what he perceived to be the smell of rotten kebab meat. The Santa lunged over his left shoulder, reaching for the book on top of the squad car.

'Give me that book!' he shouted.

'Not a chance!' Sanchez yelled back, turning around and grabbing for the book. He managed to get his hands on it before the vampire. With his chubby cold fingers he slid the book off the top of the car and clasped it against his chest ensuring his elbows protruded out to keep the Santa at bay. His attacker climbed all over his back and reached around him with both hands to try and get a grip on the book.

Sanchez twisted away from him. If he could somehow knock the fat Santa over, he might buy himself enough time to get in the car. Unfortunately gripping The Book of Death with all his might made it difficult to do anything. Although there was no way he was releasing his grip on the book (and the fifty thousand dollar reward) to some fat, out-of-shape undead Santa Claus.

Unfortunately, in terms of strength and fighting prowess Sanchez was no match for the colossal mass of the huge grey bearded fucker in the red hat. The Santa grabbed at the book and tugged at it with one hand. The two of them struggled back and forth with it like two toddlers fighting over a teddy bear. But where Sanchez continued to pull as hard as he could, the Santa suddenly surprised him by pushing. He succeeded in shoving the book hard into Sanchez's chest, knocking him off balance. He slipped and lost his footing on the ice, tumbling backwards. In refusing to let go of the book he only succeeded in pulling the obese vampire down on top of him.

Neither of them could sustain a firm grip on the book. But with each passing moment it became more evident that Sanchez was no match for his opponent. The vampire had blood-crazed eyes and where initially he had been focussed only on retrieving the book he suddenly caught sight of the ample flesh on Sanchez's neck. It was glowing red in the cold. In vampire terms it must have looked like a juicy steak.

As the Santa lunged forward to take a bite, Sanchez wrestled hard with The Book of Death, hoping to use it as a shield. With one almighty tug he managed to yank it upwards. It hit the Santa underneath the chin, knocking his head away just as he was about to sink his teeth into some flesh.

Drastic evasive action would be required to get out of this mess. Fortunately Sanchez had the survival instincts a weasel could only dream of. He pulled his hand away from the book and pulled at the Santa's beard. As he suspected it was attached around the vampire's face with elasticated string. He pulled it back as far as he could before releasing it and allowing it to snap sharply back into the Santa's face, covering his mouth and more importantly his fangs. The Santa wasn't fazed by it though and instead seized the initiative and tugged harder at the book, forgetting about biting anything for a moment. It took only a couple of seconds for him to rip the book completely from Sanchez's grip. He then sat triumphantly astride the hapless bartender, grinning maniacally. He tossed the book down on the pavement by his side and leered down at Sanchez, pulling his beard back into position.

'Time to die, fat man!' the Santa hissed, reaching inside his red jacket. He pulled out a small silver hip flask. 'I've tried your hipflask. Now try some of mine!' he sneered.

'No thanks,' said Sanchez frantically fumbling around in the snow just beneath the kerb with his free hand.

As the Santa unscrewed the lid on his flask Sanchez put Operation Weasel into action. He felt the cold metal of his Zippo lighter in his fingers. He plucked it from the snow and flicked it open, then thrust it towards the Santa's beard. The Santa never saw it coming and Sanchez watched with glee as the fat bastard's thick grey beard went up in flames.

'SHEEEEE-IIIIIIT!' the Santa screamed as the flames flew up towards his face. He rolled off Sanchez and onto the snow on the pavement, dropping his hip flask to the floor.

With the vampire rolling around face down in the snow attempting to put out the flames on his beard, Sanchez seized his chance. He hauled himself up and reached for the silver hip flask. The lid had come off it and a green liquid was leaking out onto the snow. Figuring it to be some sort of alcohol and no doubt flammable, Sanchez held it over the Santa and attempted to pour it onto the flames on his beard to ignite them further before his victim could extinguish them. He timed it perfectly. The Santa rolled over onto his back looking up at Sanchez just as he poured the liquid onto his beard and the lower half of his face. The Santa's eyes opened wide in horror as some of the liquid slid into his mouth. The flames on his beard had all but gone out but there was still a small cloud of black smoke rising up from it causing him to cough and splutter.

Sanchez put down the hip flask and prepared himself to re-enact his favourite wrestling move, The Splash. He launched himself up in the air and threw himself down onto the Santa like he'd seen his favourite wrestler, *Earthquake* do on television. Landing astride his stricken victim, he flipped his Zippo lighter open again. The Santa was no longer struggling or fighting back. He was simply laid out motionless on the ground.

Sanchez was busy congratulating himself on the effectiveness of his Splash technique when something caught his eye. Peering down at his stricken foe he noticed the green stains on his lips. He remembered the stories of the child killer paralysing kids with a green poisonous liquid. Could it be that this vampire was responsible for murdering a load of defenceless kids? Well, now it was the vampire who was defenceless. Time for some gloating and Schwarzenegger style pay off lines.

'You should lay off that green stuff, you look paralytic,' he said. The Santa didn't respond. He couldn't. The paralysis had kicked in already. His eyes said all Sanchez needed to know. He was terrified of what was to come. For once, Sanchez was going to get the chance to administer some good old retribution on behalf of all of the victims of a vicious killer. A genuine chance to be a hero and avenge the deaths of many innocent people had landed in his lap. What could possibly go wrong?

He looked down at the flame on his Zippo, then looked into the eyes of the vampire again. 'You need to lighten up!' he said smirking (while contemplating what a shame it was that no one was around to appreciate his fine pay off lines). 'Come on, give me a ho, ho, ho!' The vampire looked truly terrified but offered no fight.

Sanchez closed the lighter again momentarily and picked up the hip flask. He poured a little more of the green flammable liquid onto the Santa's clothes, then he stepped away from his prostrate victim. He screwed the lid back on the hip flask and slipped it into his inside pocket figuring it would be an ample replacement for the one he'd given away earlier. Then he flicked open his lighter again. Toying with the fat bastard by holding the flame of the Zippo over him gave Sanchez an enormous sense of power. All he had to do was drop the lighter down onto the vampire's beard and within seconds the paralysed psycho would be a smouldering pile of ash. First of all though, some more gloating was required.

'Not nice to be flat on your back with someone staring over you, threatening to kill you, is it?' he asked, kicking the vampire in the ribs for good measure.

This was turning out to be great fun. Sanchez kicked him again, harder this time. As he held the Zippo high over the Santa, readying himself to drop it, he suddenly heard a voice from behind him shout out. It was the voice of a young girl, probably no more than ten years old.

'Hey everyone! That guy is beating up Santa Claus!'

Sanchez looked over his shoulder and saw on the other side of the road a troop of Sunflower Girls, the Santa Mondega equivalent of the Savannah Girl Scouts but with some serious behaviour problems. They all wore green sweaters and blue skirts with fluffy blue pom pom hats to protect against the cold weather. Not normally a fearsome sight, but there were thirty of them. There was also the group leader, a rather large lady in her forties with a face like a giraffe's and a bowl haircut. Fortunately she was at the back of the group. The one Sanchez had to worry about was the little girl who had shouted out to the others. She was at the front of the group, pointing at him. And far from looking distressed, this little girl looked extremely angry. She reached down and pulled something from her sock. She held it up. It was a flick knife. She flipped it open and pointed the blade at Sanchez. Then she looked around at her troop.

'GET HIM!' she shouted.

Within a second, thirty screaming ten-year old Sunflower Girls had started charging towards him. The one with the knife led the way, snarling like a pit bull terrier. The leader followed on behind the pack shaking her fist angrily at Sanchez. She looked absolutely appalled at what she had seen him doing to the Santa Claus.

'It's not what it looks like!' Sanchez yelled at the onrushing mob.

It was no use. None of the girls would have been able to hear him over the noise of their own screaming. He took one last look at the vampire on the ground and dropped the Zippo onto him.

WHOOSH!

As soon as the naked flame made contact with the flammable green liquid on the Santa's red outfit his whole body exploded into flames. The sight of it stopped the onrushing girls dead in their tracks. There were gasps all round as their jaws dropped at the sight of Santa Claus going up in flames. The image would no doubt be permanently etched into their memories, scarring them for life.

Unfortunately once the initial shock passed, it only angered them further. Their screaming took on an entirely new level of aggression.

Sanchez reached down to the sidewalk and grabbed The Book of Death. By the time he'd picked it up, the Santa was a flaming ball of flesh three feet high. The flames were stretching up to the side of the squad car, blocking off any chance Sanchez had of getting into it, so with no time to lose, he turned and raced off down the icy street, praying he wouldn't slip.

Thirty hysterical Sunflower Girls chased after him, baying for blood.

Thirty

JD walked along the dusty track towards the horizon. The sun shone blisteringly in the blue sky above, yet he felt no heat from it. The temperature, much like the breeze, had been totally neutralised. For the longest time he felt like he was walking the wrong way on a conveyor belt. The scenery didn't change and the horizon seemed to come no closer. All that surrounded him was the deserted wastelands of the Devil's Graveyard. And everything seemed to be polished in an almost blinding white sheen. The only sound was that of his boots on the highway beneath his feet. Everything had been muted out. Even his breathing was silent.

Finally after an indeterminable length of time he spotted something up ahead by the roadside directly beneath the sun. It was a large building with a thatched roof. Within seconds of catching sight of it his life moved into fast-forward. The horizon raced towards him and the faint white clouds zipped by overhead all in less than two steps along the highway. And just like that, he found himself outside a large roadside bar with a solitary Harley Davidson parked outside. From the outside it looked very similar to the kind of bar found in Santa Mondega. Was this place part of his imagination? It looked like a typical gunslinger saloon. Kind of a cross between the Tapioca and the Nightjar, but ten times the size of the either of them and even less inviting. But this was undoubtedly the place he was meant to be. He was going to have to go in.

The name of the bar shone brightly in red neon letters on a large signpost above the entrance out front.

PURGATORY

He walked up a dirt and gravel covered pathway towards a pair of traditional old Wild West swinging wooden saloon doors at the entrance. A gentle murmuring noise from within the bar grew louder with every step he took. The murmur soon became a loud buzz of voices. People were inside, drinking and conversing. He felt a sense of trepidation as he approached. He had no idea who or what he would find in this place, but it sounded busy and it looked like the kind of place where the Bourbon Kid would fit in. Unfortunately, right now he still felt like JD. Maybe that would change once he was inside? One thing he sensed was a distinct possibility that some killing would be called for. The time to test out those good ol' murderous skills might be near.

He reached the saloon doors and paused for a moment. He peered over them and saw a large propeller fan hanging from the ceiling above the bar. Several feet beneath it he could see the heads of a crowd of drinkers, mostly men, but of all ages, shapes and sizes. He pressed both of his hands up against the doors and pushed them open. Then he stepped into the bar.

The second he set foot in the place, it turned deathly quiet. Everyone stopped what they were doing and turned to stare at the newcomer holding the doors of their bar open. They stood there like statues, no one moving an inch. JD took another step forward and let his hands back down to his sides. The saloon doors swung back shut behind him and flapped back and forth on their springs until they came to a stop. Still no one moved.

Directly in front of him there was a narrow opening through the crowd of drinkers. It led up to the bar where a lone barman was waiting for his newest customer to walk up and order a drink. JD walked slowly through the crowd, noting the angry looks from the men standing on both sides of him. Everyone's gaze followed him as he approached the bar. He glanced at some of the faces either side of him as he walked. These were faces he recognised.

Faces of people he'd killed.

There were many other faces he didn't recognise, but that didn't necessarily mean that he hadn't killed them too. The Bourbon Kid had slaughtered a lot of people, and not all of them had been significant enough to remember.

He could feel the eyes of all the other drinkers burning into the back of his head as he reached the bar. The bartender, a rather shifty-looking guy with straggly black hair hanging over his face, had been wiping the bartop with a towel. At the sight of JD he tossed the rag onto a shelf behind him. This bartender was another face he recognised. And it wasn't one that was pleased to see him. It was Berkley the bartender from the Nightjar in Santa Mondega. The Bourbon Kid had shot him in the face shortly after downing a glass of his finest bourbon one night. He remembered the incident with Berkley well because upon arriving in the Nightjar he had seen the dead body of his old arm wrestling adversary Rodeo Rex. Rex had been curiously positioned on top of a large rotating metal propeller fan that hung from the ceiling. He had received a serious pasting at the hands of Jessica, or Archibald Somers, or maybe even both. Who knew? Or cared?

Berkley placed a whisky glass down on the bar in front of JD and produced a bottle of bourbon from under the bar. Considering that the last time they had met, JD had blown a huge hole through the middle of Berkley's head, it seemed a fairly forgiving gesture. The head wound had vanished. The bartender looked exactly as JD remembered him. His hair was still long, dark and unwashed and he had maintained his overall *tramp in a waiter's outfit* look down to a tee. His white shirt looked unwashed and most of it was conveniently concealed beneath a black waistcoat.

'Pour me a shot,' said JD leaning against the bar and taking a look back at all the people behind him. They were still all watching his every move. Hundreds of them. Not one of them seemed remotely pleased to see him. Hardly surprising really.

Berkley uncorked the bottle of bourbon and poured it into the whisky glass. He filled the bottom inch of the four-inch high glass and then stopped pouring. JD glanced down at the drink as the bartender began to replace the cork in the bottle.

'I'm gonna want a bigger shot than that,' he remarked.

Berkley stopped corking the bottle. 'How much more?' he asked.

'You really need to ask?'

'No.'

Berkley filled the glass to the top and stepped back away from the bartop. JD looked down at the drink. This was a serious moment. If he took a sip of that bourbon his deal with the Devil was done. There would be no turning back. He would be back to the man he once was. *A man with no soul*. A man capable of killing everyone in this shitty bar. A man who had probably killed them all once before. And might be expected to do it again if he was going to get out of there alive.

He picked up the glass and inspected the contents. There was a bead of sweat sliding down the outside of the glass. *Actual sweat*. As he was watching it he heard a voice. A fairly gravelly one, as these things go, and it said: 'What are you doing in our bar, stranger? What's your business?'

JD put the glass back down on the bar. He recognised the voice. It was Ringo, a fat fuck he'd killed some years earlier in the Tapioca. Through a crowd of people on his left, Ringo appeared, barging aside anyone in his way. He looked exactly as he had done all those years before. He was a heavy set, greasy, unshaven slimeball wearing dirty brown trousers and a sweat stained baggy grey shirt. He came to a stop at the bar by JD's left shoulder and glared at him.

JD sighed. 'I'm not looking for any trouble.'

Ringo grinned menacingly and growled, 'Well I *am* trouble, and it looks like you found me.'

The bartender stepped back even further away from the bartop, corking up the bottle as he did so. JD shook his head and then turned to face Ringo, looking him dead in the eye.

'You don't fuckin' learn, do ya?'

Ringo placed a hand on JD's shoulder and squeezed hard. With his other hand he pulled out a pistol from a concealed holster at his side. He pointed it at JD's face. 'We been hearing rumours that the Bourbon Kid is headed this way. You're drinking bourbon, ain't you? Are you the Bourbon Kid?'

JD took a deep breath. 'Y'know why he's called the Bourbon Kid, don't you?'

A high-pitched male voice from the crowd of onlookers shouted out. 'I know. They say that when the Kid drinks bourbon, he turns into a fuckin' giant, a psycho, and he goes nuts and kills everyone in sight. They say he's invincible and can only be killed by the Devil himself.'

'That's right,' said JD. 'The Bourbon Kid kills everyone. All it takes is just one sip and then he goes nuts and kills everyone in the bar. And I should know, I seen it happen. Quite a few times.'

Ringo cocked his pistol and sneered at JD. 'Let's put it to the test. Drink your bourbon.'

JD looked at the glass of bourbon and thought about picking it up. It looked like pretty good stuff. He glanced back over at Berkley. 'Bartender, is this real bourbon?' he asked.

Berkley looked confused. 'Sure it is. Why wouldn't it be?'

'No reason. Just checking.'

JD picked up the glass and raised it to his lips. The whole bar watched, barely able to stand the tension of waiting for him to drink the contents. As if to torment them he didn't actually throw the contents down his throat straight away. He paused for a moment, deep in thought. Did he really want to go down this road again? He thought about making an apology for what he was about to do. The thought passed all too quickly and he smiled to himself. Then, like a man who hadn't had a drink for a week, he downed the entire contents of the glass in one mouthful, before slamming the glass back down on the bar.

And it was definitely real bourbon.

Thirty-One

Outrunning a mob of angry girl scouts wasn't as easy as it sounded. With the rather hefty Book of Death tucked under one arm, Sanchez was carrying even more weight than usual. And having just been in a fight with a vampire dressed as Santa Claus he was already feeling pretty tired. Adrenaline was the only thing keeping him going. Panting heavily as he rushed along the icy sidewalk, he took a look back over his shoulder to see if the Sunflower Girls were as close as their screams suggested. It came as no surprise to him to see that they were closing in on him. One of them (a dark haired girl who looked like she'd be a future gold medallist in the shot put) was out front and she was gaining fast. In fact she was close enough that Sanchez was able to get a look at the early stages of a moustache she appeared to be cultivating above her top lip.

He needed to think of a plan quickly. How the hell was he going to ditch this angry mob? He sure as hell wasn't going to outrun them. What he needed was an escape route. He hoped to spot a cab, preferably a passing one that he could flag down and jump into before the girls caught up with him. The streets of Santa Mondega were usually rife with taxicabs, so taking his gaze off the moustached girl at the front of the pack he began scouring the roads for one as he ran. There was no traffic about at all. Not one single car. The snow had kept virtually everyone indoors.

As he raced perilously along the icy street he made a snap decision. There was a left turn up ahead that led into a busier part of town. Unable to slow himself down as he approached the corner, he attempted to turn but instead slipped on a patch of black ice. His feet took off, leaving the ground completely. As his head fell backwards and his feet carried on upwards he instinctively dropped his arms to try and soften the fall by landing on his hands. The Book of Death came loose from his grip and bounced onto the icy ground at the same time as his ass landed on a particularly cold slab of ice. And this ice was slippery. Before he knew what was happening he was sliding along the sidewalk in some kind of high-speed race with The Book of Death. His fat ass trailed just a few feet behind it. The only good thing about his predicament was that he was now moving slightly faster than when he had been running. His major problem was that he had no control over what direction he slid in. He skidded ass first off the end of the kerb and out into the middle of the road. And he finally heard the sound of a car approaching.

The ice on the road wasn't as bad as it had been on the sidewalk, so his momentum slowed significantly. He eventually came to a stop slap bang in the middle of the road and watched in horror as The Book of Death bounced up into the air and into the path of the oncoming vehicle. There was an almighty bang as the fender of the car smashed into the book, sending it flying back up in the air and down the road. Sanchez looked on in dismay as the pages of the book blew open and it landed face down in a puddle of snow and ice in the road. The driver of the car slammed on the brakes and it came to a screeching stop in the middle of the street.

Sanchez hauled himself up into a seated position in the road. Tempting though it was to lie there and collect his thoughts as he processed just how badly bruised his ass would be, he knew that the first of the angry girls would soon be upon him (if of course she was allowed to cross the road without an adult). As he attempted to climb to his feet, only too aware that the back of his pants was soaking wet, he heard a car door open. A voice called out to him.

'Sanchez, quick, get in!' It was Flake. The car that had hit the book was her Volkswagen Beetle. It was now in front of him with the passenger side door open and Flake beckoning him to climb in. He didn't need a second invitation. He rushed over and jumped in, pulling the door shut behind him just as the biggest Sunflower Girl slammed into it. He pushed the lock down on the door and poked his tongue out at the ugly schoolgirl as Flake put her foot down on the accelerator and pulled away.

'Hold on,' yelled Sanchez. 'Pull over by that book.'

Flake drove the car down the road, swerving on the ice as she went, to where the book was lying face down in the pool of snow. Sanchez unlocked the door again and opened it, leaning out so he could grab the book. Flake slowed the car down and they came to a stop right by the book. Despite appearing to have no driving skills whatsoever (in Sanchez's opinion) Flake had in fact hit her mark spectacularly. He reached down and grabbed a hold of the book and hauled it up from the street by its front cover. He plonked it on his lap and slammed the car door closed again, then he turned to Flake.

'Okay, floor it!' he ordered.

Flake didn't wait to be told twice. She accelerated off down the middle of the road towards the city centre leaving the chasing girl scouts way behind.

'Are you okay?' she asked, not taking her eyes off the road. 'What happened back there? Why are those girls chasing you?'

Sanchez inspected the book in his hands. The cover was damaged, torn and scratched in several places, but worst of all, upon opening it he discovered that most of the pages were sopping wet.

'Dammit, Flake,' he groaned. 'The book is ruined. Your bad driving might have cost me the reward money. And Jessica will be annoyed.'

'I'm sorry, I didn't mean to. It looked like you were in trouble, so I didn't have time to show any caution.'

'It was nothing I couldn't handle.'

He blew hard on a few of the pages in a vain attempt to dry them out. Flake did not respond, and after a few seconds of flicking through pages of the book and tutting, he suddenly became aware of the fact that he may have been a little short with her. This was confirmed when he heard her sniffing. He glanced at her out of the corner of his eye. She was close to tears. She was trying to hide it, or hold it in, but she was definitely having a bit of a sob. Sanchez sighed.

'What's the matter?' he asked.

'Rick is dead. Someone killed him to get their hands on that book.'

Sanchez was taken aback. He'd given Rick a bottle of liquor the day before. What a waste! And who the hell was willing to kill to get their hands on the book? 'Oh shit,' he blurted. 'Do you know who killed him?'

Flake shook her head. 'No, but his neighbour Crazy Annie said she heard something last night.'

'Annie McFanny?'

'Yeah. I saw her this morning. She was absolutely hysterical.'

'Why, what did she say?'

'She said she heard Rick being tortured all night.'

'How's that funny?'

'It's not. She said that the killer was after a book.'

'The Book of Death?'

'I don't know, but that's the only book Rick had so I thought they might head to the library, then you'd be in trouble.'

'Did Annie see the killer?'

'I couldn't really tell. She said she thought it was Santa Claus and his helpers.'

'Whoa!' said Sanchez. 'Santa Claus, you say?'

'Yeah. Well, she is crazy. Let's face it, half of what she says is nonsense. It's just hard to tell which half sometimes, you know?'

'I think she may have been right.'

'About what? Santa?'

'Yeah.'

'Really?'

'Uh huh. Some big fucking vampire dressed in a Santa outfit just tried to get the book from me. He had a hip flask of green liquid with him too. The kind that causes paralysis.'

Flake gasped. 'Oh my God, Rick had green lips when I found him. Where's this Santa guy now?'

'I gave him a taste of his own medicine.'

'The green stuff?'

'Yep. Then I set fire to his beard. He went up in flames. Pretty sure he's dead now.'

Flake slowed the car down as they approached a red light at a pedestrian crossing. The car slid on the ice and cruised right through the crossing, narrowly missing a teenage boy who was crossing the road. It eventually came to a stop on the other side of the crossing and Flake then accelerated away again. 'Rick would be pleased,' she said wiping a tear from her cheek.

'Yeah. Those little girls weren't too grateful though.'

'Oh, that's why they were chasing you?'

'Yeah. Bitches.'

Flake took a right turn. 'We make a pretty good pair of cops, don't we?' she said.

'Huh?'

'Well, you've just located the missing book.'

Sanchez nodded in agreement. 'That's true.'

'And you've just killed the Santa who we think was the child killer.'

'Yeah.' He had to congratulate himself. He had done rather well. 'What have *you* done though?' he asked.

'I just saved you from getting your ass kicked by a Sunflower Girl.'

'Take a left up ahead.'

'Why? Shouldn't we head to the station? We should report all this to Captain Harker. He'll be really pleased to hear about this. Plus we're late for work.'

'I want to stop off at the Tapioca to try and repair this book that you ruined.'

'Oh, okay.' Flake turned the steering wheel and the car skidded around the left turn that Sanchez had pointed out. 'You need any help fixing the book?'

'No thanks,' said Sanchez staring down at the book again. 'You've done enough damage to it already.'

'I said I was sorry.'

'I know,' he sighed. 'Just drop me off. I'll make my own way to the station later when I've repaired the book.'

'Okay.'

'Don't tell anyone I've got it though, okay?'

Flake frowned. 'Why not?'

'Because I'll have Santa's angry fucking reindeer on my tail, most likely.'

'Huh?'

'People are obviously willing to kill to get their hands on this book.'

'I'm not surprised,' said Flake. 'After all, that book is very dangerous. Don't go writing any names in it!'

'I don't think I'd be able to even if I wanted to. The pages are soaking wet. This is going on the radiator when I get home. I can't return it to Jessica like this.'

Flake took an unusually long breath. 'How well do you know Jessica?' she asked.

'Pretty well,' said Sanchez. 'I nursed her back to health after the Bourbon Kid tried to kill her. Twice!'

'Yes, but what do you know about her?'

'Why do you care?'

'Well, have you considered the possibility that she might be one of the people who're willing to kill to get their hands on that book? I didn't really take to her when she showed up at the station. There's something about her I don't like.'

Sanchez couldn't believe what he was hearing. 'How can you not like Jessica?'

'She just seemed like a bit of a bitch, that's all.'

'Hey, watch who you're calling a bitch! You hardly know her.'

'Sorry, Sanchez. I just don't trust her. You should be careful. I mean, she lives in a place called the Casa De Ville. It sounds like an evil place, doesn't it?'

Sanchez shook his head. 'So you don't like her because she lives in a place with an evil name? That's ridiculous.' He turned away and stared out of the window for the rest of the journey, to ensure that Flake could see how annoyed he was.

When they reached the Tapioca, Sanchez climbed out of the car and begrudgingly thanked Flake for the ride. His top priority now was fixing up The Book of Death and delivering it to Jessica at the evil sounding Casa De Ville.

"Evil sounding," he laughed to himself. Flake was so stupid. The Casa De Ville would no doubt be a very welcoming place when he turned up there with the book.

Thirty-Two

The floor of the barroom in Purgatory was strewn with the smoking corpses of more than a hundred people. After one sip of bourbon, JD had vanished, replaced by his alter ego, the Bourbon Kid. Slaying everyone in the barroom had been exhilarating and easy. He was back, and ready to return to Santa Mondega to finish off the undead for good. No more loose ends. This time no one would be left alive.

Berkley the bartender was the only person left standing. He poured the Kid another glass of bourbon, filling the glass to the top without waiting to be told. The Kid sat back down on his barstool and dusted himself off, reflecting on how good it felt to be back to his old self. As the corpses on the floor began to smoulder and vanish into puffs of smoke, he heard the saloon doors behind him being pushed open. The doors rattled as they flapped to a close. What followed was the sound of a pair of boots crunching on the barroom floor, making their way up to the bar.

A deep male voice boomed out. 'Bartender, get me a bottle of Shitting Monkey.'

The Kid recognised the voice. This wasn't a man who was likely to be pleased to see him. They had only met once before and it hadn't gone well.

Berkley flipped the lid off a bottle of Shitting Monkey and placed it down on the bartop. The man who had entered the bar sat himself down on a stool to the left of the Bourbon Kid. He picked up the bottle of Shitting Monkey and took a large swig from it. Then he let out a satisfied *"Aaaah"* to indicate that the taste pleased him immensely. After a few seconds of uncomfortable silence, he spoke to the Kid.

'Finally, we meet again.'

The Kid looked over at his new drinking partner. The most notable feature was his right hand. It was made from solid steel. Only one man in the world had a hand like that.

Rodeo Rex.

Rex was a bounty hunter who claimed he worked for God. He was a big fucker too. He had shoulder length brown hair, mostly concealed underneath a large white Stetson. His biceps bulged out of a sleeveless blue denim jacket, showing off an array of tattoos featuring words like DEATH and CHOSEN. He also wore a pair of very tight blue jeans. They wouldn't be tight on many men, but when you had legs the size of tree trunks, like Rex did, anything was going to be tight fitting.

'You're looking a lot better,' said the Kid, referring to the last time he had seen the bounty hunter. On the previous occasion Rex had been little more than a bloodied corpse rotating round and round on a large ceiling fan in the Nightjar.

'Did me a deal with the man in red,' said Rex. He took another pull at his beer. 'I loved my work hunting down the undead so much that when he offered me the chance to carry on under his employment, I couldn't say no.'

'He keepin' you busy?'

'There's a never endin' supply of hell dodgers to be taken down. Fuckers keep on multiplying. And right now there's a revolution goin' on in your home town.'

'No shit.'

'So the man sent me to show you the way.' Rex took another sip of his beer, then he held the bottle up towards the Kid, gesturing for him to chink glasses. 'A toast,' he said. 'To killing vampires!'

The Kid picked up his own glass and duly chinked it against Rex's. 'To killing everything,' he replied. Then he poured the contents down his throat and slammed the empty glass back down on the bar again, ready for Berkley to top it up once more.

As Berkley was refilling the glass, Rex turned on his stool and looked back to the entrance. He put his non-metallic hand to his mouth, stuck his index finger and thumb in and whistled loudly. A moment later a tall dark figure appeared at the entrance, a man with a large quiff of black hair atop his head. He pushed the saloon doors open and walked slowly through them. The Kid recognised him too. They'd met before, albeit only briefly a few times. It was Santa Mondega's most well known muscle for hire.

The King. The man they called Elvis.

He wore a white suit with gold trims and a pair of large gold-rimmed sunglasses. In his right hand he was carrying a large guitar case. He sauntered up to the bar as if he was gliding across a stage in front of an audience of imaginary female fans. When he reached the bar he laid the case down on the bartop.

'Afternoon, fellas,' he said flicking the guitar case open. He reached inside and pulled out a sheet of white paper. He placed it down on the bar in front of the Kid. 'There's your contract,' he said. 'Read it and sign on the dotted line.'

The Bourbon Kid picked up the sheet of paper. It detailed all of the formalities of his deal with the Devil. Everything he required from the Devil was listed at the top followed by all of his obligations. Rodeo

Rex held out a pen. The Kid signed his name on the dotted line and then handed the pen back to Rex.

'Got yourself a good deal,' he said as he picked up the contract and slipped it inside his sleeveless jacket.

'So where's my stuff?' the Kid asked.

Elvis patted him on the shoulder. 'Take your pick from this lot,' he said.

He turned the open guitar case around on the bar so the Kid could get a look inside. It was full of weapons and ammunition. 'We got everything here you could possibly need, and then some,' he said.

Rex pointed at a small silver crossbow in the neck of the case. 'Try some of the quieter weapons,' he suggested. 'They'll be most effective for what you need.'

The Kid glanced up at him. 'I don't need any tips from you.'

'You fuckin' do. You might be a real badass, but if you go back to Santa Mondega and face up to those vampires and werewolves in your usual fashion, you're gonna get your ass kicked.'

'I doubt that.'

'If they get their hands on The Book of Death, it'll be beyond your control. They know your real name now. If Gaius retrieves the book, you're outta the game, son.'

'The Book of Death, huh. Where is it now? D'ya know?'

'Last I heard it was back at the city library in the Reference section, but that book don't tend to stay in one place for long. Make it a priority to find it and destroy it if you can.'

'A priority? I don't think so.'

Elvis intervened. 'Listen to Rex, man. He's tryin' to help you get your woman back.'

'Whadda you know about her?'

'I know she's still alive.'

'You sure?'

'Yeah man. For now anyway. But you go in through the front door with all guns blazing and they'll kill her while you watch.'

The Kid pondered what Elvis had said. 'You'd be surprised what I'm capable of when I'm in the mood.'

Rex stood up from his stool. 'Well, it's your choice how you go about it. But whether you go in quiet or loud, you've only got until midnight. Then your time is up. That's when you repay the man in red.'

Berkley had finished refilling the Kid's glass and stashed the bottle of bourbon at the back of the bar. The Kid picked up the drink and stared at his reflection in the glass for a second before downing the contents. Then he reached into the guitar case for a weapon.

'Yo, bartender,' he called out. 'What's your favourite colour?'

Berkley spun around and muttered one word. 'Shit.'

The Kid pulled a gun from the guitar case, a gold Desert Eagle with a red laser sighter on it. It felt heavy in his hand, a good weight. He pointed it at the unfortunate bartender. The red dot from the laser appeared in the centre of Berkley's head.

BANG!

Berkley's head exploded, his brains flying out through the back of his skull and splashing against the wall behind him. His body crumpled to the floor in a heap.

Elvis peered over the bar at the corpse. 'Why did he say shit?' he asked, a confused look on his face. 'Shit's not really a colour is it?'

The Kid ignored him. 'Silent weapons my ass,' he said admiring the gun. 'Get me some ammo for this muthafucker.'

'Shoulda said brown,' Elvis said, shaking his head. 'Brown's a colour. Not shit. Shit's an object. Or a state of affairs.'

Rex placed a small case of bullets on the bar next to the Kid's empty glass. 'Fine, do it your way,' he said. 'But don't say I didn't warn you.'

Elvis walked off around to the back of the bar while The Kid rifled through the weapons in the guitar case, grabbing everything that took his fancy. Rex chipped in by handing over any ammo for each weapon. The guy had deep pockets filled with all kinds of stuff. After five minutes the Kid had an array of weapons and ammo laid out on the bar. Only problem was, how was he going to carry it all? He had a few pockets in his leather jacket and he'd picked out a few holsters from the guitar case, but concealing the weapons could prove tricky.

Elvis reappeared with the answer to the problem. He threw a long dark hooded robe over to the Kid. 'There's a real shitstorm coming the way of Santa Mondega. You might wanna wear this.'

The Kid caught the robe and laid it down on the bartop. He slipped his arms out of the sleeves of his leather jacket and tossed it over to Elvis. The new robe would be perfect for carrying and concealing a small arsenal of weapons. He slid his arms into the new robe, admiring its snug fit. Then he began strapping weapons and ammunition to himself and utilising all the concealed pockets and holsters within the robe.

When he was done he turned to face Rex. 'What now?' he asked.

Rex pointed at the saloon doors. 'Head through there and you'll be right back where you started. Good luck.'

The Kid nodded at Rex and Elvis. 'I won't need luck,' he said.

He walked towards the saloon doors. When he reached them he pushed them open and walked through, pulling the hood on the robe up over his head as he went.

Thirty-Three

Rameses Gaius arrived at the Santa Mondega City library in a murderous mood. He'd received no word from the Santa Claus regarding the recovery of The Book of Death, and now the fat child-killing freak wasn't even answering his phone. It seemed he'd had the good sense to leave town rather than face the wrath of the Lord of the Undead.

Gaius strode up the stairs two at a time and barged through the double doors at the top into the reception area. Sat behind the reception desk was a teenage boy with scruffy dark hair and a white shirt that was in need of a good press.

'Where's Ulrika Price?' Gaius asked, avoiding any pleasantries.

The boy looked up. 'She didn't come in today. I'm covering for her.'

Gaius removed his sunglasses and slipped them into the top pocket on his silver suit jacket. 'Are you Josh?' he asked, glaring at the young librarian.

'Uh, yeah. How'd you know?'

'You're the one who gave The Book of Death out to a member of the library the other night, aren't you?'

'The Book of Death?'

'Yes. You know the book I'm talking about?'

Josh nodded and swallowed hard. 'I didn't give it out to anyone the other night though,' he said nervously. 'I just put it on a shelf like Miss Price asked me to.'

Gaius leaned over the desk to get into Josh's personal space. 'Take me to it then,' he scowled.

'I can't,' Josh replied. 'The cops took it away this morning.'

'What?'

'A cop came in and took it. Said he needed it for Police business.'

'What cop?'

'Sanchez Garcia. Used to be the bartender at The Tapioca.'

'Fucking fuck!'

'Everyone's after that book today,' said Josh with a shrug.

Gaius frowned. 'Who else has been in looking for it?'

'A fat Santa Claus came in looking for it just after Sanchez. Spat piss all over me.'

Gaius sniffed the air. 'I can smell it.'

Josh blushed and lowered his head to sniff his shirt. He turned his nose up as the stench of stale piss wafted up his nostrils. He glanced back up at Gaius. 'Anything else I can help you with?' he asked.

'Actually yes,' said Gaius. 'Could you show me which shelf you put the book on the other night?'

'Yeah, okay.'

Josh lifted a wooden flap on the reception desk and walked out through it. 'It's this way,' he said gesturing to Gaius as he led the way over to an aisle of books in the Reference section.

Gaius followed on behind him, taking deep breaths through his nostrils, trying desperately to control the rage that was burning within him at the revelation that The Book of Death was now in the hands of the police. Josh led him down a tall aisle full of thick hardback books and pointed to a row just below eye level.

'I put it here,' he said, proudly. 'Under A for Anonymous.'

Gaius pointed at a thick book with a green spine on the bottom shelf. 'Could you pick out that green book for me, please?' he asked courteously.

Josh shrugged. 'Sure.'

As the young librarian bent down and reached for the book, Gaius grabbed him by a thick clump of hair on the back of his head. He hauled him up off his feet and then in one swift move slammed his face into one of the hard wooden shelves. There was a sickening crack as Josh's nose broke. The boy barely had time to scream out in pain before Gaius smashed his face into the shelf three more times. Blood began pouring from Josh's nose and mouth as some of his teeth were smashed. Gaius hurled him down face-first onto the hardwood floor and leaned over him. The young librarian attempted to climb to his knees, but Gaius quickly hit him hard in the ribs, knocking him over onto his back.

Josh's eyes had filled with tears very quickly. His bloodied face revealed a look of terror. His hands were trembling and he looked ready to burst out crying at any second. Gaius leaned down and pressed his left knee into his terrified victim's chest.

'This is what you get for giving my book to the police,' he said, raising his huge right fist high above his head. Josh winced and turned his head away, clearly fearing the impact of the forthcoming blow. He had time to sob just once before Gaius rammed his fist into the side of his face, shattering his cheekbone as if it were made of glass.

For almost a minute Gaius pounded his fists into Josh's face. The boy was most likely dead after the third or fourth blow, but Gaius found himself enjoying the violence too much to stop.

When his adrenaline had calmed, Gaius paused and took a look at his bloodied fists. As he stared at them, marvelling at their power, the swelling and pain in his knuckles subsided. The Eye of the Moon, wedged firmly in his right eye socket, ensured that any pain or injuries he sustained healed up almost instantly.

He reached into his top pocket and slipped his sunglasses back on. Then he pulled out his cell phone and made a call to his daughter.

Jessica answered within one ring. 'Yes father.'

'The Book of Death is gone for now,' said Gaius, catching his breath. 'That idiot Sanchez Garcia has it.'

'Sanchez has it?'

'That's what I just said.'

'Don't worry then. That idiot will bring it straight to me. He's probably on his way here with it right now.'

'You think?'

'I have no doubt.'

'How can you be so sure?'

'Because that loser is infatuated with me. Don't worry father, if Sanchez has got it, then it'll soon be ours. Start putting your plans into action. I'll have your book for you in no time.'

'Finally, some good news,' Gaius said triumphantly. 'In that case, put the word out to everyone, it's time for us to start taking over the city. Tell them to go into the streets and kill whomever they choose, including kids.'

'*Including kids?*' Jessica sounded surprised. 'Why the sudden change of heart?'

Gaius wiped his free hand on Josh's white shirt, in an effort to get rid of some of the boy's blood from his knuckles. 'I just bashed a teenage boy's brains in,' he said, taking a deep breath. 'And I gotta tell you, it was exhilarating. At one point I think I even heard him cry out for his mom.'

He could practically hear Jessica's approving smile down the phone. 'I'll get the word out to everyone,' she said. 'Most of them are already on their way here anyway. Are you coming back now?'

'No, not yet,' said Gaius. 'I have an appointment at the museum first. Got a couple more people to kill.'

Thirty-Four

'It's no use,' said Kacy. 'He's not answering.'

Dante was sitting on the bed in their room at the Swamp, wearing his Shades jacket over a white T-shirt and a pair of blue jeans. He rubbed his forehead in frustration. Kacy had been trying to call the Bourbon Kid all afternoon. The unreliable sonofabitch wasn't answering.

'Fine. Leave him a message then. But send him a text as well. We can't just blow him off without knowing why he's not answering.'

Kacy walked over and sat down on the bed next to him. She had her cell phone pressed against her ear. When she heard a beep she reeled off her message.

'Hi, this is Kacy, Dante's girlfriend. Just so you know, we're heading to the museum tonight with Vanity. We won't be at the Casa de Ville. Vanity says that Rameses Gaius is going to the museum to have his eye polished or something. So we're going to go there and try and get it from him when he's taken it out of his head. If you want to meet us there, give me a call back. Vanity is on our side so if you do show up, don't kill him or anything. Okay, thanks. Bye.'

Dante rubbed her back. 'Good message,' he said. 'Send him a text too though. Just in case.'

Kacy handed him the phone. 'You send it,' she said. 'I need to get changed.'

'What's wrong with what you've got on?'

Kacy had on a sleeveless black top and a pair of denim shorts. 'If this plan of ours works and we end up human again, I bet it'll be freezing out there. We might need to make a quick getaway. With all that snow and hail out there, I think I'll need something more appropriate.'

'But you look hot like that.'

'The weather forecast says it's minus three out there.'

'Lightweight.'

'Fine. You can wear these shorts then.'

Dante grabbed her by the arm and pulled her towards him. He kissed her firmly on the lips. 'You just look hot, that's all I'm saying.'

She kissed him back and then pulled away. She walked over to the corner of the bedroom and bent down to pick some new clothes from her suitcase that was open on the floor. 'Just send the text,' she said.

Dante began typing a message into her phone. It would take him ages and not just because he couldn't spell some of the most basic words. He was rubbish with phones in general. As he tried to fathom out the texting system on her phone, Kacy began flicking through the clothes in her suitcase, occasionally holding something up to get his approval. He nodded at anything that would show plenty of flesh, but generally turned his nose up at anything sensible. It was all good fun though. She knew he loved watching her undress, and she in turn liked trying on new outfits in front of him. It was one of many reasons they made such a great couple. And Kacy hoped to God, they'd still be a couple come the end of the day. If anything went wrong, and it was highly probable that something would, she couldn't bear the thought of being apart from him. The moment she had seen him bitten by a vampire on Halloween still played over and over in her mind. Holding his head as blood poured from a wound in his neck where the vampire bitch had bitten him was the worst moment of her life. She dreaded the thought of going through anything like it again.

She was stripped down to her matching pink bra and panties and holding Dante's attention pretty well when Vanity suddenly burst into the room. He looked anxious, but the sight of a half naked Kacy caused him to do a quick double-take and raise a quizzical eyebrow behind his sunglasses. After staring for a little longer than was necessary he revealed the reason for his intrusion.

'Big news, kids,' he said. 'It seems that Gaius has given the order for everyone to get out in the open. The streets are already full of vampires. As of now we are at war with the whole world. There's vampires everywhere, killing any humans that aren't locked indoors. It's fucking carnage out there. And everyone's headed to the Casa de Ville.'

Kacy grimaced. 'That's where the Bourbon Kid is heading.'

Vanity nodded. 'That's why they're all heading there. Gaius knows that's where he'll go.'

'You mean it's a trap?'

'Of course. And probably the main reason Gaius's is getting out of there and heading to the museum is just in case it goes wrong.'

'How could it go wrong?' Kacy asked.

Dante answered. 'The Kid might kill everyone. I suspect he's capable.'

'Of killing a whole army of vampires?'

'Wouldn't put it past him.'

Vanity smiled. 'He's good, sure, but Gaius has covered all angles. There'll be an army of werewolves as well as vampires waiting for the Kid when he gets there.'

'How do you know all this?' Kacy asked.

'I got people on the inside, remember? I'm well connected. That's how I know that Gaius has already left the Casa de Ville. He's headed for the museum right now. This is our chance.'

A loud screeching noise from the streets outside punctuated the air.

'What the hell was that?' Dante asked.

Vanity shrugged. 'Like I said, the vampires are taking over the streets. It's murder out there.'

Dante jumped up from the bed. 'Fuck me. Let's take a look.'

Kacy grabbed a pair of jeans and began slipping them on while Vanity watched on with a wry smile on his face. Dante brushed past him on his way out into the pool hall to get a look out of the windows. He returned moments later as Kacy was slipping on a black sweatshirt. His face revealed a look of great concern, which was unusual for him.

'Vanity's right,' he said. 'He's fucking right. There's vampires everywhere out there. I just saw a gang of Sunflower Girls being chased through the streets. The vampires are picking them off one by one. Fucking horrible!'

'Sunflower Girls?' Kacy couldn't hide how horrified she was at the mental image of a group of terrified little girls being savaged by bloodthirsty vampires. 'We should do something!'

She raced out into the pool hall and looked out of one of the windows at the street below. Sure enough, the streets were chaotic. There was a group of terrified girl scouts racing down the street screaming. Vampires were grabbing civilians and dragging them into shop doorways and alleyways to feast on their blood. The girls had stayed together in a group, but they would be picked off soon enough. Kacy felt sick at the sight of it and rushed back into the apartment to grab her sneakers.

Dante recognised the look in her eyes. 'You want to try and stop them?'

She nodded. 'We all should. They're just little girls.'

Vanity grabbed Dante by the shoulder. 'There's nothing we can do for those girls. Gaius has left for the museum already. We gotta go now, or we might miss our chance.'

Kacy looked at Dante with pleading eyes. 'We've gotta try and save those kids, surely?'

He nodded in agreement. 'Yeah. Come on, let's go.'

Kacy slipped on a pair of sneakers and raced out into the pool hall after Dante. Vanity didn't look so keen. In fact he looked exasperated. He called out after them as they went. 'You can't save those kids. You're vampires. All you'll do is scare them. And maybe get yourself killed.'

His words fell on deaf ears as Dante and Kacy bounded through the pool hall and leapt over the landing, jumping down three flights of stairs to the ground below.

Thirty-Five

Dan Harker had spent much of the morning at his desk staring at his computer monitor, trawling through the previously top secret files of the last police captain, Michael De La Cruz. Almost every single one of them related to either the child killer or the Bourbon Kid. The child murders had never been investigated. Every single one of them had been filed under the list of Bourbon Kid victims. This wasn't just lazy police work, this was blatant corruption. It had been started by Archibald Somers and continued by De La Cruz. But why had they been so keen to pin every murder on the Bourbon Kid? Was it just because he was an easy target? Or was he an enemy of theirs? An enemy to the undead?

After an hour of viewing countless files containing almost identical details, Harker came across De La Cruz's file for the death of Archie Somers. And this one was interesting. It was the only case with any evidence to prove that the Kid had murdered the victim in question. It contained a link to some CCTV footage too. He brought it up onto the screen and moved his face closer to the monitor to get a good look at what was a rather grainy picture. The film footage showed the Bourbon Kid turning up at the police station and gunning down all of the on duty police officers. The only survivor initially was a receptionist named Amy Webster. The camera was positioned behind the Kid and showed the look of terror on Miss Webster's face as she followed his instructions. Unfortunately there was no audio, so Harker could only speculate on what was being discussed. It looked as though the Kid was dictating to Amy what to say on the phone. Eventually, after she replaced the phone on its handset, he issued one more instruction. Amy closed her eyes and a second later he fired a bullet through the middle of her face. Maybe it was this kind of behaviour that made Somers and De La Cruz decide to pin every unsolved murder on the Kid? After all, he was clearly a merciless killer.

Harker skipped forward through twenty minutes of film where nothing happened. He resumed play again when Archie Somers showed up at the station to confront the Kid. It proved to be fascinating viewing. Harker had to rewind and watch it several times to make sure his eyes weren't deceiving him. After a minute of heated discussion between the two, Somers transformed into a vampire and flew at the Bourbon Kid, grabbing him and plunging his teeth into his neck. The Kid embraced Somers and held him tightly, but then came the strangest part. A puff of smoke appeared from in between the two men. More words were exchanged and then Somers staggered back. He had a large hardback book stuck to his chest. A small cloud of smoke was emanating from beneath the book. Somers tugged at the book, desperately trying to rip it from his chest. The damn thing wasn't shifting though. It stayed glued to him, smouldering for a while until suddenly Somers literally exploded into a ball of flames, waving his arms wildly and screaming. Moments later he disintegrated into a pile of smoking ash on the floor. So, Somers the vampire had met a grisly end, but what was the deal with the Kid? Was he some kind of vampire slayer? And if so, why did he also kill innocent people, like Amy Webster?

As Harker pondered the answers to a multitude of questions, he heard a knock on his office door. Stood at the glass door wearing a long white coat was Bill Clay from the Forensics department. Harker gestured to him to enter. Clay pushed at the door a few times with no success before finally kicking it at the bottom and forcing it open. He walked in and closed it behind him with another kick and then turned to face the Captain.

'Hey Cap, how you doin'?'

'What can I do for you, Bill?' Harker asked.

'Switchboard is going nuts down there. Flake can't cope with all the calls.'

'Get her buddy Sanchez to help her.'

'Don't you think he'd just annoy people?'

'Yeah,' said Harker shrugging. 'Then they'll hang up. He's perfect for it.'

Clay smiled. 'Well there's one small problem. Sanchez hasn't showed up for work. In fact Flake's only just come in herself.'

'Lazy assholes.'

'Yeah, but there's a reason for their lateness.'

'It *better* be good.'

'It's not bad. Flake says they bumped into your child killer this morning.'

'What?'

'Apparently Sanchez just killed him.'

'Come again?'

'Flake says Sanchez got into a fight with a vampire dressed as Santa Claus at the library this morning. Apparently Sanchez poured the guy's green poison over him and set him on fire.'

'Fucking hell. Where's Sanchez now?'

'Up to his neck in shit, I reckon.'

'Huh?'

'Flake said he's found The Book of Death. You know, that book that's missing? He's on his way to return it to its owner.'

Harker scratched his head. 'Wow. I kinda thought Sanchez was an idiot. Sounds like he's turned into Elliot Ness.'

'More like Frank Drebbin.'

'Even so. Who'd have guessed he had it in him?'

'Not me.'

'Me either. Still, this is turning into a good news day.'

Clay grimaced. 'Yeah, well that's the good news over.'

Harker sighed. 'Oh God. What now?'

'The switchboard. It's jammed with calls reporting sightings of vampires attacking people all over the city. The local radio station is already warning people to stay indoors. I think the days of vampires attacking only by night and in back alleys are over. These black clouds over the city aren't just freak weather. It looks like this is all part of a bigger plan. Vampires are roaming through the streets of the city as we speak. And they're all headed towards the Casa de Ville. Something big is going down. This could be the start of the end of the world.'

'Please tell me you're exaggerating for dramatic effect.'

'I'm afraid not. Your plan to leak the child killer case onto the news has backfired in a big way. It's brought them all out of the shadows.'

'Thanks. I really needed to hear that.'

'Sorry Captain. But I think we should evacuate the city. Get back on the news and tell everyone to get the hell outta here.'

'Seriously? Don't you think that'll create a state of mass panic.'

Clay nodded at the window behind Harker. 'Take a look out the window. We're already in a state of panic.'

Harker got up from his chair and peered through the blinds on the window at the street below. At first it looked like nothing much was going on. But as his eyes grew accustomed to the dark outside he saw that Clay was right. On the opposite side of the road a young man who worked on a fruit and vegetable stall was being ripped to pieces by three vampires dressed all in black. He turned back to Clay.

'Holy shit.'

Clay nodded. 'It looks like we're all gonna die.'

'Fuck that,' said Harker defiantly. 'We're paid to protect the people of this city. We're gonna have to get out there and deal with this problem head on.'

'How the hell are we gonna fight an entire army of vampires? There's barely enough cops here to rescue a cat stuck up a tree.'

'That's a job for the fire department. Lazy bastards.'

'Even so. If as you say we have a responsibility to protect the people of this city then we should be advising them to run for their lives. Flake took a call just now from a Sunflower Girl Leader. She said her and her girls are sneaking through back alleys trying to avoid being spotted by the vampires.'

'Sunflower Girls?' Harker put his head in his hands. 'Oh shit, they must be terrified.'

'They've had a pretty bad day already. The leader backed up Flake's story about Sanchez setting fire to the Santa.'

'He set Santa on fire in front of a bunch of Sunflower Girls?'

'Yeah.'

'Moron.'

'Quite. As Flake was telling the leader to head to the local church, the line went dead. So for all we know, the vampires spotted them. Those girls could be dead already.'

Harker sat back down at his desk and shuddered. 'I sure hope they make it. If they can get into a church then they're probably pretty safe. They'll have crosses and holy water and shit like that to use as weapons. I don't think a vampire is gonna set foot in a church.'

'Shouldn't we send someone over there to see if they're okay?'

'Can we send Sanchez?'

'The guy who just set fire to Santa in front of them?'

Clay had a point. Sanchez was probably the last person the traumatized girls would want to see. 'Fuck. We're just gonna have to hope the church takes care of them. I'm gonna have to get back over to the news station and advise everyone to lock themselves in or get out of town.'

Clay looked deeply troubled. This city is fucking insane. 'If it's not the Bourbon Kid killing everyone, it's fucking vampires. Why would anyone want to live here?'

Harker frowned. 'Low taxes. Plenty of jobs. Nice weather, usually.'

'Even so. I'm not sure why I'm still here.'

'You're here because you love your job and you're a good guy who takes pride in protecting the citizens of this city.'

Clay smiled. 'Are you quoting the Officers' Handbook?'

'I know it off by heart.'

'That's not gonna save us though, is it?'

'Nope. But I know something that could. Here take a look at this.' He pointed at his monitor. Clay walked around to his side of the desk and peered over his shoulder.

'What is it?' he asked.

Harker used his mouse to drag the CCTV footage on his monitor back to the moment where Somers and the Kid squared up. The two men watched the monitor in silence as they witnessed the Kid send Somers to Hell in a ball of flames. When the fight was over, Harker paused the footage again and looked up at Clay to see his reaction.

'That's weird,' said Clay.

'Yeah. Freaky, right? The way he just spontaneously combusts like that.'

Clay looked puzzled. 'That's not what I meant.'

'Why? What are you looking at?'

'The Bourbon Kid. That's not the same guy that killed Bertram Cromwell.'

Harker looked closer at the man on screen in the dark robe with the hood pulled up over his head. 'You sure? How can you tell?'

'Get the footage from the museum up on screen. It's a different guy.'

Harker sifted through the database and eventually pulled up the footage of Bertram Cromwell's murder on to his screen. He and Clay watched Cromwell being butchered again. The attacker was a hooded man all right, but the psycho with the machete hacking the Professor to pieces had a completely different build to the man who had set fire to Archie Somers. The Professor's killer was tall and thin, whereas the Bourbon Kid in the Somers footage was broad of shoulder and not quite as tall.

'What do you make of that then?' Clay asked.

Harker mulled over what he'd seen. These were definitely two different killers. 'You're right, he said. 'We've got two Bourbon Kids.'

'Do you think there were two all along?' Clay asked.

'I don't know. All I know is this. One of these guys kills vampires. And he's fucking good at it. I'm not sure who the second guy is, the one who killed Cromwell. But the guy who killed Somers could be a useful ally.'

'You're thinking of asking the Bourbon Kid for help?'

'Why not? He could be the only thing standing in the way of the vampires taking over the city. Problem is, we've got to find him.'

Clay didn't look convinced. 'He'd kill you before you had the chance to make him an offer.'

'I'm not so sure. Look at it like this, Somers was a vampire. The last Police Captain, De La Cruz, was a vampire and so were his lieutenants. The Bourbon Kid killed them all. I think he might just be the hero this city needs.'

'He's a disease. We need him like we need a plague of frogs.'

'Maybe so, but I'm telling you, the Bourbon Kid could kill every vampire in this city before they even know they're dead.'

Clay furrowed his brow. 'That doesn't even make sense.'

'Maybe not, but it sounded good in my head.'

'Look Captain, what you're saying is...'

Harker stood up, sharply. 'Look, if I can put out an appeal on the local news station, I think I could maybe bring him on board.'

'You're kidding, right?'

Harker grabbed his long brown raincoat from a clothes hanger by the door and began slipping his arms into the sleeves.

Clay gestured to him to slow down. 'Captain, if you're thinking of making an appeal to the Bourbon Kid on the news, you're gonna make yourself public enemy number one in this city. It's a bad political move. He's killed relatives of everyone in town.'

Harker pulled the collar of the coat up around his neck. 'When the people of this city hear that the Bourbon Kid has actually been protecting them all along, they'll be right behind me.'

Clay shook his head. 'It's not just the people of this city you've got to worry about. It's the vampires. They'll kill you before you finish broadcasting that news piece.'

Harker pulled open the door of his office. 'Then I'll have to hope the Bourbon Kid gets to me first.'

As Harker walked out of the office Clay called after him. 'In that case, I guess I'll see you in Hell!'

Thirty-Six

The terrified troop of Sunflower Girls were racing through the snowy streets of Santa Mondega screaming for all they were worth. No wonder. Vampire clowns were picking them off one at a time and dragging them kicking and screaming into darkened side streets. The girls had set out for the day as a group of thirty but now only around fifteen remained. After the horror of seeing Santa Claus burned to death by a fat cop, their day had only got worse. Their troop leader had been one of the first to be picked off as she fought in vain to protect them.

As the remaining girls neared the church hoping to find solace there from the undead, one of the clowns, a particularly vile sort wearing a red and white striped romper suit and a bright red wig launched himself into the air and swooped down onto the back of one of the stragglers. The young girl, aged no more than ten, collapsed to the ground beneath him. Her face was thrust into the snow leaving her incapable of screaming for help.

The clown sat astride her as two of his comrades raced past in pursuit of the remaining Sunflower Girls. Ignoring them, he turned the young girl over to get a good look at her terrified face. He ran a long bony hand down her cheek, feeling the warmth of the blood flowing through her.

'Hello my pretty,' he crowed. 'You have lovely skin.' He pulled a hairband out from her long blonde hair and brushed some stray hairs away from her face. 'This will only hurt for a minute.'

He opened his mouth wide, revealing a set of huge vampire fangs. The girl closed her eyes and screamed.

SMACK!

Dante arrived in the nick of time. Just as the clown was leaning in to take a bite of the girl's neck, he ploughed into the side of him with the speed and power of an express train. He and the clown rolled through the snow. Dante had the element of surprise on his side so he was able to gain the upper hand. Behind him he saw Kacy grab the small blonde girl and pick her up from the ground. Then from out of nowhere Vanity appeared. He raced past Dante in pursuit of the other clowns that were chasing the girl scouts up to the front doors of the church.

Dante wriggled on top of the clown he had knocked down. His enemy's red wig slipped off, revealing a short crop of brown hair beneath it. Unfortunately Dante hadn't thought too far ahead with his plan to come to the rescue of the Sunflower Girls. He had acted on a rush of blood as usual. He knew he'd done the right thing; he just wasn't entirely sure what to do next. The clown had been taken by surprise and had a look of fear in his eyes, so Dante raised his right fist above his head and then ploughed it down into the clown's face. A loud crack followed and Dante winced at the sharp pain in his knuckles from the punch.

He heard Kacy's voice call out something from up ahead. He looked up and saw her shepherding the girls in through the front doors of the church. Behind her, Vanity had successfully knocked two other clowns to the floor and was doing his best to keep them both down.

The clown who was lying flat on his back underneath Dante spoke out in an anguished voice. 'Ow,' he groaned. 'You broke my nose.'

Dante looked back down at his prisoner and saw that the red plastic nose he had been wearing had snapped in half, revealing a large warty nose beneath it. There was only one thing to do in the circumstances and that was to punch the clown in the face again and break his real nose. But as he was about to throw a second punch, the clown pulled his right hand out from by his side. He was holding a gun. He pointed it at Dante's face.

Dante watched open-mouthed as the clown squeezed the trigger. It made a gentle clicking sound and a burst of warm water squirted out into Dante's his eyes. Typical clown, carrying a water pistol for comic effect. Not waiting for a second prank, Dante punched him in the face again, much harder than before. This time there was a much louder crack as the clown's real nose broke. Blood sprayed out over his face and left him looking suitably dazed and possibly concussed too. He was certainly in no state to fight back. Dante climbed back to his feet and charged towards Vanity and the two other clowns.

Vanity had bashed one of them into a state of unconsciousness. The other was clambering to his feet, looking to fight back. Dante charged over and ploughed into him the same way he had ploughed into the other clown, knocking him off his feet and back down into the snow where his head thudded against some ice.

'Quick,' yelled Vanity, grabbing his arm. 'Let's get inside. There's more of them coming!'

As they raced into the church, Dante glanced back over his shoulder. A gang of vampire clowns had seen what was going on and were charging towards the church. Some of them were armed with machetes, others just water pistols. Either way, there was no use in sticking around to get sliced up by these unfunny fuckers.

Dante and Vanity slammed shut the large wooden doors of the entrance, just in the nick of time too. A couple of the quicker clowns crashed head first into the doors as Vanity slid a large metal bolt across locking them shut from inside.

Dante looked around for Kacy. She was standing in the middle of the aisle half way down the church. On a row of pews either side of her, the faces of around fifteen terrified Sunflower Girls were peering over.

'How many of them are out there?' Kacy asked.

'About five,' said Vanity, brushing past Dante towards Kacy. 'If they decide they want to get in here we're fucked. I'll check around the back to make sure there's no other doors they can get in through.'

Vanity rushed past Kacy and the girls at lightning speed. When he reached the altar at the other end of the hall he looked both ways before dashing off out of sight down the West wing of the church.

Dante could see the fear in the eyes of the young girls and attempted to reassure them. 'Don't worry about him,' he said. 'He won't hurt you.'

The little blonde girl who Dante had rescued from the red haired clown spoke up on behalf of the others, her voice a trembling squeak. 'Are you vampires too?' she asked.

Dante looked to Kacy. 'Can you field that question, while I go help Vanity check for other entrances?'

'Sure.'

He hurried down the aisle, past Kacy and the terrified girls. As he passed them he heard Kacy attempting to explain. 'We're not proper vampires,' she said. 'We're the nice kind. We protect little girls from the real vampires. The clowns.'

He was admiring her skill and patience with the kids as he reached the end of the aisle. There was no sign of Vanity anywhere.

The church was cold and dark. The only light (or heat for that matter) was provided by a scant few candles on the walls. As Dante looked around for any sight of Vanity or any open doors that might look inviting to unwanted intruders, he heard and almighty crashing sound behind him.

It was the sound of breaking glass and it set the girls off screaming again. Dante spun around in time to see five clowns come crashing through the stained glass windows above the front doors. Shards of shattered glass fell from above and crashed down onto the stone church floor, shattering into tiny pieces.

Four of the clowns landed in amongst the pews that were hiding the screaming Sunflower Girls. The fifth clown landed behind Kacy and grabbed hold of her. He yanked her off her feet and dragged her back down the aisle with him towards the entrance. The four others each grabbed a screaming child and dragged them up out of the pews as the remaining girls ducked down crying and screaming.

Dante's instinctive reaction was to charge towards Kacy, but he'd barely taken a step when the clown who was holding her, a freak with a green wig and an evil smile, pulled a machete from up his sleeve and pressed it against her throat. He licked the side of Kacy's face and spoke into her ear.

'Why are you helping these kids?' he sneered.

'Because they're kids,' Kacy replied nervously.

Dante felt his stomach tighten. The blade on the machete was pressed tightly against Kacy's neck. One bad decision here could see her sliced up. It made him feel powerless. Kacy now looked every bit as terrified as the children she had been trying so hard to calm only moments earlier. And where the hell was Vanity?

The clown with the machete pressed against Kacy's throat seemed to be the leader. The others, hovering above the pews, holding captive schoolgirls, were clearly waiting for him to give them the signal to start the carnage. He scoffed at Dante.

'You've broken vampire code by siding with these kids,' he yelled. 'And you shouldn't have brought them here to the church. Goddamn church won't save any of you!'

Dante didn't know how to answer. But fortunately he didn't have to. From the shadows behind him, he heard a familiar gravelly voice speak out in response. 'Church won't save any of *you* either,' it said.

The clown frowned and tried his best to peer into the shadows behind Dante to see the owner of the voice. 'Who's that?' he shouted.

Dante kept his eyes glued to the machete pressed against Kacy's throat. A glowing red dot had appeared on it a second earlier. It began moving slowly up onto the clown's neck and then his face. As it travelled up through his chin and nose, the clown seemed to spot it too. It was a red laser sighter. The moving red dot eventually came to a stop between the clown's eyes, almost turning him cross-eyed as he followed its journey up his face. And then the carnage started.

BANG!

The clown's head exploded. A bullet had burst through his forehead and completely obliterated his skull. Blood and brains sprayed out everywhere. One side of Kacy's face was instantly caked in red goo. She ducked down, probably screaming, although it was hard to tell because it sounded like everyone in the church was screaming. Those screams were soon drowned out by four further extremely loud gunshots that rang out in quick succession. After each one, a different clown's head exploded and a Sunflower Girl fell to the floor screaming and covered in his blood and brains.

Dante looked back over his shoulder and saw the dark figure of the Bourbon Kid step out from the shadows behind the altar. His face was concealed beneath a dark hood as was so often the case when he was killing folks. In his right hand was a pretty heavy duty handgun. He slipped it into a holster inside his long dark robe.

Dante let out a deep sigh of relief. 'You showed up in the nick of time. Thanks, man.'

The Kid walked past him down the aisle. 'No problem,' he muttered under his breath.

Dante followed on behind him. 'Gaius isn't at the Casa de Ville any more,' he said.

'Where is he?'

'He's on his way to the museum in the middle of town. We're gonna have to go there if we wanna get the Eye back.'

The Kid stopped and turned around. 'I gotta go to a couple of other places first. Hang here for a bit. I'll meet you at the museum later.'

'I'm not sure we can wait. Gaius is supposed to be taking the Eye there to have it cleaned, or somethin'.'

Up ahead, Kacy was orchestrating some kind of group hug with the girl scouts in an attempt to calm them down and wipe the blood off them. The Kid took a look at her.

'Your girlfriend isn't ready to leave these kids yet. In about an hour the streets will be clear of vampires. Then you can leave the kids here and head to the museum. I'll meet you there when I've done a couple of other stops.'

'Where else you gotta go apart from the Casa de Ville?' Dante asked.

'First up I gotta clear the streets for you. Then I gotta stop off at the library and the police station.'

'What for?'

'Gotta find me some books and kill me some cops.'

Kacy scratched her head. 'Why kill the cops?'

'Tradition.'

Without uttering another word, the Kid walked down the aisle past Kacy and the mortified Sunflower Girls. They all backed away from him as he strode through them. The clowns had been scary enough, but this guy was way more dangerous. He walked up to the front doors, slid the huge metal bolt to one side and opened the door on the left. As he stepped through it he turned back to survey the carnage behind him.

'You might wanna secure this door behind me,' he said.

Kacy pulled herself free of the girls and hurried down the aisle towards him. 'I'll do it,' she said.

The Kid vanished through the door and out into the snow covered streets outside. He left the door open for Kacy to pull shut.

In all the chaos, Dante had forgotten all about Vanity. His vampire buddy reappeared, strolling back from the West wing of the church. He waved at Dante as he approached. 'I bolted a door to the cellar,' he called out. 'The place should be secure now.' He walked up to Dante and looked around. The church hall looked extremely different to when he had last seen it. There were smouldering corpses of clowns lying around and everyone else was covered in blood. Then of course there was the small matter of the shattered windows above the doors. 'What the hell happened here?' he asked.

Dante shrugged. 'Clowns flew in through the windows, grabbed Kacy and a bunch of the girls. Bourbon Kid showed up, killed 'em all and fucked off out into the street.'

Vanity looked surprised. 'I was only gone a minute,' he said. 'Seriously? The Bourbon Kid was here?'

'Yeah. I guess he just got back from the Devil's Graveyard.'

'What was he doing there?'

'I don't know, but whatever it was, it's made him back into his old self again.'

Vanity frowned. 'What do you mean?'

There was no need to answer his question. In the streets outside, the sound of gunshots and screams was clearly audible. At the end of the hall, Kacy was pulling the door closed. Vanity walked down the aisle towards her, with Dante following on behind. Kacy had left the door slightly ajar and was peering out into the streets outside. One of the schoolgirls spoke up.

'Is that man in the hood killing all the vampires out there?' she asked.

Kacy looked back at her and then up at Dante and Vanity. Her face, although still half covered in blood, showed great concern. She pulled the door shut behind her and looked back to the Sunflower Girl who had asked the question.

'Stay in here, honey,' she said. 'It'll be safer.'

Outside, the gunshots were becoming more frequent and the anguished howls of the Bourbon Kid's victims more vociferous. Voices were pleading to be left alone, then silenced by more gunshots.

Vanity repeated the girl's question. 'Is he killing all the vampires?'

Kacy was trembling as she slid the metal bolt back into place on the door. 'No,' she said, turning back to face the others. 'He's killing *everyone*.'

Thirty-Seven

Beth had regained consciousness in the late afternoon. She was in a fairly poky little room with a couple of heavy set soldiers who introduced themselves as Tex and Razor. She recognised them from a brief stop she had made at the Tapioca on Halloween. Her memory of events leading up to how she ended up in a room with them was extremely hazy. And her head hurt as if she'd been hit with a baseball bat.

They hadn't given her much information about why she was being held prisoner, only that it had something to do with JD or as they liked to call him, the Bourbon Kid. She was being used as bait in a plot to kill him. She'd tried explaining to them that she and JD were no longer together but her words fell on deaf ears. The soldiers weren't interested and they weren't particularly clear about what her fate might be either.

She sat on a sofa watching the news on a large widescreen television on the opposite wall. Below the television was a bank of CCTV monitors. Tex, the taller of the two soldiers, was sitting at a desk in front of the monitors, watching them intently. His hair was cut almost to the bone at the back and sides and Beth could see an unpleasant collection of red spots on the back of his neck. The other guy, Razor (who had a scar on his face twice the length of Beth's), was sitting uncomfortably close to her, watching the news with her.

In the early evening, the news reader caught everyone's attention with some breaking news. 'We now go to Sally Feldman who is with Captain Dan Harker of the Santa Mondega Police Department for a live update on the Bourbon Kid case.'

The screen switched to a picture of Dan Harker sitting at a desk in the news studio with Sally Feldman, a middle aged blonde reporter in a smart red suit. Just before the interview began, a door in the corner of the room swung open and in walked Bull, the senior member of the soldiers.

'What's up, fellas?' he asked.

'Hold on,' said Tex, pointing up at the television on the wall. 'Got some breaking news about the Bourbon Kid on here.'

On screen, Dan Harker was answering Sally Feldman's first question. 'New evidence has come to light regarding the Bourbon Kid case,' he said, staring out through the screen with a serious look on his face. 'I believe I have proof that the Kid did not murder Bertram Cromwell this morning. In fact, it's entirely possible that he's not guilty of most of the murders he is accused of. I suspect that in recent times the Bourbon Kid has been protecting this city from a group of corrupt police officials and a large army of what would appear to be vampires.'

Bull stood watching open mouthed. 'What the fuck?'

In front of him by the monitors, Tex snorted a laugh. 'Whoa, death wish!'

A smirk broke out on Bull's face. 'This idiot'll be dragged away by the men in white coats before they even cut to commercials,' he said.

On the screen, Harker continued with his outrageous revelations. 'That's right, I said it out loud,' he went on. 'There are vampires in this city. It's not just a rumour. It's not a joke. And with the darkness that has engulfed this city in recent days these creatures have now taken to the streets. Vampires are committing the riots and street muggings that are currently being reported all over the city. I advise everyone to lock yourselves insides your homes until further notice. Something or someone is the cause of these dark clouds that are hovering over our homes. And finally I have one last plea. This is for the Bourbon Kid. If you're watching this, this city needs you. Please come and find me. I am on your side. Or if you prefer, just go about your business of killing vampires. I will not send the police force after you. You have our blessing to kill them all. Please, wherever you are, come back and save our city.'

The news station cut back to the reporter in the studio who was staring wide-eyed at the screen with his eyebrows raised.

'Well, that was interesting, wasn't it?' he remarked.

Beth had listened in stunned bewilderment the same as everyone else when she heard what Captain Harker had to say. So, could it be true that the Bourbon Kid was actually a hero underneath it all? Probably not, but he was killing the vampires. She had judged JD rather hastily in the heat of the moment when she had seen him kill Silvinho. Right now it looked like he was the only chance the city of Santa Mondega had of surviving the wave of vampire attacks. She also now deeply regretted the moment when she had thrown Casper's cloth back at him.

Bull looked over at her, as if reading her thoughts. 'Don't believe all that shit,' he said. 'Your boyfriend has killed hundreds of innocent people, not just vampires. That idiot cop doesn't have a fucking clue what he's talking about.'

'I believe you're right,' she said, nodding at him. 'But look at *you*. You're holding me hostage on behalf of a gang of vampires who intend to kill me once I've served my purpose. That doesn't exactly make you a hero either, does it?'

Bull looked somewhat taken aback at the unexpected outburst. He clearly wasn't used to being spoken to in such a disrespectful manner. 'You listen to me, you stupid bitch,' he snapped. 'Me and my guys have been protecting the likes of you for years. We've fought wars to provide the freedom that you take for granted. Stuck our heads above the ground when there's bullets flying everywhere. Carried out missions behind enemy lines. And for what? A country full of people like you who don't even bother to thank us. The only reason you're alive now is because of people like us. Your boyfriend killed a war hero this morning. Silvinho died in a corridor in a shitty apartment block. That's no way for a soldier to die. Not after everything he did for his country. So when you judge me, and you judge us,' he pointed at Tex and Razor, 'remember this, it's your boyfriend killing folks for fun, not us, and not the vampires. The undead aren't out there killing innocent people for fun. They kill to survive. They need the blood to live, in the same way that you and I need food and water. They're paying us a good wage to fight for their survival. And they don't judge us on how we do it. And if you, young lady, *you* have to be sacrificed for the greater good, then I can live with that. With you as bait we can kill the Bourbon Kid and I can assure you, it will save the lives of thousands of people who would otherwise have been killed by him.'

'The vampires will kill thousands more people than he ever could,' Beth retorted.

'That's true,' Bull agreed. 'But the people who die at the hands of the vampires are dying for a reason. It's all part of the food chain. When your precious Bourbon Kid killed my father he did it out of spite. He's killed thousands of innocent people without motive. There's no honour in that. The vampires kill to survive. There's honour in that.'

'Honour? Is this what you tell yourself to ease your conscience?'

Bull frowned. 'You know, you should be a little more careful about how you speak to me, miss.'

Beth looked back up at the television screen. There was a picture of JD on a monitor behind the news reporter. She stared hard at it for a few seconds before responding to Bull. 'I'm not afraid of what you might do to me,' she said.

Bull smiled. 'Nor should you be, sweetness. When you die, I promise you it'll be quick,' he said. 'You have nothing to be afraid of.'

'Wish I could say the same for you.'

'I beg your pardon?' Bull's voice took on a more surly tone, suggesting he took offence to the remark. 'Since when did you get so cocky?'

'Since I realised my boyfriend is the Bourbon Kid.'

'That's hardly a reason to be cocky.'

'Really? Because the smart money says I'm going to live. My boyfriend has been killing vampires for years and he's still alive. He's up there on TV. I don't see you guys on TV. No one's talking about how many people you've killed, apart from *you*. You guys need to wake up to one very important fact.'

Bull's nostrils flared. She was definitely getting under his skin. 'What's that then?' he scowled.

'You're all gonna die.'

Bull stared hard at her for a few moments, clearly surprised at her brash display of confidence, and no doubt rattled by it too. He nodded at Razor. Whatever the nod meant, it triggered an instant reaction. With a deft jab from his right fist, Razor blindsided Beth with a sharp blow to the side of the head, knocking her out cold.

Thirty-Eight

'Flake, you've done a wonderful job,' said Bill Clay, patting her on the shoulder.

The switchboard on the reception desk at the police station had been overwhelmed with calls from panicked residents and Flake had done her best to keep them calm and offer advice. There had been all kinds of strange calls, including one from a girl called Caroline who claimed she'd been chased into a library by a vampire who was then killed by the Bourbon Kid. Flake couldn't tell the crank calls from the genuine ones, so she was grateful when Clay had come downstairs and dictated an answerphone message to her. They had recorded it and diverted all further incoming calls to the automated message.

'I sure could use a coffee after all that,' Flake said.

'You've certainly earned it. If I was you I'd head home.'

Flake peered over to the front doors of the station at the dark streets outside. 'I think I might stay here, if it's all the same to you,' she said.

'Can't say I blame you. We've got a few comfy sofas on the upper floors, I'll see if I can find some blankets for you.'

'What about you? Are you staying too?'

Clay shook his head. 'Nah. I'm due to meet the Captain later tonight at the museum.'

'Where's he now?'

'Addressing the city on the local news. So he's probably dead by now. Any word from Sanchez?'

'No, he never showed up.'

'That's too bad. Come on upstairs, I'll find some blankets for you.'

Flake had a few other things she wanted to attend to. Things she didn't particularly want to share with Clay. 'I'll come on up in a bit. Just got a few things to do first,' she said.

'Suit yourself. I'll see you in a while.'

Clay headed back upstairs via the stinky elevator. Flake grabbed a cup of coffee from a vending machine and settled back in at her desk. It was eerily quiet and made her long for Sanchez to show up. He had promised to drop by before heading off to the Casa de Ville with The Book of Death. She had a horrible feeling that he was about to put himself in danger by making the trip to the Casa De Ville on his own. He seemed to hold Jessica in very high esteem without any good reason. Flake didn't trust Jessica at all. The woman acted like a total bitch most of the time, yet no matter what she did, Sanchez seemed very forgiving.

Now that she finally had some time to herself Flake pulled open the bottom drawer on her desk and moved a few items aside. At the bottom of the drawer, underneath the clutter was The Book With No Name. She pulled it out and laid it down on the desk. She soon found the page where she had stopped reading the day before. She took a sip from her coffee and began scanning through the pages in the hopes of finding out anything more about vampires and cursed books.

It didn't take too long to find some more sketchy information about The Book of Death. It was described as a large black hardback book, just like the one she had hit with her car earlier. There was also a mention of the book's owner, a powerful man known as Rameses Gaius. The name sounded familiar to her but she couldn't recall where she had heard it before.

She'd been reading the occasional passage in the book and analysing some of the fine pieces of artwork for about half an hour when she finally stumbled on something that set her heart racing. It was a picture of four men and a woman. It was an old picture, but the faces of the four people in it were crystal clear. And the woman was instantly recognisable. It was Jessica. Beneath the picture she saw some lettering. It read:

Dark Lord Xavier and his family, believed to reside in Santa Mondega, a city of the New World.

Dark Lord Xavier had a face she recognised too. She had known him better as Archibald Somers, a cop obsessed with finding the Bourbon Kid for most of his career. The page next to it indicated that the people in the picture had dabbled in the dark arts. Hardly surprising when one of them was the owner of the title Dark Lord. Reading on furtively, Flake began to realise why everyone who read The Book With No Name was found dead afterwards. The book identified a whole bunch of high ranking vampires, one of which was Jessica. Sanchez obviously knew nothing about any of this and he was heading to the Casa De Ville with The Book of Death. Flake had to stop him.

She whipped her cell phone out from her trouser pocket and dialled Sanchez's number. It rang twice then the call went straight to voicemail and Sanchez's voice spoke.

"Good day to you. You have reached the voicemail of Detective Sanchez Garcia of the SMPD. I'm probably busy taking down bad guys, so please leave a message after the tone."

Flake waited for the beep and immediately started babbling a frantic message. 'Sanchez, it's Flake. Don't go to the Casa De Ville. Your friend Jessica is a vampire. It says so in The Book With No Name. I think she'll kill you as soon as she has The Book of Death. Call me as soon as you get this!'

Hopeful that he would hear her message before it was too late and not dismiss it as nonsense, she slipped her phone back into her pocket and pondered what to do. Her stomach was in knots and her mind was overflowing with different options. What if Sanchez didn't call back? Or didn't get the message?

In an attempt to keep her mind occupied she flicked through a few more pages of The Book With No Name. It didn't help much. All she could think about was how much trouble Sanchez was in. She had to figure out a way to help him. If the shoe was on the other foot, she was sure he would do the same for her.

She closed The Book With No Name. As it slammed shut, she stared at its worn brown cover and cast her mind back to the moment she had killed Ulrika Price. Of course! She had at her disposal a weapon that could kill vampires. The Book With No Name.

All she had to do was get to the Casa De Ville with it and somehow find a way to hit Jessica over the head with it as she had done with Ulrika Price. At the very least it would prove to Sanchez that Jessica was a vampire. But how would she ever get close enough to Jessica to do it?

She muttered her thoughts out loud. 'Come on Flake, think! What would Sanchez do if he was here, and it was me at the Casa De Ville with the vampires?'

Suddenly an idea came to her. She reached down to the bottom drawer of her desk once more and flicked through the clutter she had brushed aside to get to the book earlier. Sure enough, there was something there that could prove to be useful: a can of black spray paint. She pulled it out and shook it. The noise it made suggested that there was enough spray left in it for what she wanted.

She closed The Book With No Name and flicked the lid off the can. With a little trepidation she sprayed a small amount onto the cover of the book. It settled surprisingly well and looked as if it would dry quite quickly. She blew on it and then dabbed at it with her finger. It was still wet, but wouldn't smear too much. The tip of her finger had turned a little black, but for the most part, the paint seemed to have embedded itself into the book like a tattoo. With a little bit of care, such as covering the edges of the pages so that the black spray didn't hit them, she could make the nameless book look just like The Book of

Death, well, from a distance at least. There was hope for Sanchez yet. Her plan was flawed and reckless, some might even say it was shit, but it was the only plan she had, so it would have to do.

For the next twenty minutes Flake carried out an excellent piece of book camouflage. The once crusty brown cover of the book on her desk was soon a jet-black colour, unrecognisable from what it had been before. When she was satisfied that there was no brown showing through on the cover, she stood the book upright on her desk in front of a dusty old desk fan in the hope it would dry out quickly. As she watched the desk fan blow gently onto the book's cover she considered the risks of her plan to confront Jessica. It would definitely be easier if she could avoid the confrontation altogether.

She flicked through the menus on her cell phone. She had no missed calls or text messages. She took a deep breath and hoped for the best as she dialled Sanchez's number again. This time it didn't even ring. It went straight to a recorded message. A woman's voice spoke this time.

The number you are calling is either switched off or unavailable. Please try again later.

Flake ended the call before the message repeated itself. 'Casa De Ville here I come,' she said aloud, slipping the cell phone back in the front pocket on her pants.

She had been so preoccupied with planning her rescue mission for Sanchez that she hadn't noticed a new arrival in the station. A man had entered quietly via the front doors. And now his large shadow loomed over her desk. She looked up slowly and saw a figure dressed all in black with a hood pulled up over his head, concealing most of his face. She swallowed hard. She knew who this man was. It was the Bourbon Kid, the man who frequently dropped by the police station and killed all the cops, and usually also the receptionist. The memorial plaques in the staff room for previous receptionists Amy Webster and Francis Bloem were evidence of that.

'Can I help you?' she asked nervously.

The Kid responded in a gravelly voice that came straight from the depths of hell. 'I'm looking for a brown book that was left in the locker room downstairs. You know anything about it?' he asked.

Flake felt very nervous. The book he was referring to was on the desk right in front of his eyes. Only now it was black instead of brown. As she considered her response, the Kid reached inside his coat and pulled out a sawn off shotgun. He pointed it at her forehead.

'If you lie to me, I'll know,' he said. 'Choose your words carefully.'

She knew that he would kill her without thinking twice about it. She needed to give him a reason not to kill her before she gave him the answer he wanted.

She took a deep breath. 'I used the book to kill a vampire in the locker room yesterday morning.'

'Where is it now?'

'I was about to take it to…'

'WHERE IS IT NOW?'

Flake felt her legs go weak. This guy wasn't going to let her talk her way into his favour before she told him where the book was. She pointed at the black book that was standing upright on her desk.

'It's there,' she mumbled nervously, fearing a gunshot would follow the revelation.

The Bourbon Kid lowered his gun and looked down at the book on the desk. He picked it up with his free hand and laid it open on the table in order to get a look at the pages. He flicked through a few before closing it and staring at its new black cover. He ran his index finger lightly across the newly sprayed cover and then inspected his fingertip. Flake waited for his next move. For a few moments he looked around at the other items on her desk. The desk fan was buzzing gently and next to it was the black spray can. After staring at them for a short time, he looked back at Flake, his shadowed face revealing a look of puzzlement.

'Why did you spray it black?' he asked.

'I was trying to pass it off as The Book of Death. I was going to take it to the Casa De Ville to kill the vampire Jessica.'

'Why would you do that?'

'To save my friend Sanchez. He's gone there now with the real Book of Death. But he doesn't know that Jessica is a vampire.'

The Kid's shadowed face revealed nothing. 'I wouldn't worry about Sanchez,' he said. 'He's probably dead already.'

'But he might not be there yet,' said Flake, desperation creeping into her voice.

The Kid raised his gun again and aimed it at the end of Flake's nose. 'Close your eyes,' he growled.

'Why?'

'Because this is gonna sting.'

Flake did as she was told. Maybe he was kidding around?

BANG!

Maybe not.

Thirty-Nine

Jessica stood at the front entrance to the Casa de Ville and looked out into the courtyard. Everything was in place. Vampires and werewolves were concealed behind every bush, tree and statue in sight. If the Bourbon Kid came in through the front gates at the end of the driveway (and she suspected he was pig-headed enough to try it) he wouldn't make it far before the entire undead army swarmed all over him.

The only two vampires out in the open were Lionel and Nate from the Panda clan. They were standing guard on the front gates to make it look as if the Casa was operating as normal. But behind them was an army of over a thousand, all concealed in the dark.

She stepped back inside the building and closed the large double doors behind her. On the reception desk in the entrance hall was a female member of the Panda clan. Jessica didn't much care for her, if truth be told. She looked stupid sitting there at the desk wearing a bright red baseball cap with her face covered by the two large black patches around her eyes. Not many females ever joined the Panda clan simply because of the awful eyeliner.

Jessica called over to her. 'You, Panda Girl.'

'Yes ma'am.'

'I'll be up in my father's office if you need me.'

'Yes ma'am.'

Panda Girl watched on as Jessica flew up the staircase on her right, vanishing out of sight within half a second. She didn't like Jessica much either. Being referred to as Panda Girl had been annoying the first time it had happened, but Jessica had done it so many times that everyone in the Casa de Ville now called her that.

Jessica had only been gone for a minute when the phone on Panda Girl's desk rang. Rather than pick up the receiver she reached over and pressed a button to take the call on speaker.

'Reception, who is it?' she asked.

'Lionel on the gates. Got a cop here called Sanchez Garcia. Says he's come to see Jessica.'

'She's not seeing any visitors at the moment. Tell him to come back tomorrow.'

'Hang on.'

Panda Girl waited while Lionel had a muffled conversation with someone else in the background. Eventually, he came back on the line.

'This Sanchez fella says he's brought her a book she's been looking for.'

'Is it The Book of Death?'

'He's not saying.'

'What's this guy look like?'

'A fat version of the guy from the TV show CHiPs, except he's in a car, not on a bike.'

Panda Girl sighed. 'Okay, send him on through. Tell him to park up around the back and come to the front doors. I'll deal with him.'

'Okay.'

The line went dead and Panda Girl dialled the number for Rameses Gaius's office. The call went through to his answer phone, so she left a message.

'Jessica, this is Panda Girl on reception. Got a Sanchez Garcia on his way up the drive. Lionel on the front gate says he's brought a book for you. Call me when you get this.'

A couple of minutes passed before there was a knock on the front doors. Panda Girl hauled herself up out of her chair and made her way over to the peephole to see who was outside. She peered through it and saw a chubby fellow in a highway patrol outfit. He had a black satchel over his right shoulder. He fitted the description that Lionel had just given her. She opened the door.

'You're Sanchez Garcia?' she asked.

'Yes I am, thank you,' he replied.

'You've got something for me?'

'No. I've got something for Jessica.'

'What is it?'

'It's The Book of Death,' he said holding up his satchel.

'In that case, you can leave it with me.'

Sanchez shook his head. 'I'm a friend of hers. She'll be pleased to see me. Plus she said there's a fifty thousand dollar reward for the return of this book.'

Panda Girl sighed. 'Fine. Come on in.'

'Thank you, my good man,' said Sanchez as he brushed past her on his way in.

She closed the door behind him. 'My name's Panda *Girl!'* she snapped.

'Of course it is. Where can I find Jessica?'

Panda Girl pointed to a crimson coloured sofa at the back of the foyer next to a door that led into one of the dining rooms. 'Take a seat there,' she said. 'I've left a message for Jessica to say you're here. She'll call for you when she's ready.'

'Fair enough.'

Sanchez wandered over to the sofa, admiring the paintings on the walls all around the foyer. 'Nice place you've got here,' he remarked.

Panda Girl ignored him and sat back down at her desk with her back to him. The phone rang just as she sat down. She reached over and pressed the speaker button again. 'Hello, reception.'

'Panda Girl, it's Jessica. I just got your message. Did you say Sanchez is here?'

'Yes. He's got The Book of Death for you.'

'He has?' Jessica sounded surprised.

'I haven't seen it, but he says he's got it in his satchel.'

'Who'd have thought it?' said Jessica, snorting a laugh. 'That idiot hasn't even worked out I'm a vampire yet, but somehow he's found The Book of Death. Brilliant. I bet he didn't even notice all the vampires and werewolves in the courtyard on his way in, did he?'

Panda Girl lowered her voice, knowing Sanchez was within earshot behind. 'He drove right past them all,' she said.

'What a fucking loser.'

'Want me to send him up?'

There was a slight pause as Jessica mulled over the suggestion. Eventually she replied. 'No. He'll get lost, you'd better bring him up. Once I've got the book, he's all yours.'

'Okay, see you in a minute, Jessica,' she said, ending the call.

She was already envisaging how much fun it would be to drink the blood from Sanchez's juicy neck. There was plenty of flesh there to take a bite out of. She stood up and turned around. The crimson sofa at the back of the foyer was now empty. Sanchez had fled. She sniffed the air. His scent, and that of some barbecue chicken wings was still floating in the air. It wouldn't take long to find him.

'Sanchez,' she called out. 'Oh, Sanchez. Come out, come out, wherever you are!'

Forty

'It's like the fucking North Pole here!' Lionel yelled over the sound of the howling wind.

'When have *you* ever been to the North Pole?' Nate called back.

'Huh?'

Standing guard at the front gates at the entrance to the Casa De Ville was a shit job at the best of times, but in a blizzard like the one they were caught up in right now, it was as bad as it got. Nate was no big fan of snow. He could handle the cold just fine. Being a vampire made cold weather perfectly bearable. But the wind blowing through his ears and the three inches of snow underfoot was irritating in the extreme. And it was bloody difficult to hear his buddy Lionel over the noise of the wind. It wasn't that easy to see him through the blizzard of snow either. The highlight of their evening so far had been opening the gates to let Sanchez through to see Jessica. Other than that the evening had been extremely uneventful. Their task was simply to keep an eye out for the approach of the Bourbon Kid, if of course, he was foolish enough to show up and allow himself to be spotted from the front gates.

'I said, when have you ever been to the fucking North Pole?' Nate repeated, a little louder than before.

His fellow Panda, Lionel, was renowned for a total lack of enthusiasm in every task he undertook. So even though Nate was hacked off at their current assignment, it was a safe bet that Lionel would be hating it even more.

Behind them, every other surviving member of the local undead scene was concealed behind a tree, bush or statue in the courtyard, ready to ambush the Bourbon Kid if he did show up.

'Well I've never actually *been* to the North Pole,' Lionel yelled back. He took his baseball cap off and shook the snow from it, before securing it tightly back on his head. 'I've seen it on telly though. And it's got a fuckin' lot of snow!'

The pair of them had been instructed like everyone else to wear dark clothes to help camouflage themselves in the dark, but against the backdrop of snow the camouflage was largely redundant. Nate reached into his thick dark coat and pulled a pack of cigarettes from his inside pocket. 'Wanna smoke?' he called over to his buddy.

'Nah. I'm good, thanks.'

Nate fumbled around in his pocket for his lighter and then held it up underneath the rim of his baseball cap to shield it from the snow. It was a shitty disposable red lighter that he'd snagged from a victim a few days earlier. It took four flicks to ignite the damn thing and even then the flame was pretty pathetic. After puffing hard on the end of the cigarette four or five times it eventually lit up. The flame on the lighter flickered and went out completely a second later.

As he took a drag on the cigarette, he saw Lionel poking his head through the bars on the gates, peering out into the road.

'You seen something?' he shouted over to him.

Lionel looked back and shook his head. 'Just snow. And more snow.'

The sound of someone moving behind him distracted Nate for a second. He looked back and heard a few of the other vampires and werewolves fidgeting in their hiding places and talking among themselves.

'At least we get to stand on the driveway,' he called over to Lionel. 'It sounds like everyone else is knee deep in waterlogged shit back there!'

Lionel stepped back from the gates and shrugged. 'The werewolves probably like that.'

'I bet the clowns hate it though.'

'Why the clowns?'

'Those big shoes will get filled with muddy water. Ruins their socks.'

Lionel looked surprised. 'I didn't know clowns wore socks.'

'Some of 'em must do. I've got some new socks on today so I'm glad to be up here at the gates. This is probably the safest place to be as well.'

'How d'ya figure?'

'Think about it. If the Kid really is gonna show up here, then coming in through the front gates would be pretty fuckin' stupid wouldn't it?'

'Yeah, we'll see him coming down the road long before he gets to the gates,' said Lionel, once more peering through the gates and down the road.

'Five bucks says he doesn't even show.'

'I'm not taking that bet. Of course he won't show. I wouldn't be out in this weather if I had a choice.'

Nate sucked hard on his cigarette and blew a lungful of smoke out into the cold night air. It vanished instantly within the downpour of snowflakes. Lionel had a good point. Only thing was, where most people would stay indoors in such abysmal weather, the Bourbon Kid wasn't most people. He was a fucking psycho with no fear of anything or anyone. A few drops of snow wouldn't keep him away if he was intending on showing up.

'You hear that?' Lionel shouted over to him.

'No. What?'

'I think I heard something just now.'

Nate took another drag on his cigarette. 'I didn't hear anything. What did it sound like?'

'A rustling in the bushes over there,' Lionel pointed at a row of bushes that ran along the inside wall of the grounds, over to his right. He took a step towards them, his back turned on Nate.

'Whoa, hold on a sec!' Nate shouted. 'Just stay here. This isn't fuckin' Camp Crystal. You don't walk off on your own to investigate a noise. Stay here where I can see you. And make sure you're in view of the CCTV cameras too. No one can help you if you do something dumb like wander off on your own!'

Lionel kept his back to Nate and craned his neck around to see if he could make out anything over by the bushes.

'It's fucking hard to see anything in those bushes, man,' he complained. 'Shouldn't we have some lights on down here?'

'Quit bitchin'. If anyone sneaks up on us, the guys watching on the cameras will turn on those big fuckin' spotlights. But if you go wandering off behind a bush out of sight of the cameras, I'm not following you in.'

Lionel turned back to face him. 'What if I need a piss?'

'Piss through the fuckin' gates!' He took another drag on his cigarette. 'You don't actually need a piss, do you?'

'No. I was just askin', is all.'

Nate leaned his head back and blew a lungful of smoke up at the sky again. This time he was able to watch the smoke escape in a snake like shape upwards. The snowfall was slowing. The wind had eased ever so slightly, but it still made a gentle whistling noise. The dark clouds up above were beginning to part and a narrow shaft of light from the moon began to reveal itself. Nate took one last drag of his cigarette and tossed it down into the snow. As he heard the cigarette hiss and fizzle out, he looked up again and was pleased to see that the snow had stopped completely. A few flakes still floated around in the wind, but there was no more blizzard. *"Finally, thank God for that,"* he thought.

'Looks like Gaius is bringing the moon out for the werewolves,' he called over to Lionel, his voice suddenly a lot clearer over the calming winds.

Lionel didn't respond. He was stood still, just staring back out through the gates.

Nate called over to him again. 'I said, it looks like Gaius is bringing the moon out for the werewolves.'

Still no response.

Nate could only see him from a side angle and couldn't tell if he had heard him or not. 'Lionel? Are you listening—'

Before Nate could finish his sentence, Lionel's legs buckled at the knee. He collapsed towards the ground in slow motion. It reminded Nate of the moment Charlton Heston slumped to his knees in front of the Statue of Liberty at the end of Planet of the Apes. As he mulled over the insignificance of it, he received a shock.

Lionel's head drooped forward. And kept going. It slid clean off his shoulders and landed with a gentle thud, face down in the snow. The rest of his body remained kneeling upright. A fountain of thick red blood began gushing out in all directions as if someone had turned on a garden sprinkler between his shoulders. The snow behind his decapitated head was sprayed blood red and a dark patch began spreading quickly towards Nate. The rest of Lionel's body slumped forward landing just short of his head. Nate watched the events unfold in stunned bewilderment before suddenly coming to his senses and reacting.

'Oh fuck!' He grabbed his walkie-talkie and raised it to his mouth. He pressed the button to speak, but before he could utter a word he felt a razor sharp blade pressed against his Adam's apple. He tried his best not to swallow too hard. The last thing he wanted was to feel that blade cut into his throat as a result of his own actions. A body pressed up against his back and he felt the warm breath of a man at his right ear. A hand appeared out of the darkness and grabbed a hold of the walkie-talkie, removing it from his grip. Then he heard a voice. A gravelly whisper.

'How many vampires in the courtyard?' it asked.

Nate took a short breath before sensibly replying. 'Hundreds.' The blade pressed harder against his throat. 'Possibly thousands,' he added.

'And werewolves?'

'The same.'

The blade that had remained pressed to his throat was loosened and pulled away. Nate breathed a gentle sigh of relief.

'So what now?' he asked.

The knifeman did not respond.

Unsure if his attacker was still behind him or not, Nate tried to reason with him. 'I won't say I saw y…'

A horrific ripping sound interrupted his speech. He felt an agonising pain in his lower back. The pain rapidly shot through to his stomach. Gasping for breath, he succeeded only in chasing after some oxygen like a kid trying to bite an apple in a barrel. His chin dropped forwards suddenly as he found his neck muscles no longer able to hold his head up. And as he looked down he saw the blade of a sharp knife protruding through the front of his stomach.

It was covered in blood.

His blood.

His legs buckled in the same way as Lionel's had. As he began to fall face first into the snow a hand grabbed his head to stop its downward trajectory. Blood was rushing up through his lungs into his mouth. Thick lumps of it began sliding over his tongue and seeping out through his lips. He could see it dribbling onto the white snow below.

Then the blade in his stomach began to move again. His attacker pulled the knife upwards, through his stomach and up through his rib cage. The blade sliced his undead vampire heart in two, splitting his chest open. As he exhaled his last breath he saw his guts fall out onto the snow.

Forty-One

After a particularly stressful and tiring day, Elijah Simmonds was at last able to relax. The museum was closed for the evening so he finally had a chance to wander around the displays and decide on what changes to make. First up, he decided, there were far too many boring paintings. Definitely more nudes were required. At present there were far too many paintings by the expressionists. Simmonds couldn't stand the expressionist paintings. The only redeeming feature they had was that they were worth a lot of money, so there was a possibility that he could sell a few of them off and bring in a few hundred thousand dollars revenue, maybe more.

In fact, he decided, the entire hall containing the expressionist paintings could probably be replaced by something far more entertaining, like a mini theatre with a cinema screen. If the museum showed films about the expressionists rather than stocking their dull works it could generate some much needed extra revenue. As he strolled around the halls he began to feel great excitement at the project that lay before him. Transforming the museum into something much more modern would see him hailed as a visionary. Most of the locals didn't visit the museum any more because it had become so damned dull under the stewardship of the now deceased Bertram Cromwell. A redesign could bring them back.

On his way through the main hall on the ground floor, he came across Cromwell's favourite display, the Tomb of the Egyptian Mummy. It was a vast display that took up enormous space behind a large glass wall. A year earlier this monument had been trashed and the mummy stolen. Cromwell had spent vast sums of the museum's resources having it restored, against Simmonds's better judgement. But now that he was in charge he had visions of turning it into a kind of House of Horrors attraction, perhaps set in a giant plastic pyramid. It could even feature a mini fairground ride with mummies and other creepy creatures.

It was while he was staring at the tomb that Simmonds's night took an unexpected turn. He heard footsteps coming down the main stairs at the far end of the hall on his right. He looked around and saw James the security guard. He was being followed by a group of men. One man in particular stood out above the others. He was a broad fellow with a shaved head. He wore a smart silver suit and a pair of sunglasses. The other four men who flanked him, two on either side were dressed all in black with their faces largely concealed behind black headscarves. They looked like ninjas.

James waved at Simmonds. 'Mr Simmonds, I have a gentleman here to see you.'

Simmonds sighed inwardly. It seemed that the day was not quite over after all. The group of men made their way up to him and then James introduced the big fellow in the suit.

'This is Mr Gaius,' he said. Then he turned to Gaius and gestured back at Simmonds. 'This is Elijah Simmonds.'

Simmonds held out his hand. 'Hi, I'm the manager here,' he said. It felt so good to say it out loud.

Gaius took his hand and shook it firmly. 'I'm the new owner,' he said.

'Excuse me?'

'I'm the new owner of this museum. So good to meet you, Mr Simmonds. I'm a big fan of your work.'

Simmonds couldn't hide his shock. 'How did this... I mean, umm, will I still be manager?'

Gaius placed his right arm around Simmonds's shoulders and steered him away from the rest of the group, walking him away to a corner where there was a large piano with a mannequin dressed as Ludwig van Beethoven sat behind it on a stool.

'Ever seen Beethoven play?' Gaius asked.

'Um, no.'

Gaius raised his left hand. A gentle glow seemed to emanate from his fingertips. He waved his fingers gently in several directions like a puppeteer. It generated a reaction from the wooden figure seated at the piano in the purple suit and grey wig. Beethoven was coming to life. The figure of the composer began moving in an awkward, clunky manner. His head perked up and his fingers began tapping away on the keys of the piano.

'Recognise the tune?' Gaius asked.

It did sound vaguely familiar to Simmonds, but he wasn't entirely sure where he'd heard it. 'Is it Thank you for the Music by Abba?' he asked.

'No, it's concerto number five, you ignorant prick.'

Gaius squeezed Simmonds's shoulder tightly as they watched the pianist perform. About thirty seconds into the performance Simmonds heard the sound of glass cracking behind him. He twisted his head around to get a look at where the noise had come from. He saw the four ninja guys were taking turns kicking the glass cover around the tomb, using their bare feet. The glass was several inches thick and not the sort that would normally break easily, but as Simmonds watched on, held back by the firm grip of Gaius's hand on his shoulder, the four ninjas kicked at it repeatedly until after four or five seconds the whole thing came crashing down. James stood by helplessly, looking to Simmonds for advice on what to do.

'What the hell?' Simmonds blurted out. 'You can't just do that.'

Gaius twisted him back around again to watch the wooden figure of Beethoven performing at the piano. He leaned in and whispered into Simmonds's ear. 'Did Bertram Cromwell die easily?' he asked.

'What?'

'When you killed Bertram Cromwell, how did it make you feel?'

'What are you talking about?'

Gaius smiled, not a warm smile by any means, but a smile nonetheless. 'I know you killed him,' he said. 'But I'm not mad. As it happens you did me a favour. He would never have allowed me to come down here and mess with his precious tomb, would he? But you, you Mr Simmonds, have wisdom beyond your years. You don't mind if my boys here spend a bit of time rearranging the tomb do you?'

'Um, well…'

'I thought not. We've got business here this evening you see. I'm having a couple of kids mummified and condemned to hell for all eternity. I think you know them, Dante Vittori and Kacy Fellangi?'

'I know them,' said Simmonds, recalling the brief time that Dante had worked at the museum. 'That asshole Dante smashed a vase over my head once.'

'Good,' said Gaius, slapping Simmonds hard across the back. 'Then you're in agreement?'

'Umm, I guess so.'

Gaius wrapped his arm back around Simmonds's shoulder and turned him back towards the middle of the hall. Then he began walking him back through the hall towards the main stairs.

'So, did you get what you were after in the end?' Gaius asked.

'What's that?'

'The combination to Bertram Cromwell's safe, of course. That must have been one of the reasons you killed him. Keeps a lot of cash in there, doesn't he?'

'I wouldn't know about that.'

'Elijah, my dear friend, if you want to stay alive and run this museum for me, you're going to have to start being a little more honest with me. Cromwell's job was never guaranteed to be yours permanently was it? But if you could get your hands on the cash in the safe, it wouldn't matter, would it?'

Simmonds smiled. Gaius had obviously done his homework. 'That safe is impossible to break into,' he said. 'Cromwell took the security combination to the grave with him.'

Gaius laughed heartily. 'My dear Elijah, let me show you what I'm capable of. While my friends are down here preparing the tomb, why don't you and I go upstairs and I'll show you how to crack open a safe?'

Forty-Two

From the control room up in the East tower of the Casa De Ville, Bull continued to stare out of the long narrow window down at the courtyard below. The snow had begun to ease up, but the moisture on the outside of the window was still slightly obscuring his view. Even though it was difficult to make much out in the dark due to the added hindrance of the falling snow, he had to admit he was impressed at how well the vampires and werewolves had concealed themselves in the bushes and trees. These creatures were like chameleons once they stood up against anything in the dark. Occasionally he thought he caught sight of one moving, but as he stared at what he thought was a member of the undead the movement would instantly cease, as if they could tell he was watching them. But as Bull knew only too well, the Bourbon Kid could move in and out of the shadows with great skill too. He could blend into his surroundings as well as any creature of the night.

Behind him Beth had just regained consciousness after Razor's blow to the temple earlier in the day. She wasn't so chirpy now that she had a bruise the size of an egg, swelling above her right eye. Razor was sitting next to her with his left arm stretched along the back of the sofa behind her, ready to clip her around the ear if she attempted to move without asking first.

Tex was still sitting in front of the bank of monitors on the other side of the room, staring at them intently, looking for any signs of an intruder on the premises. All of the cameras around the grounds were beaming their signal into the control room. Entry into the Casa De Ville undetected ought to be an impossibility.

Through the window Bull saw a sliver of blue light filter through the clouds above. The moon was finally making an appearance. This was a signal. Night was here. And in Santa Mondega, the beginning of night usually meant the beginning of carnage.

The snow quickly eased and soon stopped falling from the sky altogether. As his view of the courtyard below became clearer, he heard Tex call out from behind him. 'I got somethin' for ya, boss.'

'What is it?'

'Message from Jessica.' Bull looked around to see Tex reading an email on one of the monitors. 'She says the Bourbon Kid is heading this way. One of her sources says he's just come back from the Devil's Graveyard.'

'Devil's Graveyard?'

'Yeah. Ever heard of it?'

'Only in folklore. It's s'posed to be a place people go to make deals with the Devil. You know, sell their souls for immortality and all that shit.'

'You think that's what he's done?'

Bull shrugged. 'Won't make a blind bit of difference. We've got an army of immortals down there. Anything else?'

'There's one other thing you should know,' said Tex.

'What's that?'

'It's stopped snowing.'

'Yeah, I can see that.'

'Well it's made it a hell of a lot easier to see what's going on out there,' said Tex. 'What's the view from the window like?'

'It could be better. But I can just about make out the front gates.'

'He won't come in through the front gates... will he?'

Bull continued to stare hard out of the window at the courtyard below. 'I'm convinced that's what he's gonna do.'

'That's pretty dumb though,' said Tex. 'He's cleverer than that, surely?'

'He's cunning all right,' Bull agreed. 'But he's also pig headed and a show off. Likes to face down an army head on. You keep your eyes on those monitors. I'll keep mine on the courtyard.'

Tex stared at the monitor that was showing the front gates. 'There's fuck all happening at the gates, boss,' he said. 'Just them two Pandas. One of 'em's smoking a cigarette.'

'Smoking, huh? No wonder they're an endangered species,' said Bull.

Tex didn't laugh. Instead he shouted out. 'OH SHIT! Man down!'

Bull spun around. 'What? Where?' he snapped.

Tex was pointing at the monitor showing the front gates. 'We have a Panda down,' he said. 'No wait, hang on.' He squinted hard at the screen, trying to piece together what he was seeing for a few seconds before adding, 'We now have *two* Pandas down. Both guards on the gate are down.'

Bull peered out of the window at the gates. It was hard to see clearly what was going on. 'What the fuck has happened to them?' he asked, hoping for some guidance from Tex.

'They're down. Permanently.'

'Dead?'

'Yes sir.'

'This is it then. He's here.'

212

Tex squinted at the monitors in front of him, hoping to get a better view of proceedings. 'One guy's head fell off,' he said. 'Other guy kinda split in two down the middle.'

'Split in what?'

'Two. Down the middle. You know, fell in half. Like sliced bread.'

'Fuck!'

'Yeah. That's gotta hurt.'

Bull couldn't validate any of what Tex was telling him from his view at the window. He trusted Tex though and he knew that a quick response was required. 'Okay Tex, switch on the central spotlights. Let me see what we're lookin' at!'

Tex reacted to the order instantly. He flicked a switch on a panel beneath the bank of monitors and the outside sky suddenly lit up as a spotlight shone down on the courtyard. Tex had the controls for the spotlight at his fingertips. He guided the light over to the gates, watching its progress on the monitors.

From the window Bull watched the huge beam of light shine down twenty feet in diameter. It showed up the silhouettes of some of the previously hidden vampires and werewolves as it searched the grounds for the killer of the two guards at the gates.

Bull and Tex suddenly both shouted out at the same time. 'THERE HE IS!'

Tex had stopped the spotlight directly on a man dressed all in black standing on the driveway. The man was wearing a long dark coat with a hood pulled up over his head. Where Tex has spotted him on a monitor, Bull had seen it at the same time as he stared out of the window.

From behind them, Razor piped up. 'Is it the Bourbon Kid?'

Bull nodded. 'Who else was it gonna be?'

'I dunno. Thought maybe he wouldn't show.'

'You just keep a hold of that little lady,' Bull ordered. 'She's the reason he's here.'

Down below in the courtyard the Bourbon Kid was standing motionless in the centre of the spotlight. The gates and the two dead Pandas were roughly twenty feet behind him. As Bull focussed momentarily on the dead guards and the blood red snow around them, he spotted something else moving, behind them. 'He's set the gates in motion,' he mumbled half to himself as he tried to make sense of it. Then realising he couldn't make sense of it he raised his voice and alerted the others. 'The gates are opening! What the hell is he doing?'

Tex looked baffled. 'I don't get it. Why is he opening the gates when he's already inside?'

Razor offered a suggestion. 'Maybe he's looking to escape, seeing as we've spotted him?'

Bull shook his head. 'Not without the girl. He won't leave without her. What the fuck is he playing at?'

'Shall I sound the siren?' asked Tex.

'Yeah. As soon as the vampires hear it, they'll swarm on him.' He turned to Beth. 'I figure your boyfriend has about ten seconds left to live. Wanna come and watch?'

Beth shook her head. 'I can watch it on the monitors from here, thanks,' she said.

Tex pressed a button on his control desk and a loud siren blared out in the courtyard outside. On the monitors, Beth was able to see the hoards of vampires and werewolves react to it. They began creeping out from their hiding places in the bushes and trees of the courtyard. And there were lots of them. A hell of a lot. They began edging towards the Bourbon Kid.

Bull snapped at Tex. 'Okay, now turn on all the lights.'

Tex flicked a few switches on and in an instant the whole courtyard lit up. Beth watched the situation unfold on screen. Literally thousands of vampires and werewolves in the courtyard were advancing on the Bourbon Kid, who no longer had a spotlight to himself. He stood motionless facing down an entire army of the undead.

'Get ready,' said Bull. 'Any second now, he's gonna do something.'

'Like what?' asked Razor.

'I dunno, but be ready, because when he does, they'll rip him apart.'

The vampires and werewolves continued to edge closer to the Kid. He had obviously seen them, but he had not reacted. The vampires at the front of the crowd eventually stopped just a few yards away from him. The whole undead army stood as one, stretching the length of the courtyard, waiting either for the Kid to make his move, or for a signal of sorts from Bull.

'We got about three thousand guys down there,' Bull said, smirking. 'It hardly seems like a fair fight.'

Beth stared at the monitors and allowed herself a half smile. 'You're right,' she said. 'You're gonna need way more than three thousand for it to be a fair fight.'

Bull ignored her and continued staring out of the window.

Although Beth wasn't entirely sure what they were seeing on screen, she heard a shout from Tex loud and clear. 'GRENADES!' he shouted.

From one of the other monitors A huge ball of smoke blew up from the ground around the Bourbon Kid, obscuring him from view completely.

'Shit!' Bull yelled. 'They're smoke bombs!'

Beth kept her eyes glued on the screen, waiting to see what became of JD. The army of vampires and werewolves began slowly forming a perimeter ring around the ball of smoke.

'What's he doing?' Bull asked. He sounded puzzled. 'Why isn't he shooting at them, or something? What the fuck is he waiting for?'

'Haven't you figured it out yet?' said Beth, scornfully.

Bull spun around. Everyone else was staring hard at the bank of monitors. Tex and Razor were looking at one of the monitors on the left. It showed the huge ball of smoke, but there was still no sign of the Kid coming out of it.

'He's still in that ball of smoke, right?' said Bull.

'Yep,' said Tex, still squinting at the screen.

Beth cleared her throat to grab their attention. 'You're looking at the wrong screen,' she said.

Bull looked over at her, failing to mask the annoyance on his face. 'What?' he snapped.

Beth pointed at a monitor on the far right. 'Look at that one,' she said.

All three of her captors looked over at the other monitor. It was showing live footage of the grounds just outside the front gates, so it had been of little interest to them once the Kid had showed up inside the grounds.

'What the fuck is that?' Tex said, frowning. He had the best view of the screen from his spot at the desk. Bull raced over to his side, and Razor jumped up from the sofa to join him. On the monitors it was evident that something huge was moving outside the gates. In fact there was a vast amount of movement. It was coming from the woodland on the other side of the road like a tidal wave surging towards the gates of the Casa de Ville. All three men watched aghast at what they saw on the monitor.

When what was happening began to sink in, Bull spoke on behalf of everyone. 'Oh sweet Jesus,' he whispered. 'God have mercy on us all.'

Forty-Three

After fleeing from the Casa de Ville's reception area Sanchez had wandered into a large dining room. The place was impressive, much nicer than his own dining room. It had probably been the scene of many fine banquets over the years, or centuries. There was a long varnished oak dining table in the centre of the room with posh high-backed chairs lining the sides of it and a chair at either end. The walls on either side were adorned with shelves of expensive looking ornaments, the likes of which would be worth sneaking out with if he could make it out in one piece. Right now though the best thing about this room (in Sanchez's opinion) was the fact that it was empty. The revelation that Jessica was a vampire and that she had an undead army lurking outside in the courtyard had come as a real shock. And the way she had spoken about him suggested she didn't care for him in the slightest, other than maybe as a potential snack. He needed help, big time. He pulled his cell phone from his pocket and switched it on. He had two missed calls. Both from Flake. She had also left him a message. He pressed for voicemail and listened to it –

"Sanchez, it's Flake. Don't go to the Casa De Ville. Your friend Jessica is a vampire. It says so in The Book With No Name. I think she'll kill you as soon as she has The Book of Death. Call me as soon as you get this!"

Dammit!

Why hadn't he listened to her before? Flake was so smart. And he was so stupid—not the other way around as he had foolishly believed earlier. Some kind of apology might be in order, eventually. For now, Flake was most definitely the first port of call to get him out of this mess. He had to call her back, *and quick*. He pressed dial and put the phone to his ear. The dialling tone that followed went on for what seemed like an eternity before the call was answered. Flake's voice came through loud and clear.

"Hi this is Flake. I'm not available to take your call right now. Please leave a message after the tone. Or beep. I'm not sure whether it's a tone or a beep. Is a beep considered a tone? Oh well, just leave a message anyway. After the tone."

Okay, so maybe she was a *bit* stupid. But Sanchez left a message for her anyway. He spoke in a hushed voice in case anyone was within hearing distance outside of the room. 'Hi Flake, it's Sanchez. I just got your message. You were totally right. I'm really sorry I doubted you. Thing is, I'm stuck in a dining room at the Casa De Ville. There's vampires and werewolves everywhere. I still have The Book of Death with me, but I can't get out of here. See if you can get the cops to send everyone here. There's something big about to go down. So, if you get this message, give me a call, or see if you can work out a way to get me out of here. Um,' he realised he was babbling and wasn't exactly sure what he was trying to say, but he wanted to make sure he got his message across clearly. 'If you do come here yourself, watch out for all the vampires and werewolves in the courtyard. I think they're after the Bourbon Kid. He's around here somewhere too. If you see him, steer clear. He's dangerous and would kill you just for fun. I really hope you get this message. Miss you. Bye.'

Sanchez considered what he'd just said. Not only had he apologised for doubting Flake, he'd also warned her to steer clear of the courtyard, and then told her he missed her. That last part was particularly alarming. Probably because it was genuinely true. He really did miss hanging out with Flake when she wasn't around. Who knew how that had come to happen? All the time he'd been obsessing about Jessica, Flake had been like a rock for him. Hell, the woman had saved his ass when Ulrika Price tried to kill him, then she'd come to his rescue when the Sunflower Girls had been chasing him, baying for blood. And most important of all, she knew how he liked his sausage cooked. Right now, given the choice of hanging out with Jessica or Flake, he'd pick Flake any day of the week. Of course, there was no guarantee that she would want to hang out with him right now. He'd been a bit of a shit to her of late, what with blaming her for the mess The Book of Death was in after she'd hit it with the car. He promised himself if Flake could get him out of this latest scrape, he'd even stop tipping her with fake one dollar bills when she waited on him in the Ole Au Lait.

He slipped his phone back into the hip pocket on his pants and considered his options. He needed to find somewhere to hide.

But where?

There was nowhere suitable within the dining room, other than maybe under the table. At the far end of the room was a large black door with a shiny brass doorknob on it. Hopefully it would lead to an exit of some kind, or at least a bathroom with a lock on the door. If he could find a bathroom he might be able to lock himself in it and wait for Flake to call back.

He quickstepped over to the large black door and turned the brass knob. It opened inwards and behind it he saw a long narrow corridor. Thankfully an empty one. There were doors on either side of the corridor every ten yards or so. Bedrooms? Bathrooms? Only one way to find out. He scurried over to the first door on the right and opened it. He peered inside. There was a double bed in the middle of the room with a bedside table and not much else, other than a set of walk in wardrobes and a small door in the corner. He checked both ways down the corridor to make sure no one saw him, then he slipped inside the room and closed the door behind him. He headed over to the door in the corner. This had to be an en suite bathroom, right? He poked his head around the door and was pleased to see that he was correct, for once. There was a long royal blue bath against the far wall and a matching toilet and washbasin on his left. A light blue shower curtain hung down from a rail above the bath. He stepped inside and bolted the door shut behind him.

He thought about the phone conversation he had overheard between Panda Girl and Jessica. Jessica had indicated that he would be of no further use to her once she had her hands on the book. What a bitch. After all he had done for her. That book was the only thing keeping him alive. The minute he gave it up he would become food for the immortals.

In the interest of keeping himself alive he made a snap decision.

He would hide The Book of Death.

He took his satchel off and laid it on the floor. Then he pulled the book out. The cover was still a little bit damp and edges of the pages were looking a bit crusty courtesy of Flake hitting it with her car and knocking it into the snow earlier in the day. He carefully placed it down in the bathtub. He didn't want anyone hearing him place it there, and in the hopes of making it reasonably difficult to find he pulled the shower curtain across to conceal it from the sight of any casual passer-by dropping in for a shit. It wasn't the best plan by any means, but it was a plan. If he bumped into Jessica he could pretend he'd forgotten to bring it with him and claim he had to head back to the Tapioca to get it from his safe.

As he was busy congratulating himself on coming up with a half decent plan he heard the door to the bedroom open. It seemed that someone may have found him already. He heard footsteps coming towards the bathroom door. Then the handle shook. Someone was trying to open the door from the other side.

A muffled voice called through the door. 'Who's in there?'

Sanchez panicked. 'Just a minute!' he called out to buy himself some time.

There was no sense in looking like he had anything to hide, so he crept over to the toilet and flushed it. Then he picked up his empty satchel from the floor and hung it over his shoulder again. He unlocked the door and strolled out in as calm a manner as he could in the circumstances.

Standing outside the bathroom with a fierce look on her face was the Panda Girl with the stupid black eye makeup and the baseball cap.

'All done,' said Sanchez. He waved his hand in front of his nose and added, 'I wouldn't go in there for a while if I was you.'

Panda Girl looked down at Sanchez's satchel and then back up at him. 'Your satchel's empty!' she scowled. 'Where's the book? What have you done with it?'

Forty-Four

Bull spoke on behalf of everyone. 'Oh sweet Jesus,' he whispered. 'God have mercy on us all.'

He rushed back to the window and stared down into the courtyard below. His eyes confirmed what he had seen on the monitors. Swarming into the courtyard through the large iron gates at the end of the driveway was an army of flesh hungry zombies. And there appeared to be an infinite number of them piling in from the woodland opposite the Casa de Ville.

Tex confirmed it verbally. 'Fucking zombies!' he said, staring at his bank of monitors. 'Thousands of the muthafuckers. Where the *hell* did they come from?'

'Devil's Graveyard, I'm guessing,' Bull replied.

The zombies had charged in and there was now one almighty scrap taking place in the courtyard. The vampires and werewolves were hopelessly outnumbered and the sudden onslaught had completely overwhelmed them.

Bull had seen some violence in his time. He'd been in the thick of some pretty serious war zones along with the rest of his team, but as he watched the carnage in the courtyard below, he knew he was witnessing something utterly unlike anything he'd ever encountered before. The sounds that made their way up to the window in the Control room were quite sickening. Crunching bones, ripping flesh, screaming beasts. This was not a place he really wanted to be. All he wanted was the Bourbon Kid, but since the exploding smoke bombs and arrival of thousands of zombies it was now impossible to see the serial murderer anywhere. Bull's quest for revenge was not going according to plan.

Tex remained glued to his seat staring at the bank of monitors in front of him, watching and commentating on the events as they unfolded. Razor took up his position standing guard over Beth. He had drawn a pistol from its holster by his ribcage and had it aimed at her in case she had any thoughts of escape. Of the three, he was the most on edge. This was a man that followed orders and when there were none being barked out, he got anxious.

'What are we gonna do, boss?' he asked.

'I'm trying to spot the Kid in this crowd,' said Bull craning his neck to get a better view out of the window. 'Hang on, I see something.'

'What is it?' asked Razor. 'Is it him?'

'It's a fucking car,' said Bull. 'Someone's driving right through the middle of the zombies and vampires, toward the front doors.'

'Is it the Kid?' Razor asked again.

'I can't tell.'

Tex interrupted. 'The Kid is already inside the building,' he said. 'Look!' He pointed at one of the monitors on the top row. It showed the view from a camera in one of the Casa de Ville's outer corridors.

Bull strode over to take a look. He recognised the figure on screen. 'How the hell did he get inside?'

'He must have smashed a window or something,' said Tex, flicking a few switches on his control panel. The image on screen changed as a different camera angle came into play, this one showed the Kid from behind. He was walking towards a large black door at the end of a corridor.

'Where exactly is he?' Bull asked.

'This is a corridor in the East wing,' said Tex. 'He's heading towards the reception area.'

Bull pulled his pistol from its holster and double-checked that it was fully loaded. He'd checked it less than an hour earlier and not used it since, but he needed to remind himself exactly how many bullets he had at his disposal. The bullets were still there. He tapped Tex on the shoulder. 'Come on, let's get to the main hall. There's a group of Jessica's personal bodyguards in there. We can send them down to the reception area to deal with him.'

Tex didn't look convinced. 'How many of them are there?'

'About ten, mostly werewolves I think.'

'In that case, he'll probably kill them all, right?'

Bull nodded. 'Most likely, but they'll slow him down. By the time he gets up to this floor, you and me can be concealed in the main hall, waiting for him, armed to the teeth. He won't know what hit him.'

Over by Beth, Razor still looked on edge. 'What about me?' he asked.

Bull pointed at Beth. 'You stay here with her. Keep the gun pointed at her head. And watch what's happening on the monitors. If you see me get taken down, you put a bullet through her face. Understand?'

'You got it, boss.'

Forty-Five

Kacy had been doing her best to keep the group of young girl scouts calm. In the wake of the Bourbon Kid murdering just about everyone who had been out in the streets outside the church, she was able to assure them that there wouldn't be any more vampires flying in through the windows any time soon. She had the girls all seated in the pews at the front of the church and was doing her best to give some kind of off-the-cuff sermon about how the Good Lord would spare their lives. She was making it up as she went along because in all honesty she wasn't the religious type. As she began to run out of stories to tell, the girls' attention began to waver and one of them asked a question.

'Why does the Bourbon Kid kill people?'

Kacy grimaced. This was a tough question that needed to be handled tactfully. 'Well,' she said. 'The Bourbon Kid was sent by God to protect us all. When we came to the church and begged for God's help, he sent us the Bourbon Kid, and it worked out pretty well for us all, didn't it?'

'Does that mean he's like Jesus?' one of the girls asked.

'Yes. He's exactly like Jesus,' Kacy replied.

It was a lie, of course. But it seemed to make the girls feel a lot better about their predicament. Some of them even looked like they believed her. Ever since the Kid had finished shooting up anything moving in the streets outside, things had gone pretty quiet.

Dante helped out by explaining to the girls that no harm could come to them while the Bourbon Kid was alive. He even regaled them with a tale about how he'd seen the Kid stick a shotgun up a vampire's ass once in an elevator. The girls laughed, probably because they thought he was kidding.

Vanity seemed more on edge than anyone. He was spending a lot of time on his phone, regularly texting or chatting in a far away corner of the church where no one could hear him. After one particularly long call he came back to where Dante and Kacy were. He looked worried.

'Whassup, man?' Dante asked.

'I just spoke to Moose. She says Gaius left the Casa de Ville half an hour ago. He's probably at the museum already. We're gonna have to go now if we want to catch him with his eye out. We'll have to leave the girls here.'

Kacy balked at the suggestion. 'We can't do that. They'll be all on their own. It's not safe.'

Vanity turned to Dante. 'We gotta do something. If you two are really serious about ever becoming human again then we have to go now.'

Dante puffed out his cheeks. 'He's right,' he said, rubbing Kacy's back. 'What do you wanna do, babe?'

Kacy looked at the troubled faces of the Sunflower Girls. It had taken almost an hour to calm them down. If she now announced that she was leaving them they would be in tears again pretty quickly.

'I'm staying here,' she said. 'Why don't you two go. If you can get the Eye from Gaius you can bring it back here, can't you?'

'That's not such a bad idea,' said Dante. 'You'll be safe here. If things with Gaius get ugly I wouldn't want you there anyway. Me and Vanity can go on our own. Right, Vanity?'

Vanity didn't look convinced. 'I think the three of us should go together. We'll be stronger.'

'I can't leave the girls,' said Kacy.

Vanity shrugged. 'Why don't you bring them along with us?'

'That's a shitty idea,' said Dante immediately. 'They're Sunflower Girls, not Ewoks!'

'Fine,' said Vanity. 'Just us two should go then. But we've gotta go now.'

Kacy sensed that Dante just needed some reassurance that she would be okay without him. She slipped her arm around his waist and leaned her head against his shoulder.

'Go do what you gotta do with Vanity,' she said. 'You don't need me. I'll text the Bourbon Kid and let him know what you're doing. Hopefully he'll get there and be able to help you out.'

Dante kissed her then ran his hand through her long dark hair. 'This'll be a piece of cake,' he said. 'We'll be in and out of the museum and back here before you know it.'

'You'd better be.'

Vanity interrupted their tender moment. 'Let's get moving,' he said, nodding toward the front doors.

Dante kissed Kacy on the forehead and pulled himself away. 'See you soon, babe,' he said.

Vanity started jogging down the aisle towards the front doors with Dante following on just behind. Kacy watched them go and wondered for one awful moment if she would see them again. She'd acted calm so that Dante wouldn't worry, but deep down she was terrified of what might happen to him when he confronted Gaius. She was also having suspicions about how trustworthy Vanity was. Why was he being so secretive with his phone? Had he really been talking to his friend Moose? And if so, why did he have to do it out of earshot?

As Dante was following Vanity through the door and out into the street, she called after him. 'I love you.'

Dante stopped and looked back. 'I love you too, babe.'

As he pulled the door shut behind him, Kacy made one last plea that he probably didn't hear. 'Try not to get yourself killed this time!'

Forty-Six

Bull's palms were sweating. He'd been in far more dangerous predicaments than this and remained completely calm. But this was different. He was standing in a giant hall in the Casa de Ville waiting for the conclusion to a plan he'd waited over half his life to complete: the opportunity to avenge his father's death. On a couple of previous occasions he'd come close. Two days ago he'd even sawn off a man's head only to find he and his men had been outwitted and had killed the wrong guy. This time would be different. With all the chaos and carnage going on outside there was a feeling of finality about this situation. It would all end tonight. Unfortunately at this point, the outcome was unclear. Either he would kill the Bourbon Kid, or die trying.

   He kept his stare fixed on the doors at the end of the hall. Any second now his nemesis could come storming through those doors. For that reason, he was glad to have Tex with him. Tex specialised in counterintelligence and would have every possible route into the hall etched into his mind. From the obvious selection, the doors, right through to the less obvious possibilities, like air vents, if there were any. And Tex had his own reasons for wanting to kill the Kid. He wanted to avenge the death of Silvinho.

   Bull concealed himself behind a white concrete pillar on the left hand side of the huge hall. Tex was a few yards further back, tucked out of sight behind a large unsightly statue of a centaur situated by the side of the flight of stairs that led up to the control room where Razor was guarding Beth.

   Bull kept his gun pointed at the doors. Every second felt like a minute as he waited for his enemy to arrive. He only took his eyes off the doors momentarily to glance over at Tex. Tex was checking all around him, his head constantly on the move. If anything or anyone tried sneaking up on them, he would see it. The two men's eyes met for a fleeting moment. They'd shared looks like this many times over the course of their careers. It was a look of trust and mutual respect. Bull turned his gaze back on the doors, secure in the knowledge that he had his best man with him, watching his back.

   Then in one horrible moment the whole scenario changed. The entire hall was plunged into total darkness.

   Bull analysed the situation immediately. Either the power had been cut or someone had switched off the lights from within the hall. He listened carefully. Unfortunately the only sounds were coming from far away. The undead war in the courtyard outside was not relenting. But inside the main hall, things were very different. Nothing moved. Nothing made a noise.

The lights had been off for almost thirty seconds before he finally heard something. From behind him there was a quiet slapping noise, followed by a muffled yelp. He swivelled around, the toes of his boots turning on a dime. All he could see was pitch darkness. He still knew his bearings. He knew exactly how far he was from every pillar, every statue and every wall in the hall. But was Tex still with him?

'Tex,' he whispered loudly. 'You okay?'

Tex did not respond. Bull was no fool. He knew what that meant. Tex was most likely dead. That would explain the muffled yelp. The Bourbon Kid was in the hall with them. In the darkness.

Another sound broke the deathly silence. It came from high above on the opposite side of the room. It sounded like glass breaking. Two more almost identical sounds followed moments later, from different areas of the giant hall. Bull had no choice. He had to get some lights back on. On the wall behind him there was a light switch. He just had to get to it before the Kid got to him. Drawing on much of the experience he'd picked up working behind enemy lines, he moved silently across the floor with his free hand outstretched until his fingertips touched the wall. He scoured the smooth plastered wall, hoping to find the light switch. With his other hand, he continued to point his gun out into the hall, his finger ready on the trigger, itching to fire if he heard even the faintest sound.

As soon as he felt his fingertips brush against the light switch, he flicked it on. The room lit up, the sudden brightness dazzling him for a split second. As his eyes grew accustomed to the light he scoured the room for any sign of his enemy. The first thing he saw was the body of Tex, slumped on the floor in a heap behind the statue of the centaur. His neck had been broken. It only took a millisecond for Bull to recognise that. He didn't have time to dwell on it though. His eyes continued scouring the room, moving at a million miles an hour. He could see statues, staircases, pillars and all kinds of other things in the hall. But no Bourbon Kid.

He exhaled hard, suddenly realising that he had been holding his breath for an unusually long time. As he inhaled again, a shadow flashed before his eyes.

It came from above.

And just like that, the face of the Bourbon Kid appeared right in front of him. From nowhere, suddenly the two of them were only inches apart. Before he could react, Bull's gun hand was knocked back against the wall. His nose cracked too, courtesy of a head-butt from his enemy. His skull crashed back against the wall behind him and his gun slipped from his grip as his knuckles bashed against the wall. The lightning speed of the attack dazed him and by the time he'd reacted and attempted to lunge forward into his attacker, the Bourbon Kid had a hand wrapped tightly around his throat.

Bull instinctively shaped to throw a punch into the Kid's ribs. But then he spotted a small silver crossbow pointed at him. The Kid had it in his right hand. He slowly lifted it towards Bull's face, stopping just below his nose with a silver dart aimed up his left nostril.

Bull had seen weapons of its kind before. It was a specially designed semiautomatic lightweight crossbow, the kind that made no noise when fired and could easily be concealed within a baggy sleeve. A fine weapon to have in the dark, or when trying not to make a sound.

And in the face of the man he saw before him he recognised his father's killer. The hood pulled over his face covered much of it in shadow, but he was still easily recognisable. A gravelly voice from within the hood spoke out.

'How did you get mixed up with all these vampire cunts?'

Struggling for air due to the Kid's grip on his throat, Bull only just managed to splutter out an answer. 'Given the choice between them and you, I choose vampires every time.'

The Kid nodded at the body of Tex behind him. 'And now your men are dead. Do you like the way I broke that guy's neck? Very symbolic don'tcha think?'

He eased his grip on Bull's neck, allowing him to take in a decent breath of air. After taking in a lungful Bull responded, all the while eyeing up the crossbow that was aimed up his nose. 'You're fucking scum, man. I did nothing to you,' he said wheezing. 'You're the one that killed my father. It should be me here killing you, not the other way around. I don't deserve this.'

'Stop bitching about what you deserve,' said the Kid. 'Tell me where the girl is.'

Bull glanced over at the staircase in the middle of the hall. 'She's upstairs in one of the rooms. You should hear a gunshot any minute now. As soon as my buddy in the control room sees you kill me on his monitors, he'll waste her. And he won't think twice about it. He's already punched her in the face once today.'

The Kid raised half a smile. 'You think by telling me this, I'm not gonna kill you in case your buddy sees it on a monitor,' he said.

'Yeah. You'd be a fool to kill me. He sees you kill me and she dies. Are you willing to take that risk?'

The Kid tightened his grip on Bull's neck again. 'Since I just shot down all your cameras, you bet I am.'

Bull suddenly realised what the earlier sounds of breaking glass had signified. All three of the CCTV cameras in the hall had been disabled. 'What if you missed one?' he suggested, a hint of desperation creeping into his voice.

'I never miss.'

With that remark the Kid thrust the end of his crossbow further into Bull's left nostril. He flicked the trigger. The silver dart flew out and vanished up into Bull's nose, through the back of his eye and into his brain. The sharp tip of it pierced through the top of his skull as it came to a stop, blood spurting out of the top of his head like a volcano erupting.

Before allowing Bull's dead body to fall he reached over to the light switch and flicked it off again, plunging the room back into darkness. Confident that the murder had gone unseen he released his grip on Bull's throat and allowed his dead body to slide to the floor.

Out of sight on a balcony high above, Jessica the Vampire Queen had watched on with interest. So far, everything had gone exactly the way she had expected. She had the Kid right where she wanted him. Now she would finally have her revenge for all the pain he had inflicted upon vampires she cared about. It was time to put the final part of her plan into action: executing Beth while he watched.

Forty-Seven

Dan Harker had been parked across the street from the museum for thirty minutes waiting for William Clay to call him back. He'd left three messages on Clay's cell phone and he'd also tried calling the police station numerous times. But Flake was no longer answering the switchboard. Maybe his trip to the local news station had backfired? Perhaps the vampires had gotten to the police station? Who knew? Certainly not Harker.

Thirty minutes of mulling over his options was long enough. There was nothing else for it. He was going to have to go into the museum with no back up and arrest Elijah Simmonds on suspicion of the murder of Bertram Cromwell. Arresting a murder suspect on his own wasn't part of protocol, and for good reason. It was dangerous. Especially when the suspect in question was accused of such a brutal slaying.

There wasn't a soul in sight as he stepped out of his car and trudged through the snow and up to the front doors of the museum. He rang the doorbell in the wall three times and waited for an answer. Just as he was about to give up and try to find another way in, the doors were opened by James the security guard he had met on his earlier visit.

'Hi,' said Harker. 'Mind if I come in for a minute? Wanna see Mr Simmonds about something.'

'Sure. Come on in.'

James stepped aside to let him through and then secured the doors shut behind him. 'Is it as cold out there as it looks?' he asked.

'It's as cold as I can ever remember this city being.'

'Want me to take your coat?'

'Nah, that's okay. Just tell me where I can find Mr Simmonds, please.'

'He's down in his office. Want me to walk you there?'

Harker shook his head. 'That won't be necessary.'

'Okay. I'll buzz down and let him know you're on your way.'

Harker took a step towards the corridor that led down to Simmonds's office. He hesitated a moment then turned back to the security guard. 'Actually, would you mind not calling him? I've got some good news for him and I'd like it to be a surprise.'

'Are you sure it's good news?'

'It's good news.'

'Good luck to you then, Captain.'

Harker continued on his way down the corridor to Simmonds's office. As soon as he was out of sight of the security guard he hurried up his pace. If the guard decided to ignore his request and call ahead to Simmonds, he would lose his element of surprise. As he approached the large black door at the end of the corridor and saw the bright silver lettering that read SIMMONDS he pulled his pistol from its holster by his ribcage.

He stopped outside the door and considered knocking on it, but just as his knuckles were about to rap against it, he thought better of it. He needed every ounce of surprise on his side. He reached out for the doorknob and twisted it quickly. He pushed the door and flung it as far open as he could, keeping his pistol at the ready. Directly in front of him Elijah Simmonds was sitting behind his desk in his large black leather chair, counting money. Lots of money. On the desk in front of him was a huge mountain of cash. Bundles of fifty dollar bills were stacked a foot high. He looked shocked at the sight of Harker appearing at the door.

'Captain Harker,' he spluttered. 'What can I do for you?'

Harker pointed his gun at Simmonds and stepped inside the office. 'I'm gonna have to ask you to stand up and put your hands on your head,' he said.

Simmonds raised his hands defensively, a nervous look across his face. 'Don't shoot,' he said. 'This isn't what it looks like.'

'Stand up,' Harker repeated taking another step towards the desk.

'Okay, okay,' said Simmonds. He began to slowly rise from his seat, taking great care not to make any sudden movements. Harker stared down at the bundles of cash on the desk. It was more money than he'd ever seen. 'What's with all the cash?' he asked.

Simmonds didn't respond. Instead the next sound Harker heard was that of the door slamming shut behind him. He spun around to see who or what had shut it. Stepping out from behind the door was a giant of a man in a silver suit. He had a shaved head and wore a pair of sunglasses.

'So you're Captain Dan Harker,' the man said. 'You're the smartass detective who's been on the news warning the public about the possibility of vampires taking over the city.'

'That's right. Who are you?'

'I'm Rameses Gaius, the leader of the undead army whose plans you tried to wreck.'

Harker could feel his fingers twitching on the gun. 'Well, Mr Gaius, I'm gonna have to ask you to get on your knees. You're under arrest.'

'I don't think so.'

Gaius raised his right hand. His palm began to glow a bright blue colour. A source of electrical energy seemed to be generating in the centre of his hand, and from behind his sunglasses a similar blue glow appeared around his right eye. Harker decided to take his chance and squeezed the trigger of his gun.

BANG!

The gunshot was deafening in the confined space of Simmonds's office. The bullet ripped through the chest of Rameses Gaius. But the man didn't fall. He stood there and smiled, his hand still glowing.

BANG!

Harker fired another shot into his chest. Again it seemed to have no effect on Gaius, other than to broaden his smile.

'My turn,' Gaius sneered.

Harker's eyes bulged with fear as he saw the blue light in Gaius's hand generate into a sphere the size of a bowling ball. With one flick of his wrist Gaius then unleashed a blue laser bolt from his hand. It struck Harker in the chest, lifting him off his feet and sending him crashing back into the wall behind him, The wall was made up of shelves of books and the impact of him crashing into them caused a bundle of them to topple from the higher shelves down on to his head.

Feeling dazed and severely stunned by the blow, Harker fought to regain his breath. His lungs felt like they had collapsed and his eyesight had temporarily failed him. He tried blinking furiously in the hope of clearing his vision and seeing what might be coming his way next. His gun had slipped from his grip and he scrambled around on the floor with his right hand hoping to relocate it.

As his eyesight slowly returned, the face of Elijah Simmonds appeared above him. The museum's new manager had a smirk on his face. He had picked up Harker's gun and was now waving it in his face, taunting him with it. Where Simmonds had looked terrified only moments earlier, now he looked smug and dangerous. 'Looking for this?' he asked, grinning.

Harker opened his mouth to answer, his lungs sucking in a huge gulp of air as he did so. Simmonds seized his opportunity and was upon him in an instant. He grabbed Harker around the throat and thrust the barrel of the gun into his mouth.

'Not so tough now, are you, Captain?' he jeered.

Harker stared back up at him with pleading eyes, hoping and praying that Simmonds wouldn't have the guts to pull the trigger. In spite of the gun in his mouth he managed to splutter out a barely audible *"please don't"*. The plea fell on deaf ears. Simmonds squeezed the trigger on the gun and blew his brains out.

Forty-Eight

Since Dante and Vanity had departed for the museum, Kacy had found it tough going sitting with the girl scouts. Her biggest problem was that her vampire instincts were hard to control. Each of the girls was beginning to look like an ideal snack, and Kacy was feeling hungrier with every passing moment.

One of the girls, a tiny little thing with long dark pigtails protruding from underneath her blue pom pom hat, had gone to find a toilet. Kacy remained with the others and tried to keep them entertained with a game of charades. Lucy, the head Sunflower Girl with the blond pigtails, was acting out the name of a film. Kacy sat in amongst the rest of the girls on the front pews, encouraging them to guess the answer. For the past five minutes they had been stuck on a film title and only had the words *Butch* something *and the Sundance Kid.* The girls couldn't get the missing word from the actions Lucy was performing. Kacy wanted to just shout out *"It's Cassidy for fuck's sake!"* but the girls' determination to work out the answer for themselves was keeping them occupied and therefore taking their minds off all the horrible things they had seen earlier.

Then came another problem. Veronica, the girl who had gone to the bathroom, returned with a concerned look on her face. She was hopping around from foot to foot too, suggesting she hadn't actually managed to use the bathroom yet.

'What's up, honey?' Kacy asked her.

'There's a man in the toilet,' Veronica replied. 'He's locked himself in and won't come out.'

'What?' Kacy stood up and walked over to her. She placed her hands on the girl's shoulders and looked her in the eye. 'Did he say who he was?'

Veronica shook her head. 'No.'

'Okay, wait here. I'll be back in a minute.'

Kacy headed off in the direction Veronica had come from. It was the area Vanity had dashed off to earlier when he was supposedly securing any doors and windows to prevent anyone from getting into the church. The door marked "Toilet" was on the right. She walked over to it, glancing back at the girls to give them a reassuring smile. They were all now ducked down between the pews peering over them.

Kacy knocked on the toilet door. 'Is there someone in there?' she asked.

A man's voice replied. 'Who's that?'

'My name is Kacy. Who are you?'

'I'm the priest, Father Papshmir.'

'Why are you locked in the toilet then?'

'I locked myself in here when the vampires came in. Have they gone?'

'Yes, they're all dead.'

'Are you sure?'

'Positive. It's just me and a group of Sunflower Girls here now.'

'Has Vanity gone?'

Kacy frowned. 'How do you know Vanity?'

'Has he gone?'

'Yeah, he's gone.'

She heard the sound of the toilet door unlocking. The door opened inwards and the face of an elderly priest peered around it. 'Thank God for that,' he said.

'Hi,' said Kacy stepping back to allow him to come out. 'I could sure use your help out here. I've got some terrified little girls. They could use some guidance from God right now.'

The priest stared hard at her. 'Are you a vampire?' he asked.

Kacy felt herself blush. He'd obviously rumbled her and with him being a priest and all, he might have a crucifix on him, so she figured it was best not to lie in case he decided to use it. 'Yes, but I won't hurt anyone. My boyfriend Dante has gone with Vanity to find a cure to make us back into humans again.'

Papshmir stepped out and closed the toilet door behind him. He was dressed in his official black church robe as if ready to give a sermon. He looked Kacy up and down. 'Well, *you* look harmless enough,' he said. 'But I can't believe for one minute that Vanity would want to quit being a vampire.'

'How do you know him?' Kacy asked again, curious as to how a man of the cloth could be so clued in to the local vampire scene.

'How do I know Vanity?' Papshmir almost laughed. 'Fuck me, that cunt,' he looked up to the heavens and added a quick *"Forgive me, Lord,"* under his breath before continuing. 'He's been married in this church by me on no less than six occasions. He's a serial bride killer. As well as a total cunt. *Forgive me, Lord.*'

Kacy was shocked at the revelation Vanity had been married so many times (and also at the fact the priest had used the word cunt). 'I saw his wedding video this afternoon,' she said. 'With his wife Emma. He really loved her.'

Papshmir scoffed. 'Did you see the film of the wedding reception?'

'No, just a minute or so of the ceremony. I didn't notice if you were the priest marrying them though.'

'Well I was,' said Papshmir. 'And if I remember correctly, Emma was wife number five.'

'He really loved her though didn't he? I could tell by the way he was looking at her in the video.'

'Oh yeah. He loved her all right. He loved her so much that him and his vampire buddies killed her and her entire family and friends at the reception.'

'What?'

'That's the reason he gets married all the time. He comes in here at least once a year and threatens to kill me and my entire flock if I don't perform a marriage ceremony for him and whoever he's decided to slaughter at his next big wedding function.'

Kacy swallowed hard. Vanity had lied to her. If his wife Emma was dead, killed by him, then he would have no desire to become human again and return to her. If he'd lied about that then there was a very good chance he'd also lied about Gaius taking his eye to the museum for cleaning. Dante was most likely heading into a trap.

She grabbed Papshmir by the arm. 'Can you look after the girls out there for me? I've got to go after my boyfriend. He could be in trouble.'

'Sure thing,' said Papshmir. 'I've been listening to them playing charades for the last half hour. I'll just carry that on. You go do what you have to do.'

'Thanks.'

Papshmir walked off to the main hall where the children were peering out over the tops of the pews. Kacy grabbed her phone and began frantically sending a text to Dante, warning him that he could be in danger and urging him to get away from Vanity and call her as soon as possible. She considered calling him, but decided a text would be more discreet. As she was doing it she heard Papshmir addressing the Sunflower Girls.

'Right then girls,' he bellowed. 'It's Butch *fucking Cassidy* for fuck's sake!'

There was a chorus of "Ohhhh" from the girls. Then Papshmir spoke again, much quieter this time. 'What's that smell?' he asked.

One of the girls spoke up in response. 'Veronica just shit her pants.'

'Where?'

'In your confessional box.'

'Holy shit. Not again!'

Kacy hit send on her text and thought hard about what to do. Drastic action was required. A text to the Bourbon Kid might be a good idea too, she decided. But with Dante possibly in grave danger and the confessional box in the church filled with shit, she decided her best option would be to get out of the church and head to the museum as quickly as possible.

Forty-Nine

Normally the museum would be closed by five o'clock. And in light of all of the murdering going on in the city it made more sense than ever for the place to be shut. But as Dante and Vanity walked up the steps at the front of the building Dante was surprised to find the front doors were wide open.

'That's kind of odd, don't you think?' he remarked.

'I'd say it's a stroke of luck, personally,' said Vanity coolly.

'You'd think that security would have the place locked up though, right? I mean when I worked here the place closed on time every day. They were hot on that kind of thing.'

'It's under new management though isn't it?'

'I guess so. Rotten news about Professor Cromwell getting killed. I really liked him. I never quite got around to apologising to him for calling him a cunt last time I saw him either.'

'You called the Professor a cunt?'

'Yeah. In my defence, though, he had just stabbed me.'

Vanity looked somewhat perplexed. 'I'd have done more than just call him a cunt.'

Dante reached the front doors and peered around them. The reception hall was empty. 'I don't like the look of this,' he said. 'Something's not right.'

Vanity strolled confidently past him into the reception area. 'Don't be such a wuss. This is a good omen,' he said. 'All we've gotta do is find Gaius and we're home. This couldn't have worked out better.'

Dante frowned. 'I'm no genius, but this looks a bit fucking suspect to me. Don't you think this whole thing is a bit odd? I mean, what if Gaius knows we're coming? We could be walking into a trap.'

Vanity smiled. 'You're right about one thing.'

'What's that?'

'You're no genius.'

'Thanks. You're hardly Alfred Einstein yourself.'

'Albert.'

'Huh?'

Vanity shook his head. 'Look man, you're just being paranoid. Come on, let's try downstairs and see if he's around. We should hurry. Don't want to miss our chance.'

Vanity seemed very keen to get down to the main hall. Now Dante was relatively aware of the fact that most people thought he was a moron. Kacy frequently warned him about rushing headlong into trouble. And his gut instincts were telling him this was trouble. Why on earth should he trust Vanity? Kacy had been convinced by his story about wanting to be human again because she'd seen his wedding video. Dante hadn't seen it. All he'd ever seen was that Vanity liked killing people and drinking their blood. And he could kick a clown's ass as well as anyone. But Dante hadn't really seen any signs of remorse from him. He seemed to love being a vampire. Some clarification was required.

'Vanity.'

'Come on man,' Vanity said, once more waving him along to the corridor at the end of the reception area.

'Are you on the level here?'

'What?'

'Are you setting me up?'

Vanity looked puzzled. 'What do you mean?'

'I mean, I smell a rat. I really don't see you desperately wanting to be human again. What I do see is you leading me into a meeting with Gaius. And let me get this straight, you're telling me he comes here to have his eye cleaned?'

'Polished.'

Dante took stock of what was being said for a moment. Kacy had been so excited about this opportunity to get their hands on the Eye that he had allowed himself to get caught up in it all without really thinking it through.

'Surely he can polish his own eye. Jeez, it's gotta be like wiping the lenses on your glasses, surely. He could polish it with a fucking handkerchief, for fuck's sake.'

Vanity frowned. 'Are you calling me a shit?'

'No. I'm just saying that something's not right here. This doesn't add up.'

Vanity walked aggressively towards him. 'You're calling me a shit. You're accusing me of setting you up! After all I've fucking done for you. You muthafucker!'

Dante responded to the aggression the best way he knew—by responding in kind. He stormed towards Vanity and the pair of them stopped inches apart, staring one another down.

'I *am* calling you a shit,' Dante retorted. 'What the fuck is going on here? Are you my fucking friend or what? Because right now I've got this feeling like you're Rameses Gaius's bitch and you're using me to get in his good books.'

There was an awkward silence as he waited for Vanity to reply. The two of them stared at each other fiercely for a few seconds until quite by surprise, Vanity's face broke out into a huge beaming smile. He laughed heartily and slapped Dante on the shoulder.

'Haha, good one,' he said. 'You almost had me then. I thought you were serious for a second there. Come on. The time for joking around is over. We've gotta go pick a fight with a mummy before it's too late.'

He slapped Dante on the shoulder again and then bounded back to the corridor at the back of the reception area. Dante couldn't work out what to make of it. Vanity seemed to think he was kidding when he accused him of double crossing him. But he hadn't been kidding. He started following on after his laughing buddy, unsure of whether or not he was making a terrible mistake.

As he reached the corridor he felt his phone vibrate in his pocket. Someone had sent him a text message. He pulled his phone out of his pocket and flicked to the message. It was from Kacy. It read –

VANITY LIED. GET AWAY FROM HIM. I THINK IT'S A SETUP! CALL ME!

He read the message twice to make sure he wasn't misunderstanding it. He'd been right. Vanity *was* a shit. And a bit of a cunt for that matter. He stopped walking and looked up to see Vanity striding along the corridor up ahead with his back to him. He had a chance to turn and run before Vanity noticed. He slipped his phone back in his pocket and turned back to the museum's front entrance.

As he turned he heard the sound of the front doors being slammed shut. His eyes confirmed it. Standing in front of the now closed doors in his shiny silver suit was Rameses Gaius. And his precious blue stone was still lodged firmly in his right eye socket.

'Mr Vittori,' he said stepping forward. 'We meet again.'

'Pardon?' said Dante, pretending not to have heard him.

Gaius looked irritated. 'I said, Mr Vittori, we meet again.'

'Sorry, I still can't hear ya,' said Dante, his eyes desperately searching for an escape route as Gaius walked towards him.

'I said, we meet again!' Gaius raised his voice, almost shouting.

'What?'

Gaius stopped in the middle of the reception area, approximately ten metres away from Dante. 'Let me put it another way,' he said.

The giant mummy raised his right arm. In the palm of his hand was a bright blue glowing light. Dante stared at it, unable to work out what it was. It was unlike anything he'd ever seen. Suddenly Gaius jolted his arm and the blue glow formed into a laser bolt. It flew from his palm straight at Dante. It blasted into his chest. The sheer force of it lifted him off his feet and he flew backwards through the air until his head crashed into a wall behind him with a sickening crack. Everything went black and as he drifted into a state of unconsciousness and slumped to the floor, Dante hoped Kacy wouldn't come looking for him without the Bourbon Kid.

Vanity dashed back to the reception area to find Gaius standing over the collapsed, unconscious figure of Dante. The Lord of the Undead looked mighty pleased with himself, which meant that he was most likely pleased with Vanity too.

'Too easy, huh boss?' Vanity said, grinning.

Gaius grinned back at him. 'There's nothing as simple as defeating the gullible, is there?'

'Uh, yeah. So what's next? You still need me?'

Gaius glanced over Vanity's shoulder. 'No,' he said coldly. 'We've no further need for you.'

Vanity didn't like Gaius's tone. He spun around to see what it was that his boss was looking at behind him. Four vampires from the Black Plague were approaching him from behind. He turned back to Gaius.

'I thought we had a deal,' he said, failing to mask the concern in his voice.

Gaius raised his right hand. His palm was glowing blue. "I don't make deals with people who double cross their friends,' he said.

'Oh shit.'

Fifty

Beth could feel Razor's gun pressed into the base of her spine. In front of her she could see the outline of Jessica. The Vampire Queen was leading the way into the darkened main hall.

By the time they had reached the top of the staircase Beth's eyes had gradually become accustomed to the dark. She was able to make out the shapes of several statues and pillars in the hall below. There was no sign of JD, but she knew he must be near. As if reading her thoughts, Jessica spoke aloud.

'He's down here. I can smell the bourbon on his breath.' Raising her voice she called out into the darkness. 'Show yourself! You can't hide from me in the dark.'

What followed was the sound of a door opening at the far end of the hall, quite some distance away. Beth made out the sound of some muffled voices and then suddenly all of the lights in the hall came on at once, lighting up everything brightly. Her eyes darted around her surroundings, looking for JD. All she saw at the end of the room was Sanchez the bartender being shoved in the back towards the centre of the room by one of the Panda vampires. It was a female wearing an all black outfit, with the exception of the red baseball cap on her head. Under her left arm she was carrying a large black hardback book.

Jessica called out to her. 'Is that The Book of Death you've got there?'

Panda Girl nodded. 'Yeah. This guy brought it with him.'

Jessica reached the bottom of the stairs and stepped onto the marble floor. She hissed at Sanchez. 'So, you found my book. How good of you, Sanchez.'

Sanchez shrugged. 'Well, it was nothing really. Perhaps you could just give me the reward and I'll be on my way?'

'Why the rush?' Jessica asked, a mischievous grin breaking out on her face. 'Why don't you stay a while? We're having a party. Your friend the Bourbon Kid is here too. He's about to show himself to us any second now.'

Sanchez didn't look too keen to take her up on the invite. 'It's okay. I've got places to be,' he said, turning back towards the door through which he had come. Panda Girl wasn't letting him get away that easy. She grabbed his arm and yanked him back. Then she shoved him hard, back toward the middle of the hall.

Jessica walked towards him, looking all around her, no doubt waiting for the reappearance of the Kid. Razor pressed his gun harder into Beth's back and then gave her a push to indicate that she should follow Jessica.

Panda Girl shoved Sanchez again, a little more ferociously this time. She nodded at Jessica. 'He wasn't planning on giving you the book at all,' she said. 'He found out you were a vampire and had a change of heart. When I found him he was cowering in a bathroom and trying to hide the book.'

'That sounds like typical Sanchez all right,' said Jessica scornfully. 'We'll deal with him later. For now I think it may be time to call out our mystery guest.' She stared all around the hall, looking once more for sign of the Kid, then she called out loud. 'Very well then. Razor, *kill the girl.*'

Beth felt a lump in her throat. Razor's gun had been pressed against the small of her back but the pressure was relieved as he pulled it away. Although he was behind her, she could see his arm moving out of the corner of her eye. He was about to shoot her in the head. She closed her eyes and waited for the moment of truth. Would JD make his move and reveal himself before Razor pulled the trigger?

She heard the safety click on the gun as Razor released it, ready to fire.

'WAIT!' A gravelly voice called out from behind them.

Beth looked over her shoulder. Razor too, twisted around pointing his gun in the direction of where the voice had come from. Stepping out from within the shadows of one of the many statues in the hall was the Bourbon Kid, his long dark robe identifying him to everyone, the hood pulled up over his head.

Razor pointed his pistol at him.

The Kid raised his hands in surrender. 'Hey, don't shoot,' he said calmly. 'I came here to make a deal.'

Jessica swiftly appeared at Beth's side, her lightning dexterity making it seem as though she had appeared out of thin air. This bitch was quick.

'Drop your weapons!' she hissed at the Kid.

The Kid ignored her and pointed at Razor. 'Put your gun down,' he said.

Razor had plans of his own. His three best friends had all perished at the hands of the Kid so he wasn't about to pass up the opportunity for some payback. 'No fucking way,' he grumbled. Then without waiting for permission from anyone he squeezed the trigger on his gun. The loud bang that followed was deafening. Beth covered her ears and winced.

JD had ducked out of the way of the bullet before it was even fired. His response to the attack was emphatic. As he rolled to one side he aimed his right arm in Beth's direction. A silver dart flew out of his sleeve. Before she had a chance to move the dart flashed past her hip. It missed her by less than an inch and embedded itself into Razor's crotch. He doubled over and slumped to the ground howling in agony clasping at the dart.

From behind her, Beth heard Sanchez sum up the events in one overstated sentence.

'*SHIIIIT!* He just shot that guy in the dick!' the bartender exclaimed.

Realising that she was suddenly free of Razor's grasp, Beth turned to flee. She had no idea where she was intending to run to, but anywhere away from Jessica was a start. Unfortunately Jessica was fully expecting such a move. She stepped in behind Beth and grabbed her by the hair, yanking her head back. A moment later Beth felt the Vampire Queen's razor sharp fingernails pressed against her throat.

'That was a mistake!' Jessica hissed at the Kid.

The Kid stood up and spoke calmly. 'Let her go. This is between you and me. Leave her out of it.'

'Drop that fucking crossbow you've got up your sleeve!' Jessica demanded.

'Fine.'

The Kid lowered his arms. From the right sleeve of his coat he dropped a miniature silver crossbow to the floor. It clattered against the hard marble and bounced away from him.

'Got any other weapons?' Jessica asked. 'Because now's the time to drop them.'

The Kid opened his coat. Underneath it he wore a simple black T-shirt and black combat trousers. 'I have nothing else. Now let her go.'

'Take off your coat and get on your knees,' said Jessica.

'You'll let Beth go?'

'Get on your knees.'

The Kid took off his coat and tossed it onto the floor. But instead of dropping to his knees he made a swift movement with his right arm. He reached back and whipped out a gun that had been strapped across his back. He pointed it at Jessica's head, its red laser sighter aimed at the centre of her face. Jessica was lightning quick though. As the Kid was about to squeeze the trigger she yanked Beth's head into the line of fire. For several seconds the Kid continued to re-aim the gun at Jessica. Each time he did she moved a part of Beth into the line of the red sighter.

Behind her, Beth heard Razor groaning. It distracted the Kid momentarily too. He took his eye off Jessica, pointed his gun at Razor and fired off a shot.

BANG!

Although Beth didn't see what happened, she heard the unpleasant sound of blood splattering against the marble floor. And then the red laser was aimed back at Jessica again and the ritualistic dance began once more. The Kid tried in vain to line up a clean shot at the Vampire Queen who was revelling in the challenge.

After numerous failed attempts to line up a clear shot, he gave up trying. It was obvious that she was too quick. Firing a shot would be far too risky. He stopped re-aiming the gun and lowered it to his side.

'You've got no intention of letting her go, have you?' he said.

Jessica smiled. 'I want you to watch this,' she said. 'I'm going to make your darling Beth into a vampire. She's going to be my new bitch. And you can be her first victim, unless you choose to kill her of course. You know, like you did with your mother?'

'And like I did with Archie Somers. Shoulda heard him scream. What a bitch.'

Beth felt Jessica's grip on her throat tighten. The claws on the end of her fingers were on the verge of drawing blood. 'I'm going to enjoy this,' she hissed.

The Kid seemed unfazed. 'I knew it would come to this. Quit stalling and do it now. What are you waiting for?'

'Very well. As you wish!'

Jessica opened her mouth wide, revealing a set of huge vampire fangs, thirsty for blood. Beth looked over at JD, her eyes pleading with him to save her. And that was when it finally hit her. This was not JD who had come to her rescue. This was the Bourbon Kid, the man who cared for no one.

As that thought raced through Beth's head, Jessica's fangs ripped through the skin on the lower part of her neck, plunging deep into her flesh.

Fifty-One

Flake looked into the eyes of the Bourbon Kid and watched him raise his gun again and aim it at the centre of her face. 'Close your eyes,' he growled.

'Why?'

'Because this is gonna sting.'

She did as instructed and closed her eyes. Maybe he was kidding around?

BANG!

Maybe not.

He'd fired the gun all right, just as she had expected he would. But she was still alive. At least, it felt like she was still alive. Somewhere behind her, near the elevators at the back of the reception area she heard a body slump to the ground. The Kid had killed someone, but she had no idea who. Maybe the next bullet would be for her? She winced, readying herself for what was to follow.

And she waited.

Was the Kid deriving some sick pleasure from prolonging the agonising wait? After what felt like an eternity but was most likely about five seconds, she heard another sound. A rattling noise. It was a familiar sound to Flake. She recognised it immediately. The rattling lasted three or four seconds then stopped. It was followed by a hissing sound, coupled with something splashing on to her eyelids and across the bridge of her nose. What sick twisted shit was this guy pulling? Much of the upper half of her face from the tip of her nose, up to just above her eyes felt the impact of the spray. This renowned psychopath, the Bourbon Kid was spraying her face with the can of black spray paint she had left on her desk.

When the spraying came to an end and she heard him place the can back down on the desk, she squeaked out a question from the corner of her mouth. 'What are you doing?' she asked.

'I'm making you look like a vampire,' came the reply.

She opened her eyes and blinked a few times.

'Keep your eyes shut,' said the Kid.

She snapped them shut again, closing them tightly. The paint had a strong vapour that had stung her eyes when she opened them.

'Is this some kind of sick game?' she asked.

'You wanted to help your friend Sanchez, right?'

'Yes.'

'Well, if you wanna get into the Casa de Ville, you're gonna need to look like a vampire. There's a clan called the Pandas. They paint part of their faces black. You can pass off as one of them.'

Keeping her eyes closed, Flake grimaced. 'Surely there's a better way of doing this than using spray paint?' she reasoned.

'It's short notice,' said the Kid. 'It was either this or I punch you in both eyes.'

'This is good.'

Flake heard the Kid shuffling around for a while before she suddenly felt him grab her left arm. He began rolling up the sleeve on her shirt. Feeling relatively confident that he no longer planned to kill her, she pulled her arm away. 'What are you doing?' she asked.

'I'm going to inject you with a serum. It lowers your blood temperature so you can walk undetected amongst the undead. You'll have a free run of the Casa de Ville.'

Flake wasn't a fan of injections. 'Oh,' she sighed. 'Is it absolutely necessary? My doctor always struggles to find a vein when giving me injections and my arms bruise easily.'

'Open your eyes.'

She opened her eyes slowly, blinking a few times to make sure it didn't sting too much. The Kid's face was in front of hers. He was holding a long syringe in his right hand and he had a serious look on his face.

'This is necessary,' he said. 'Otherwise the vampires will spot you for a phoney straight away. And they'll eat you alive.'

Flake pulled a face like a sulky teenager. 'Seriously, my arms bruise easily. There's got to be another way to do this?' she groaned.

'There is,' said the Kid. 'Pull your pants down, bend over the desk and I'll stick it in your ass.'

Flake could see from the expression on his face that he wasn't kidding. She rolled the sleeve up a little further on her left arm. 'Just below the elbow is probably good,' she said.

As the Kid squeezed her arm, looking for the best spot to inject her with the serum, Flake readied herself for the inevitable pain and bruising that would follow once he stuck the needle in. Glancing over her shoulder so that she didn't have to see the needle as it penetrated her skin, she saw the dead body of William Clay. He was spread-eagled on the floor by the elevator behind her, lying in a pool of his own blood. The blood was seeping out from a gaping head wound. Clay had obviously walked in at the wrong time. He had been the poor sucker on the receiving end of the gunshot she had heard while her eyes were closed. In the grand scheme of things, she now considered two black eyes and a bruised arm from the Bourbon Kid wasn't so bad after all. In fact some might say she'd gotten off lightly.

Fifty-Two

The drive to the Casa de Ville wasn't exactly a fun road trip. Flake sat in the passenger seat, thankful that she was still alive. The Bourbon Kid was in the driver seat of the black Ford Mustang, which Flake figured was most likely stolen. He kept his dark hood pulled up over his head, concealing his face all through the journey as he explained in curt detail exactly why they were going there and what he expected from her when they arrived. She nodded in agreement mostly, and added the occasional *"Okay"*. The rest of the journey was filled with uncomfortable silences during which she regularly checked out her reflection in the mirror on the back of the sun visor on the passenger side. She sure did look weird with the black paint across her face.

Eventually the Kid pulled over at the side of the road not too far from the entrance to the huge Casa de Ville. He turned off the engine and turned to Flake. 'You okay?' he asked.

'I think so.'

Before she could add anything else her cell phone rang.

'Turn that off.' the Kid ordered.

Flake fumbled around in her trouser pocket for the phone. She pulled it out and took a quick look at the screen. 'It's Sanchez calling,' she said.

'I don't care. Turn it off.'

'But he might…'

'Turn it off.'

The phone stopped ringing and the call went to voicemail. Without waiting to listen to the message she turned the phone off and slipped it back into her pocket.

'Right,' said the Kid, tapping the steering wheel. 'The key's in the ignition. Once you see the gates open, wait for the zombies to swarm in, then drive through the gates and up to the front entrance.'

'Where exactly *are* all these zombies?'

'They'll show themselves the minute the gates open. They're waiting in the woods on the other side of the road. When you get to the front of the building, get out of the car and make sure you've got that book in your hands. That's all you've got to fight the vampires off with.'

'And how do I get into the building once I'm there?'

'Ring the doorbell.'

'What about you? Where will you be?'

'I'll be where I need to be.'

'What if you get killed? How will I know what to do?'

The Kid let out a deep sigh. 'Me, get killed? Really? Worry about yourself. When you drive up to the entrance, don't stop for anything. If a vampire or a zombie or anything else gets in your way, mow that fucker down!'

'I can do that,' said Flake with a degree more confidence. Her driving skills were decent and she wasn't afraid to put her foot down on the accelerator when necessary.

The Kid opened his car door and stepped out. 'Good luck,' he said. 'I'll see you on the other side.'

'Good luck to you too!' Flake called out. He had already slammed the door shut by the time she'd finished speaking so chances were he hadn't heard her.

He vanished off into the shadows and Flake manoeuvred herself over to the driver's side of the car. The Book With No Name had been resting by her feet on the passenger side. She leaned over and picked it up. She laid it down on the seat beside her she considered her predicament. She was about to drive into a war between several thousand vampires, werewolves and zombies, and God knows what else, and she was doing it with nothing more than a book, some face paint and a Ford Mustang. *"I must be insane,"* she thought to herself. *"But Sanchez is inside there somewhere."*

Just as the Kid had predicted, the large iron gates at the front of the estate began to open. A series of lights then came on within the grounds of the Casa de Ville. The whole place lit up brightly. And within a second of the lights coming on, she saw the arrival of the zombies. On the opposite side of the road, which was made up of thick woodland, they suddenly began swarming out from the trees.

In their thousands.

She checked that all the doors were locked on the car and watched in disbelief as hordes of the grotesque creatures lurched past her and through the gates up ahead. Their arrival in the courtyard caused havoc, just as the Kid had predicted. Screams and howls began ringing out from within the walls of the estate as the battle commenced.

When eventually most of the zombies had made their way through the gates, she started up the engine on the car.

'Here goes nothin',' she whispered.

She slammed her foot down on the accelerator and stormed towards the front gates, knocking aside some of the zombie stragglers on the way. One or two bounced up onto the hood of the car and flew over the top. By the time she'd steered through the gates and started haring up the driveway, Flake was having the time of her life. Mowing down pedestrians for fun was the kind of thing most people only ever got to do in video games. This was the same thing, but with real life victims, only this was perfectly legal and morally right too.

When she reached the huge mansion at the end of the driveway, she slammed on the brakes. A werewolf who had been clinging onto the roof of the car went flying off and into a bush at the side of the entrance. There was a loud thud as his head smashed into the wall behind the bush.

She had no time to lose reflecting on what was going on around her though, so she turned off the engine and pulled out the ignition key. She grabbed the book from the passenger seat and opened the door to get out. There were a number of vampires near the entrance, mostly dressed in black. They were backing away from the army of zombies, most of whom hadn't made it this far down the drive. As Flake stepped out of the car, the noise of the on-going battle was brutal. Horrific high-pitched screams from vampires, howling wolves and groaning zombies filled the air, punctuated by the sound of snapping limbs and teeth crunching into flesh. Clutching The Book With No Name tightly to her chest, she kicked the car door shut and raced up the steps at the front of the building. No one seemed to pay her much attention. Hardly surprising considering self-preservation was probably top of everyone else's agenda. Plus of course she looked like a vampire and she'd been injected (in the arm, thank you very much) with the cooling serum. She reached the top step and pressed the doorbell in the wall. Instead of a ringing sound, the song Saturday Night by Whigfield began blaring out from inside the building. Hardly the most appropriate doorbell chime, but Flake had more important things to worry about. She turned her back on the door to make sure nothing was creeping up on her as she waited for someone to let her in.

Spotlights from above her shone down on the fighting undead masses in the courtyard. Blood was spraying in all directions. Arms and legs were being ripped off. There were quite a few casualties from her driving too. Someone's leg was still on the roof of the Mustang. As she winced at the horrors going on in front of her, she heard the door open behind her. She turned around, hoping to see someone wave her in. Standing in the doorway was a woman with the same kind of look as her. It was one of the Panda vampires. She was wearing a red baseball cap and an all black outfit. She pulled the door completely open and stared at Flake, frowning.

'Who the fuck are you?' she asked.
'One of you,' Flake replied nervously.

'No way,' Panda Girl replied. 'I know all the Pandas. You ain't one of them. And why are you dressed as a cop?'

'I'm new,' Flake said attempting to step inside, keeping the book clutched tightly against her chest. 'And I just killed a cop to get this uniform.'

Panda Girl shook her head. 'You're not coming in,' she hissed.

Flake was about to attempt barging her way in when just in the nick of time, she saw a figure appear behind Panda Girl. It was the Bourbon Kid. He grabbed the unsuspecting vampire. One of his hands slid around her waist, the other around her neck. He dragged her back from the door and in one swift movement snapped her head to one side, breaking her neck with a loud crack.

Flake dashed inside the door and slammed it shut behind her. With the sound of the carnage outside closed out, all that could be heard now was the irritating singing of Whigfield. Flake turned back to the Bourbon Kid. He had dragged the body of the Panda Girl back to a door at the far end of the reception area. He kicked the door open and backed through it.

'Through here,' he called to Flake.

She hurried over and followed him through into a large dining room. He chucked the body of the Panda Girl onto the floor by a set of tables and chairs. Flake closed the door shut behind them again. No one had seen them. At least, she hoped no one had.

'What now?' she asked.

'Take your clothes off,' said the Kid.

'What?'

'Get your clothes off.'

'Are you just obsessed with seeing my ass?'

'Get your clothes off,' he repeated. He pointed at the dead Panda on the floor. 'Put hers on. You need to look like her.'

'Oh right,' said Flake. 'Sorry.'

'I'll see you upstairs when you're done. Don't be too long.'

'How will I know where to find you?'

'I'll kill everyone I see on my way there. You can follow the trail of dead bodies.'

With that, the Kid headed over to a door at the far end of the room and disappeared through it.

Flake placed The Book With No Name down on the floor and began stripping the clothes off of the dead Panda. Then she pulled her own clothes off in a hurry, hoping not to be interrupted by any fleeing vampires that might pass through.

The vampire's clothes fitted her almost perfectly. She slipped on the red baseball cap and tucked her hair back underneath it as the vampire had done. Did she look convincing though? She really wasn't sure how she looked, which made her a little nervous. She needed to check out how she looked, but she had to make her way up to the main hall as the Bourbon Kid had instructed.

She picked up The Book With No Name and hurried out of the room through the door that the Bourbon Kid had disappeared through. The long narrow corridor outside had at least ten doors on either side. She grabbed the handle on the first door on the right. It opened easily enough. She just hoped that there was a mirror inside and not a gang of vampires.

She peered around the door. It was a fairly small bedroom. In the corner was a door, most likely for a bathroom. There was no sign of a mirror in the bedroom so the bathroom would be her best bet, if indeed vampires had mirrors in their homes. She tossed The Book With No Name onto the bed in the middle of the room and hurried over to the door. She tried the handle. It was locked. Someone must be inside. Sanchez possibly?

The sound of a toilet flushing inside confirmed that it was a bathroom. Flake backed away from the door, unsure what she was about to be confronted by. She reminded herself that she looked like a vampire (hopefully), so she had nothing to fear.

'Who's in there?' she called out tentatively.

A few seconds passed before the bathroom door opened and Sanchez strolled out nonchalantly.

'All done,' he said. Flake stared amazed at him. He seemed so casual. Before she could speak he began waving his hand in front of his nose. 'I wouldn't go in there for a while if I was you,' he added.

Flake was relieved to see him alive, but noticed that the satchel he was carrying over his shoulder looked empty. Had he given Jessica The Book of Death already?

'Your satchel's empty!' she gasped. 'Where's the book? What have you done with it?'

Sanchez stared hard at her, a look of puzzlement on his face. 'Flake? Is that you?'

'Yeah.'

'Are you a vampire?'

'No, numbnuts. I've come here to save your ass!'

Sanchez frowned. 'Oh, wow. Thanks.' He pointed into the bathroom. 'The Book of Death is in there,' he said. Glancing over her shoulder, he spotted the identical looking black book on the bed. 'What's that book then?' he asked.

Flake grabbed him by the hand. 'We've got to go help the Bourbon Kid,' she said, picking up The Book With No Name in her other hand. 'Come on, I'll explain on the way.'

Sanchez held back. 'Can't you explain here?'

Fifty-Three

Sanchez followed Flake back out into the corridor. Although he was extremely keen to go home, or even lock himself back in the bathroom, he had a feeling he'd be better off with Flake. Before leaving the bedroom, she had briefly explained her plan to him, a plan she claimed to have concocted with the Bourbon Kid who she said was "an all right guy" in spite of the fact he had shot William Clay in the face when he had dropped by the police station. Sanchez listened intently until she had finished explaining the plan and his part in it. He mulled it over for a while before voicing his thoughts.

'It's a shitty plan,' he declared as he hurried along the corridor behind her. She stepped over the decaying corpse of a recently murdered clown and then turned back to face him.

'You got a better one?' she snapped.

'Yeah. Let's get the fuck out of here!'

Flake stepped back over the clown and slapped Sanchez across the face. Quite hard too. Rather uncalled for, in his opinion.

'Man up, Sanchez, for goodness' sake,' she barked. 'We've got a chance to kill Jessica. She's a vampire and by the sounds of it, she's the worst one of all. If we can play a part in helping the Bourbon Kid to kill her then I think it would be pretty silly not to.'

'Kind of dangerous, though, isn't it?' said Sanchez. 'Job for the police, I figure.'

'We *are* the police, you idiot!'

'Damn.'

Flake headed back down the corridor again. 'Come on, hurry up,' she called back. 'You're either coming with me, or you can take your chances with the thousands of vampires and zombies outside.'

She had a point, and more importantly, Sanchez noted, she had The Book With No Name. And that fucking thing killed vampires. Wherever that book was going, he was going too.

He followed her along the corridor, occasionally stepping over the remains of a dead vampire or werewolf. Flake seemed to be following the trail of corpses. She led the way up a flight of stairs to the next floor. It was similar to the previous floor, all bloody corridors and corpses. This was not a fun place to be. Flake continued to dash around, opening doors, peering around them and then closing them again. She didn't seem to know exactly where she was going, and although Sanchez was tempted to point this out, he had a feeling she'd snap at him again, or worse still slap him around the chops again.

After seeming to check every single room on the second floor they headed up another flight of stairs that was strewn with dead bodies. By now Sanchez was breathing heavily. It was bad enough dashing around everywhere, but hurdling dead bodies and piles of smouldering ash was making it even more testing. This was a lot more exercise than he was used to. Fortunately the next floor up was totally different. There were no more corridors, for starters. At the top of the stairs was a small landing and a huge set of large wooden double doors with a pair of hideous statues of naked men on either side.

'This'll be it!' said Flake pointing at the doors.

'How can you be so sure?' Sanchez asked.

'There's no more dead bodies. And these are the only doors on this floor by the looks of it. This must be the end of the trail. Follow me, and remember, you're my prisoner.'

Sanchez sighed. 'I can't see how this is going to be believable,' he moaned. 'You'd never be able to take me prisoner.'

'A *Sunflower Girl* could take you prisoner. And I look like a vampire, remember,' said Flake, shaking her head. 'Now shut up and just play along!'

She carefully turned the handle on one of the doors and pulled it open. It creaked slightly as she pulled it out towards her. Sanchez peered over her shoulder and around the door. There was a huge hall on the other side. But it was extremely dark. Someone had obviously forgotten to turn on the lights.

'Looks like no one's here,' said Sanchez. 'Maybe we should go home?'

Flake grabbed his arm and pulled him into the huge hall with her. She pulled the door shut behind them, making it even darker than before. Sanchez groped around on the wall inside the doors to see if he could find any lights. His hand quickly settled on some switches and he flicked them all at once. The room lit up brightly. Several sets of chandeliers hanging from the ceiling breathed light into the room. And it immediately became evident that they weren't alone. Coming down a wide flight of stairs at the other end of the hall was Jessica and a big soldier guy that Sanchez recognised as Razor, one of four military guys who had dropped by the Tapioca on Halloween. Razor had a firm grasp on a rather distraught looking lady in a blue dress. Sanchez recognised her too. It was Mental Beth.

Flake grabbed Sanchez by the arm again and pulled him away from the light switches then she shoved him forward towards the centre of the hall. She really was treating him like a prisoner. *"How degrading,"* he thought. He was about to tell her to ease up on the shoving when Jessica called out to them from the far end of the hall.

'Is that The Book of Death you've got there?'

Flake nodded. 'Yeah. This guy brought it with him.'

Jessica reached the bottom of the stairs and stepped onto the marble floor. She hissed at Sanchez. 'So, you found my book. How good of you, Sanchez.'

He shrugged. 'Well, it was nothing really. Perhaps you could just give me the reward and I'll be on my way?'

'Why the rush?' Jessica asked, a mischievous grin breaking out on her face. 'Why don't you stay a while? We're having a party. Your friend the Bourbon Kid is here too. He's about to show himself to us any second now.'

It suddenly became glaringly obvious to Sanchez that Jessica was an evil vampire bitch. He couldn't fathom how he'd never spotted it before. Maybe he'd been blinded by his infatuation with her. Either way, he didn't feel like hanging out with her any more. 'It's okay. I've got places to be,' he said, attempting to turn back towards the door. Flake shoved him hard in the back again pushing him even further into the hall.

Jessica walked through the middle of the hall towards them, looking all around her, no doubt waiting for the reappearance of the Kid. Behind her, Razor and his hostage Beth followed on tentatively.

Flake shoved Sanchez once more, a little harder than was necessary. Then she called out to Jessica again. 'He wasn't planning on giving you the book at all,' she said. 'He found out you're a vampire and had a change of heart. When I found him he was cowering in a bathroom and trying to hide the book.'

'That sounds like typical Sanchez all right,' said Jessica scornfully. 'We'll deal with him later. For now I think it's maybe time to call out our mystery guest.' She stared all around the hall, looking once more for sign of the Kid, then she called out loud. 'Very well then, Razor, kill the girl.'

"What a bitch," Sanchez thought inconsequentially.

'WAIT!' It was the Bourbon Kid. Sanchez recognised the gravelly tone immediately. He spotted the mass murderer step out from the shadows behind the large staircase.

For the next twenty seconds or so, the Kid exchanged insults with Jessica and Razor and tried to persuade them to give up Beth. Sanchez prodded Flake in the arm and nodded at The Book With No Name which she had tucked under her arm.

'You gonna do it now?' he whispered.

Flake grimaced. 'Not sure. I'm waiting for some kind of signal.'

'Like what?'

'I don't know. The Kid said I'd know when the time came.'

Sanchez's eyes opened wide as he saw some action up ahead. 'SHIIIIT!' he yelled instinctively. 'He just shot that guy in the dick!'

The Bourbon Kid had fired a silver dart from a miniature crossbow and it had hit Razor right in the privates, doubling him over and taking him out of the equation completely.

In the confusion, Beth made a break for it. It was a futile attempt because Jessica grabbed hold of her before she'd taken barely two steps. The Vampire Queen wrapped one of her hands around Beth's neck. Her fingernails had lengthened into rather unpleasant looking claws, razor sharp ones.

'Do you think that was the signal?' Flake whispered.

'It could be. You're gonna have to do something pretty quick, or she's gonna kill Mental Beth.'

Up ahead, Jessica and the Kid continued to trade insults. Jessica seemed to be calling all the shots though because the Kid dropped a crossbow from the sleeve of his coat. It clattered onto the floor. Maybe he was surrendering?

'Got any other weapons?' Jessica asked. 'Because now's the time to drop them.'

The Kid opened his coat. Underneath it he wore a simple black T-shirt and black combat trousers. 'I have nothing else. Now let her go.'

'Take off your coat and get on your knees,' Jessica ordered.

'You'll let Beth go?'

'Get on your knees.'

The Kid took off his coat and tossed it onto the floor. But instead of dropping to his knees he made a swift movement with his right arm. He reached behind him and whipped out a gun that had been strapped across his back. He pointed it at Jessica's head, its red laser sighter aimed at the centre of her face. Jessica was lightning quick though. As the Kid was about to squeeze the trigger she yanked Beth's head into the line of fire. For several seconds the Kid continued to re-aim the gun at Jessica. Each time he did she moved a part of Beth into the line of the red sighter.

In the middle of all this the guy on the floor with the silver dart in his nut sack let out a gentle groan. It distracted the Kid who took his eye off Jessica for a second and took aim at the stricken soldier on the floor.

BANG!

The guy's head exploded as a bullet flew through his forehead. Blood and brains splattered out onto the marble floor behind him. It created an almighty mess. *"That'll stain if it doesn't get cleaned up soon,"* Sanchez thought, remembering a similar incident that had taken place in the Tapioca once.

The Kid turned his attentions back to Jessica and tried once more to line up a clean shot at her. He had no success. Jessica was just too damned quick. But all the while he had Jessica distracted it allowed Flake to edge ever closer to her, brandishing The Book With No Name. As Flake tiptoed almost to within touching distance, the Kid lowered his gun and addressed Jessica once more.

'You've got no intention of letting her go, have you?' he said.

Jessica smiled. 'I want you to watch this,' she said. 'I'm going to make your darling Beth into a vampire. She's going to be my new bitch. And you can be her first victim, unless you choose to kill her of course. You know, like you did with your mother?'

'And like I did with Archie Somers. Shoulda heard him scream. What a bitch.'

Jessica tightened her grip on Beth's neck. The claws on the end of her fingers were on the verge of drawing blood. 'I'm going to enjoy this,' she hissed.

The Kid seemed unfazed. 'I knew it would come to this. Quit stalling and *do it now. What are you waiting for?'*

Flake stopped creeping towards Jessica and literally charged at her.

Sanchez watched on in horror as Jessica, the woman he had been infatuated with for the best part of six years, opened her mouth wide, revealing a set of huge vampire fangs, thirsty for blood. She plunged them deep into Beth's neck, right at the moment Flake ploughed The Book With No Name into her back.

Jessica and Beth both screamed out in pain at the same time. It was hard to tell how far Jessica had managed to dig her fangs into Beth's neck, but as soon as Flake hit her with the book, the Vampire Queen reeled back. Flames erupted all around her back where Flake was pressing the book up against her. These were big fucking flames too. Sanchez could feel the burning heat from them back where *he* was. In a matter of seconds Jessica had erupted into one giant fireball. Flake too was caught up in it.

Sanchez felt his blood run cold when he heard Flake join in the screaming. He rushed forward and grabbed her, wrapping his hands around her waist. He tugged hard at her and succeeded in pulling her free from the flames and the book, which had glued itself to Jessica's back. Pulling Flake free hadn't been easy and the recoil caused Sanchez to fall back, dragging her onto the floor on top of him.

The Bourbon Kid dragged Beth clear of the flames, although unlike Sanchez he didn't lose his footing. He laid Beth down on the marble floor and then once again took aim with his gun. This time he had a clean shot. Jessica had nothing to shield herself with. He fired off a succession of shots. They rang out so quick that Sanchez couldn't be sure exactly how many times he fired. But every shot seemed to plough right into Jessica's chest as she writhed around in agony within the ball of flames. The final bullet flew into her face. Her screaming stopped and her body seemed to implode. The flesh all but disappeared from her body in one quick flash of light. The Kid stepped back away from the flames and Sanchez watched in awe as what remained of Jessica slowly disintegrated, her bones crumbling away into ash as she fell.

And then she was gone. Forever, this time.

The flames where she had once stood flickered lightly on the floor before extinguishing themselves completely, leaving nothing more than a pile of grey ash. Behind the dissipating smoke Sanchez could see the Bourbon Kid. He was crouching over Beth who was slumped in a heap on the floor at the bottom of the stairs. Blood was dribbling from a large bite-mark in her neck.

Flake freed herself from Sanchez's vice like grip and stood up, racing over to the Kid's side. Sanchez slowly climbed to his feet.

'How's Beth?' Flake asked. 'Was I too late?'

Sanchez couldn't get a good look at Beth to see what kind of state she was in. The Kid summed it up for him.

'She's either about to die, or turn into a vampire,' he said.

'Oh God,' said Flake. 'Is there anything we can do?'

The Kid leaned down and picked Beth up in his arms. He had one arm under her knees and another beneath her shoulders. Her head hung back limply over his arm. Sanchez could see that she was either unconscious or dead.

The Kid looked down at Beth, his face showing some genuine concern. 'We've got to get her to the museum,' he said.

'What's at the museum?' Flake asked.

'Not much,' said Sanchez. 'I went once. It's mostly paintings and old statues. Crap really.'

The Kid ignored Sanchez and headed towards the double doors at the end of the hall, carrying Beth in his arms. 'The Eye of the Moon is at the museum,' he said. 'I'm gonna need your driving skills, Flake. You coming?'

Flake picked up The Book With No Name from the floor, brushing some of the remains of Jessica from its cover. 'You bet,' she said, hurrying after him.

'Me too!' Sanchez called out, making sure they hadn't forgotten about him.

He took one last look at the pile of ash that had once been Jessica. How had it come to this? Jessica was dead and now he was heading off to a museum with the Bourbon Kid.

Fifty-Four

It took Kacy less than twenty minutes to race across town to the museum. By the time she arrived she was in a state of panic. Dante still hadn't replied to her text. She'd even tried calling him as she raced through the deserted streets, but his phone was switched off. In desperation she had also called the Bourbon Kid's cell phone. He hadn't answered either, so she left him message, a rather garbled, stupid and incomprehensible message by all accounts, but she hoped the general gist of it had gotten through. She needed him to get his ass to the museum as soon as possible.

When she reached the museum she scoped the area outside for any sign of the Kid's car. It was nowhere to be seen, and there was no trail of bodies leading up to the museum entrance, which was a likely indicator that he hadn't arrived yet. She was on her own.

Her legs felt weak with nerves as she raced up the steps to the front entrance. The double doors were open. She peered through them into the reception area and saw that it was empty. At least, it looked empty from the outside, but as she stepped inside she saw a body lying flat on its back at the far side of the reception hall. She recognised it immediately. It was Vanity.

After first checking both ways for any lurking enemies, she hurried over to him. Someone had worked him over real good. His face was bloodied and bruised, his once handsome looks gone forever. His eyes were closed and very badly swollen. In a strange kind of way Kacy hoped that Dante had inflicted this beating on the leader of the Shades clan. But somehow she doubted it. Her gut instincts were telling her that regardless of what had happened to Vanity, Dante was in trouble. If he was still alive.

She reached down and prodded Vanity in the chest to see if he was conscious. As her fingertips touched his chest she felt sure she saw him breathe in, ever so slightly.

'Vanity,' she whispered tentatively. 'Are you alive?'

He didn't respond so she nudged him in the chest again, a little harder this time. His eyes snapped open and his left hand reached up and grabbed hers, grasping it tightly. It startled her momentarily, but once the shock of it had subsided she reminded herself that he was practically dead and in no condition to be a threat to her.

'What happened here?' she asked. 'Where's Dante?'

Vanity's mouth opened slightly. His teeth were covered in blood, mostly his own by the looks of it. A great deal more blood was stuck in his chin beard, drying rapidly. He stared up at her, his eyes almost lifeless.

'Kacy?' he croaked.

'Yes. Where's Dante?'

Vanity coughed up a little blood and it dribbled out onto his chin. 'I'm sorry,' he said. 'Gaius has him.'

'Where? Where did they go?'

'Downstairs.' He swallowed a mouthful of blood, before spluttering out a few more barely audible words. 'They're burying him in a tomb.'

Kacy started to stand up, ready to rush downstairs to find Dante, but Vanity (with every last ounce of strength he had) kept a grip on her hand and pulled her back down.

'Wait,' he croaked. 'There's too many of them. You'll need this.' He pressed a small solid object into Kacy's hand. Then he released his grip on her and let both his arms fall to his side.

'What am I supposed to do with this?' Kacy asked.

Vanity swallowed hard once more. His time was coming to an end. He took in a short sharp intake of breath and muttered two words. 'Use it...'

'Use it for what?'

He took another short breath. As he exhaled he coughed up a few more words. 'Use it to…'

'To what? Use it to what?'

'Use it to…' He couldn't muster up the rest of the sentence. Instead he exhaled one last time and then his head slid to one side. Kacy squeezed his cheeks and turned his head to face her.

'Use it to what?' she pleaded. 'What's it for?'

Vanity didn't respond.

'What's it for?' she repeated. 'Vanity! Vanity! Use it for what?'

It was no use. Vanity was no longer breathing. He was dead. Who or what had killed him she wasn't entirely sure, but she had neither the time nor the patience to stop and worry about it. Instead she climbed to her feet and hurried over to the stairs that led down to the lower floor and the Egyptian Mummy's Tomb.

As she made her way down the stairs, she felt her cell phone vibrate in her pocket. She pulled it out and checked the display.

NEW TEXT MESSAGE

She opened the message. It was from the Bourbon Kid. It was only four words long, but it was exactly what she had hoped for.

I'm on my way.

She breathed a sigh of relief. The feeling of respite, however, lasted only momentarily. When she reached the bottom of the stairs she saw Rameses Gaius. He was stood with his back to her in the middle of the giant hall. In front of him were four vampires from the Black Plague clan, dressed from head to toe in black ninja style outfits. On the floor in the middle of them was Dante. It was clear that he was either unconscious or dead. The ninjas had managed to wrap him in bandages from his feet up to his waist. His clothes had been stripped off and thrown to the floor by the tomb entrance. Vanity had been right, they were preparing to bury him alive, all bandaged up like a mummy.

None of them had seen her arrive and she quickly concealed herself behind a large statue of Napoleon Bonaparte. She had to decide what to do quickly. Was there time to wait for the Bourbon Kid? What could she do on her own? As she was mulling over her options she heard the voice of Rameses Gaius. He hadn't even looked around, but he'd become aware of her presence.

'Miss Fellangi, how good of you to join us!' he called out to her.

She pretended not to hear him and stayed concealed behind the statue. The four ninja vampires looked around. None of them spotted Kacy spying on them from her spot behind the statue.

Gaius called out again. 'Please come out from behind Napoleon.'

The game was clearly up. Kacy stepped out from her hiding place behind the statue. Her only option was to try and stall Gaius long enough for the Bourbon Kid to arrive and hopefully fix things.

'Is Dante alive?' she asked.

Gaius turned around slowly and faced her. He took off his dark sunglasses and tucked them into the breast pocket on his silver suit jacket. Kacy got a good look at his right eye. In its socket was the Eye of the Moon. So much for taking it out to have it polished. While she stared at his eye, Gaius raised his right arm. The palm on his hand was glowing a bright blue colour and it was aimed at her. She sensed something bad was coming her way and darted back behind the statue.

A blue laser bolt from Gaius's palm blasted into the floor right where she had been standing. After striking the ground, it ricocheted up and disappeared out of sight up the staircase behind her. His face showed signs of irritation. He redirected his aim, pointing his hand at the statue of Napoleon. Another laser bolt flew from his palm and crashed into the head of the statue. The sheer force of the bolt knocked it off its concrete stand. The statue tumbled down onto Kacy. She tried to dive out of the way but Napoleon's hat butted her on the side of the head, knocking her to the floor.

As she lay dazed and disorientated underneath Napoleon, she heard Gaius speak out again. He wasn't talking to her this time. He was addressing the four vampires he had brought with him.

'Go get her,' he ordered. 'Wrap her up and throw her in the tomb with her idiot boyfriend.'

'Yes sir,' one of the vampires replied.

She felt a pair of cold hands haul her up from the floor. Her cell phone fell from her pocket and clattered onto the floor. She was still seeing stars so she had no idea where it landed. As she was dragged across the floor by one of the ninjas, she heard one of the others speak out.

'Hey Gaius, according to this bitch's phone, the Bourbon Kid is on his way here.'

Fifty-Five

Sanchez opened the front door of the Casa de Ville and peered out into the courtyard. Just as he feared, there were still vampires, zombies and werewolves tearing each other apart and spraying blood and guts all over the snow on the ground. Worryingly, there were also quite a few of them scrapping in the space between him and the police squad car Flake had parked near the bottom of the concrete steps below him. Getting to the car was going to be difficult and dangerous.

He turned back to see where the others were. At the back of the reception area Flake was holding open a door so that the Bourbon Kid could carry Beth through it. He had her in his arms, resting her head against his left bicep to stop it from drooping back and causing her any discomfort. The woman's time on earth was limited, that much was evident to Sanchez. She was barely conscious and seemed oblivious to all that was going on. Lucky bitch.

Flake let go of the door and rushed past them towards him. 'What's it like out there?' she asked.

'Not too bad,' he replied. 'Here, why don't I hold this door open for the others while you go start the car.'

'Okay,' said Flake. 'Good thinking.'

Sanchez held the door open for her and ushered her out into the courtyard. She had The Book With No Name tucked under one arm, so he figured she was probably pretty safe. As she charged down the steps to the car, she held it up in front of her in case anything lunged at her.

Sanchez turned back to see the Bourbon Kid approaching with Beth. 'Flake's just starting the car,' he said. 'It's right out front. You head on through. I'll cover your back.'

The Kid peered around the door at the carnage outside. Then he looked back at Sanchez. 'You sure you don't want me to carry you out too?' he asked.

It was a tempting offer, but Sanchez sensed he was just being sarcastic. 'I'll be okay. Come on, let's go.'

The Kid stepped through the door, taking great care not to bang Beth's head against the door's frame. Sanchez drew his nightstick from his belt and followed him out.

Flake had already started the engine on the car and was reversing it back up against the steps to ensure their journey from the front door to the car was as short as possible. She flicked on the headlight too which drew the attention of a few of the nearby undead creatures. Sanchez shoved the Bourbon Kid in the back to hurry him along in case any of the vampires or werewolves decided to lunge at him. The Kid strode quickly down the steps towards the car. Most of the undead knew full well who he was and steered clear of him. Sanchez took advantage of the situation and was able to follow along behind in the Kid's slipstream, pausing only to thump a legless zombie over the head with his nightstick.

They made it to the car untouched. Sanchez rushed around the Kid to open the back door, hoping to dive in before any vampires swooped. As he pulled the door open, he lost his footing on the icy driveway and fell back on to his ass. The Kid sidled up and carefully placed Beth onto the back seat of the car. He climbed in after her and pulled the door shut behind him.

Sanchez staggered to his feet and saw a huge werewolf bounding across the driveway toward him. It was a big hairy beast that had taken on the shape of a giant wolfhound. It was probably a pure breed, born a werewolf under a full moon. The worst kind. It had great big fangs and bloodthirsty eyes that were focussed on him. There was no sense in hanging around waiting for the bastard to get any closer. But as Sanchez lumbered forward to the car the beast leapt up in the air, swooping towards him, fangs wide open, ready to take a bite out of his face.

Luckily, Flake had seen the werewolf approach. She reached over from the driver's seat and flung the passenger side door open. It hit the wolf in the face, making a sickening crunching sound. It knocked the beast back down the driveway, eliciting an agonised yelp.

Sanchez needed no second invitation and dived into the front passenger seat, slamming the door shut behind him. He looked over at Flake. 'Get us the fuck out of here!' he screamed.

Flake didn't really need to be told. She pressed her foot down hard on the accelerator and the car zipped off down the driveway. Vampires, zombies and werewolves bounced up onto the hood of the car as it screeched along the icy path towards the front gates.

'Are you trying to hit them all?' Sanchez asked as a Panda's face splatted against the windscreen directly in front of him.

'It's kinda hard to avoid them,' said Flake, fighting with the steering wheel.

Sanchez looked over his shoulder to the back seat. The Bourbon Kid had Beth draped across his lap. He was brushing her hair away from her face and wrapping a white rag around her neck to stem the flow of blood from the wound Jessica had inflicted upon her.

'How's it look, man?' Sanchez asked.

'Not good. We need to be at the museum in a matter of minutes if we're gonna have any chance of saving her.'

'It's eleven thirty already!' Flake shouted back.

'Then I've only got half an hour,' said the Kid. 'Put your foot on it, Flake.'

'You got it.'

Sanchez shuffled back around in his seat and watched Flake steer the car through the front gates and turn left onto the road. 'Jesus Flake, Stevie Wonder drives better than you!' he yelled.

'And he plays the piano better than you, so shut up,' came the reply.

Sanchez ignored the insult. He was just relieved to see that the road into town was free from undead monsters. He hadn't exactly approved of Flake's driving on previous occasions when he'd been in a car with her. She had a habit of hitting something every thirty seconds, whether it be a vampire, werewolf, zombie or simply a book. At least when Sanchez hit something like a snowman, it was intentional. With Flake at the wheel he had to take up his default position, gripping the dashboard tightly with both hands and hoping for the best. By some small miracle, Flake didn't crash into anything else for the rest of the journey to the museum, in spite of the icy roads and her high speed driving.

After a ten-minute rollercoaster ride across town, she parked up right outside the front of the museum.

'We're here,' she yelled back to the Kid.

He was already opening the back door and climbing out. He slammed it behind him and stepped onto the pavement. Instead of racing straight into the museum he tapped on Sanchez's window. Sanchez wound it down a few inches.

'Whassup?' he asked.

The Kid leaned as far into the space at the top of the window as he could. 'Flake, take care of Beth for me. I'll be back as quick as I can.'

'Sure thing,' said Flake. 'Good luck!'

The Kid dashed off up the stairs to the museum. Sanchez wound his window back up and peered over his shoulder at the back seat. Beth was laid out in a state of unconsciousness, her head rested against the seat. She was barely breathing. It was entirely possible that she might either die or transform into a vampire at any minute. 'We best stay up front,' he suggested.

Flake scowled at him. 'She's *dying,* for goodness sake. I'm gonna go sit in the back with her to make sure she's okay.'

'Fair enough,' said Sanchez. He reached down and picked up The Book With No Name, which Flake had thrown onto the floor by his feet when she got into the car. 'I'll keep hold of this book in case she transforms and we have to kill her.'

Flake had just opened the driver's side door to climb out. She hesitated and looked back at The Book With No Name in Sanchez's hands. 'Oh shit!' she said, wide eyed. 'The Kid's gone into the museum without the book! You'd better take it and run in after him!'

'What?'

'I promised I'd stay here with Beth. You'd better run on in after the Kid and give him the book. He'll never get the Eye of the Moon back without it!'

Sanchez looked out of his window. The front door of the museum was open. The Kid had already gone through it. If Sanchez wanted to catch up with him before he confronted Rameses Gaius he was going to have to get a move on. He tucked The Book With No Name under his arm and opened the car door. As he climbed out, Flake raced around from the other side of the car. She opened the back door so that she could climb in and attend to Beth. Before she climbed in she hesitated. Then she reached out and grabbed a hold of Sanchez's arm. She pulled him over to her.

'What now?' he asked.

'I wanted to say thanks for pulling me clear from the fire earlier.'

'Oh. Yeah.' He found himself blushing as he thought back to the moment he had dragged her away from the fire. 'Well, y'know,' he mumbled, 'you're my ride home.'

Flake poked him playfully in the stomach. 'They need you in there,' she said, pointing to the museum. 'Go be a hero again. Good luck.'

Fifty-Six

Kacy's head hadn't cleared. She felt nauseous and totally dazed from the impact of being hit on the head by Napoleon's concrete bicorn hat. Her eyesight had temporarily deserted her too. But she could hear voices. They were the voices of the ninja vampires who had dragged her over to the tomb where Dante was laid out on the floor in an even worse state than her.

'Yo! Save some bandages for us. We've got to do the girl.'

'Just strip her off. We'll bandage her up.'

'Why do *you* get to bandage her up?'

'Because I've got the bandages, numbnuts.'

A third voice butted in. 'I'll help you strip her.'

'Okay. Hold her up while I take her pants down.'

'All right, but hurry up. She looks like she's getting her wits back.'

On hearing that she was about to have her pants pulled down, Kacy was indeed trying her best to clear her head and get her wits back. She felt a pair of hands slide under her armpits and haul her up from the floor. Another figure bent down in front of her and began unbuttoning her jeans. He got to work pretty quick too. Her jeans were tugged down past her knees with ease.

'Fuck me, look at those legs.'

Kacy blinked a few times and slowly began to get her sight back, albeit somewhat blurred. Her jeans had been pulled down to her ankles. The ninja who was bent down in front of her was in the process of frantically pulling her sneakers off.

As her sight was returning, the guy who was holding her up from behind reached down and grabbed the bottom of her sweatshirt. He yanked it up over her head, where it got stuck and smothered her face, blinding her again. She was now being twisted in all directions by two vampires who couldn't care less how it made her feel. Even if she hadn't been totally dazed it would have been difficult to put up much of a struggle.

She felt her sneakers come off and heard them being tossed aside. Moments later her jeans were tugged hard and came off completely. She felt the touch of the vampire's cold, crusty hands making their way up her legs towards her underwear (a pair of tiny pink panties Dante had bought for her with the words FREE ENTRY sewn into the back in black lettering). Behind her, the other ninja was still fighting hard to get her sweatshirt over her head.

As she felt the cold vampire fingers tug at her panties, she heard a loud crack. The grip of the vampire's fingers on her underwear loosened, then his hands fell away, leaving her underwear in place, albeit only just.

The guy behind her stopped tugging at her sweatshirt. 'What the fuck?' he said, sounding puzzled.

BANG!

Kacy's felt the whoosh of a bullet speeding past her head. The guy behind her immediately relinquished his grip on her and she fell backwards, her head crashing down hard on the floor. She lay there on her back feeling even more dazed than before, wondering what had happened. After a brief moment wincing at the pain of yet another blow to the head, she came to her senses and remembered her predicament. She grabbed at her sweatshirt and set about pulling it back over her head to cover at least part of her modesty.

The blast of the gunshot was still ringing in her ears. As she wrestled with her sweatshirt she heard two further shots, followed by the sound of two more bodies dropping to the floor. A few moments of quiet were followed by the sound of Rameses Gaius's distinctive booming voice.

'Show yourself, you cowardly sonofabitch!' he yelled.

Kacy finally managed to poke her head back through the top of her sweatshirt. She took a deep breath and looked around. Her vision was still blurred but she was able to get an idea of her bearings. Dante was laid out on the floor a few yards away. She expected to see the Bourbon Kid somewhere too. He was definitely in the hall because the results of his handiwork were in evidence. She could see a pair of dead vampires on the floor either side of Dante. Both of them had suffered fatal head wounds courtesy of the Bourbon Kid's deadly aim with a gun. Two others were on the floor, not far from her. One had a broken neck, the other one only had half a head.

As Kacy continued to survey the carnage around her, a flash of bright blue light suddenly dazzled her. She saw the source of it. Gaius was firing off blue laser bolts from both hands, aiming blindly in all directions. But where was the Bourbon Kid? There were numerous statues and displays within which he could conceal himself, and it seemed that Gaius was unable to locate him.

As if the laser bolts and gunshots weren't enough to contend with, one of Gaius's mistimed attacks had created another problem. A set of red curtains had caught fire and burst into flames. So as well as being stuck in a room with an angry mummy, a serial killer, an unconscious boyfriend and not knowing for sure where her pants were, she now had to contend with the fact that the place was on fire too!

She hauled herself forward onto her knees and stared around the hall. Her jeans and sneakers had been tossed across the floor and had landed not too far from an antique piano with a mannequin of Ludwig Beethoven sitting at it. She took in another deep breath and groggily began crawling on her hands and knees towards it.

Behind her she could hear Rameses Gaius cursing and firing laser bolts off in all directions. Occasionally a gunshot would ring out in response. Gaius and the Kid were taking shots at each other but, where the Lord of the Undead was out in the open, the Kid was hiding within the shadows of the museum's displays.

Kacy reached out and grabbed her jeans with her fingertips. As she did, a blue laser bolt hit the floor nearby and ricocheted up, flying a few inches past her nose. Clearly, time was in short supply. Her jeans were almost completely inside out where the vampires had yanked them off so hurriedly. As she picked them up off the floor, something fell out of the one of the front pockets. It was the small object Vanity had handed her. She cast her mind back to the moment when he had slipped it into her hand. "*Use it...*' he had said.

Fifty-Seven

Sanchez made his way tentatively down the stairs to the main hall. Below him he could hear gunfire and all kinds of stuff breaking. That was a sure sign that the Bourbon Kid was already taking on Rameses Gaius, and doing it without The Book With No Name. Sanchez hoped he wasn't too late.

At the bottom of the stairs he saw the actions that went with the noise. A pair of curtains had been set on fire too, and the flames were spreading. There were dead bodies lying around on the floor, which was nothing unusual in all honesty. Over by a shattered glass display he saw the unconscious figure of Dante, wrapped up in bandages from his feet to his shoulders. There was also the strange sight of a rather attractive brunette in her early twenties crawling across the floor on her hands and knees, wearing just a black sweatshirt and a pair of pink panties with the words FREE ENTRY across the back. In any normal situation Sanchez would be checking the spelling quite rigorously, but this wasn't the time. The large shaven headed figure of Rameses Gaius was standing in the centre of the hall with his back to Sanchez. He was firing off blasts of blue lightning from his hands, aiming them at just about anything. They were ricocheting off the floor and walls, blasting into statues and displays. Everything he hit either snapped in half or burst into flames. This was one destructive bastard.

Out of the corner of his eye, Sanchez caught sight of the Bourbon Kid. He was hiding in the shadows behind a black curtain that covered a statue of a fat naked guy. He had a large gun in his hand. He saw Sanchez and nodded at him. Then he vanished into the shadows. His disappearance was followed by a loud gunshot that drew Gaius's fire. The giant mummy launched a laser bolt at the curtains where the Kid had been hiding.

Sanchez had no fucking idea what the Kid had nodded at him for, but he suspected it was some kind of signal. It probably meant he was supposed to do something important. Something brave. The Kid had drawn Gaius's attention away from the stairs so Sanchez could sneak in undetected. This was obviously his big moment. Gaius was only twenty metres in front of him. Time to be a hero, like Flake had suggested.

He tiptoed as quickly as he could up behind Gaius, only taking his eyes off the back of the mummy's head briefly to check out the ass on the girl with the pink underwear one last time, just in case he never got another chance.

When he was less than a yard behind Gaius he raised The Book With No Name up above his head and smashed it down towards the back of the mummy's skull. Unfortunately, as he plunged it down, the Lord of the Undead suddenly spun around. There was no time for Sanchez to pull out of the attack and neither was there time for Gaius to duck out of the way. The book crashed down, right into his face, hitting him hard on the bridge of his nose.

Sanchez thought back to the moment Flake had hit Jessica with the book. It had set the Vampire Queen alight almost instantly. The same thing couldn't be said for Rameses Gaius. For what felt like an awfully long time, Sanchez stood motionless, pressing the book against the face of the mummy. But Gaius didn't burst into flames. He simply reached up with both hands and grabbed the book. Then he shoved it back into Sanchez's face. The impact was immense. It sent Sanchez sprawling back onto the floor behind him. His feet bounced up over his head and he rolled back until he eventually came to a sudden halt with his head almost wedged between his own ass cheeks. As he sat back up, he saw Gaius throw The Book With No Name at him. The magical book hadn't wounded Gaius at all. The mummy had no interest in it either. He nonchalantly flung it at Sanchez's head. Sanchez ducked out of the way of it and raised his hands defensively, in readiness for a violent assault from Gaius's now glowing blue right hand.

And then behind his attacker, he saw a ray of hope. The Bourbon Kid had stepped out of the shadows and was pointing his gun at the back of Gaius's head. A red laser sighter was aimed precisely at the back of the eye socket that held the Eye of the Moon. As Gaius prepared to fire a laser bolt at Sanchez, the Kid fired off a shot.

BANG!

It was a damn fine shot. Sanchez watched in awe. He saw everything clearly as if it were in slow motion. The back of Gaius's head spurted out a few spots of blood as the bullet pierced his skull. A clanging sound followed as the bullet hit the back of the Eye of the Moon and then like a dream, the blue stone flew out of his eye socket, spraying blood all around it.

Sanchez's joy at the sight was short lived.

Rameses Gaius had reflexes every bit as quick as the laser bolts he fired from his fingertips. His left hand snapped into action. He reached up and caught the blue stone as it flew out of the front of his head. The stone had travelled less than half a yard before he had recovered it.

Gaius looked down on the stone with his remaining good eye. For a moment Sanchez almost thought he saw the mummy smile. The moment passed all too quickly and Gaius turned around to face the Bourbon Kid. In the back of Gaius's head Sanchez saw the hole where the bullet had entered. As he stared at it, the hole closed up quickly, vanishing courtesy of the healing powers in the Eye of the Moon.

"Fuck me," Sanchez thought. *"This guy is fucking invincible."*

Gaius snarled at the Kid. 'You had your shot. Now it's my turn!'

He raised his right hand and fired one of his blue laser bolts at the hooded figure in the long dark coat. It hit the Kid in the chest and lifted him off his feet. He flew back twenty feet through the air and crashed into the Egyptian Tomb display behind him.

Holy crap!

Sanchez gawped at the sheer power of Rameses Gaius. This man was a walking army of Iron Man, General Zod and the Incredible Hulk all rolled into one.

Fortunately Gaius seemed to forget all about Sanchez as he took several giant strides towards the Bourbon Kid, ready to finish him off.

If Gaius succeeded in killing the Kid, it wouldn't be long before he turned his attention back to Sanchez and the semi-naked girl. One of them would be the next to die. At least Sanchez had his pants on, so he'd probably be less likely to catch Gaius's eye first.

Any hopes they had of surviving rested with the Bourbon Kid and his renowned fighting prowess. Sanchez needed to come up with a way to distract Gaius before he killed the Bourbon Kid. He had to buy the Kid some time because right now the hooded slayer looked dazed and vulnerable on the floor by the tomb.

Sanchez saw the girl pick something up from the floor by a pair of jeans. It was a small dark object and she was preparing herself to throw it. Throwing stuff at Gaius was a relatively lame idea, but it was probably the only option open to any of them right now. Flake had told Sanchez to go be a hero; the only problem was, she wasn't there to tell him the best way to go about it. So with no decent ideas of his own Sanchez decided to join in with the throwing idea. He reached inside his breast pocket and pulled out his hipflask. With its lid slightly loosened it could at least cover Gaius in piss. That might distract him a bit, or cause him to electrocute himself, perhaps?

As the girl took aim, Sanchez finally got a look at her face. He recognised her as Kacy, Dante's girlfriend and a former chambermaid at one of the local hotels. He decided it would be best to let her throw first. That way he could see how Gaius reacted. And he really hoped her throwing was as impressive as her ass. As she lined up her throw Sanchez inwardly wished her luck. She drew her arm back, then with all her might threw the small dark object in her hand.

Sanchez had seen girls throw before and had never been particularly impressed. And Kacy's throwing skills were abysmal. She missed Gaius completely. In fact she ended up throwing the small object at the Bourbon Kid's head. *"Useless,"* Sanchez thought.

The Bourbon Kid was climbing to his knees as the object flew at him. He reacted quickly and reached up, catching it in his right hand. It was just a small rectangular shape the size of a playing card. Maybe the Kid could throw it at Gaius with more accuracy and power than Kacy had done—if he had time.

Gaius stopped a few yards away from the Kid and raised his right arm again. His palm glowed bright blue. This was the moment of truth. In one almighty show of force he thrust his arm at the Kid, unleashing a bright blue laser bolt at his fallen enemy.

What followed happened quickly. As the laser bolt shot out from Gaius's hand and surged towards the Bourbon Kid's head, the Kid held up the small object Kacy had thrown at him.

And he flipped it over in his hand. Where one side of it had been black, the other was shiny.

It was a small hand mirror.

The blue laser bolt blasted into the mirror and its bright light reflected sharply back on itself. A flash of blinding blue light filled the room and the laser bolt shot back into the face of Rameses Gaius.

The impact caught him completely off guard and the sheer power of his own furious bolts of lightning lifted him off his feet. The Eye of the Moon flew out of his hand and bounced onto the floor as he flew backwards through the air. Sanchez watched on wide-eyed as Gaius's ass came flying towards him. Fortunately the Dark Lord landed on his back just short of him. The smooth polished floor caused him to slide along on his back until he came to a stop with his head in Sanchez's lap.

Gaius was clearly dazed. Sanchez could see him blinking furiously with his one good eye. He was seriously disorientated, although that probably wouldn't last for long. After a few seconds he stopped blinking and seemed to focus his stare up at Sanchez.

"Uh oh," thought Sanchez. *"He's about to get back up."*

There was nothing else for it. Sanchez's only weapon was his hipflask. He pulled the lid off and held it up over Gaius's face. He poured the contents out and tried to direct some into Gaius's empty eye socket.

However, as the piss came out of his flask Sanchez was surprised to see that it was a green colour. That was unusual. His piss was normally a dark yellow colour, occasionally a bit brown, sometimes even quite clear, but not usually green.

He suddenly remembered he had picked up the Santa's hipflask after their altercation earlier in the day. This was the green liquid that paralysed folks. He poured it over as much of Gaius's face as he could, some of it into the eye socket and some of it into his mouth. It trickled onto his tongue and down his throat. It was evident from the look in his good eye that the liquid was having a negative effect on him.

Sanchez watched Gaius's face slowly numb up, in the same way that the Santa's had done. He recognised the look of fear in his victim's eye. Gaius managed to cough just once as the liquid trickled down his throat. But that was the last function his body performed. Very quickly his movement stopped altogether. And without the Eye of the Moon in his eye socket, or his hand, he wasn't going to be healing up any time soon either. Realising that Gaius was now powerless, Sanchez took great pleasure in holding the Dark Lord's head down with one hand while he waited for some assistance.

Over by the wrecked tomb display the Bourbon Kid climbed to his feet and staggered over to Sanchez and Gaius. He looked in fairly bad shape. That laser blast from Gaius had clearly taken something out of him. He stooped down to pick the Eye of the Moon up from the floor, then turned and tossed it through a few small flickering flames on the floor over to Kacy. She caught it and shouted a quick thanks back at him. Then she crawled over to Dante with it.

The Kid dragged himself over to Sanchez and Gaius. He practically fell down onto Gaius's chest. Sanchez edged back to allow him room to do whatever horrible things he had planned. The Kid reached down and grabbed the Dark Lord by the face and squeezed his cheeks hard.

'I saw what you did to the young boy in the library,' he growled.

'What did he do?' Sanchez asked.

'Bashed a boy's head in. Had himself some real fun at that kid's expense.'

Sanchez shook his head in disgust. 'Well, you know what they say?' he said.

'No. What do they say?'

'It's all fun and games until someone loses an eye.'

The Kid nodded. 'That's true.' He stopped squeezing Gaius's face and looked up at Sanchez. He had blood dribbling from his mouth. 'What was in that flask?' he asked.

'Eggnog, I think.'

'Evil stuff.'

Turning his attentions back to the stricken and now terrified figure of Rameses Gaius, the Kid clenched his right fist and raised it up above his head. He looked Gaius in the eye, making sure he had his full attention. He took a deep breath.

'This is for the boy in the library.'

Fifty-Eight

Dante felt the touch of Kacy's hand against his cheek. He opened his eyes. There weren't many things better in life than waking up and seeing Kacy's face looking down at him.

'You okay?' she asked.

He tried to move his arms only to discover that they were wedged tightly against his sides. In fact he couldn't move at all from his shoulders down. He was lying on his back on a hard floor. He craned his neck and looked down at the rest of his body. He was wrapped in bandages from his feet right up to his shoulders.

'What the fuck have you done to me now?' he asked, frowning.

'It wasn't me, silly.'

'So why the fuck am I dressed as a giant worm?'

Kacy looked confused. 'When have you ever seen a worm dressed like this?'

'Cartoon porn.'

'We'll talk about that later.'

As his senses came back to him, he caught sight of something out of the corner of his eye. 'The fucking floor is on fire too! Have you seen that? The fucking floor is on fire!'

'I know.'

'What the fuck?'

Kacy seemed remarkably calm considering there were a bunch of three-foot high flames just a stone's throw away.

'Here, let me help you up,' she said, lifting his shoulders up from the floor and getting him into a sitting position.

He looked around. Behind Kacy and to the right of the fire he saw the Bourbon Kid and Sanchez. They were leaning over the body of Rameses Gaius. The Kid was busy slicing Gaius up with a bone handled knife. There were other bodies lying around too.

'Okay, I can't remember fuck all. Seriously, what's happened this time?' He looked closer at Kacy. 'And why aren't you wearing any pants?'

'They got ripped off. And before you say anything, you should know your clothes are on the floor behind you.'

'All of my clothes?'

'Yeah.'

Dante lowered his voice. 'Were we *fucking* in here?'

'No. You got stripped naked by some vampires. They tried to make you a mummy.'

'They were trying to fuck me?'

'No, *mummify* you. You know? That's what the bandages are for. Hold still while I unwrap you.'

She grabbed some of the white bandages around his shoulders and began unravelling them. He'd been bound up pretty tight. While she got to work, he tried desperately to cast his mind back to how he'd ended up in this current ludicrous predicament. It wasn't coming back to him no matter how hard he tried to concentrate.

'Hurry the fuck up!' he snapped as he caught sight of the fire spreading towards them.

'Stay still then.'

'I am still.'

'Okay, just shut up then.'

As soon as Kacy freed his arms he began ripping off the rest of the bandages himself. He'd unwrapped them down to the knee when Sanchez came rushing over to them. The bartender-cum-cop grabbed at Kacy's arm.

'You still got the Eye of the Moon on you?'

'Umm yeah.' She reached down to the floor by Dante's side and picked it up. She held it up to show Sanchez. 'Here it is. Do you need it?'

Sanchez nodded. 'Got a dying girl in the car outside.'

Kacy tossed the stone to him. 'Don't sniff it,' she warned. 'Dante sat on it just now.'

Sanchez took a look at Dante's naked body and grimaced. 'Why would I sniff it anyway?' he asked.

'I don't know. You look the sort.'

'Yeah well, your pants are on fire.'

'Shit!'

He was right. Over by Beethoven's piano, Kacy's jeans had just caught fire. The flames were spreading towards her sneakers too. And it was starting to get pretty fucking hot. She left Dante and dashed over to her grab her sneakers before they went the same way as her jeans.

Sanchez rushed off with the Eye of the Moon, heading for the stairs at the far end of the hall, ducking out of the way of a few flames that seemed to deliberately lunge at him as he ran.

Dante freed his feet from the last of the bandages and grabbed his clothes. He managed to pull on his jeans and shoes and was reaching for his black T-shirt when he spotted the Bourbon Kid. The serial killer had dragged the body of Rameses Gaius across the floor towards the tomb. He dropped the once proud mummy on the floor by Dante's feet. The self-proclaimed Lord of the Undead now had *two* empty eye sockets and a huge hole in his face where his nose had once been. The Kid had removed his clothes too. The naked body wasn't a pretty sight. It was covered in blood and some pretty deep cuts, courtesy of the knife he'd been taken apart with. As Dante was slipping his T-shirt over his head he greeted the Kid with a thumbs up.

'Hey man, thanks for coming back for us.'

'Thank your girlfriend. She really came through for us.'

'Yeah she's cool like that.' Dante reached over to Kacy and grabbed her by the back of her head, pulling her towards him. He didn't need to pull hard. She reached forward and their lips locked for several seconds before Dante pulled away. 'Love you, Kace,' he said.

'Love you too. Now let's get the fuck outta here.'

The Bourbon Kid grabbed Dante's arm. 'Hey, I need help wrapping this muthafucker up in these bandages.'

'What for?'

'We need to get him in that fucking tomb.'

'Isn't he dead already?' Dante asked.

'The guy's been dead for hundreds of years. He needs to go back in the tomb to be sure he won't come back.'

'Even with the fire?'

'Would you just do as you're fuckin' told?'

'Have we got time for this?' Kacy asked.

Dante gave her a peck on the cheek. 'Why don't you get outta here?' he said 'I'll meet you outside in a minute.'

'Are you kidding?'

'No. Go on, I'll be fine.'

Kacy shook her head. 'No you won't. The last two times I've left you on your own you've gotten yourself turned into a vampire and a mummy. If I leave you again I'm worried you'll turn into a zombie or a werewolf!'

The Bourbon Kid grabbed some of the bandages by Dante's feet. 'If you two don't get a move on, we'll all be turned into ash. Quit bitchin' and help me wrap this fucker up.'

Kacy grabbed Gaius's feet and lifted them off the floor so that Dante and the Kid could start wrapping the bandages around his legs.

By the time they had wrapped every inch of Gaius's body in bandages the flames in the hall had spread towards the stairs at the other end. The oxygen in the hall was becoming thin, due in no small part to a considerable amount of smoke that was beginning to blow up towards the ceiling.

They hauled Gaius's body over to the open sarcophagus in the tomb display. He had escaped from that same tomb a year earlier. Now it was time so send him back. The Kid stood Gaius's mummified body upright and the three of them pushed his body inside the sarcophagus.

'He's a perfect fit,' Dante commented. 'You'd think it was made for him.'

'It was,' said Kacy.

'Really?'

'I'll explain later.'

A loud crash behind them served as a reminder that time wasn't on their side. The legs on Beethoven's piano had given way and it had crashed to the floor, engulfed in flames. Other displays all around the hall were rapidly catching fire and breaking apart.

'Are we done?' Dante shouted above the din.

The Kid nodded. 'Get outta here. I'll stick the lid on this sonofabitch.'

Kacy tugged at Dante's arm and started heading towards the stairs at the end of the hall. The fire was spreading swiftly enough that their window of opportunity for escape would soon be closed. Dante began to follow, but took one last look back to see how the Kid was coping.

'Hurry up, man, there's not much time!' he yelled.

The Kid was securing the lid onto the front of Gaius's tomb, imprisoning him once again for all eternity, or until the fire got to him, whichever came first. He looked back at Dante and waved him away.

'I got one more person to kill,' he yelled back.

'What? Who?'

'Elijah Simmonds. He's around here somewhere.'

'Are you nuts? He'll be long gone by now. There's not enough time for that. You'll burn in here!'

The Kid took one last look at the Mummy's Tomb, checking it was closed. He turned back to Dante and pulled the hood on his coat up over his head.

'There's always time to kill one more.'

Fifty-Nine

It had been a pretty great day all round for Elijah Simmonds. After killing the local Police Captain he'd spent twenty minutes packing all the cash from Cromwell's safe into a pair of suitcases. As he sat contentedly at Cromwell's old desk in his new office drinking a large brandy he contemplated his options. He could stay on as manager of the museum, a job he had always coveted, or simply skip town with all the cash. Life was good.

He'd had two large glasses of brandy already as he waited for James the security guard to call and let him know when Rameses Gaius had finished the job of mummifying Dante and Kacy in the hall downstairs. It was almost midnight when his desk phone rang. He allowed it to ring three times before casually answering it.

'Hello.'

'Hi boss, it's James.'

'Is it done?'

'No. Things have gone all to shit down there.'

Simmonds let out a deep sigh. 'Oh fuck. What's happened?'

'Gaius and his vampire buddies are toast. The Bourbon Kid just wasted them all. And the place is on fire.'

Simmonds sat up sharply in his black leather chair. 'What?'

'They're dead. I saw it all on the monitors here in front of me. I say we get the fuck out of here, boss. That fire is spreading. And I've lost sight of the Bourbon Kid.'

'Shit. Call the fire department. And then get your ass down here!'

'Are you kidding? I'm getting the fuck out of here! See ya later. And good luck.'

James sounded panicky. Hardly surprising really. He'd already had his nose broken by the Bourbon Kid on their only previous meeting. He probably wanted to be as far away from him as possible.

'James, don't hang up!' Simmonds yelled. 'I've got a hundred grand in cash up here for you. Just come down here. Don't leave without me. We can leave together. We'll be safer that way. James? Jimmy? You still there? Jim?'

The line went dead. He hoped James had heard him. Surely a hundred grand was enough of an incentive to come down to the office?

Simmonds glanced over at the dead body of Captain Dan Harker on the floor to his left by a wall of bookshelves. He'd had the guts to blow Harker's brains out. The evidence was still all over the wall to prove it. Could he kill again if he had to? He opened the top drawer on his desk and reached into it. The gun he had used to kill Harker was still there. He pulled it out of the drawer and checked the chamber. It still contained four bullets.

He tucked the gun in the back of his suit trousers and picked up the two suitcases full of cash from the floor by the desk. Both cases were heavy. He placed them down on the desk in front of him. This was quite a dilemma. If he carried both cases he wouldn't have a free hand to carry the gun. His mind was racing as he tried to figure out the best thing to do. The smart thing would be to leave one suitcase behind and walk out with the gun primed and ready to fire.

As he was contemplating what to do, he heard a knock at the door. He pulled his gun out and pointed it at the door, his hand trembling.

'James?' he called out. 'Is that you?'

From the other side of the door he heard James's voice. 'Yeah. You seriously got a hundred grand in there for me?'

'Yes. Shit yeah. Come on in!'

Simmonds kept his gun pointed at the door and watched as the handle twisted. The door clicked and opened slowly inwards. Standing in the doorway was James. He looked nervous.

'Here,' said Simmonds, gesturing to one of the cases he'd plonked onto the desk in front of him. 'Grab one of these.'

James looked down at the case on the desk. He looked like he was about to cry. Nerves or a conscience had clearly gotten the better of him. Simmonds put his gun down on the table and grabbed a case. He tossed it over to James. It landed at the security guard's feet.

'Come on, Jim. We haven't got much time!'

James swallowed hard and stared down at the case at his feet. Then he slowly leaned forward. At first it looked like he was leaning down to pick up the case. It soon became evident that he had no intention of picking it up.

He couldn't.

He fell to his knees, landing with a gentle thud on top of the case full of money. Blood trickled from his mouth and he gazed up at Simmonds for a moment. Then his upper body fell forwards and his face crashed into the floor. Sticking out of the middle of his back was a large bone handled knife. Simmonds stared hard at it for a moment, the shock of it paralysing him.

He slowly looked back up. Standing in the doorway right behind where James had been stood was the dark shadowy figure of the Bourbon Kid. Simmonds's jaw dropped.

'Hey, it was nothing personal,' he said, nervously.

The Kid did not respond He stepped into the room and leaned down to retrieve his knife from James's back. He didn't seem to have seen the gun on Simmonds's desk.

The museum's manager needed no second invitation. While his intruder was busy pulling the knife out of James's back, he reached for the gun.

Sixty

Clutching the Eye of the Moon tightly in his left hand, Sanchez charged out through the front doors of the museum and onto the snow covered steps outside. The dark clouds above were breaking up and shafts of blue light from the moon were beginning to shine through. The demise of Rameses Gaius would have far reaching effects, the first of which would be a rapid change in the weather.

Flake poked her head out of the back of the police squad car where he'd left her. Behind her, Beth's feet were sticking out over the end of the back seat. Flake called out to him. 'Sanchez, hurry!'

He looked down at the icy steps and decided it would be easier to throw the blue stone to Flake, rather than risk slipping on the ice.

'Here, catch!' he yelled to her.

He tossed the Eye through the air to Flake. He overthrew it slightly, but she reacted like a short stop and reached up, plucking it out of the sky. The years she had spent catching the tips that were thrown at her in the Ole Au Lait had clearly paid off. She ducked back inside the car and set about working out how to use the Eye to cure Beth's gaping neck wound.

Sanchez hung back at the top of the steps for a while, bent over and trying to get his breath back. He began to realise just how tired he was from all the running.

Flake called up to him. 'Sanchez, give me a hand here. I'm not sure what I'm supposed to be doing!'

'Coming.'

He trudged down the last few steps and then over to the car. A feeling of dizziness had come over him. To stop himself from collapsing he steadied himself by resting his hand on Flake's butt which was conveniently poking out of the back door of the car.

He peered over her shoulder to see what was going on. She was leaning over the body of Beth, wiping the other woman's brow with one hand and pressing the glowing blue stone into her chest with the other.

'Come on Beth,' she whispered. 'Hang in there.'

From what Sanchez could see, not a lot seemed to be happening. Beth's eyes remained closed and it was hard to tell if she was breathing or not.

'Try pressing the stone into her hand,' he suggested.

'Is that how it works?'

'I think so.'

Flake grabbed Beth's right hand and pressed the blue stone into her palm. At first nothing much seemed to happen, but after a few seconds the stone began to glow a light blue colour from within. The glow intensified with each passing moment and gradually some colour returned to her face. She opened her eyes and smiled up at Flake and then looked over at Sanchez and smiled at him too.

'Where am I?' she asked.

'Back seat of a car,' said Sanchez.

'A police car,' Flake added, brushing Sanchez's hand away from her ass. 'You're safe now.'

Beth took a short sharp breath. A worried look washed over her face. 'I was kidnapped,' she said. 'They were going to kill me. That's about all I can remember.'

'It's all okay now,' said Flake, stroking her face. 'They're all dead.' She turned to Sanchez. 'Aren't they Sanchez?'

He nodded. 'Oh yeah. They're very dead.'

'See,' said Flake turning back to Beth. 'No one can hurt you now.'

Flake's calming words seemed to have the desired effect because the look of panic on Beth's face softened a little.

Sanchez considered his part in all the events. He'd done pretty well. 'I knew it would all be okay,' he said, casually. 'I wrote the names of the bad guys in The Book of Death the other day. It seems that if you write someone's name in that book then pretty soon they're history. I should get a medal for this.'

Beth didn't seem to hear what he said, rather annoyingly. She gripped Flake's hand tightly. 'What about JD? Did he come for me? I don't remember.'

'Who's JD?' asked Flake.

'The Bourbon Kid.'

Flake smiled at her. 'Oh yeah. He came after you in a big way. There's a lotta dead people thanks to him.'

A tear appeared in the corner of Beth's left eye. 'He killed more people?' she half stated, half inquired.

'Shot one guy in the dick,' said Sanchez.

Flake stroked Beth's head again. 'They all deserved it,' she added. 'He did it for you.'

'I know,' said Beth, wiping away the tear in her eye. 'It's just, you know…'

'Hard to take in?' Flake suggested.

'No, it's not that. I feel kinda goofy saying this. You'll think I'm nuts.'

'*Everyone* in this town is nuts,' said Flake.

Beth finally smiled. 'I just love him when he kills people,' she said.

Flake grinned. 'He killed a hell of a lot of people, so he must *really* like you, too.'

The ground beneath them suddenly shook and a deafening booming noise filled the air. It sounded like a bomb had gone off inside the museum. The loud boom was followed by the sound of glass shattering. A sudden rush of heat burst from the building. It caused Sanchez to reel back. Smoke was now billowing out of the windows on the ground floor.

'Holy shit! That fire spread quick,' he said, raising a hand to cover his eyes.

Flake took a step towards the front entrance. 'Oh God. Who's still in there?' she asked.

Before Sanchez could answer, Dante and Kacy came rushing out of the front entrance and down the steps to the street. They both looked shell-shocked. Their faces were covered in black soot. And Kacy still wasn't wearing any pants.

Sanchez nudged Flake. 'They look worse than you.'

'What?'

'I mean their faces are covered in black stuff, you know, bit like yours, but worse.'

Flake sighed. 'How do you stay single?' she muttered.

Before Sanchez could respond, Kacy screamed out. 'Shit! My back is on fire!'

The back of her sweatshirt had caught fire and the flames were flickering dangerously close to her hair. Dante reacted quickly and dragged her to the ground. He rolled her over in the snow to put the flames out. Flake rushed over to help him pat out some small flames that were flickering underneath the arms on her sweatshirt.

Kacy screamed out. 'Get it off me. It's burning!'

Sanchez hurried over to help Flake and Dante pull the sweatshirt over Kacy's head. Fortunately before he got there they had succeeded in ripping the sweatshirt off and throwing it to one side. Black smoke still poured from it as it lay simmering in the snow. Kacy was left lying in the snow in just her underwear.

'You okay?' Dante asked. 'Any burns anywhere?'

Flake hauled Kacy up into a seated position and brushed some debris from her back. Kacy began rubbing her arms. 'I think I'm okay,' she said. 'It's a good job I'm not feeling the cold.'

Dante kissed her on the forehead. 'You look hot, always.'

Once they'd come to the conclusion that Kacy had escaped unscathed from the flames, she stood up and dusted herself down. Dante slipped an arm around her shoulder and pulled her in tight, brushing some snow off her chest. Sanchez noticed that her underwear had gotten rather wet in the snow and was now looking decidedly see-through. Out of politeness he chose not to mention it.

Flake looked over at the entrance. 'Where's the Bourbon Kid?' she asked.

Dante shrugged. 'He went after the museum's manager. Had a score to settle with him, I think.'

Beth poked her head around from the back seat of the car. 'He's gone after Elijah Simmonds?'

Dante nodded. 'Yeah. He'll get him, don't worry.'

'But what about the fire?'

Another loud explosion from inside the museum drowned out everything. Some windows on one of the upper floors shattered and glass fell down onto the street not far from where they were gathered.

Dante grabbed Kacy by the arm and pulled her out into the road, away from the falling debris. 'Look,' he said pointing to the sky. 'There's a blue moon coming out through the clouds.'

Kacy looked up. 'Does that mean we can go back to being human?' she asked.

Dante nodded. 'Yeah. We should do it now. Where's the Eye?'

Flake pointed over to the car. 'Beth should have it back there.'

'Is this it?' said Beth, holding the blue stone up.

'Yeah,' said Dante. 'Mind tossing it over here?'

Beth tossed the stone over to him. He caught it in his free hand and planted a kiss on Kacy's forehead. 'You ready to do this babe?'

'Sure. What we gotta do?'

'Stand under the moonlight and hold it up. It kinda lights you up real bright so everyone can see you for miles around. After a while you just go back to being human, I think.'

Kacy gave him a gentle dig in the ribs. 'Can we do it somewhere a little more private then? I already look kinda naked here. Not sure I need to be lit up for everyone to see.'

The sound of a distant fire engine approaching with its siren blaring made the decision an easy one.

'We're getting the hell out of here,' Dante announced. 'Shall we all meet up somewhere later?'

Flake looked to Sanchez. 'How about we all go for a drink at the Tapioca? We can work out what story we're gonna tell the Captain.'

Sanchez shrugged. 'Fair enough. Although, I usually just make up the story as I go along when the cops question me about anything.'

'How do you get away with that?' Flake asked.

'I'm renowned as a bullshitter. They expect it.'

'So it's settled,' said Dante, interrupting their trivial aside. 'We'll head there once we've fixed ourselves up?'

'Sure,' said Sanchez. 'See you there in about an hour.'

Dante and Kacy hurried off across the street and down a back alley, disappearing out of sight just before the fire engine pulled up at the scene. As the firemen started preparing to fight the fire Sanchez made a suggestion to Flake.

'We should really get out of here,' he said. 'We should probably get Beth to a hospital after all she's been through.'

Beth called out from the back of the car. 'Can't we wait to see if JD is all right? I'm feeling okay now.'

Flake walked over to Beth and leaned down to take a closer look at her. 'Have you seen yourself in the mirror?' she asked.

'No,' Beth replied tentatively. 'Do I look bad?'

Flake smiled. 'That scar you had on your face, it's gone.'

Beth swallowed hard. 'What?'

'Take a look in the rear view mirror. You look beautiful.'

Sanchez peered over Flake's shoulder to see if she was telling the truth. Beth's scar had indeed vanished courtesy of the healing powers of the Eye of the Moon. 'She's right,' he said, agreeing with Flake. 'You look gorgeous. It's a shame about all that blood on your top though. Spoils the look a bit.'

Beth took a look at her reflection in the car's rear view mirror. She ran her fingers across her cheek where her scar had once been.

'I don't believe it,' she whispered. 'After all this time, it's gone.'

She was so overjoyed at the sight of her new reflection that she barely heard the sound of a gunshot from within the museum.

Sixty-One

Special Agent Richard Williams had seen some bullshit during his twenty years in the FBI, but the report he'd just read about the events in Santa Mondega bordered on farcical. A former colleague of his, Detective Miles Jensen, had been assigned to this same shithole town a year earlier and had vanished without trace amidst rumours of supernatural activity. Williams had kept an open mind about the whole thing, but now as he sat in the Captain's glass walled office with two halfwit cops who had filed a report on the latest of the city's many massacres, he was convinced someone was having a joke at his expense.

'Is this a joke?' he asked.

The two cops sitting opposite him looked like halfwits. The first one, Sanchez Garcia, was proudly wearing a highway patrolman's outfit, with the sunglasses and Stetson hat still on. The other, Officer Flake Munroe, clearly took herself seriously as a cop, but looked too inoffensive for it. She answered Williams's question soberly. 'That's the events exactly as they happened,' she said.

Williams forced a fake smile. 'Right,' he said leaning back in his chair. 'Let me just summarise this out loud, so I can be sure I'm getting it right. According to you, this city was taken over by a mummy who created an army of vampires and werewolves to carry out his plot to take over the world.'

'That's right,' said Sanchez.

'Uh huh. And these vampires and werewolves are responsible for all the murders in this city.'

'Most of them,' said Flake. 'A lot of the kids were killed by Santa Claus.'

Williams took a deep breath and loosened his tie. 'Of course. Santa was responsible for all the child killings. And then of course there's the Bourbon Kid who you say was responsible for saving the city from the undead.'

'He played a part,' said Sanchez. 'It was a team effort though.'

'A team effort, huh.' Williams stopped fiddling with his tie and ran his fingers through his thinning silver hair. This was exasperating. 'So which one of you guys set fire to the museum?'

'That was the mummy,' said Sanchez. 'He did it with laser bolts from his hands.'

'Laser bolts, of course.' Williams stared hard at Sanchez. The idiot cop in his stupid highway patrol outfit was keeping a straight face throughout the interrogation. 'I find it interesting that the report also says you set fire to Santa Claus in the street, in front of a group of Sunflower Girls.'

'That's right.'

'Nice work. You sure you didn't set fire to the museum too?'

'Quite sure, thanks.'

Williams tried to eyeball Sanchez, but could see nothing through the other man's dark glasses. 'Interesting,' he mused. 'The Casa de Ville burned down too. No survivors there either. You were there that night too, before you went to the museum, right?'

'Correct.'

'Seems like these fires follow you around, Mr Garcia.'

'Yes it does. Better than being followed around by flies though.'

Williams resisted the urge to lunge over the desk at Sanchez. He wanted these two idiots out of his office and off the police force as soon as possible. He took a moment to calm himself before continuing. 'You're also claiming that a book called The Book of Death which you stole from the library was causing the death of everyone whose name was written in it.'

'Yep.'

'This book also burned in the fire, along with another book, sorry,' he paused for dramatic effect, 'another *magic* book that you say kills vampires.'

Flake jumped in. 'I can vouch for the magic bit. I used it to kill the Vampire Queen. And a librarian.'

'Did you?' Williams's voice dripped with sarcasm. He was convinced they were taking the piss, yet the pair of them maintained their straight faces. 'And yet all of the evidence that could back up anything you've said in this report burned in the fires at the museum and the Casa de Ville. Isn't that convenient?'

'On the contrary,' said Flake. 'I think it's somewhat inconvenient. You clearly don't believe anything we've put in that report. The evidence would have come in handy. Wouldn't it, Sanchez?'

'Yep.'

Williams reached forward and closed the report folder on the desk in front of him. 'Right,' he said. 'Let me get this straight. You two are proudly claiming to have used a pair of books to defeat an army of vampires.'

'And werewolves,' Sanchez chipped in.

'And werewolves,' Williams repeated, wearily.

'Come to think of it,' Sanchez went on, 'I hit a zombie over the head with a stick at one point too.'

Williams ignored the latest boast from Sanchez and carried on. 'So how many names did you write in The Book of Death, Sanchez?'

'Just the names of the mummy and the Vampire Queen,' said Sanchez proudly.

'Just the bad guys, huh? What about Elijah Simmonds? Did you write his name in the book?'

'Who?'

'The museum's assistant manager. His charred remains along with that of a security guard named James Beam were found in the fire. Autopsy reports say Simmonds blew his own brains out with a Desert Eagle, and Beam was stabbed to death. It's hard to tell though, because there wasn't much left of either of them after the fire. Neither of you two have mentioned anything of this in your report. Were Simmonds and Beam vampires too?'

Sanchez raised an eyebrow. 'Jim Beam is dead?'

'Yeah. Know anything about it?'

'Nope.'

Flake gave Sanchez a gentle shove. 'Jim Beam,' she said with a laugh. 'I meant to tell you, that bottle of Jack Daniel's you gave to Rick was full of Jim Beam. I tried some of it last night.'

Sanchez shrugged. 'I didn't have any Jack Daniel's left, so I took an empty bottle and filled it with Jim Beam. Figured Rick wouldn't know the difference.'

Williams slammed his hand down on the desk. 'Hey, do you two mind? I'm trying to establish what happened in this case.'

'It's pretty simple,' said Sanchez. 'Everyone died. The end.'

'You're an idiot,' Williams snapped. 'I have no idea how they let you wear a uniform.'

'Are we done?'

'Not yet,' said Williams. 'One last thing in your report that I want clarification of. What happened to the Bourbon Kid? Your report says he was in the museum when it burned down.'

'That's right,' said Sanchez.

'Well we've got no body for him. All the bodies we pulled out of the fire have been identified. He's the only one not accounted for.'

Sanchez and Flake both shrugged. 'Come on,' Williams demanded. 'What happened to him?'

Sanchez raised a hand tentatively. 'Maybe he's still in the museum.'

Williams frowned. 'What?'

'I read about a cat once that survived for six months in a house that was burned down. Apparently it survived by eating the ash.'

Williams had had just about as much as he could take. He wanted out of Santa Mondega as soon as possible. His main priority was simply to resolve this case as discreetly as possible and employ a new police force. These two idiots were the last remaining links to the old regime. He forced a broad smile at them.

'Okay, we're done,' he said, breezily. 'You two are dismissed. Your services on the police force are no longer required.'

Flake looked surprised. 'But I haven't got another job to go to.'

'That's not my problem. You were only here temporarily anyway. I've shipped in thirty new experienced officers from out of town. They'll be taking over from here. Hand your badges in at reception on your way out. The city would like to thank you and blah blah blah.'

'But that's not fair!' Flake complained. 'I need this job. The Ole Au Lait is closing down. This is all I have.'

Williams shrugged. 'That's too bad. Life's not fair, honey.' He picked up the report and waved it at her. 'Anyway, I think you missed your true calling. Judging by the report you've written, I'd say you could get yourself a job writing horoscopes. It's an easy job. You just make shit up and expect people to believe it.'

Flake faked a smile. 'Thanks for nothing.' She stood up to leave, but took one parting shot at Williams. 'You shouldn't joke about horoscopes, you know. I already read mine this morning. It said I should have sex with my boss. But as you've just fired me, I guess that won't be happening now. Looks like you missed out.'

'I'll get over it.'

Sanchez perked up in his seat. 'I could use a new catering manager at the Tapioca.'

Flake looked down at him. 'Really?'

'Yeah. With the Ole Au Lait closing down, there's a gap in the market for a new breakfast place.'

Her face lit up. 'I'd love to do that!'

'Good. The job's yours then. It'll be nice having you around in the mornings anyway.'

Williams looked bewildered. 'Excuse me, but would you two mind getting the fuck out of my office. I just fired you both, remember?'

Sanchez stood up. 'Can we keep the uniforms?'

'Sure. Now get the fuck out.'

Flake slammed the door shut behind them. Williams breathed a sigh of relief. Spending his morning with a pair of tiresome morons had been exasperating. He closed the cardboard folder containing the report and opened the top drawer on his desk. He slipped the report into it and pulled out his copy of the local newspaper, The Santa Mondega Universal Times. He flicked through the first few pages, checking out the reports about the aftermath of the latest massacre. When he reached the page with the horoscopes on it, he smiled to himself. He wasn't normally one for reading horoscopes, but having just spoken about them with Flake he decided to break with routine and read one for a change. The astrologer writing the horoscopes was named "Big Busty Sally". *"This'll be funny,"* he thought to himself.

He scoured the page for the Pisces report. It read:

Uranus will give you the strength to make an important decision. If you want to further your career, take a chance and have sex with your boss. It could be the start of something special.

Williams's jaw dropped. Flake hadn't been kidding when she'd said her horoscope had told her to have sex with her boss. For a few moments he visualised himself fucking her over the desk in his office. She was pretty fit and probably a fun shag too. After a few seconds of thinking about it, he shook his head and laughed to himself. Flake seemed pretty stupid, but even she wouldn't be dumb enough to follow a horoscope *that* literally.

Sixty-Two

Rae's Diner was a hive of activity for the first time in a long while, and all of the customers seemed to be in a sociable mood for a change. Everyone was wishing each other a good day, whereas in the past, no one ever spoke to anyone they didn't recognise. Times had changed in Santa Mondega. The sun was shining outside and the days of the undead lurking in dark corners were a distant memory.

Kacy picked one of her French fries from her plate and nibbled on the end of it. Dante was sitting opposite her in their booth by the window, wearing one of his indiscreet red Hawaiian shirts. He was shovelling fries into his mouth three and four at a time with one hand. His other hand was sometimes forcing in an occasional bite from his cheeseburger. When it came to eating fast food, Dante had it down to a fine art. As well as shoving in the burger and fries he was drinking a large coke through a straw.

'You enjoying that?' Kacy asked.

Dante made an approving noise and nodded. He hadn't noticed that she was barely touching her food. Even though the burger and fries was far more nutritious than her previous diet of blood, Kacy's appetite hadn't really returned since she'd become human again. She was still worrying about things that Dante had long since stopped caring about. Things like what to do with the Eye of the Moon. She finished eating the French fry and began twiddling with the blue stone that hung around her neck on a silver chain. It was visible for everyone to see, resting nicely above her ample cleavage on her low cut white T-shirt.

'I don't think I want this any more,' she said.

Dante shrugged. 'Shove it over here then. I'll eat it.'

'Not the food. The Eye of the Moon.'

Dante stopped cramming food into his mouth and looked up at her, his face showing an unusual degree of concern. 'What?' he said, revealing a half chewed burger in his mouth.

'I think we should get rid of it.'

'But it's worth a fortune.'

'I know, but it's bad luck. Look at how many people have died because of this thing.'

Dante wiped his hands together and picked up a napkin from the table next to his plate of food. He used it to wipe some grease from his fingertips. 'That stone can stop you from ever getting sick. No one can hurt you when you're wearing it. Why get rid of it?' he said. He took another suck of coke through his straw before continuing. 'Neither of us'll have to worry about getting seriously ill ever again.'

'Maybe not,' Kacy reasoned. 'But we'll always have to watch our backs, because people will kill for this thing. The Mystic Lady told us that, remember?'

Dante looked deep in thought for a moment. 'Is that the old woman whose head fell off?'

'It didn't fall off. Someone beheaded her.'

'Same difference. She was as mad as old cheese.'

'Even so, she was right. A lot of people have been killed because of this stone.'

Dante picked up a French fry, but for once didn't stick it straight into his mouth. 'Well I thought the Bourbon Kid would have come looking for it by now.'

'It's been over a week. I think he was coming back for it, he'd have done so already.'

'I guess so. So what do you wanna do with it then?'

Kacy looked out of the window at the street outside. The diner they were eating in was situated on the promenade in the harbour. She nodded at the sea. 'Thought maybe we could throw it off the end of the pier,' she said timidly, hoping that Dante wouldn't react angrily to the suggestion.

He sat blinking at her for a few moments, as if he was checking to see if she was serious. Eventually he wiped some ketchup from the corner of his mouth. He looked at the red sauce on his fingertip and licked it up. 'If we throw it away and you get sick one day, are we gonna have to come back here and look for it at the bottom of the sea?'

Kacy shook her head. 'No. The healing powers of this thing mess with the forces of nature. I want us to grow old together and take whatever life throws at us.'

Dante smiled. It was his boyish smile. The one he used whenever he wanted to get her to do something she might not be keen on. 'Grow old together, huh?' he said.

'Yeah.'

Dante called over to the waitress. 'Check please!' He turned back to Kacy. 'Let's take that stone and throw it the fuck away then. I don't want anything as much as I want to grow old with you. Let's get the fuck outta here and go throw it off the end of the pier.'

'You sure?'

'Fuck yeah.'

After paying for their food, they left the diner and strolled along the promenade towards the pier. The sun was back out in the sky and all traces of the snow had long since vanished. Dante kept his arm around Kacy's shoulder the whole time, occasionally squeezing her in tight for no particular reason. It was great to be back together as humans again, and not to be in any danger for a change. There were lots of other love-struck couples and families strolling along the promenade too and everyone looked happy and carefree.

'You know,' said Kacy tentatively. 'We never got around to arranging a date for the wedding, did we?'

Dante stopped walking. 'What wedding?' he asked.

'You proposed to me right before we got into all this shit, remember?'

Dante scratched his head. He looked puzzled. 'Really?'

'Yeah. When we went to the fortune teller at the fairground.'

'Huh? Where's your engagement ring then?'

'I haven't got one.'

Dante stuck his hand into one of the front pockets on his jeans and pulled something out. He held it up in front of her. 'Are you sure?' he said.

Kacy's eyes lit up. He was holding a small ring in between his index finger and thumb. It was a slim gold band with a small pink heart-shaped diamond in its centre.

'Oh my God,' Kacy spluttered, struggling to find words to describe how she was feeling.

He reached out and grabbed her left hand. He pulled it towards him and slipped the ring on her finger. 'I'd get down on one knee,' he said, 'but I'll be honest with you, I really can't be fuckin' bothered.'

Kacy barely heard him. She stared at the ring on her finger. It was beautiful, exactly the kind she would have chosen herself. And it fitted too. Feeling herself welling up with joy she threw both arms around him and planted a huge kiss on his lips. He in turn slipped both his hands onto her ass and squeezed hard. After a few seconds she pulled herself away and stared at the ring again.

'How did you know I'd like it?' she said, failing to mask the surprise in her voice.

Dante shrugged. 'It's pink, gold and expensive. Even I could figure that out.'

'I love it,' she said, still unable to take her eyes off it.

'Nothing's too good for my woman.'

They carried on walking along the promenade until they reached the old wooden pier that led out into the sea. As they walked across the rickety wooden panels on the pier, Kacy stopped staring at her engagement ring and looked up. Standing at the end of the pier, looking out at the horizon was a solitary figure she recognised. It was Beth. She was wearing a pair of torn black jeans and a blue hooded cardigan, her hands tucked into its pockets.

'I wonder what she's doing here?' said Dante.

'I expect it's a nice place to come when you want to get away from everything and collect your thoughts,' Kacy suggested.

'Probably a good place to get mugged, too.'

Kacy elbowed him in the ribs to remind him to keep his voice down. 'Don't be like that,' she said.

Beth may have heard them because she turned around as they approached. Kacy could see that she had been crying. As they walked up to her she wiped her eyes on her sleeve.

'Hi, Beth,' said Kacy with a sympathetic smile.

Beth smiled back. 'Hi, what you guys doing here?'

Kacy held up her hand to show off her new engagement ring. 'Dante just gave me this!'

Beth's eyes lit up. 'Wow, that's beautiful,' she said as she moved in for a closer look.

'Thanks.'

As the two of them marvelled at the ring, Dante butted in. 'Beth, we've still got the Eye of the Moon. But we got no need for it any more. Do you want it?'

Beth stopped staring at Kacy's new ring and shook her head. 'That thing brings nothing but trouble,' she said.

Kacy unclasped the silver chain around her neck and held it out to Beth, the Eye of the Moon rested firmly in the palm of her hand. 'We were thinking of throwing it off the end of the pier.'

'Do you mind if I do it?' Beth asked.

'It's all yours.'

Beth took the blue stone from Kacy. 'Do you still want the chain?' she asked.

'Nah, it's okay,' said Kacy. 'It's worthless. Throw the whole thing in the sea if you want.'

'You sure?'

'Yeah. Go nuts. Chuck it as far as you can.'

Beth took a long look at the chain in her hand. The Eye of the Moon was a beautiful stone, but it had been the cause of many, many deaths in Santa Mondega. To keep possession of it was dangerous. She looked back up at Kacy, her eyes close to tears again. 'You know, the last time I threw a necklace off the end of this pier, JD came back to me.'

Kacy reached out to Beth and rubbed her arm gently. 'Then you should definitely do it. It could be the sign that brings him back again.'

The two women embraced for a few seconds. Kacy could sense from the way Beth clung tightly to her that she'd made a good friend. Eventually, Beth peeled herself away and walked back to the end of the pier. Kacy watched her take one last look at the Eye of the Moon in her hand before, with one almighty throw, she tossed it out into the sea. It hit the surface of the water and made a gentle plopping sound. Then it vanished beneath the waves.

Beth didn't turn back right away. Instead she continued to stare out to sea, looking to the horizon, as if she hoped it would bring her some answers.

Dante sneaked up behind Kacy and slipped his arms around her waist. 'It's just like the end of Top Gun isn't it?' he said. 'You know, when Maverick throws Goose's dog tags out to sea?'

Kacy rested her head on his shoulder. 'Sweetie, it's nothing like Top Gun.'

'No. I think it is.'

They argued about the relevance of Top Gun for a while longer as Beth stared out at the sea. Eventually the three of them left the harbour and headed to the Tapioca for a celebratory drink.

Sixty-Three

Six months later

Sanchez hated strangers coming into his bar. Unfortunately for him, Flake fucking loved them and was regularly organising events to encourage new customers into the Tapioca. It made Sanchez livid, but he had to grudgingly admit that Flake had transformed the place and profits were up because of her efforts.

For the first time ever, the Tapioca was hosting a wedding reception. Dante and Kacy had just been married at the Church of the Blessed Saint Ursula. Sanchez quite liked Dante and Kacy, so out of respect (and as a promise to Flake) he'd hidden the piss bottle away and was serving only proper drinks for a change.

Flake was out back with one of his other new employees, Mental Beth. The pair of them had been bridesmaids at the wedding. They were still wearing the pink dresses Kacy had picked out for them, but instead of enjoying the festivities they were busy preparing a finger buffet for the rest of the guests.

Beth had actually turned out to be a lot less mental than Sanchez had been led to believe. She was hard working and got on really well with Flake, so he'd had to stop referring to her as Mental whenever Flake was around otherwise he tended to get a clip around the ear. He kind of felt bad for Beth too. The Bourbon Kid had vanished and it was pretty evident that she was lonely and desperate to know what had become of him.

Dante was seated on a stool at the bar. He was wearing a smart black tuxedo and drinking a bottle of Shitting Monkey beer. He chatted with Sanchez whenever the bartender had a free moment. Sanchez had never seen him look so smart. Then again, Sanchez had rarely been dressed smarter himself. He too was wearing a suit, a fine bright yellow one he'd picked out for himself at the local flea market.

Dante had barely taken his eyes off Kacy all day. Sanchez recognised the look too because he'd begun to look at Flake the same way in recent months.

'She sure does look beautiful in that wedding dress,' Sanchez remarked.

'Yeah,' Dante nodded. 'Look at how happy she is, mingling with all them people.'

Kacy was standing by a table in the corner. She was wearing a glistening white wedding dress and chatting with a few of the other drinkers. In her hand she had a large glass of red wine.

'Who are those people she's talking to?' Sanchez asked.

'I have no fuckin' idea,' Dante replied. 'She's shitfaced, man. She'll talk to anyone when she's like that. I don't even think those people were at the wedding.'

'What about this guy?' Sanchez asked, nodding at a stranger who had just entered the Tapioca and was making his way up to the bar.

Dante took a long look at the new arrival. 'I hope he's not a long lost uncle or something,' he said. 'Look at the state of him.'

As with all strangers in Santa Mondega, this guy was weird looking. He was in his early forties and walked with a bit of a limp. He was unshaven and scruffily dressed. He wore a dirty grey overcoat that needed a trip to the dry cleaners and a pair of black pants held up by a piece of string.

The stranger took up a place at the bar on a stool next to Dante. 'Yo, bartender, can you get me a dark rum please?' he asked.

Sanchez was immediately annoyed that he'd left the piss bottle out back. He begrudgingly picked up a clean glass and poured out a measure of real rum. He placed it down on the bartop.

'Three bucks.'

The man reached inside his coat and pulled out a five dollar bill. As he handed it over to Sanchez he asked another question. 'You know where I can find someone called Beth Lansbury?'

A quiet hush descended over the bar and before Sanchez could answer, Beth and Flake both came out from the kitchen to see who had asked the question.

'Who wants to know?' Sanchez asked.

'Me, obviously,' said the man. 'That's why I asked.'

Sanchez wasn't particularly one for looking out for other people, but he knew that any enemies of the Bourbon Kid might come looking for Beth, so he played it cool. 'What you wanna see her about?'

'You know where she is?'

'That depends on what your intentions are.'

'I've got something for her.'

'You can give it to me. I'll pass it on.'

The barroom remained quiet. The large heavy duty propeller fan hanging from the ceiling was the only thing making any noise as it whirred around at a lazy pace.

The man sniffed his glass of rum, then took a sip. 'You're Sanchez, right?' he said, placing the glass back down on the bar.

'I might be.'

'Yeah, I was told you'd be an awkward prick.'

Dante leaned over and nudged the man's arm. 'Hey, buddy. Watch who you're calling a prick.'

Sanchez waved Dante away. 'It's all right, I've been called worse.'

The stranger sighed. 'Let me explain to you why I'm here.'

Sanchez picked up a white towel from under the bar and began wiping the bar to give the impression he was disinterested. 'Here we go,' he said. 'He's gonna tell us a story now.'

The stranger looked around, and noticing that he had the attention of everyone in the bar, he raised his voice so that everyone could hear what he had to say.

'I've come from a small community down South. A place called Lakeland. Anyone heard of it?'

No one answered.

'Well anyway, for years we had an issue there with a group of bikers. These guys were somethin' else. Not Hell's Angels. Nah, they were worse 'n that. They only ever came out at night. In the mornings we'd find villagers lying dead in the streets, well, that is, we'd find what was left of 'em. These bikers did unspeakable things to the people of our community. Cannibalistic shit. Like stuff you've never seen. For as long as I can remember we all lived in fear. Sometimes they'd leave us alone for a few months, then all of a sudden they'd come back. They'd break into houses and drag people's kids from their beds. We were powerless to defend ourselves and anyone who stood up to them was ritualistically tortured and killed. Some were even eaten alive in the streets.'

Sanchez coughed. 'You know there's a wedding going on here, right?'

'Yeah, I'm sorry about that,' said the man, raising his hands apologetically. He looked over at Kacy. 'Nice dress,' he said.

'Thanks,' said Kacy, beaming. 'Got it specially made for me by Franck Summers.'

'That's nice,' said the man. He looked at Dante and added. 'Is she drunk?'

'Yeah.'

'Well, anyway,' the man raised his voice. 'About a month ago this guy comes into town. Real nasty looking dude, not the kinda guy you'd wanna fuck with. And, well, he changed everything.'

Beth had been standing behind Flake throughout the man's tale. She stepped forward. 'What did he look like?'

'Hard to say. Never really showed his face much. Kept it hidden underneath a dark hood most of the time. Had a real gravelly voice though.'

'What was his name?'

The man shrugged. 'Never told us his name. We only knew him as the man who drank bourbon. At least that's how we knew him before he went out into the street and faced down all the bikers on his own. No one in the village will ever forget that. What he did, it makes me shudder to think about it. We thought the bikers were bloodthirsty and merciless. This guy was worse than all of them put together. These days we know him better as the guy who saved our village. Lakeland's a nice place to live again now. Hell, people can even go out at night.' He picked up his glass of rum and took another sip before adding, 'Although they don't.'

Beth sneaked forward and nudged Sanchez to one side so she could speak to the stranger. 'I'm Beth Lansbury,' she blurted.

The man smiled at her. 'I'm very pleased to meet you, Beth,' he said.

'The man you speak of, his name is JD. Do you know where he is now?'

The stranger took another sip of his rum and set the glass back down on the bar. 'Can I get another drink?' he asked Sanchez.

'Rum again?'

'Uh huh. Make it a double this time.'

Sanchez grabbed the bottle of rum from the back of the bar and hurriedly poured the man's drink so he could hear the rest of the conversation. The man accepted the drink and made no attempt to pay for it. He turned back to Beth.

'He said he'd made a deal with the Devil. It didn't make a lot of sense but he said he had to travel around the world, ridding places like Lakeland of the undead. Guess he'll do a good job of it.'

'Did he say if he was coming back here any time soon?' Beth asked, her voice revealing a hint of desperation.

'Not any time soon. He said he won't stop until every last undead muthafucker is in Hell where they belong. I guess he's got a lifetime's work ahead of him.'

Beth looked disappointed. 'And he asked you to come here and tell me this?'

The man reached inside his jacket and pulled out a small piece of cloth. 'Nah, he just said to give you this. Said you'd know what it meant.'

Beth snatched the cloth away from him and unfolded it. Her fingers were trembling. Sanchez peered over her shoulder to get a good look at it. It was just a brown cloth with a red heart sewn into the middle. Within the heart, sewn in blue letters, were the initials JD. Beth turned around, clutching it tightly against her chest. There were tears welling up in the corners of her eyes.

Sanchez understood how she was feeling and offered some comforting words. 'As messages go,' he said, 'it's a bit vague, isn't it?'

THE END (maybe…)

Printed in Great Britain
by Amazon